I0693010

SUNDERED SOUL

A GREYMANTLE CHRONICLES SERIES

SUNDERED SOUL

BOOK ONE

J DAVID BAXTER

Silver Paw Publishing

Copyright © 2025 by James D Baxter

All rights reserved.

No part of this book may be reproduced in any form or by any electronic or mechanical means, including information storage and retrieval systems, without written permission from the author, except for the use of brief quotations in a book review.

Disclaimer:

This is a work of fiction. Any resemblance to action events or persons, living or dead, is entirely coincidental.

Design, production by Silver Paw Publishing.

Editing services by Dale McDowell.

Cover design by J David Baxter.

HARDCOVER: 978-1-953708-39-7

PAPERBACK: 978-1-953708-38-0

EBOOK: 978-1-953708-37-3

For more on the Greymantle series, see: JDavidBaxter.com or GreymantleChronicles.com

CHAPTER
ONE

Several men loomed over Mara, their gazes filled with exactly the kind of interest no one wants directed at them—especially while sprawled on unfamiliar cobblestones, wearing nothing but pajamas in a dark alley.

Dark alley? Wasn't I just in bed, safe behind locked doors and wards? How the hell did I end up here? Her mind scrambled to make sense of what was happening.

"And who are you, creeps?" she demanded sharply, struggling to grasp how her comfortable bedroom had suddenly become this damp, shadowed street.

The best-dressed of the group sneered, clearly amused. "We're creeps? What's a noble lady such as yerself doing half-dressed in a Daggerport alley behind a disreputable pub like the Murky Waters?"

He glanced meaningfully at the others. "Seems to me you're looking to entertain us tonight. Right, boys?"

Grunts and chuckles of agreement rose from the other four. The tallest, stubble-shadowed and smirking, stepped closer. "Only one type of 'lady' hangs around a place like this at night, dressed like that. I don't care what she says—she's obviously after some fun."

Fear might have gripped Mara if she weren't so confident in her own power. If she'd still been mortal, she'd be terrified, but a century of vampirism had replaced any vulnerability with annoyance, confusion, and steadily mounting anger.

Her thoughts were interrupted when a sudden, overwhelming hunger twisted sharply through her gut, nearly doubling her over. *Impossible—I fed just hours ago! Why am I starving again already?*

It wasn't merely anger or confusion she felt.

Make that hangry, she thought grimly.

She hadn't felt hunger this intense since the earliest nights after her turning. She was no fledgling struggling to manage her bloodlust; she'd fed recently and well. How could she have grown so weak, so quickly?

Her frustration boiling over, she growled at the men surrounding her. "Are you freaking kidding me? You'll be lucky if I don't leave you all broken and bleeding. Five-to-one odds—pathetic!"

She started to move, focusing on the man in the dark cloak embroidered absurdly with a dragon emblem. *Seriously? A cloak?* Before she could strike, he jabbed her sharply with a metal-capped wooden rod.

Mana-charged electricity surged violently through Mara, driving her body hard into the ground. Her muscles convulsed, seconds dragging into unbearable eternities before the pain finally ceased.

Laughter echoed harshly from the cloaked attacker as he exchanged smirking glances with his companions. "That ought to make her more agreeable, eh, boys?"

Shock and rage battled within her as she gasped incredulously, "A damned taser?"

This guy has a death wish.

Through gritted teeth, Mara hissed, "I'm gonna shove that stick up your butt and turn it on high!"

The man's smug expression faltered into confusion, clearly startled she could still speak. "How are you even conscious after being hit with my shockrod?"

Some of the other men were starting to look nervous, but the cloaked man smirked. "Guess it needs to be recharged. No matter. I don't need no magic to handle a little thing like you."

He reached down, grabbed a handful of her nightshirt, and pulled her forward, his other hand rearing back to punch her in the face.

Mara wasn't about to allow that. Instead, she calmly reached over and tapped him in the sack, using only a fraction of her vampiric strength. Still, it was enough that his eyes bugged out, and he doubled over, letting go of her instantly as he reached for his injured privates.

Reaching up, she grabbed his hair and stared into his eyes. "Kneel and do not move."

She slammed her will into his mind, not being gentle. After what he was about to try and do to her, she didn't care if she left the bastard as a vegetable; he deserved whatever she did to him.

The other men, not sure what was happening, thought she was simply fighting back. A couple looked as if they were having second thoughts about the whole situation. However, two of the men wore armbands with dragon heads stenciled on them, similar to the one on the cloaked man's chest. They seemed bolder and followed their leader's actions. Taking out copies of the wooden shockrods, they tried to stun her. The tall, scruffy one took the lead now that Cloak Guy was out of action.

This time she was ready and knew to avoid the weapons. She leaped up to her feet but had to dodge rather than attack.

Mara might be confident in her fighting abilities, but was still worried. She was in an unknown situation, in an unfamiliar place, but worst of all, these people weren't pushovers. She was used to dealing with slow, pathetic humans who would easily fall to her enhanced speed and strength. However, unlike regular mortals who might have guns or knives, these guys had weapons that could actually incapacitate her, and all it took was a touch.

She had been lucky with the first guy. She would have been helpless if he had held that taser to her longer instead of just making a quick hit.

Worse, they were fast and seemed to know what they were doing, indicating a decent level of combat training. Seeing her avoid their thrusts, they started coordinating their attacks, trying to drive her back against the alley wall so they could score a hit.

"Bitch, you got lucky Drevan's rod wasn't working right, but mine is. Once I get you, I'm not gonna let go!"

That was stupid of him. Now she had their leader's name.

Mara couldn't help the snarky reply, "I bet he has that problem a lot. I bet you do, too."

Scruffy snarled at her comeback and lunged again with his magic taser. "Once I hit you, I'm gonna put this someplace real uncomfortable too!"

These people did not know who they were dealing with!

"Oh, that's it, sunshine! You just signed your death warrant, and I will not make it quick!"

She wasn't about to let herself get hit with one of those magic taser again. Unlike a human, she wouldn't need more than a couple of seconds to recover. Still, a taser would lock her muscles just like anyone else, so she had no intention of getting hit. She willed the blood in her system to fuel her vampiric speed, making her fast enough to be a total blur to their unenhanced vision.

For an instant, the world seemed to slow down. She could easily see the two shockrods coming in from either side. She gracefully stepped forward and slammed an elbow into Scruffy's face, the one who had just made such an indecent threat. There was a satisfying crunch as his body was hurled backward from the force of her blow.

Then, the world lurched to a halt.

Instead of the super speed continuing, Mara found herself staggering as her vampiric speed cut off, and she returned to normal. Worse, a wave of weakness washed over her. She felt a stab of hunger so intense it frightened her. Never in the all the years since she was first turned had she felt such intense emptiness.

Instantly realizing the problem, she felt real fear for her existence. Somehow, she had burned too much blood and did not have enough left to power her vampiric abilities. She was as weak as a regular mortal and had only enough blood left to keep from falling unconscious. Any more loss, and she could die here; her body would simply shut down, and she'd never wake.

Now it was three against one, and one of her attackers had a damned taser that could leave her helpless; the other two had long daggers and stood with the bearing of experienced fighters.

Come on, Mara, you've been in worse spots than this! Pull it together, you just need to take out three mortals!

In one hundred years of secret warfare against the Cabal's supernatural forces, she had faced hideously overpowered opponents and terrible odds. That fight against the werewolf stormtroopers during the fall of Berlin had been terrifying. Still, the little voice in the back of her head whispered that she had never fought without her vampiric abilities. She'd never been as weak as a mortal, no matter the odds.

Damnit, I may not have powers, but I'm not going to meekly give up and let them do what they want!

She had trained in a dozen different martial arts. She might not be a grandmaster black belt from some ancient tradition, but she knew how to kick ass.

Unfortunately, skill didn't entirely even out the fight.

The second armband-wearing creep might have missed his strike, but he wasn't slow. While she was adjusting and realizing the problem, he reset and thrust again.

Electricity arched through her side and almost caused her knees to buckle, but she was already in motion as he struck her. Her momentum carried her away from the magic rod, making it a glancing blow instead of a solid hit.

It hurt like hell, and she knew she would be writhing on the ground if she were still mortal. Those things were more potent than regular tasers.

The thing that saved her was the man's surprise at not seeing her collapse. In his shock, he didn't follow through with a second attack.

Unfortunately, she couldn't capitalize either, as it took a second to recover from the hit.

The two men with daggers looked nervous, and she had a feeling they weren't willing to commit murder. Otherwise, they could have gutted her when she was recovering from that last hit from the shockrod. Instead, all they had done was move to surround her, provide a threat, and prevent her escape. They were leaving the dirty work to the armband guy.

The asshole seemed pretty unhappy about that judging from his expression. "Don't just stand there like idiots! What are we paying you for?"

One of them grumbled just loud enough for Mara's enhanced hearing to pick up. "Damned Dragon Followers! It's one thing to have a little fun, but they ain't paying us enough to murder some silk-wearing noble woman in an alley."

Great, he's got enough of a conscience not to want to be a murderer, but he doesn't mind a little sexual assault... What a saint!

With the two flanking her not seeming to make any moves, she focused on the guy in front, the one with the magic taser.

He lunged in, confident, now that she was surrounded and unarmed.

Mara fell back on years of training; she sidestepped and brought her right forearm upward in a block to knock the rod to the side. She was careful not to let her arm touch it near the metal tip. That meant the rod came a little closer to hitting her than she would like, but it worked. She was inside his guard and free to strike.

With her left arm still extended to prevent a counter, she swung her right fist in with all the force her weakened body could muster. She focused on her form, her fist palm upward, and rotated her hips and body to transfer all the power she could. At the last instant, just as her knuckles were making contact, she snapped her wrist around in a twisting motion, sending every ounce of force into the point of contact.

Even at mortal levels of strength, the punch was effective beyond her expectations. She had aimed not at his jaw, but at his Adam's apple and felt a crunching from the man's throat.

Pain and shock bloomed on her attacker's face, followed by panic as he tried in vain to pull air into his lungs. Henchman #2 was definitely out of the fight.

Mara wasn't going to wait for the other two men to hit her from the side and back. She stepped forward, pulling the Dragon Follower in front of her. She had no idea what that name meant, but she intended to use the bastard as a human shield to prevent the other two from attacking.

They looked uncertain and glanced at each other.

She didn't have much time left. She could feel her body starting to shut down from the lack of vital energy in her blood. It was how vampires fueled their existence; it was what animated them and gave them their powers. Her father had taught her about it, but this was the first time in her long life that she had ever come close to collapse.

She needed this fight to be over, and she needed blood, right now!

Unable to wait any longer, she bared her fangs at the two men, then sank them into the neck of her dying meat-shield. Still, she stared at the dagger-wielding men, even as she drank to let them know she was coming for them next. It was half bluff, and half intimidation, but it worked!

They took one last look at one another and at the men they were hired to serve, and fled the alley like the devil was chasing them.

Mara would have laughed in relief if she weren't busy draining her attacker.

Normally, she would never kill this way; the Cabal would hunt her down and end her for revealing the existence of the supernatural to morals. However, she had a feeling the Cabal was the least of her worries at the moment. She wasn't sure what was going on, but she had been transported from her locked and warded bedroom to some dark alley where people dressed differently than she had ever seen before and carried long wooden magic tasers and daggers with blades the length of her forearm. She was starting to think she was not in Texas anymore.

When she had finished with the armband-wearing attacker, she let his body fall to the ground. She had enough blood now that she felt recharged. She might have taken more from the other two downed men, but she felt that she was on a clock now. The two henchmen had fled, but would they call the police or come back with reinforcements to rescue their employers?

She glanced at the guy she had elbowed in the face before she had lost her strength and speed and chuckled.

He was going to have a severe concussion if he survived. His body lay crumpled next to a wall.

She smiled maliciously as she walked over to the kneeling man, still grabbing his balls. He had dropped his shockrod, so she scooped it up, looking it over.

It was almost entirely wood, but she noticed that the end had two bands of metal, with simple but unrecognizable sigils engraved in them. They seemed to be coated in a greyish fog, as if they were cooler than the surrounding air, causing them to produce a vapor. It was a little cool out, so she didn't think much of it.

She was careful to only touch the rod by the handle. She didn't know exactly how the device worked, but she wasn't dumb enough to grab the business end. It must have already been charged, because when she jammed it into the man's crotch, he jerked like he'd been hit by a lightning bolt.

Her smile faded only after he collapsed to the ground, writhing and clutching himself.

"Threaten to use that rod on me? How's that for karma, you piece of shit?"

She shook off the surge of vengeful satisfaction, forcing herself to focus. I need to hurry. They might have sent someone to get help, and while these bastards deserved every second of this, I don't have time to deal with the police.

Mara leaned over the cloaked man, who was still moaning and cradling himself as he lay on the ground. She grabbed him by the throat and slammed him hard against the wall.

The desire to end him was a living thing in her chest, hot and demanding, but she forced it down. She needed answers—and while one of them was already dead, it would be better if she didn't kill them all.

His mouth moved as he started babbling excuses about how they hadn't "meant nuthin' by it," but she cut him off sharply.

"Please!" he gasped, voice barely a wheeze. "I'm sorry... I'm sorry. Just let me go, and I'll forget this ever happened."

His words came in a desperate rush, a torrent of promises and pleas. Coins clinked as he fumbled at his belt, offering her his money pouch. Yet for all his groveling, there was a sliminess to his voice, a hint of deceit that curled around his words like smoke.

"Shut up!" Her voice was low and dangerous. She couldn't stand another pathetic lie.

Mara arched a brow and let out a dry, humorless chuckle. "Funny how polite you get when the woman you tried to assault turns out not to be helpless, after all."

Confusion warred with her anger. How could she have gone to bed and ended up here? The cold cobblestones under her bare feet felt all too real.

She leaned in, close enough for him to smell the iron on her breath. "You're not sorry. You're scared. There's a difference, and I'm not feeling very forgiving after what you just tried to do."

No way they hadn't meant anything by it. From their practiced arrogance, she'd bet good money she wasn't the first woman they'd tried to victimize.

"Now listen up," she snapped, eyes narrowed. "Strip down to your underwear and pile every valuable you've got on your cloak. Then take your friend's valuables and add them too. You have two minutes. Move!"

The last word rang with fury, echoing off the narrow walls of the alley.

She didn't know who they were, and she wasn't sticking around to find out. That dragon symbol burned in her mind—who knew what it represented?

Mara risked a glance up at the night sky framed by the jagged rooftops. One look at those two pale moons told her everything she needed to know.

This wasn't some alley in Houston. And it sure as hell wasn't Earth.

CHAPTER
TWO

She was still staring at the sky, stunned at the sight of two moons, when the creep finished stripping his companions of their valuables and knelt back where she had commanded him before.

There was a small pile of junk on top of the cloak. She blinked in surprise. On Earth, men didn't typically wear much jewelry, but there were many rings, earrings, and necklaces, certainly more than she would have expected. Chalking it up as a difference in cultures, she swept all the jewelry into a belt pouch, not really concerned with their valuables at the moment. She cared more about covering herself.

Looking at the men, Mara had no desire to take and wear their clothes. However, she also didn't want to be walking around the streets of some strange world in nothing but the shearest of silk pajamas. Making a decision, she picked up the long woolen cloak and draped it around her shoulders, then grabbed one of the men's belts. Belting the cloak around her waist covered her entirely and ended up making her look like a medieval monk or a Jedi.

Unfortunately, she had no boots or shoes, and the ones the men wore were not her size, even if she would have been willing to wear them.

On the other hand, this alley was surprisingly clean. Now that she noticed it, she couldn't help but be amazed. She had never been in any city on Earth where alleyways weren't grimy and filled with trash. Being barefoot on Earth in a place like this, her feet would have probably been cut up with broken glass. And yet, there wasn't so much as a speck of dust to be seen. It was almost enough to make her question whether this whole experience was even real.

An alley behind a shady pub not stinking of stale beer spilled onto the ground? Not a chance!

Even knowing she should hurry to get away from the scene, she had to pause for a moment to soak in the experience. She touched the building walls and scented the air, but they seemed both solid and real. The air might not be filled with the sour smell of a back alley, but there was a taste of salt in the air. She was near an ocean. Wherever this was, it was a port city.

She was focused on her senses when she almost doubled over. Another wave of intense hunger swept over her. It wasn't quite as bad as before, but it was close. She was experienced enough to know the signs. Her body was nearing its limits; the magic of the blood that sustained her was almost exhausted again. It was as if she had been using her powers continuously until she was out of energy.

Except, she had just drained a guy dry and filled up. There was no way she should have used up all the power in her blood. Not that quickly!

What the hell?!? I haven't even been using my powers since draining that guy!

With absolutely no remorse, she looked at the man she had smashed in the face. Without a hospital soon, he might not survive anyway.

Besides, he had intended to assault her and place that shockrod somewhere unpleasant. She bared her fangs again. The police might be on the way, but she didn't hear anyone yet, so there was still time....

Several moments later, she wiped a tiny drop of blood from the corner of her mouth, looked at the men, and smirked. They might be disgusting pigs, but their blood had tasted just fine, and now she was full and wouldn't need to feed for another couple of days so long as she didn't have to exert herself and use her powers.

Assuming that whatever had drained my energy before doesn't happen again....

Surveying the scene one last time, she was torn regarding what to do about the last bastard, the one she had questioned. He was still alive.

There was a war inside her over whether to kill him or not. On the one hand, she hated leaving an enemy like this alive for fear he might come back at her later. On the other, committing murder in a new world when the guy was helpless wasn't exactly self-defense at this point. If the authorities caught her, she wouldn't be able to honestly claim justification. He did try to cross a line that deserved death in her opinion, but still, she wasn't in immediate danger now.

"They called him Drevan. I've got his name if I have to find him."

With a growl in her throat, the decision was taken from her. Before she could worry too much, she heard people in the distance hurrying this way.

It was past time to leave!

She would have wiped the creep's memories, but there was no more time.

Growling, she turned down the alley in the opposite direction from the noise and hurried away. Still, she didn't run; she just walked fast while trying to look as casual as possible. She took several turns before she exited onto an actual street.

Being nighttime, however, there weren't many people walking around, so she decided to duck into another alley on the opposite side of the road and a little way down.

After several more twists and turns, she eventually found a street perpendicular to the other road she had previously seen. She didn't know north from south or east from west, but she could tell that the main streets of this city were aligned with surprising precision. For what it was worth, this city had been planned and laid out impressively well. On Earth, that would have meant it was either a newer city or one in the United States. Most of the old-world towns had grown up much more organically over centuries and did not have grid-pattern layouts.

Sadly, that theory was at odds with the fact that the buildings around her looked old. Not in the sense that they were covered with hundreds of years of grime and dirt, the way many European cities were. Instead, the construction's thick stone looked weathered enough that it couldn't be modern. Of course, with two moons visible in the sky, neither of which looked like Earth's moon, she was certain she was not on Earth anymore. Therefore, any rules of thumb about Earth construction probably didn't hold weight here.

On the plus side, judging by the sky, it didn't look like dawn was about to break anytime soon, so it must still be early in the evening, hopefully not too long after sunset. There were still people out on the streets, which meant she could ask someone about where she was. Her biggest issue at this moment was a lack of information.

Well, that and needing a place of safety to sleep before the sun came up!

She was going to need money. Looking down at the dark leather belt pouch at her waist, she opened it. The jewelry didn't look terribly expensive, but it didn't look like worthless costume jewelry either. She hoped it would be worth something. That thought led to her next problem.

Where could she sell the jewelry without questions being asked? There had to be pawnshops or illegal fences that would buy stolen merchandise. As a vampire, she had a network of places back in Houston where she could sell any 'found' items, but this wasn't Earth.

Judging from the buildings around her, she was definitely not in a rich part of town. That meant she needed to find a dive bar and ask around. That would be the easiest way to find the types of contacts she needed.

She wandered for nearly fifteen minutes before she realized the town was too big for her just to meander aimlessly, hoping to find what she was looking for.

Grumbling, she approached a man walking down the other side of the road. "Excuse me. Can you tell me where I can find a bar near here?"

"Pardon, what?" The man looked startled and glanced at her up and down, trying to figure out who she was. Confusion was evident on his face.

"A pub? A place to get a drink?" He checked her out but seemed unsure of her. She was wearing a belted cloak but no shoes, walking around the city streets barefoot.

"Uh..." He struggled to think for a second, then added, "Most of the pubs around here are not very nice. This is the Dockside, the port area outside the city walls. You should head north, further into the city. I assume you just came to Daggerport from a newly arrived ship?"

She nodded. "That's right. I was robbed and need to learn more about the city to find out where to go next. I've got friends to stay with, but I need to find them, and I'm lost. I thought a pub would be a good place to find someone to help me."

Holding back a chuckle, she couldn't help but think, "If this were a video game, my deception skill would have just increased."

The man looked relieved to have an explanation of why someone would be wandering around barefoot and looking lost. He suddenly looked sympathetic, "I can escort you to a Watch Station. They can help you from there and make sure you find the people you are looking for."

She rolled her eyes. That was not what she had asked. *I just want directions to the nearest pub, is that so hard?*

Hating to use her compulsion after what had happened before, she hesitated to risk it. What if she ended up feeling empty again? She would have to attack this man right in the middle of the street and take some of his blood. She was already at risk because of killing two men in the alley and baring her fangs at the two who had escaped.

Mara shook her head, "No, I just want to find a pub and get a drink, even if it isn't a nice one. Then I can worry about finding my friends. Can you please point me to the nearest one, even if it isn't safe? I've already lost my valuables; there's nothing else for someone to rob."

Looking like he wanted to protest, he complied instead, "Fine. Two streets over and a couple of blocks to the west, you'll find the Ship's Bilge." He pointed in the appropriate direction.

It was clear on the man's face what he thought of the place. Plus, it didn't take a genius to get that the name of the place was questionable. Who in their right mind would eat or drink at a place called the Ship's Bilge?

The man shook his head as he walked off.

To Mara, it sounded perfect. With a name like that, it had to attract a questionable clientele. Hopefully, it would be filled with the kind of people who could point her to illegal pawn shops or dealers in stolen goods.

CHAPTER

THREE

IN JUST A COUPLE OF MINUTES, Mara found herself standing in the doorway of the pub in question. It was just as bad as the name implied. The smell hit her like a two-by-four to the face. The city streets were so bizarrely clean, she had forgotten the lack of odor until she opened the door to this place. Coughing, she adjusted to the new environment.

Honestly, it's really not that bad, no worse than any dive bar back home. It's just that everything is so odorless in this strange world that it makes it seem terrible.

She was no werewolf to spend her unlife sniffing at everything around her, but vampire senses were definitely keener than human's, and she had become accustomed to knowing when someone was nearby just by their scent. It had helped her innumerable times over the decades during a hunt or a mission.

Note to self: Don't rely on scent in this world.

Even in this place, most of the patrons were strangely odorless.

Those thoughts had kept her immobile a bit too long, and people were staring at her now. She hurriedly moved, planning to head over to the bar and order a drink, but realized she had no money. She had been rich on Earth and hadn't needed to worry about buying anything since her death in 1915. Besides, people didn't believe in vampires there, so she could always use her compulsion ability if she ever desired something badly enough. Unfortunately, she didn't know what people here might be aware of, so it was best not to risk it.

Halfway to the bar, she stopped and quickly scanned the room. She picked her target and headed for his table. Unlike many of the drinkers, he seemed to be clear-headed and looked focused, like a man waiting for a business partner.

Mara chuckled to herself. *Except, who in their right mind would be in a place like this to do business? Someone nefarious, of course!*

Sliding into a seat opposite the man, she gave him a closer evaluation.

He had greasy hair and tired eyes that darted around the room suspiciously. He had a stubbly beard and wore faded clothes that had seen better days. They were covered with a dark overcoat that could easily conceal weapons or contraband. He seemed to be in his element in the dive bar as if he belonged there. Despite his somewhat ragged appearance, there was an air of menace about him, and it was clear to Mara that he was there to do something illegal.

In one hand, he clutched a tall glass filled half with dark, warm beer; in the other, he played with a short dagger, spinning it around like a top, like someone playing a deadly version of Spin the Bottle.

Ignoring the spinning knife, he looked at Mara as she took a seat at his corner table. He looked her up and down, not disguising his interest. His eyes roamed over her curves, which were all that was visible thanks to the belted cloak. However, when his eyes reached her chest and alighted on the dragon's head symbol embroidered on the left breast, his interest turned to disgust.

"What do you want, Follower?" The last word was laden with scorn.

That surprised Mara. She didn't know what the symbol represented, and the guy in the alley was an attempted rapist, but still. For some low-life in a scummy dive bar to look down on others so thoroughly....

She waved her hand dismissively. "I'm not one of those creeps. I kicked his nuts up into his throat when he tried to do something he shouldn't have and took his cloak to cover up with."

It took a second, but when Mara's words sank in, the guy sat back and laughed as if he'd just heard the best joke. When he was done, his eyes actually were on her face. "So what do you want with me?"

Mara had considered using compulsion, but she was still a bit wary of what effect that might have on her, so she opted for the truth. If the guy was stupid enough to try to rob her, then his little pig-sticker of a knife wouldn't help him.

"After so generously donating his cloak, the guy and his companions decided to compensate me by giving me all their jewelry. I need to find someone to sell it to who won't ask questions."

After another round of chuckling, Scruffy got serious. "I might know a guy...."

She wanted to roll her eyes but restrained herself. Of course, it wouldn't be free. She sighed, "For obvious reasons, I don't have any money on me. I could give you one of their pieces of jewelry as thanks for your help."

There were a few coins in the pouch, she had heard them clinking in the alley when Drevan had begged for his life. Still, she wanted to save those in case of a real need.

Since he wasn't offering his name, she had decided he would be known as Scruffy from now on. This was the second scruffy guy of the night, but this one seemed much less likely to make her feel stabby, although she would withhold her judgement on that for the moment.

Scruffy frowned slightly. "When you say jewelry, you mean their magic items, right? They aren't really just decorative jewelry; hardly anyone wears things that aren't practical."

It took a moment for Mara's brain to catch up. *Magic items? Toto, I definitely don't think we're in Texas anymore!*

"Uh, I guess. I just shoved their donation into a pouch and decided to leave before the police showed up."

Nodding sagely, Scruffy agreed, "Yeah, you definitely don't want to deal with the Watch. Not even if you are the victim, not if you have anything on you they shouldn't find at least."

He seemed to be weighing a decision in his mind, and Mara could practically read his thoughts from the way his eyes were looking at her. In the end, he shrugged and shook his head before saying, "About three streets to the west, you'll find the main road that goes up the hill to the city gates. When you pass the gates, go to your right, east toward the mountain. Follow the wall until you see the road with an Inn on the corner called the Sea View."

Scruffy grumbled under his breath, "Idiot name... like they could see the ocean with the wall in the way!"

"Anyway, head north on that street for six blocks, and you'll see a small shop with a green stone front. That's the place you're looking for. Tell him Nargant sent you. He'll try to cheat you, but he doesn't talk and never gives up information on his customers to the Watch."

She reached into the pouch and pulled out a gold chain with a small jade pendant, and passed it over, covering it with her hand so that others in the bar wouldn't see what she was giving Scruffy, aka Nargant.

He pulled it down into his lap before glancing down and then frowned. "This is a bank token. I can't do anything with this! The Makers Guild ward them so that only the owner can transfer coins, and even then, you can't make someone give up their money by force. Even if the guy were here right now with a dagger to his throat, I couldn't force him to hand over his money; the magic would detect that."

That was all news to Mara and a harsh reminder that she needed information almost as much as she needed money. She tried not to let the shock at his words show on her face as she replied.

"The chain is gold. Weighs maybe half an ounce; that ought to be more than enough to compensate you for the information."

Again, the man seemed to weigh the idea of whether or not it would be worth his effort to rob her. In the end, he shook his head. "Fine. But take the token with you. I'm sure the guild can track it if the guy reports you to the Watch, and I don't want 'em coming here." He fiddled with the chain for a second, then passed the jade token back just as surreptitiously as she had handed it to him.

Mara looked the man in the eyes, "Thanks Nargant. I remember those who help me, and never forget those who cross me."

She didn't use compulsion or bare her fangs, but she knew how to intimidate people; she'd been doing it for a hundred years. Nargant shivered and looked away first before grumbling. "It's nothing. The chain is fine. Is there anything else?"

Mara smiled, but there wasn't any warmth to it. "No, that's it. I just needed that information."

Without another word, she stood and walked out of the pub. She could feel more than one set of eyes on her as she exited and would take precautions to make sure she wasn't followed. Rather than directly heading in the direction she was given, she walked a couple of blocks north before turning down a narrow street heading west. She waited a moment before a pair of footsteps turned down the dark street.

She had specifically chosen the narrow road, which wasn't much bigger than an alley, specifically because it wasn't well-lit. Her borrowed cloak was a dark color, and her belt was black. Only her arms, feet, and face were pale, but she had decades of practice at hiding in the dark.

Her would-be assailant quietly and cautiously turned the corner to follow, but soon stopped when he didn't see anyone on the street ahead. He looked around in confusion, but it was already too late for him.

Mara had one arm locked around his throat and the other wrenching his wrist behind his back in a hold she'd learned from an oilfield worker who hadn't believed in pulling punches—just arms.

"I don't know what your plan was, but tailing me? That was your first mistake."

She'd half-expected it to be Nargant, but nope—just one of the burly drunks from the bar. She could smell the rotgut on his breath even from behind him. Real smooth.

"Ow! Bitch, let me go or I'll hurt you!"

She rolled her eyes. "Seriously? That's your line?" She twisted his arm a little further, just until he whimpered. "Buddy, I'm the last girl you want to try that crap with."

"Don't make me break your arm. Or your neck. I'm going to put you on the ground, and then you're going to hand over everything valuable. Got it?"

"Yeah! Oww!" he yelped, the picture of drunken eloquence.

She eased him down without effort. It would've been easy to sweep his legs and drive his face into the dirt, but why make a mess? He wasn't worth the cleanup. Just another drunk idiot who thought he saw an easy target. He'd learn. She wasn't about to let him off without paying a toll.

Knowing about bank tokens, she ignored the leather cord on the man's neck and focused on anything else that might be magic. He had three earrings and two rings, which quickly disappeared into her pouch, followed by a small handful of actual coins. They were silver and copper, judging by the sound they made.

It had been a few years since the US stopped using actual silver and copper in its coins, but she fondly remembered the tones of those old coins jingling. Those, too, ended up in her belt pouch.

When she was done, she flipped him over and looked the sailor in his eyes, and flexed her will. "You will not remember me. You got tired of drinking at the Ship's Bilge and decided to find a pub with better drinks. However, you were too drunk and stumbled and fell. The ground seemed comfortable, so instead of getting up, you fell asleep. You will not wake up until morning unless someone finds you."

She waited a long moment to see if the hunger would return the way it had before. Sure enough, after a couple of minutes, her body felt as if it had used up most of its energy. It was the equivalent of going several days without feeding, and it had only been a super tiny use of her abilities. She quickly dragged the sailor over to a wall and bit his wrist, and drank. Unlike earlier, the hunger wasn't as bad, so she didn't need to kill the man in order to replenish her vitality. Still, she did take more than was strictly healthy for him, but not so much as to be life-threatening. He would feel weak for a few days but should recover.

Her first thought was how foul his blood tasted. She really hated feeding on people who were drunk or high—it always tainted the flavor. Bitter, sour, and sharp in all the wrong ways. Even after a century as a vampire, that part hadn't gotten any easier.

The disgust didn't come from the act itself. She'd gotten over that squeamishness long ago. Drinking blood wasn't something she craved or enjoyed like a fine meal—it was fuel, nothing more. Necessary, not pleasurable. Still, some part of her remembered how horrifying the idea had been in those first few months after she turned. Back when she'd still felt constrained by mortal sentiment.

When she finished, she licked the punctures clean and waited just long enough to make sure the wounds closed. No bleeding, no mess. Just a passed-out drunk with no memory and a mild case of anemia.

With a final glance to make sure the street was still clear, Mara left him slumped against the wall, snoring softly. It was still early, and she'd gotten lucky—this part of the city wasn't busy yet. No witnesses. No one sees the predator in the dark.

Mara still wasn't sure what to make of the idea of all the jewelry in her pouch being magic items, but this was clearly a different world, so maybe magic was a thing here more openly than on Earth. One thing was sure, she was eager to find out.

CHAPTER

FOUR

HER ADOPTIVE FATHER, Davin, had magic. He was the only vampire she had known in her unlife who had it. He had sworn her to secrecy, even going so far as to bind her with a magic oath in order to keep mages or elder vampires from being able to pry the knowledge out of her with compulsion or magic. According to him, Vampires with magic had been hunted and exterminated. He only survived the purges by faking his own death and hiding his abilities. Mages despised blood magic, considering it an abomination, and other vampires, those without the ability, killed them out of jealousy.

Mara could understand that. There had been times over the decades when she had desperately wanted what Davin had, and she loved him like family, her only family. Even so, she couldn't help envying him.

"And now here I am in a world that seems to be practically swimming in magic."

Now that she was looking and walking down a busier street, she couldn't help but see evidence of it everywhere around her.

Streetlights were glowing crystals suspended in globes atop decorative pillars. Floating hover carts passed up and down the streets among the pedestrians, while others rode horses. Even the streets, themselves, had to be cleaned with magic; there was no other explanation for why things were so spotless and odor-free.

Shaking her head, she followed the flow of people going uphill toward the wall and the massive gates of the city.

Looking up and down the main thoroughfare, she could see the harbor in one direction, with tall ships moored at docks or anchored in the bay. In the other direction, a city loomed over her, built at the base of a massive mountain that seemed to stab at the sky.

What had that creep in the alley called this place? *Dagger-something... Daggerport!*

From her vantage outside the city gates, Mara couldn't see much beyond the sprawl of the outer town, but even this Dockside district was massive. She guessed it was at least the size of Galveston, Texas —back home, that meant over fifty thousand people. This seemed significantly more densely packed.

And this was just the part outside the walls.

How big is this city if the overflow alone could swallow an entire American town?

Beyond the stone ramparts, the mountain loomed, its slopes alive with scattered lights. Her vampiric vision picked out details normal eyes would miss—walkways clinging to cliff sides, windows cut directly into the rock, faint movement in the glow. It reminded her of looking at the Houston skyline at night from a distance.

Okay... maybe not quite that many lights, but it gave the same impression—like the mountain itself was a living, breathing city.

Weird that people here would dig into the side of a mountain instead of building up. Maybe magic changed the way architecture evolved? Skyscrapers with spellwork instead of steel? Her thoughts wandered as she walked, but they snapped back into focus as the gates drew closer.

She didn't know what kind of welcome she'd get. She was barefoot, for one thing— guards, even in magical fantasy cities, probably didn't appreciate vagrants strolling in after dark. Earth's police sure didn't.

The walk from where she woke had only taken about half an hour, and she figured it was still reasonably early in the evening–nine, maybe ten o'clock. The traffic in and out of the gate was steady, not frantic but far from dead. Carts rolled by, merchants argued, guards checked documents but rarely stopped anyone.

No reason to sneak. So she didn't.

Chin up, stride steady, she joined the flow and walked through the gates like she belonged.

As she did, Mara couldn't help but be impressed. The walls were extremely thick, at least 100 feet, and had obvious defensive measures built in that would allow the guards to defend against invaders while remaining safe. There were murder holes in the ceiling that would allow arrows to be fired down from above—or whatever projectile weapons these people used. Or they could pour boiling oil or acid. She couldn't help but notice there were some kind of weapons mounted above the gates as well that seemed to be manned and ready for use.

She had no idea what those weapons were, but they had long bodies with large crystals on the ends. They were on stands that allowed them to pivot and raise up and down the way you would have mounted a machine gun. Overall, it was pretty intimidating, and that didn't even account for the guards themselves. There were easily twenty-five men in sight, either on the wall above or in the passageway, stationed at key locations. Each wore light armor, a sword at their waist, and on the other hip, they all carried one of those shockrods.

The impression she had of the soldiers was "competent." They looked like a group of men and women who knew how to fight and had the experience to handle difficult situations. They were the kind you didn't want to mess with. On the other hand, they were posted to a duty that saw them scanning thousands of people passing their checkpoint every day. Even competent soldiers couldn't catch everything illicit moving in and out of their gates.

Such as herself.

Davin had taught her early in her new life as a vampire that people would treat you the way you presented yourself. If you cringed and worried that every mortal you met would see through your pretense of being one of them, then they surely would. However, if you walked with confidence, head held high, and acted like you belonged there, you could walk into a room full of vampire hunters, and they'd be convinced you were Van Helsing's great-granddaughter.

One hundred years of practice not only fooling mortals, but fighting a shadow war against an enemy with overwhelming numbers and power meant Mara didn't so much as flinch when the inner gate guard called her over.

The man was wearing an odd-looking pair of glasses and carrying a grapefruit-sized crystal orb in his hand. He wasn't alone either; two stout-looking soldiers flanked him, seeming ready for violence.

Cool as a cucumber on the outside, Mara tensed inwardly. They had clearly detected something about her, and with magic items being a thing on this world, she had to believe they knew what she was. Those glasses and that orb both seemed to have that weird grey vapor-looking stuff clinging to them, more so than his shockrod or anything else he was wearing.

She stepped up to the trio and nodded respectfully, but otherwise presented a confident front. "Yes?"

The brown-haired soldier with the magic items frowned. "Are you new to the city?" He hadn't failed to notice her bare feet and unusual attire.

Hmm... how should I play this? Honesty. Always the best policy, and you couldn't be caught up in lies if you didn't tell any.

Still, that didn't mean telling the whole truth.

"I just arrived tonight."

The man nodded almost imperceptibly to himself, as if he had a way to detect the truth. Mara patted herself on the back for deciding not to lie. But that meant she would need to get creative with the truth, depending on what questions the guard asked.

"Why are you not wearing shoes? Even with the cleaning magic, while your feet might not get dirty, you could still injure yourself on something sharp."

This guy asked questions like a police interrogator. She could easily sense that he didn't care about her safety but was simply asking to see how she would react. Would she get nervous and act suspicious?

Such games would not work on her; she had too much experience with situations like this.

With calm nonchalance, she replied, "Unfortunately, my belongings didn't arrive with me, but a man was kind enough to give me his cloak and point me to a shop inside the city where I can acquire what I need. I was on my way there now."

That garnered a raised eyebrow, but her attitude seemed to satisfy. His next question was more business like. "Name, and how long do you plan to stay in the city?"

"Mara, and honestly, I don't know yet. I thought I would have a look around and decide if I like it or not before making a decision."

The man's frown deepened. "Name and image have been registered. Be aware—your kind is not permitted to live above ground in the city. If you leave Daggerport, you will report to the gate and submit to questioning. Should we learn that you've committed any murders or violent crimes while inside the walls, you will be punished accordingly. If you intend to stay, keep your nose clean. As a vampire, you are subject to questioning at any time."

Hmm. That was a lot to unpack.

From the sound of it, every guard in the city would now know exactly who and what she was. And if they knew that much—and still allowed her inside—then Mara had to assume they were also equipped to deal with vampires. The 'above ground' comment stuck out. The way he'd said it, with that little edge in his tone, made it sound like the good, decent people lived up here. Vampires, clearly, were expected to keep to the shadows—literally and legally.

There was more to this city than met the eye. That much was clear. An underground existed—and it wasn't just metaphorical.

Still, he hadn't forbidden her entry. No threats. No posturing. Just rules and expectations. That was... unexpected.

Dismissed with a flick of the hand, Mara stepped away from the checkpoint, her mind spinning with the implications. This world was strange—vampires weren't hunted or feared, but were instead tolerated under strict terms. Second-class citizens, maybe. But citizens, nonetheless.

Mara hadn't made it more than twenty steps beyond the gates when she stopped in her tracks.

A massive boulevard stretched before her, straight as an arrow and glowing in the early evening light. For the first time, she got a proper look at the city itself.

It was beautiful.

Just inside the gates was an open square, but beyond that, the boulevard came alive. Shops and cafés lined both sides of the road, their lanterns casting a warm glow across the cobblestones and onto the faces of laughing patrons. More striking still was the series of parks running down the center of the thoroughfare—lush, manicured islands of green filled with trees, hedges, and quiet little paths. Wrought-iron lanterns dangled from curved posts, casting golden light over stone benches, bubbling fountains, and bursts of color from blooming flower beds. Somewhere nearby, the scent of night jasmine drifted through the air, mingling with the smell of roasting meat and fresh bread.

It reminded her of Paris in the 1920s—of moonlit walks and jazz spilling out of open windows—making her long to stroll the boulevard and soak it all in.

Unfortunately, I don't have that luxury right now. The mess in the alley might already be on its way to the city guard, if it hadn't been reported already. She needed to disappear—fast. That meant getting out of this cloak and into something less conspicuous.

With a sigh, she turned down the much smaller road that ran along the inside of the city wall. Shops and businesses lined this street too, but they were quieter, more utilitarian. A travel agency sat on the corner, followed by a fishmonger, a moneylender, and a string of nondescript storefronts. A few inns and taverns dotted the block— none as divey as the Ship's Bilge, but not what she'd call upscale either.

She followed the directions she'd been given and turned left when she found the Sea View Inn. Judging by the cluster of men loitering near the door, it wasn't a place she'd be staying. They didn't approach her physically, but the things they muttered as she passed made her fingers twitch with the urge to break a few noses.

The city might be beautiful, but some things never change.

Putting vengeful thoughts aside, Mara frowned, her mind catching on something odd. The men outside had spoken clearly—too clearly. She could understand every word as if it were spoken in perfect English. But some of the idioms they'd used made her brain itch.

Those phrases... they were the same kind of garbage she'd heard from construction crews on Earth. The slang, the tone—it was *precisely* the kind of sleazy catcalling she'd learned to ignore a hundred years ago.

But how would they have the same idioms here? In another world, speaking another language?

One more mystery to figure out when I'm not in a rush, she told herself, filing it away under "problems for later."

Luckily, the pawnshop wasn't hard to find. It turned out it wasn't six blocks north of the wall like she'd been told—it was seven. But she hadn't gotten lost.

There it was: a squat building with a green stone façade and a carved wooden sign reading *"Greenstone"* swinging overhead.

Mara rolled her eyes at the lack of originality, grabbed the handle, and stepped inside.

It was time to sell some stolen goods.

CHAPTER

FIVE

A SCOWLING CUSTOMER stormed toward the door just as Mara stepped inside, forcing her to sidestep quickly to avoid a shoulder check. Judging by the fury on his face, he wouldn't have blinked at plowing straight through her.

Not exactly a glowing review, she thought, watching the man shove the door open hard enough to rattle the hinges. *Still, I'm short on options, and I need a safe place to hole up before sunrise. Might as well give it a shot.*

Her second impression of Greenstone wasn't much better.

For a place claiming to be a pawn shop, the merchandise left a lot to be desired. A few dull-edged blades hung on hooks along the walls, while a mismatched pile of dented armor lurked in one corner. Shelves were crammed with what looked like broken tools, odd trinkets, and the kind of junk even a street vendor would hesitate to touch. The only thing that looked halfway professional was the long glass case at the back of the shop.

Behind it sat a man with the slick look of someone who measured people in coin weight. He was already eyeing her with an amused smirk that made her skin crawl.

Slimy bastard.

"If you're here for shoes," he said, gesturing lazily toward her bare feet, "I'm afraid you're out of luck. I don't sell clothing."

No shit. Like I couldn't tell that at first glance.

The pawnshop owner was a lean, sharp-featured man with greying dark hair tied back at the nape of his neck. His deep-set eyes were keen and calculating and a bit hot, and he seemed to be weighing, estimating her worth to the nearest cent, and maybe what he could get from her, not involving coin.

He was dressed in a simple but well-tailored vest over a linen shirt unbuttoned halfway down, displaying greying chest hair, and he had a few rings on his fingers. Despite the skeeziness, he carried himself with the quiet confidence of a man who always knew the true worth of a deal, whether or not he let on.

Mara wasn't sure what to think. Most men focused on her body, or perhaps her face, and got distracted, but this guy seemed at least equally as interested in her purse. A man of appetites, but from the look in his eyes, gold was his true mistress.

She gave him a grin, hiding her mild annoyance. After a hundred years of unlife, slimy men barely registered. If she'd punished every creep who gave her a look she didn't like, there'd be a mountain of bodies trailing behind her. She had better things to do.

"Selling, not buying. Nargent sent me."

That name changed the man's face like someone flipped a switch.

"That rat bastard still owes me three gold marks, and now he's sending people my way?" Gavian scowled, then huffed. "Figures."

36

She almost regretted dropping the name, but it did get his attention. The irritation faded as quickly as it came, and he shifted into professional mode.

"I'm Gavian. First things first: is this your own business?"

She frowned. "Yeah. It is."

"Are you in any way affiliated with the city watch, any investigative organization, or the Seers' Guild?"

She noticed the flicker of vapor—magic—flutter near his face. Subtle, but unmistakable. Some kind of truth spell, perhaps. Interesting.

"Nope. No affiliations. I was attacked earlier tonight. Luckily, the bastards who tried it became overwhelmed with guilt and decided to donate their worldly possessions. At least, everything they had on them."

Gavian blinked, then let out a bark of laughter. "Is that where you got the cloak, too?"

She nodded. "I was in my nightclothes when they decided to 'have a little fun.'"

His amusement faded fast. "Followers of the Dragon broke into your home and tried to assault you?"

"It's... complicated." She shrugged. "Let's just say I went to bed somewhere safe and woke up somewhere I definitely wasn't. Then those pricks stumbled across me."

"Hmm... either way, I'm surprised those people would be so brazen. Considering they go around preaching how all humans are brothers and sisters, that's pretty hypocritical."

"I don't know anything about them other than what I experienced tonight. They are scumbags in my book. Now, do you want to buy their stuff or not?"

The man gave a dark chuckle. "Yeah. I'll buy, if it's any good. Show me what you've got."

She didn't hesitate, pulling the various pieces of jewelry out of the pouch and laying them on the counter one by one. Considering there were only three guys, they had a lot of jewelry. There were nine rings, seven earrings, three bank tokens, a brooch, and four other pendants. All of it was crafted of metals and gemstones or crystals. The metals were a mix of precious ones like gold and silver, and the more mundane steel or bronze.

The man frowned, "Well, they aren't anything special, I can tell that just by looking. Give me a moment to examine them, and find out what they do."

He pulled out a gorgeous wooden rod marked with numerous symbols and hash marks. She got the distinct impression that those marks acted as a ruler for measuring things although it didn't resemble Earth rulers beyond the marks.

Fanciest damned ruler I've ever seen!

However, the man did some more magic mumbo jumbo and held the rod over each item, examining them closely.

Gavian let out a slow whistle as he spread the jewelry across the counter, fingers flicking through the rings and pendants with casual expertise. He plucked up a gold band set with a blood-red stone and held it to the magic field that the rod was emitting, then glanced at Mara with a knowing smirk.

He separated the items into small piles, picking up one of the rings first as part of his explanation.

"Three storage rings. Nothing special, maybe five cubic feet each. Basic enchantments, nothing like the high-end stuff Master Elegar produces for the nobles, but handy for keeping your hands free even if they were made by a lesser Maker. Worth something, but not as much as you'd hope. They are also more than halfway through their guaranteed lifespan. If they were brand new, they would probably be worth a good bit, but not when they are that old."

He set them aside and grabbed a simple silver brooch, turning it over in his palm.

"This thing? Fire resistance charm. Low tier, probably only useful against small flames or keeping your soup from scalding you." He snorted. "Might save a fool from burning his fingers, but it won't do much against real fire magic. Still, better than nothing."

Next, he picked up a few pendants, tapping one against the counter.

"Ah, data crystals. Could be anything in here—messages, records, spell notes if they were stupid enough to carry something valuable. But they are keyed to the owner; unless they transferred the ownership to you, they're just fancy rocks. Worthless. Worse, if the men hire a Seer, they will be able to track them directly to you. You'll have to dispose of them somewhere soon."

Mara stayed quiet, watching as he moved on to the earrings, reserving her judgment on his honesty until she had heard more.

"These?" He lifted three gold earrings with small gems. "Cleaners, they'll remove all unwelcome dirt and odors. I'm surprised you didn't use one before bringing them to sell. Still, they are extremely common. Every citizen has one; it's the law in Daggerport, like most places in the civilized world. Except you, of course, since you just got... well, whatever happened to you, you clearly are in need of pretty much everything. You're not wearing a single magic item." He almost looked scandalized by that and was clearly making assumptions.

"If you didn't need to launder all of this to keep the Seers from tracking you down, keeping one of these would be useful. Unfortunately for you, that's not an option due to your circumstances."

The next set of earrings was silver with faint engravings. Gavian tapped one against the counter, shaking his head.

"Speech Stones. Lets the wearer communicate with someone over long distances. They look decent enough, able to be attuned to ten other speech stones, and they aren't keyed to the owner. I'll have to go to the trouble of de-attuning them, though. That will be a pain."

He moved to the remaining rings, picking one and rolling it between his fingers, squinting as if he had to concentrate to identify it. "Hmph. This one's just a Ring of Steady Hand—helps with keeping your grip steady, maybe good for a scribe or someone who works with delicate tools, but nothing special. This one here?"

He tapped another with a dull, scratched gemstone. "Minor Warding Ring—barely worth the metal it's made of. Might turn a dagger into a bruise instead of a cut, but don't count on it saving your life." He flicked his fingers over the last two with a smirk. "Ring of Silent Steps—makes you a little quieter, but you're not sneaking past any real pros with it. And this? Just a simple light ring—hovering glow follows you around, about as bright as a lantern."

He pushed the rings into a pile dismissively, as if they had no value.

Mara wasn't buying his act. Those rings were all handy utility items and something anyone would be happy to have at their disposal.

Then, the pawnshop owner eyed the last few pendants. Three of them were bank tokens, but the last one was something different.

"This pendant," he muttered, rolling one between his fingers. "This one's got a ward on it—feels like it blocks scrying or weak tracking magic. Not bad, but not foolproof."

He set it down with a casual shrug.

"Now, none of this is high-end, mind you. Just the usual trinkets people like that carry. Still, I can take them off your hands for a fair price, or we can talk trade if you're looking for something specific."

Mara arched a brow, unimpressed. "And by 'fair price,' you mean what, exactly?"

Gavian chuckled, leaning on the counter. "A price that won't make either of us walk away feeling cheated—too much."

Not that she would have trusted him anyway, but she was getting the distinct impression he was about to lowball her. She had dealt with enough crooks in her time to feel it.

"Alright, what's your offer?"

"Well, let's see..." He was making counting gestures with his hands as he muttered unintelligibly under his breath.

When he had finished, he looked her in the eyes and said, "I think nine gold marks is fair for the lot. Keeping in mind that I not only have to deal with using magic to cleanse them of their connections to their past owners, and who knows how long these will take to sell, I'm taking quite a big risk here."

Mara knew bullshit when she smelled it. Without hesitation and tapping into her vampiric speed, she stepped forward and reached over the counter, grabbed Gavian's collar, and yanked him close. She looked deeply into his eyes and pressed her will into his mind.

He didn't have time to react, his eyes barely beginning to go wide before Mara's power overwhelmed his brain.

She smirked in satisfaction as she commanded, "Now tell me what these are really worth, and what is the highest price you would give if you were an honest merchant."

With a dazed expression, he seemed to be struggling as he answered, "Forty-one Gold Marks. But I don't have that much gold on hand. Normally, I would transfer the money to your bank token, but you don't have one."

Wow, he must really love his gold to be fighting her will this much. "How much cash do you have on hand then? And tell me about money here. I'm from a long way away."

He pulled a pouch full of coins from his own storage ring and handed it to her with great reluctance. A mother would have an easier time giving up a child for adoption than this man had giving up his coins. "That is all I have, but I'll give it to you for your items, like an honest merchant."

CHAPTER

SIX

Mara wanted to laugh, he almost sounded pained at that last. "And how does money work here in Daggerport?"

"Money is in the form of coins. Ten Copper coins equal one silver piece. Those are the small silver coins. Ten of those, in turn, are worth one silver mark, the big silver coins. Ten silver marks are worth one gold piece. Take ten of the small gold piece coins, and it is worth a gold mark."

Mara poured the pouch of coins Gavian had given her onto the counter and looked at them. There was a mishmash of mintings, but she quickly noted that no matter what face or image was depicted on the coin's faces, they all seemed to be remarkably similar in size and weight. Familiar with Earth coins and weights, she figured the 'mark' coins were about the same as a 1 oz silver coin on Earth or maybe a little heavier. Likewise for the gold.

A gold mark, with the face of some queen, weighed exactly the same as the one with a mountain range on one side and a logo that translated to 'The Dwarven Sovereign Bank' on the other. The same was true with the different types of coins.

For a brief moment, she was surprised by her ability to read that. She was absolutely sure she shouldn't be able to recognize a foreign symbol like that at a glance, but it was as easy to read as if it were in English. Something to wonder about when she had more time. For now, it was just another weird piece of a strange puzzle that her night had become.

Seeing her interest, the merchant continued, still sounding dazed, "The dwarves set the standard for all coins, and all of the nations follow their regulations. In fact, most of the cities or countries pay the dwarves to mint their coins for them."

Scooping the coins back into the pouch, she figured she had around thirty-five gold marks worth of coins.

"What's the value of a gold mark in some form I would understand? What can one of these big gold coins buy?"

The man thought for a second and replied, "A member of the City Watch will earn around ten gold marks per year—an officer around fifteen. A common laborer mucking stalls might only make four gold marks per year."

Doing some quick math, she estimated that one gold mark was worth the Earth equivalent of around $10,000 US dollars, and a single copper was roughly a single dollar. That would help her keep things straight as she handled these coins.

Needing to understand why these magic items were so valuable, she asked the merchant.

"Well, the Makers Guild guarantees all their work for at least twenty-five years, but most good items last for fifty or even one hundred, so people buy their magic items and keep them for a long time. It just makes sense that they would be expensive. Only the

Makers and some Wizards are even allowed to create magic items. It's illegal for any other mage due to the dangers if an enchant were to fail."

Hmm... that was actually good information. It sounded like, at least for magic items, they did not have a 'throw-away' economy.

"I don't want all of this, just the stuff I can cleanse and sell. You need to take the bank tokens and other useless things and find some way to get rid of them. Otherwise, the Seers will use their magic to find you."

That brought her to another question: "Alright, and you say I have to leave all this with you; otherwise, I can be traced by some... What did you call them? Seers? Explain the Seers."

Still dazed by her compulsion, he continued as commanded, "The Seers are one of the top ten mage guilds. They are employed by the city and governments all over the continent to act as magistrates and investigators; the regular citizens can also commission them. In your case, if the Watch gets involved and anyone is killed or seriously injured, they will bring in a Seer as part of their routine. The Seer will create an image of you, and it will be posted to all of the guards in the city. If you really were attacked and only defended yourself, then maybe they won't chase you down, but just post up an arrest warrant. Then you will have the Watch and bounty hunters after you.

If you still have their things, then the Seers will be able to track those right to you. Without them, they would need to be actively looking for you within range of where you are currently. Unless some bigshot in the guild gets involved, that is. One of those high-rankers has the power to scry the whole city at once, but you should be safe as long as all they have is your image."

"Well, shit." This night had gone off the rails fast. She was stranded on a new world where vampires were a known quantity, magic was

45

as common as cell phones, and apparently, *everyone* had it—except her. Worse, she'd already managed to rack up a potential criminal record just for defending herself against a pack of would-be rapists.

And the cherry on top? She probably would've let the bastards live— maybe even walked away unscathed—if she hadn't been starving. But no, the magical kidnapping that brought her here had wrung her dry, leaving her empty of power and too ravenous to hold back.

And now this asshole was trying to lowball her.

"Do you have the means to destroy the items you won't take, so the Seers can't trace them back to me?"

"Yes." The answer was clipped and flat, but he was still under compulsion. She doubted he would've admitted it otherwise.

"Good," she said, voice cool. "Then you'll do so immediately. Consider it compensation for shorting me on the payout."

Even bound by her will, Gavian looked like he'd bitten into a lemon.

"But if they trace the goods to me, they'll question me. The Seers will know I helped you. That could implicate me."

She gave him a cold smile. "Don't worry. I'll make sure you don't remember a thing. Burn the cloak and belt too, then find me something—*anything*—I can wear over these pajamas. Something plain, something forgettable. That way, if anyone comes sniffing around, you can say you took pity on a woman who'd been attacked and had nothing left. No magic items, no possessions. Just a sob story and bare feet."

Gavian gave a slow nod, visibly relieved at having a cover story he could sell. He might be a seasoned fence, but even in a city with magical investigators, plausible deniability went a long way.

"Alright," she said, waving a hand. "Get to it."

The man led her into a back room and down a narrow flight of stairs into a stone-walled basement. Unlike the barren front of the shop, this place was packed—floor to ceiling—with racks, crates, and shelves overflowing with gear. Weapons, armor, magical odds and ends... all of it looked just valuable enough to raise questions, and none of it looked like it had ever seen a legal ledger.

This was the real Greenstone. And judging by the faint shimmer of magic in the air, she had no doubt the room was heavily warded, probably to keep the Seers from catching wind of his little treasure trove.

The center of the room had been kept clear, and at its heart was an arcane circle inlaid into the stone floor. Even with her limited magical awareness, Mara could see the misty grey energy clinging to the etched metal symbols. The magic practically hummed in the air.

Gavian stepped into the circle and dumped the rejected items into its center. Then, with a few muttered words and a wave of his carved wooden rod, the circle flared to life. A dome of shimmering energy snapped into place just as the junk began to crackle and dissolve in a furious burst of light and sound.

Mara flinched despite herself. It looked disturbingly like someone had tossed a CD into a microwave—if the microwave was powered by arcane hellfire and had a flair for the dramatic.

When the light show finally ended, the discarded goods were gone. In their place, faint tendrils of grey mana hung in the air, caught within the containment field like smoke in a glass dome.

She tilted her head. "What happens to all that energy?"

"The magic?" Gavian glanced at her as he stepped out of the circle. "The array lets it dissipate slowly. Keeps it from building up and drawing attention."

Smart. He might be a greasy, lowballing fence, but the man clearly knew his business.

After seeing that the destruction was completed, the man moved to a rack and pulled off a cloak of the cheapest, roughest fabric he had. "Here, the covering you asked for."

She almost wanted to laugh. His subconscious was fighting her hard for every copper despite the compulsion she had put him under.

"Sandals or shoes for my feet? I don't want to draw attention."

Woodenly, he moved to a shelf, pulled out a pair of heavily worn leather sandals, and presented them.

She adorned her feet with the proffered footwear, and then draped the cloak over her shoulders and buttoned it at the neck with its cheap wooden buttons. It had a hood, which would keep her face mostly hidden, so that should help avoid notice long enough to get some real clothes.

"Now, tell me where I can stay that's actually safe."

"The Dragon Inn," Gavian said without hesitation. "Pretty much everyone who passes through the city goes there at least once—it's something of a landmark. But for someone like you? It's safe because of the owner, Zakkarius Ironeater. He's an old Dwarf with deep connections. Nobles, guilds, even the Watch—no one crosses him."

Mara arched a brow. "And they wouldn't drag me out if I'm staying there?"

"Not a chance," he said. "As long as you've paid for a room and stay inside, even the Watch won't touch you. That place is neutral ground, untouchable. Pricey, though. But with what I'm giving you, you'll have enough to stay there a good while. Long enough to get on your feet—assuming you don't blow it all on gear."

He gestured around at the shelves. "As you've probably guessed, magic isn't cheap. You'll need a cleaner at the very least. It's the law, and you'll stand out fast without one."

That was a lot for someone under compulsion to say, but apparently the man's subconscious was no longer fighting her will now that money wasn't on the line. Mara also thought that it was about time to leave the building. She had been here awhile already, and if the Watch really was after her, it would be best to put some distance between her and the last place she had been connected with the stolen items.

"Just three more questions and I'll be out of your hair," Mara said. "First—how do I get to that inn you mentioned?"

"Easy enough," Gavian replied. "Head west 'til you hit North Road, the main north-south boulevard through the city. Can't miss it—it's the widest thoroughfare in any city on the continent. Divided lanes, with trees and parks running right down the center, stretches from the Docks Gate in the south all the way to the Forest Gate in the north.

"From there, go north until you pass Castle Road—another monster of a street, east-west this time. When you see it, you'll know. Ornate stonework, statues, banners, the whole show. Keep going north, and about halfway to the Forest Gate, look for Dragon Street. There'll be a sign on the corner pointing east. Take that turn, follow it down. You'll know the place when you see it. Supposedly, a dragon fell out of the sky and crushed a noble's estate right there. Dwarf bought the ruin, hollowed out the corpse with magic, and built an inn inside it."

Mara snorted. "Well, you're downright chatty now. Eager to be rid of me?"

He wisely didn't answer.

"Second question—where do I shop for what I need tonight? Preferably on the way to the inn."

"The Mile," Gavian said without hesitation. "Runs along that North Road. Once you pass Castle Road, that's where the real shopping starts. Locals call it the Merchant Mile, and it lives up to the name. You need clothes, cleaners, gear, even a forged identity; someone there is selling it. They say if you can't find it on the Mile, it can't be bought."

Mara again felt something was off between the words she was hearing and what the man was saying. She had noticed a few small things that seemed odd so far, but 'Mile' was an Earth term for distance measurement, and it made no sense here—not unless whatever was translating their language for her was also converting their unit of distance into miles.

That's awfully convenient.

"Third and last—how do I get one of those Bank Tokens you mentioned?"

"Not too far from Dragon Street, before you get to it, you'll see a big white stone building, looks like a big fortress, except it has no windows or any other entrance except the front doors. It's got a big symbol on the front for the Dwarven Sovereign Bank. It's not open this late, but you can go there tomorrow. They will take your coins and hold them for you, and issue a bank token. With it, you can magically transfer money from your vault to that of anyone else who has a token, which is everyone."

"Excellent. You have been very helpful. Now, you are going to lead me upstairs, and as I leave the building, you will forget we did any business together in stolen magic items. You will only remember that a young woman who had been robbed and assaulted came in, and you took pity on her and gave her a cloak to cover herself with. You will not remember anything unusual about me, nor be able to give a good description. You were put off by having to provide charity to someone who couldn't afford any of your merchandise, and just wanted me to go away. You will not have any idea where I might have gone."

Interestingly, she did not feel much resistance from Gavian's will to these suggestions. No doubt because he knew he was better off not being able to get involved in the event that the Watch or other Followers of the Dragon came looking for her.

"Now, escort me to the door, and I will leave."

She thought with some excitement, *I've got some shopping to do!*

CHAPTER

SEVEN

THE WALK across town turned out to be far less stressful than Mara had expected. Daggerport was massive—easily stretching for miles —and laid out in an almost obsessively perfect grid of north-south and east-west streets. What caught her attention most, though, was how clean everything was. Not just tidy, but spotless. No trash, no grime, no graffiti.

She had traveled all over Earth during her century as a vampire— conducting covert ops, infiltrating enemy organizations, waging a hidden war against the Cabal. She'd seen cities across the world in every state of chaos and decay. But this place? This place was alien in its precision.

Downright bizarre, she thought. *Although... the people don't seem like they've got sticks up their butts, so that's something.*

When she reached the broad, bustling thoroughfare that cut north to south across the city, she knew she was on the fastest route to cross Daggerport. A weathered street sign labeled it the *Great North Road,* but according to Gavian, it seemed everyone just called it the *North Road.*

The evening crowd meandering along the boulevards only added to the city's strange appeal. People strolled, laughed, browsed through shops, and dined in open-air cafés under soft, magical lanterns that cast a warm glow. For a city this well-kept, she would've expected coldness or rigidity, but instead, the atmosphere had a relaxed cosmopolitan energy, like a place where cultures blended without friction.

A nearby group sharing wine and laughter around a café table caught her attention. The food on their plates sent up aromas that teased her senses—rich, savory, delicately spiced. It was rare for anything to smell truly appetizing to her anymore, but this... this was tempting. Whoever the chef was, they knew what they were doing.

That's impressive, she mused. *Most mortal cooks can't manage anything that doesn't taste like wet cardboard to me.*

Not only did they smell yummy, but exotic as well, seasoned with spices with which she was completely unfamiliar.

She chucked to herself at the thought, *Note to self, indulge in some foodie style exploration when I have a chance!*

It was odd, she always had enjoyed good food, even after becoming a vampire, but she didn't really *crave* it. Maybe it was the situation and the uniqueness of the smells, but she actually felt a mild hunger craving. Just one more oddity of this absolutely insane evening.

Mara received another shock while walking north along the park-lined avenue and watching the people. She had been taking note of fashions to understand how people dressed in this city when she noticed an Elf sitting on one of the park benches. He was tall and lithe, and he had the classic angular face and pointy ears from fantasy, although not the super long ones that some game franchises made popular.

She couldn't help herself—curiosity tugged at her feet—and she drifted closer to get a better look.

After a few seconds, the Elven man turned slightly, his eyes meeting hers with a calm, knowing expression. She hadn't made a sound, but somehow he was aware of her stare.

"Oh! Sorry," she said, caught off guard. "I'm new to the city... and from pretty far away. I've never seen someone like you before. I didn't mean to stare." A faint blush touched her cheeks—embarrassment, not from fear, but from being caught acting like a tourist.

He smiled, serene and unbothered. "Even in Daggerport, Elves are uncommon. We don't often linger in cities. For myself, I find the evenings here peaceful, especially when the crowds thin. The parks are my favorite part of this place."

His eyes moved to the rows of trees lit by soft light crystals. "In a city shaped by Dwarven minds—so precise, so structured—this is the closest I've found to the harmony of nature. One of my kin helped design the green spaces here, just after the last war."

Mara glanced at the trees with fresh eyes. "They look ancient. Did your people use magic to grow them like that?"

Chuckling, the Elf gestured around him, "No, no, the war was a bit over four hundred years ago; it just seems recent to me. I remember visiting the city before that, when it was still part of the Human kingdom to the west, and even earlier still when the Dwarves first began building it as a trading town at the outskirts of their mountain kingdom."

He gestured toward the mountain range to the east, at the foot of which the city had been built.

"The Human world changes so quickly, if you'll pardon my saying so."

That was a lot to unpack.

Apparently Elves really did live forever—or close to it—just like in the stories. And this guy had casually mentioned Dwarves like it was no big deal. If Elves and Dwarves were real here, what else had bled into Earth's myths? Dragons? Demons? Gods?

Focus, she told herself. *One existential crisis at a time.*

Out loud, she kept it polite. "I see. Thank you for the explanation. Are you visiting the city too, or do you live here?"

"I am Arden, and I have a residence and business here in the city." He looked at her closely, seeming as if he could see into her soul, although she didn't detect any malice or ill intent.

After a long, thoughtful moment, the Elf raised his arm in a smooth, fluid motion. A small engraved plaque shimmered into existence in his hand, which he offered without flourish. "I match properties with people who need a place to make their home. If you find yourself in need, I will help."

Her first instinct was to decline—on principle if nothing else—but something about him made her hesitate. There was no sales pitch in his tone, no hustle in his body language. The offer felt genuine. Like he'd seen something in her during that soul-searching glance he'd given her earlier. She didn't feel pitied—just... acknowledged. As if he'd recognized someone adrift and offered a line without asking questions.

"Thank you," she said, accepting the plaque with a nod. "If I decide to settle here, I'll come find you. But for now, I've got nothing but the clothes on my back and a few coins in my pouch. Might be a while before I'm looking for anything as permanent as a home."

Arden gave a slight shrug and a kind smile. "Then I wish you luck—and success in your search. When the time comes, I'll be there."

She gave a slight nod of her head and a wave, and walked away, glancing down at the fancy engraved copper plaque. It had Arden written in big letters surrounded by vinework decorations. It was in a script that she could somehow magically read, and below it in what she was coming to recognize as the local common language was an address.

Unfortunately, she had no pockets, so she was forced to place it in her coin pouch, hoping that the coins wouldn't scratch up the beautiful invitation too much.

The Elf wasn't the only non-human race on the streets. Now that she was aware of their existence, she did notice quite a few Dwarves among those out and about. When she first heard mention of 'dwarves,' she thought Gavian was just being rude about the owner of the Dragon Inn being a little person. Now, however, she understood she was in a world with actual fantasy races.

Well, not fantasy here. They are clearly real on this world. Still, this is pretty wild.

The Dwarves she saw were almost the stereotypical race from video games and novels back home. They were super broad and stocky and looked very strong. However, unlike some of the stories from Earth's fiction, these Dwarves did seem to have distinct male and female genders, and the women did not have beards! In her opinion, they were cute with their wide faces. They had a feminine look to them, very different from the rugged, bearded males.

Another thing she noticed right away was that the Dwarves she was encountering were all very well dressed. Better than the Humans around them, that was for sure.

The humans, on the other hand, were much more diverse. This city seemed to be a melting pot of nationalities and cultures, with individuals and groups from all over the world coming to the city to trade and do business.

Mara was paying close attention to this, in particular, because she wanted to know what kind of clothes to buy.

The poorer folk dressed plainly—boots, pants, shirts, and often some kind of coat or cloak. The night air was cool, and she didn't spot many bare arms. Interestingly, dresses seemed uncommon. Aside from a few noble-looking women in flowing gowns, nearly everyone wore some variation of trousers and blouses.

The most striking difference between men's and women's fashion was the fit. Women's clothes hugged their figures—tight pants, cinched waists, and corsets that emphasized curves. Men, by contrast, wore looser pants tucked into tall leather boots, with long-sleeved shirts and vests. A few showed off with tighter shirts stretched over muscles, and wide belts hung heavy with knives, tankards, pouches, or other useful bits.

She noticed those knives weren't just for show. Plenty of people had sheathed swords at their hips or those damned magical cattle prods like the ones the Follower bastards had used on her earlier.

So much for relying on the city Watch. Despite the clean, orderly appearance of Daggerport, the citizens clearly believed in being prepared. Nearly everyone had some kind of blade—belted, booted, or tucked somewhere easy to reach. It wasn't paranoia. It was culture.

Well, who was she to judge? She was from Texas, after all.

That thought made warmth stir in her chest. Davin, her adoptive father, the vampire who'd saved her from death and raised her like his own. He was the one who'd drilled her in swordplay and daggers, who'd taught her not to rely on guns alone when facing werewolves or rival vampires. Even though she'd grown up with lever-action rifles and Colt revolvers, she'd learned that sometimes, steel was the only thing that kept you alive.

And now, on this strange new world, those hard-won lessons might be the only thing that kept her alive. As she topped the rise where the main road met Castle Road, Mara finally got a true sense of the city's scale. Lights stretched across the horizon in every direction.

Seeing it from this vantage point, she could only guess at how many people lived within the walls—but it had to rival the major cities back on Earth. Maybe not packed in like Tokyo or sprawled out like Dallas or L.A., but Daggerport was no small town. Judging by the distance she'd walked from the southern gate just to reach the city's center, it had to span at least twenty miles north to south. Castle Road sloped upward from the river in the west to the mountain base in the east, maybe ten miles across on its own.

It was hard to judge in the dark, even with her enhanced vision, but if the districts she'd seen so far were any indication, this place could easily house over a million people—maybe even two or three. There were no skyscrapers, no towering apartment blocks, but many buildings stood three stories tall, and she'd seen quite a few rising as high as seven.

She pushed those thoughts aside as she neared the intersection. City guard posts sat at each corner, and a tall, ornately built observation tower rose from the center of the massive square. From the top, someone could probably see the entire city, or at least anyone foolish enough to cause trouble here.

Years of infiltration and black ops had taught her one critical truth: never act like you don't belong. The moment you started slinking and skulking, people would start watching. So she didn't pull her hood lower or duck her head. She walked with purpose, shoulders relaxed, posture confident, as if she had every right to be there and absolutely nothing to hide.

Sure enough, the Watchmen's eyes slid right past her, scanning the crowd for pickpockets, beggars, or anyone who looked like trouble.

Still, there was a moment—just one—when she approached the northeast corner. A young guard glanced her way, then did a double take. His brow furrowed like he was trying to place her. Recognition flitted across his face, but when she caught his gaze, smiled warmly, and offered a polite wave, he blinked, flushed, and quickly looked away.

And that's how you do it.

She smiled contentedly to herself as she passed the north/east guard post without incident and finally reached the famed 'Merchant Mile' that the sleazy pawnshop owner had told her about. Sure enough, the streets were much more packed with businesses. Surprisingly, more than a few were still open even as late as it was getting.

Mara assumed she had woken up just after dark in that shaded alley, and it had taken around three hours to walk up from the south gate, and maybe another three before that since the fight with the creeps that had attacked her. That would put the hour around midnight or maybe 1:00 AM, assuming this world even had 24-hour days.

Which is maybe not a reasonable assumption to make since this world has two moons and clearly isn't Earth.

She would need to make a point of learning more about this world, but that could wait.

Now that she had reached her first destination, it was time to find some clothes and then go settle into that Inn before the sun came up.

CHAPTER

EIGHT

MARA'S first stop was a clothing store—a two-story boutique nestled in the lower half of a four-story building. Thankfully, it catered exclusively to women and had an impressive variety of ready-made garments on display—just what she needed.

She had been born into a time when most clothing was handmade. Her mother had sewn all their clothes by hand, and later, Mara had learned to do the same out of necessity. They hadn't been rich enough for luxuries like a sewing machine. After Davin turned her and brought her into his higher society lifestyle, she'd discovered shopping was one of life's unexpectedly delightful pleasures. He had money, and he hadn't minded spending it—especially when it brought her joy.

Through the 20th century, she'd come to see shopping not just as survival but as a rare indulgence. She wasn't a fashion addict, not exactly—just someone who appreciated nice things.

Well... okay, maybe there was one room full of clothes. But it was dwarfed by my armory, tactical gear, and stealth suits. So I had priorities. That's not so bad... right?

Still, she was getting a thrill looking at all the interesting foreign clothing in styles different from what she had back on Earth. She had to remind herself that this was only her first stop, and she still needed to get to that Inn before the sun rose.

Once inside the story, a woman in bright, expensive-looking fabrics approached, her posture graceful and practiced. She held out her hand, palm down, in a slow, ritual-like gesture. "How may I serve?"

Mara smiled, but hesitated, uncertain. Was she supposed to shake the woman's hand? That didn't seem quite right. Better to just explain. "I'm sorry—I don't know the local customs. I just arrived in the city today, and none of my belongings made it with me. I'm hoping you can help me find something to wear."

Then, as if remembering something obvious, she added, "Also, how long until sunrise? I don't even know what time it is."

The woman blinked, caught off guard, then gave a warm smile as the implications sank in, the potential size of the sale. "Of course! Sunrise is in about five hours. We're closing soon, but I'm sure the owner will let me assist you as long as it takes to get you properly outfitted."

She gave a friendly nod toward Mara's earlier confusion. "On the Mile, we hold our hand out like this—palm down—to signify we serve your needs. You respond by holding your hand palm-up under mine, to show support for our trade."

Odd custom, Mara thought, *but no stranger than handshakes, I suppose.*

"Thank you for explaining," she said aloud. "I'll remember that while I'm in the city. As for clothes, I'm looking for two outfits for now. One should be something nice—stylish, but not too expensive. I want to look respectable, not noble, since I'm still getting on my feet. The second should be dark and practical for after dark. I do work that sometimes requires me to follow thieves and criminals, and it's best to stay out of sight when I do."

The woman's eyes widened. "Oh! You're a bounty hunter? That must be so dangerous! And you're so young for it!"

Mara gave her a crooked grin. If the woman wanted to think that, she wasn't about to correct her. Let her imagination fill in the blanks. Mara might look young—forever in her late teens or early twenties, no thanks to the vampire who'd killed her—but she'd lived at least four lifetimes longer than this saleswoman.

"You could almost say I was raised to fight bad people in the dark and drag them to justice."

She nearly laughed at herself. The line sounded way too much like something out of a comic book—and *not* the good kind. Images of a dark clad figure with a bat-like symbol on his chest flickered through her head, and for a moment. She pictured herself skulking across rooftops in a cape. *Yeah, no.*

Her life hadn't been anything so noble.

Sure, she'd fought against the Cabal—those overreaching bastards who ruled Earth's hidden supernatural world with iron laws and zero empathy. That part was true. But the rest? The rest was murkier.

She'd owned a restaurant. Lived a quiet life in Houston. Kept mostly to herself in the vampire community. And between her more righteous missions, she'd spent more than a few decades moonlighting as a cat burglar and art thief. Elegant, lucrative, and morally flexible. She told herself it helped fund the resistance, and it did. But it also paid for a really nice sofa and an unnecessarily large collection of boots.

The saleswoman interrupted her thoughts, "You must be super brave! Come, let's find you some good outfits then!" She hurried Mara off to another room filled with outfits in darker colors, apparently taken by her imagination of the glamorous and dangerous life of a bounty hunter.

The woman had initially tried to put her in something that wouldn't have looked out of place on a comic-book hero—tight, black, and dramatic, like something Black Widow would wear. It might have been flattering, but it also screamed *Look at me, I'm trying to be sneaky!*—which, ironically, would make her stand out even more.

With a few nudges and some strategic vetoes, Mara managed to put together something more practical. The pants were a dark charcoal grey in a sturdy, slightly stretchy fabric that hugged her legs without restricting movement. Suitable for running, climbing, or fighting—she'd tested enough clothes over the decades to know what worked. The blouse was a lighter shade of grey, soft and breathable, helping break up the silhouette without looking mismatched. Over that, they added a black leather corset—stylish, but also surprisingly functional.

The saleswoman beamed as she adjusted the fit. "This leather is strong but supple. You won't get the discomfort of proper armor, but it'll take a beating. The beast it comes from produces hide that resists cuts and scratches—very popular with women who have difficult jobs but still want to look nice. And the straps and buckles? Mostly decorative, but they give it flair."

Mara gave a half-smile. *Stylish and stab-resistant. What more could a girl ask for?*

The woman's tone dipped regretfully. "If your budget were a little higher, I'd point you to our partner shop through the Maker's Guild. They specialize in enchanted fabrics—real defensive gear. Some pieces can even shrug off magic. It would be perfect for someone in your line of work. If you ever have the means, I'll make sure they offer you a discount for tailoring."

That actually *would* be worth following up on, once she wasn't one step from sleeping in an alley. "Thanks. I'll keep that in mind. For now, I just need a jacket or cloak to go over this."

"Of course, this way." The woman led her into another room filled with outerwear. A dark grey wool tone-on-tone hooded cloak was soon presented. It could be belted at the waist and buttoned at the neck or worn open on the shoulders like a cape if desired. It had options, and Mara felt confident she could configure it so that it wouldn't interfere with fighting or running through dark alleys.

The saleswoman stroked the fabric: " High-quality Gak wool. Not scratchy at all, and very weather resistant. We get our fabric from the Clan lands to the north. They have the best Gaks, much better than the stuff you can get from Valentros, and much more affordable, too."

Mara smiled encouragingly at the saleswoman. "It's perfect; I'll take it. Now, let's get me outfitted for social settings rather than work."

Grinning, the saleswoman led her away, and half an hour later, Mara was parting with two small gold coins and a silver mark. The woman seemed pleased with the sale, and Mara, now dressed in her new dark outfit, felt infinitely more comfortable. She'd gladly discarded the cheap cloak the skeezy fence had thrown at her, and good riddance to it.

With a bag in one hand, stuffed with her pajamas and a more colorful social outfit, she continued her journey in search of decent footwear. Finding a cobbler at this late hour wasn't easy, but this *was* the largest city in the region—famous for its trade, or so the clothing saleswoman had assured her.

Fifteen minutes later, she spotted a wooden sign with a boot swinging above a warmly lit storefront. The shop was smaller than the department-store-like place she'd just left, but as soon as she stepped inside, she was greeted by the comforting scent of leather. The walls were lined not just with boots, but with belts, pouches, bags, and packs. Most importantly, the shopkeeper gave her a tired but genuine smile before showing her a pair of tall black leather boots that buckled up the sides, and just so happened to go perfectly with her corset.

He tapped her boots with a tool filled with a bit of magic, and thy snugged themselves to her feet like they'd been made just for her. They were instantly, almost suspiciously, comfortable.

Seeing her reaction, the man raised a hand reassuringly. "They're not enchanted," he said. "I've got a fitting tool—adjusts 'em to match your feet. They're regular leather and will stretch naturally over time. You ever need a refit, just come back—I'll readjust them for free."

She added a few pairs of socks, a sturdy new belt, and a proper belt pouch to her haul. With that, she threw away the last remnants of the garbage Gavian had let her walk out with. It wasn't just about quality—it was the principle. Even if the city's magic kept everything sparkling clean, those items felt tainted.

After the stop at the leather shop, she was down another six silver marks and three small silvers, but it felt like a bargain.

Maybe it was just a dumb, lingering human reflex, but being ripped from her homeworld and dropped into a strange city in nothing but her pajamas had been more than a little unsettling.

Now, clothed from head to toe in gear she'd chosen for herself, Mara finally felt like she had some control again. The new outfit wasn't armor, but it *felt* like it. She left the store thankful for the cobbler's warm friendliness and that magic item that had made these the absolute most comfortable footwear she'd ever worn!

Her spine straight and her stride steady, Mara moved through the streets like she owned them. Outwardly, she'd been projecting confidence from the start—hell, she could've walked down the boulevard buck naked and made it look intentional. But now? Now she didn't have to fake it. The new clothes helped, sure, but it was more than that. She felt equipped, in control—herself again.

She continued on, passing shop after shop until she spotted a weapons dealer with its lanterns still lit. Ironically, this made the third or fourth she'd seen still open, even at what had to be 2:00 AM. Apparently, Daggerport had a thriving market for tools of violence—or defense, depending on your perspective.

Armor was tempting—but also a little premature. She didn't want to walk around looking like she was itching for a fight. That could wait until she had a better read on the city's social rules. No need to spook people—or worse, invite trouble.

What she *did* want was a couple of weapons that would serve as both protection and deterrent. A long dagger, for starters. Something practical, intimidating, and familiar. And one of those magical cattle-prods the Followers had used—shockrods, she'd heard someone call them. Apparently, they were perfectly legal to carry, and from the way they hung from belts all over the city, no one batted an eye at them.

People were a lot less likely to mess with a woman who looked like she could light them up with a stick and gut them before they hit the ground.

She'd already learned the hard way that being perceived as defenseless after dark in this city was an open invitation for the worst kinds of attention. Sure, she could handle herself—against regular people, even groups of them; her vampiric strength and speed made her a one-woman wrecking crew—but the Watch was another story. Avoiding conflict was smarter, at least until she figured out how deep the hole she was in really went.

Finding a likely shop, Mara stepped inside, seeing walls and cases full of various weapons, from swords to halberds and daggers to clubs. The proprietor was a Dwarf, the first she had seen up close. It was hard to tell, but she thought he was young. His beard wasn't as long as others she had seen, and he just didn't look quite as craggy and weathered as some of the others she had passed in the streets.

Unlike the cobbler and the young woman from the clothing store, this shopkeep didn't bother with pleasantries. He eyed her with a gruff demeanor and asked, "What d'ye want?"

She blinked in surprise at the near rudeness. "I'm looking for a dagger, and perhaps one of those magic rods."

The Dwarf spat on the floor. "Ye won't find no shockrods here. This shop deals in proper Dwarven steel, not flimsy magic trinkets."

He was giving her a look that said she just might not be worthy of the least item in the shop if she was asking for anything but his merchandise.

"I see. I didn't realize that. How much would just a dagger be?" She went on to describe what she was looking for in the weapon.

Seeing that she knew her mind and wasn't just some idiot looking to impress others, the young Dwarf softened toward her just a bit. "I'm Rurik Ironhand, and this here is Stoneheart Armory—proud affiliate of Grinor Brightiron himself."

He said it as if she should know the Grinor name, but spoiled it by stating with a rye smile, "Sorry, but I just arrived in town, and I'm not familiar with Grinor."

Rurik let out a scoff. "Ye don't know Grinor Brightiron? Bah! He's the finest metal merchant in the city! One o' only five folk in all the world sellin' true Adamantine."

Unwilling to express more ignorance by admitting she didn't know what Adamantine was, Mara just tried to look suitably impressed. "I see, thank you. I wasn't aware of that. That's quite the impressive connection then."

The young Dwarf practically preened at her response, no doubt happy that the stupid human had recognized the greatness of his shop.

Down to business!

"Now about that dagger. How much would one like I described run, and how would that compare to a lesser blade from some other shop that doesn't carry fine Dwarven Steel?"

Rurik stroked his beard, nodding with pride. "Aye, I can sell ye just what ye asked for—balanced true for throwin', but with enough blade to serve ye well in a fight. Mark me words, this steel'll last ye a lifetime. Won't break, won't dull, an' ye'll not find finer craftsmanship this side o' the mountain!"

He quickly retrieved a dagger that fit the bill and presented it, placing it on a sturdy wooden table covered with black fabric to show off the blade's beauty.

She tried to keep just how impressed she was off her face, not wanting to give away her eagerness. She had owned some quality weapons back on Earth, but this dagger was a thing of beauty. The Dwarven Steel it was made from was like some type of Damascus Steel back on Earth, but it was more beautiful. The layers of the blade seemed somehow distinct, and had a depth almost like a Hamon line on a Japanese blade.

She had no idea how they managed that, but if she were back on Earth, she would buy this dagger, put it in a display case, and make it the prized possession in her extensive collection. In other words, she wanted it.

He gave a dramatic pause before ending, "Three gold marks."

Mara almost choked. That was the equivalent of around $30,000 back on Earth. They sure prized their Dwarven Steel.

Wanting to understand how expensive that was, she asked, "How much would a similar dagger run that wasn't Dwarven Steel?"

Rurik scoffed, his thick brows furrowing in offense. "Bah! Five silver marks? Ye'd get a lump o' pig iron for that price, not a proper blade. If ye want somethin' that even comes close to Dwarven steel, ye'd need enchantments stacked on it, an' that'd cost ye no less than two gold marks. This here's a bargain, lass—quality, craftsmanship, and beauty all in one."

Sensing that they were now haggling, Mara narrowed her eyes and countered, "I really just need the weapon for show to keep men from annoying me. As beautiful as your weapons are, I don't really need something so fancy."

As if reluctantly, she added, "Still, I could give you a single gold mark, and even that is more than I planned to spend."

Rurik let out a bark of laughter, shaking his head. "A single gold mark? Lass, ye wound me. This here is dwarven steel, finest craftsmanship ye'll lay hands on. If I let it go for that, I'd have to pack up me shop and take up beggin' in the streets."

Mara smirked. "Oh, come now, you'd never let yourself fall so low. And let's not pretend you're taking a loss on it."

The Dwarf snorted, stroking his beard. "A loss? Nay, but I've got a reputation to uphold. If I start lettin' highborn lasses talk me down to near scraps, next thing ye know, every greenhorn that walks through me door'll be demandin' the same."

She gave a casual shrug. "I doubt many greenhorns come through here looking for weapons they can't afford. Besides, if I walk out with this, people will see your craft in action. Consider it free advertisement."

Rurik eyed her, unimpressed. "Bah. I don't run a charity, girl."

She met his gaze evenly. "And I don't pay extra for the sake of a merchant's pride."

For a long moment, the Dwarf considered her, then exhaled through his nose. "One mark and seven gold pieces," he finally said, voice gruff but firm. "That's as low as I go. Ye'll not find a better deal for steel that won't dull nor break, no matter how many skulls ye split."

Mara pretended to consider, then nodded. "Now that's a price I can work with."

Rurik grumbled, but there was a glint of satisfaction in his eye as he took her payment and handed over the dagger. "Try not to get yerself killed with it, eh? Bad for business."

"Now hold on! You're not done yet. I need a sheath to go with that. Preferably one that I can strap to my thigh to keep it from bouncing around if I'm running down an alley chasing some creep that tried to do something nefarious."

Rurik let out a deep chuckle, shaking his head. "Aye, aye, can't have a fine blade like this rattlin' around like a loose coin in a beggar's cup." He turned, rummaging through a wooden chest behind the counter, muttering to himself as he sifted through various sheaths.

After a moment, he pulled one free and set it on the counter with a *thunk*. It was made of thick, dark leather, reinforced with sturdy stitching and accented with faint dwarven runes too worn to be decorative, but still lending an air of quality.

"This here's solid work," he said, giving it a firm pat. "Good retention, won't let the blade slip loose unless ye mean to draw it. Straps'll fit snug on the thigh, won't bounce about even if ye're sprintin' full tilt after some fool who's about to regret their life choices."

Mara inspected it, testing the feel of the straps and the draw. It was practical, well-made, and—more importantly—wouldn't hinder movement. She nodded in approval.

"And the price?" she asked, already bracing for another round of negotiations.

Rurik grunted. "Five silver marks."

She narrowed her eyes. "That seems a bit steep."

He crossed his arms. "Aye? Well, perhaps ye'd rather take that fine dagger o' yers and shove it in a belt loop like some amateur cutpurse. Or let it slap yer leg raw every time ye run."

Mara rolled her eyes. "Fine. Five silver marks."

Rurik smirked, taking her coin and handing over the sheath. "Pleasure doin' business, lass. Try not to lose yerself in an alleyway, eh? Blade's no good to ye if ye ain't around to wield it."

She quickly added the sheath to her new belt and strapped it down to her leg. Its comfortable weight felt reassuring hanging from her hip.

It wasn't lost on Mara that she'd just dropped the equivalent of seventeen grand on a dagger and sheath. In her current situation— with more unknowns than certainties—some might call that reckless extravagance.

I don't care, she thought. The blade was exquisite, and she wanted it. *If I ever get this thing back to Earth, it'll be the centerpiece of my collection.* That was her story, and she was sticking to it.

Maybe it was a skewed perspective, but money had never really been a concern back home. Between her absurdly wealthy adopted father and the ability to "encourage" deserving donors to provide whatever she wanted, she'd rarely had to pinch pennies. She told herself she'd be more frugal at the next shop.

One more stop, and then she could hole up somewhere safe before sunrise.

CHAPTER

NINE

ASKING A FEW QUESTIONS OF PASSERSBY, Mara soon found what she needed—a Maker's Guild shop for magical items.

The moment she stepped inside, she knew this wasn't going to be cheap. The polished stone walls gleamed under soft ambient lighting, and immaculately arranged glass display cases lined the space, each showcasing an array of enchanted wares. Above the entrance hung a banner bearing the guild's logo—a hammer inside a circle, or perhaps an orb—set against a field of deep blue and gold.

Two guards flanked the door, their sharp eyes ready to scan every customer who entered. Unlike the usual hired muscle she'd seen in other cities, these men were well-dressed, their tailored jackets embroidered with the Maker's Guild insignia. But it was the weapons at their belts that held her attention—shockrods, sleek and dangerous, she could imagine them almost humming with restrained power.

This place reeked of money. Mara felt her stomach sink as she thought of the dent this was about to put in her purse.

A man approached, his smile as polished as the glass counters, as oily as a street vendor peddling counterfeit relics. "Ah, a pleasure, my lady! Welcome to this Maker's Guild affiliate shop. I am Faflir, at your service. How may I assist you this evening?" His voice dripped with honeyed obsequiousness, but his sharp eyes were already sizing her up, calculating her worth to the last copper.

Suppressing a sigh, she stated her need plainly. "I need a Cleaner. My belongings were lost in transit."

He blinked, momentarily thrown off by the statement, but recovered instantly. "Ah, most unfortunate! But not to worry—you've come to the perfect place. Right this way."

He led her to a set of three long glass cases, each one lined with velvet and framed in polished wood so fine it gleamed under the store's lights. Inside, an overwhelming selection of jewelry lay neatly arranged: rings, earrings, pendants, hairpins, and brooches. However, Mara quickly noticed that rings and earrings dominated the display. It made sense. Items worn directly on the body were harder to lose and ensured constant access to their magic.

She scanned the selection, considering her options. A Cleaner was a necessity, but if she was going to spend a small fortune, she might as well get something practical. Her gaze landed on a pair of diamond studs, each about a carat in size.

"What about those?" she asked, pointing.

Faflir's smarmy grin widened as if she had just displayed the most exquisite taste imaginable. "Ah, an excellent selection! This pair includes both a Cleaner and a Speech Stone, a matching set designed for utmost convenience. No need to worry about coordinating your accessories—diamonds, after all, go with everything." His tone was smooth, almost patronizing. "And, of course, purchasing them together ensures perfect magical attunement. Truly, a refined choice."

Mara arched an eyebrow, unimpressed. "And how much will they cost?"

"Four gold marks and five gold pieces," Faflir declared smoothly. "As you can see, the stones are of exceptional quality, free of any visible flaws. They are guaranteed to provide a full century of flawless service. The Cleaner can function in autonomous mode, discreetly removing any soil from your person as needed, or it can be activated on command for a more thorough cleansing—purifying not just you and your worn items, but also anything you're touching, up to the size of a small personal carriage."

From the way he said *soil*, she understood that to mean *more* than just dirt. *Eww.*

"And the Speech Stone?"

"Ah, yes. Madam is wise to ask." Faflir's smile widened as if she had passed some sort of test. "This particular stone can be attuned to up to fifteen others, allowing seamless communication across any distance. Unlike lesser models, its enchantment ensures that your conversations remain private unless you choose to project them aloud. A truly remarkable piece—boasting half again as many connections as the standard variety. A rare find, indeed."

The sheer unintentional condescension radiating from this man was starting to piss her off.

She hated to ask—knowing full well he was itching to fleece her of every coin—but walking around unprepared wasn't an option. With a sigh, she relented. "What other basics would you recommend for someone who's lost all their belongings and only has a pittance of coins to their name?"

"There are so many essentials a Lady might require that we could provide, it's difficult to narrow it down to just a few." Faflir made a show of scrutinizing her, as if appraising a rare but slightly battered artifact. "However, I do see that you lack a Bank Token, meaning your means are currently limited to whatever is in your pouch. Given that—and considering you're new to our fair city—I would strongly suggest a Data Crystal pre-loaded with a comprehensive map of Daggerport, as well as key information on the Free Trade Cities. It should serve you well during your stay."

He turned, leading her to another gleaming glass case filled with pendants, each cradling some form of crystal. With a practiced flourish, he retrieved one and draped it across his palm like it was a royal heirloom.

"This fine piece," he continued smoothly, "not only contains the aforementioned data, but can also store up to 10,000 documents or five hours of recorded speech or images. A truly invaluable resource."

Unlike the diamond earrings, the crystal in this pendant was semi-precious—clear but with a subtle shimmer—something elegant yet practical. It was set in white gold and hung from a black leather cord, accentuated with small white-gold beads spaced along its length.

She might have been thoroughly icked out by this guy, but she had to admit—he knew his business. The necklace and pendant would complement her current outfit perfectly, and their neutral tones meant they would pair just as well with the more colorful clothes she had picked up earlier. Fashionable and functional—a rare combination.

The relatively short cord ensured the crystal would sit high on her chest, easy to access, and perfectly positioned to capture whatever she needed. The thought of taking pictures with a magic crystal, storing moments with a simple command, was strangely thrilling. If she ever found a way back to Earth, showing her father actual images from another world would be nothing short of incredible.

Davin would be amazed; he didn't have anything like this among his collection of magic items. Although, to be fair, he also didn't have

Cleaners or Speech Stones, so she was pretty sure he would love all of this.

Seeing that she was pleased with the suggestion, he moved in for the kill. "There are so many things you might need, but their pinnacle would be a storage item." His smile widened, oozing practiced sympathy. "For someone who has already lost all their worldly possessions under such tragic circumstances, what could be more essential than ensuring it never happens again? A Storage Ring or Pouch would keep everything you own secure—always within reach, yet never weighing you down."

There it was. The other shoe had dropped.

He hadn't even told her the price of the Data Crystal yet, and now he was bringing out the big guns—hitting her where it hurt. A storage item would be beyond useful, but from the way he was practically glowing, she already knew it was going to be well out of her reach.

He led her toward the back of the shop, where the most exclusive and heavily guarded merchandise was displayed. The sheer concentration of magic in this section was nearly palpable. Shelves and cases held everything from saddle bags and belt pouches to intricately crafted rings, each one practically humming with enchantment.

The salesman picked up a ring, presenting it with the same flourish as if he were unveiling a priceless artifact. "Ah, now this—this would be a perfect complement to your other selections. And as a bundled deal with the Crystal and Earrings, it's yours for only fifty-three gold marks."

Boom. The real price drop. She had expected it to be bad, but that was worse than she feared. Even if she *had* that much, she still needed to afford a room at that Dragon Inn where she could sleep safely during the day.

"That's more than I have," she said, keeping her tone neutral. "And while I'm sure it's incredibly useful, I'll have to pass."

For a moment, disappointment flickered across his expression. It was the first genuine emotion she'd seen from him. He studied her, realizing she wasn't just haggling—she genuinely didn't have the coin. Adjusting his pitch, he gestured toward a plainer ring. "Hmm... perhaps this one instead? A more modest design, but still quite functional. I could let it go, along with your other items, for a mere forty-five gold marks."

That was still way too high. After her earlier purchases, she was down to just under thirty-three. She knew he was overcharging, but she doubted there was enough wiggle room in his price to get him to drop twelve gold marks without some serious effort.

"Still too much, I'm afraid. If I had access to my resources back home, buying this trinket wouldn't be an issue. But with what I have on me, I just can't go that high."

His frown deepened, this time entirely genuine. He tapped his fingers against the display case, considering his options before sighing. "I see. Well, perhaps a belt pouch then. They run significantly lower than a ring while still providing secure storage." He gave a knowing smile, slipping back into his usual smarmy sales tone. "Of course, do keep in mind the convenience factor. With a ring, you can simply summon an item directly into your hand. With a pouch, well... you'll have to reach in and retrieve it yourself." He let out a regretful sigh. "It's a *significant* difference in ease of use, truly."

Mara barely stopped herself from rolling her eyes. *Of course, he'd try to make a glorified coin purse sound like a massive downgrade.* But at least it sounded like they were finally in a price range she could work with.

"Fine. Let's take a look. And while we're at it, I'd like a shockrod as well." She made sure to hold his gaze, letting him see exactly what she was thinking—she'd *love* to test one out on *him*.

A few moments later, she was the proud owner of a plain black leather belt pouch, reinforced with steel accents. It didn't look like much, but it could hold about as much as the bed of a full-sized pickup truck. Alongside it, she now carried a sleek shockrod—an elegantly carved wooden baton, about an inch in diameter, capped with engraved blued steel. Like her knife, it was secured to her thigh in a sheath, but this one was equipped with a magical snap, designed for a quick draw. One flick, and she'd be ready to put it to use.

Unfortunately, her newly acquired pouch felt depressingly light, carrying just five gold marks out of the thirty-five she'd started with after fencing her loot. Still, it wasn't an insignificant sum. According to the pawnshop owner's offhand explanation, an unskilled laborer would be lucky to earn that much in a year.

But Mara wasn't naive. Surviving in Daggerport—especially the way she would need to—was bound to be a lot more expensive than living hand-to-mouth.

A weariness tugged at her spirit, heavier than any coin pouch. It had been one hell of a night, and she'd barely scratched the surface of the world she'd been dropped into. Time enough to worry about money and enemies later. Right now, she needed a safe place to hole up before sunrise—and a little time to figure out what the hell to do next.

CHAPTER

TEN

ANOTHER HOUR of walking brought Mara to a sight so bizarre she had to stop and stare. The skeezy pawnshop owner hadn't lied—if anything, he had undersold it.

This section of town was filled with neighborhoods of well-off families and small estates, each sprawling across anywhere from a quarter of a block to a full one, often surrounded by privacy hedges or stone walls.

At the heart of one such estate stood the Dragon Inn, occupying an entire block behind its battered, half-collapsed walls. Or rather, what had once been a grand manor was now partially crushed beneath the body of an enormous dragon.

Just as Gavian had described, the dragon's wings had flattened the gardens and outbuildings, its massive tail and hindquarters disappearing out of sight behind the estate. On this side, the creature's long, scaled neck had slammed straight through the outer wall, and its massive head lay with jaws agape, fangs the length of her arms or legs gleaming like ivory but honed sharp as dwarven steel.

Most absurdly, a thick red carpet rolled from its open mouth like a lolling tongue, welcoming guests inside.

A big human guard lounged on a stool beside the dragon's head, chuckling at her expression.

"Welcome to the Dragon Inn," he drawled. "All are welcome, but keep any violence to the arena in the courtyard. Draw a weapon inside or disturb a guest, and you'll be removed. Maybe permanently, depending on how much you piss off the boss."

He jerked his thumb toward the dragon's gaping maw—the entrance.

Seeing her hesitation, the guard grinned and added, "Don't worry about the teeth, lass. They're enchanted. You couldn't hurt yourself on 'em if you tried. Just walk the 'tongue' and head on in."

Still, Mara didn't move for a long moment. She had read about dragons all her life, but reading and standing before one were two very different things. This beast was so massive that she could easily walk right into its mouth—maybe two big men could walk side-by-side, even three smaller people, and still not brush the teeth. It was a lot to take in.

Even the creature's eyes glowed a molten orange-red, flickering slightly as if it might yet rise and bite her in half. Probably another enchantment. Still, at night, under the flickering streetlights, the whole thing looked disturbingly alive.

She shook her head, forcing her feet into motion. *It would be pretty damn pathetic to stop outside a safe place just because it looks scary. Move your butt, Mara.*

No sooner thought than done. She marched up the 'tongue' and into the dragon's maw. There, tucked behind the fangs and tongue, was a polished wooden door set into the dragon's throat, lit by a pair of wrought iron sconces.

Opening it revealed a dark-paneled hallway sloping downward, warm light spilling from lanterns set along the walls.

Mara let out a breath and chuckled under her breath. *So it's not actually inside the dragon's belly. Clever. The place is really underground, hidden by some masterful construction.*

She passed a coat check—or maybe it was a weapon check—where a young woman sat behind a counter. The attendant repeated the same rule about no trouble and offered to store any weapons or valuables during Mara's stay if she wished.

"Zakkarious Ironeater—Zak, if you value your teeth—owns the place," the woman added with a wry grin. "He keeps a careful eye on everything and doesn't tolerate mischief."

Mara nodded politely but declined, continuing through a set of heavy double doors into the heart of the inn.

She stopped short. She hadn't been sure what to expect, but it hadn't been this!

The place had the feel of an old English pub, all dark wood paneling and warm lantern light, but on a scale far bigger than anything she'd seen back home. One long side of the room housed an expansive bar, with sections built for Humans and Elves, and shorter portions built for Dwarves. The center of the room was filled with tables, spaced generously to allow for private conversations, and the opposite wall was lined with booths offering cozy seclusion.

At the far end, a low stage sat bathed in soft light, where musicians played a quiet, intricate melody that wafted through the room like smoke.

Despite the late hour—well past three in the morning—the Dragon Inn thrummed with life. Unlike Earth, where bars shut down at two, Daggerport either didn't have such regulations or simply ignored them. But this wasn't the chaotic mess of last-call drunks she would've expected at this hour. No shouting matches, no spilled drinks or staggering fools. Just quiet conversation, measured laughter, and the kind of clientele who knew how to mind their own business.

Her boots made a soft sound against the polished stone floor as she crossed to the bar.

The dwarf behind the counter stood like a fortress, solid, battered by time, but utterly unbroken. His thick beard, iron-grey and shot through with black, was neatly braided with dark metal beads. His deep-set eyes, sharp and cold, gleamed like hammered steel under the lantern light. There was a gravity to him, a presence that spoke of battles fought and burdens carried without complaint.

Though shorter than a man, he stood atop a raised platform behind the bar, making him appear nearly human height. A trick of construction—but Mara doubted he needed tricks. He radiated a quiet, immovable authority, the kind that settled into the bones of a place and refused to be dislodged. Seeing him, she was starting to understand why the City Watch wouldn't cross him.

As she stepped forward, he caught sight of her and scowled.

She opened her mouth to speak, but the dwarf beat her to it.

"You've been gone for ages, then show up twice in one day—at the same time—and now you're pretending to be a vampire?" His voice was a low rumble, the sound of thunder grumbling behind distant mountains. He squinted at her, more annoyance than curiosity sharpening his gaze. "I don't know what game you're playing, boy, but it better not bring trouble to my bar."

Mara blinked. *What the hell?*

She hesitated, studying him. He wasn't just mouthing off—there was weight behind those words, something old and knowing. But she had no clue what he was talking about, and right now, she wasn't in the mood to play twenty questions with a cryptic dwarf.

"Look," she said, keeping her tone even and steady, "I just want a room. One with no windows. No disturbances during the day. I'm not here to cause trouble."

The dwarf grunted, the sound thick with disapproval but grudging acceptance. "Fine."

He ducked under the bar and came back up with a small brass token, its surface engraved with sigils she didn't recognize. He slid it toward her with a hand that looked like it could have crushed rocks for fun. "West hall, third door on the left. Bed's solid. Walls are thicker than your skull. No one'll bother you unless you go looking for it."

Mara picked up the token, feeling the faint tingle of magic humming through the metal. She let out a slow breath. One thing solved, at least.

Then he spoke again.

"There's an entrance to the Undercity through the broken manor inside the courtyard walls. You're welcome to use it."

That stopped her.

The Undercity.

The fence she'd met earlier had mentioned it—said most of the vampires lived down there, out of sight, out of mind. It was tempting, but she wasn't about to throw herself headfirst into an unknown vampire den without knowing who ruled the roost. She needed time. Information. Allies.

She gave a cautious nod. "I'll keep that in mind."

She turned, scanning the main room for a quiet corner where she could sit and plot her next move. Before she could take a single step, Zak's voice carried after her, low but cutting through the murmur of the inn.

"And no using your vampire tricks on my patrons. You wanna play your little bloodsucking games, do it somewhere else."

Mara's jaw tightened. *Great. Another person telling me what to do.*

She kept walking, her spine straight, her expression unreadable.

But inside?

Inside, the fight was already starting to smolder.

She muttered an obscenity under her breath but didn't argue. Sunrise was creeping closer, and she wasn't about to gamble with her first full day on this world by testing how the sun would treat her now. Better to hole up somewhere safe and deal with everything else tomorrow.

With one last glance around the room, she strode toward the hall leading to the guest quarters.

As she turned, her sharp hearing caught the dwarf muttering under his breath.

"Twice in one day. Same damned soul. One in the afternoon, the other in the dead of night..."

There was a pause, followed by the quiet clink of a bottle against glass.

"This ain't natural."

Mara frowned but kept walking.

What the hell was that supposed to mean?

The crazy dwarf acted like he knew her, but his words were pure nonsense. She'd met people like that back on Earth—people who 'saw things' that weren't there and spun whole worlds of conspiracy inside their heads. Of course, on Earth, those types were usually marginalized, living on the edges of society. Not running Inns and casually tossing out room tokens like candy.

Still, she wasn't about to look a gift horse in the mouth. He hadn't asked for payment, hadn't tried to stop her—and in her book, that made him a good kind of crazy.

Maybe tomorrow, if she ran into him again, she'd ask what the hell he thought he saw.

Assuming she even wanted to know.

The next evening, Mara woke feeling more ready to tackle this strange new world. It would be a challenge—far tougher than surviving on Earth, where magic was rare and most people didn't even believe vampires existed. Here, not only did they believe, but a lot of them seemed very prepared to deal with her kind.

Unfortunately, that was the least of her worries. She had killed members of some group called the *Followers of the Dragon*, and from the name alone, she didn't like her odds if they actually had a real dragon to throw at her. After seeing the dragon that formed the entrance to this inn—and realizing just how massive those beasts could be—she had no interest in meeting a living one anytime soon.

Worse still, it was likely there was already a warrant out on her for the murder of the two who tried to assault her.

Despite the whole mess being the fault of the bastards who had attacked what they thought was an innocent mortal, she knew better than to hope for sympathy. In a world this saturated with magic, they probably had ways to divine the truth—and the truth was, she hadn't just defended herself. She had killed them because she was starving. The law would see her actions as indulgent and unnecessary. They'd argue someone with her strength should have been able to restrain herself, resolve things peacefully.

She let out a frustrated sigh.

Okay, Mara, nothing you can do about that now. Deal with what's in front of you first, worry about the rest later.

The first order of business, now that she had a safe place to hole up during the day, was to get one of those Bank Tokens everyone seemed to carry. After that, she needed to start building up some real money and buying better magical protections. She already had a cleaner, a storage pouch, and a data crystal, but could she get her hands on something that let her walk in the sun or shield her from fire?

That would go a long way toward surviving in this strange new world.

Back on Earth, carrying items like that would've gotten a vampire *ashed* by the Cabal's agents. Magic artifacts were rare back home and dangerous to possess openly. Her father, Davin, had secretly kept a few such items hidden, but then he had spent centuries waging war against the Cabal. He alone among Earth's vampires came from a bloodline that still had access to magic, and he had the skill to conceal it.

Unfortunately, Davin hadn't turned her—he had only rescued her from the bastard who had been in the process of killing her. She had fought back with everything she had, clawing at his face. Some of that creature's blood had gotten into her wounds, completing the grim, accidental transformation herself.

She had spent years debating with herself over that twist of fate, hating it at times, resenting it at others. But in the end, she had come to terms with what she was. No, she didn't carry Davin's bloodline magic—but she had built a life she could be proud of, and that was enough.

As she slipped her room key into her pouch, Mara glanced toward the bar and spotted the same gruff dwarf from the night before on shift again.

Does this guy ever sleep?

She gave him a nod on the way out, but he motioned her over with a flick of his thick fingers.

His face, though locked in its usual scowl, carried something else this time—genuine concern, buried under layers of stubborn gruffness.

"Be careful of the Blood Mages," he said, voice low and firm. "They went after the boy this morning. I don't know what game you're playing, but I'll be damned if Joram dies over something you dragged him into."

She blinked. *The hell was this cryptic bastard on about now?*

Her patience snapped. "Listen, I don't know what you're talking about."

Zak's scowl deepened, but something flickered behind it—hesitation, like he'd expected a different answer. He muttered under his breath, "She really doesn't know... but there's no way that's a coincidence."

Then, louder: "Just steer clear of the Blood Mages. They're riled up after Joram and the boy killed two of their men this morning. They're up to something nasty."

That didn't clear anything up. But it sounded like well-meant advice.

She should've just walked away—but something about this dwarf made her skin itch. Like he knew something about her she didn't even know herself. Which was impossible. She'd arrived here yesterday.

Not knowing what else to do, she asked, "Will you keep my room for another day? I'll be back before dawn."

Still, she couldn't help herself. The Blood Mages? That name alone sounded bad. And if they were hunting people, she needed to know why.

"What are these mages you mentioned? I just got here yesterday, and I don't know anyone in this city."

Zak studied her for a long moment, as if weighing something far heavier than her words. His frown deepened, thick brows knitting in open skepticism.

"Red robes, bad attitudes, always with a squad of soldiers dogging their steps," he said finally. "One of their top agents is in town. Took an interest in your other half yesterday. Now two of his men are dead, and they're off chasing the boy to who knows where. If you see one of 'em—or their lackeys—just keep walking."

That was... even less helpful.

She crossed her arms. "Look, I get that you know I'm a vampire. But I'm over a hundred years old, not some kid. And I definitely don't have a husband, let alone an 'other half.' If you think you know something, just spit it out already."

The cryptic bullshit was wearing thin. He didn't seem crazy. Which meant he thought he knew something about her. But he was wrong. He had to be.

Zak gave her a long, unreadable look. Then, flatly: "Fine. If that's the way you want it." He exhaled sharply, the sound halfway between a sigh and a growl. "Out of respect, I'll let you stay here, so long as you don't cause trouble. Now go do whatever you're planning, and let me watch my damn inn in peace."

Dismissed.

Mara clenched her jaw, resisting the urge to throw a retort over her shoulder. Instead, she turned on her heel and strode out, no closer to understanding anything.

She wanted to get into it with the strange dwarf, demand he explain himself, but she couldn't afford to antagonize him. Not yet. He was offering her a place of safety, even if it was over some bizarre case of mistaken identity. And at three silver marks a night, she wasn't about to slap her confused gift-horse in the mouth and get tossed out onto the street.

Besides, if he really was powerful enough to offer sanctuary even against the City Watch, he was the kind of ally she couldn't afford to alienate.

No sense in pissing him off. Yet.

Thankfully, Mara didn't run into any Blood Mages on her way to the Dwarven Sovereign Bank.

Not that I'd know a Blood Mage if one walked up and bit me on the ass.

Still, they sounded scary enough, judging by how serious that dwarf had been about it—and two of them being killed outside the inn this morning? That was crazy, even by her standards.

The good news: it had nothing to do with her.

The bad news: she was still a wanted criminal, and there were probably revenge-hungry friends of the dead Followers of the Dragon prowling the city searching for her.

Note to self: research the Followers and figure out exactly what kind of crazy I've gotten myself tangled up in.

She shoved the thought aside as she walked through the towering front doors of the "bank."

Calling it a bank felt like a stretch.

It wasn't some friendly corner branch like she'd known on Earth. It was guarded by dwarven warriors who looked like they could single-handedly dismantle a tank—head-to-toe armored in gleaming Dwarven Steel, weapons bristling from their belts and backs. There wasn't a single window anywhere, only the massive two-story doors that looked like they could hold off an army.

The entire place, inside and out, was carved from polished stone that looked suspiciously like marble. Fixtures of gold and inlaid gemstones gleamed from the walls and ceiling.

Okay, on second thought, Mara mused, *maybe it is precisely like banks on Earth.*

The biggest difference?

How damn serious the dwarves were about their business.

The ones working behind the counters weren't the rough, grimy tunnelers she'd imagined from books and movies. No, these dwarves were immaculate—every hair in place, every bit of their tailored clothes sharper than a razor's edge. They looked every inch the world's premier bankers.

They were also ruthlessly efficient.

In less than fifteen minutes, she'd handed over four gold marks and walked out with a bank token of her own. She also got change for her last gold mark, so that she would have some smaller denomination coins on her for things she might not want to use the token for.

The process had involved a human mage in a private room, where he'd conducted the attunement behind a veil of magic Mara couldn't even see through. She found it interesting, but it mostly just cranked up her curiosity about how magic worked in this world.

Another thing to add to the research list, she thought. *Right under "Don't get eaten by a dragon."*

Still, this wasn't the time for research. At least, not that kind.

Right now, she needed to build up her resources. Living modestly on a few gold marks was fine for a normal citizen. She wasn't normal. If she stayed an outlaw—or worse, a target—she'd need a hell of a lot more help.

Help that came easier with a fat stack of cash.

She had considered just leaving—moving on to another city, starting fresh—but there were two problems with that.

First, this was the place she'd been *kidnapped* to.

That couldn't be a coincidence.

Whoever had dragged her here—and for whatever reason—was probably still lurking somewhere nearby. If she bailed now, she'd never find out why.

Second?

Mara didn't run.

Oh, she might "advance to the rear" if strategy demanded it, but not because some cult's lowlifes got what they deserved. She wasn't about to slink out of town like a beaten dog just because a few jackasses picked the wrong target.

Decision made, she slipped the new token into her pouch, adjusted her belt, and smiled faintly to herself.

It was time to hunt.

CHAPTER

ELEVEN

On Earth, a vampire like Mara could use compulsion to get whatever she needed, whenever she wanted, so long as she didn't expose the supernatural to the mortal world.

That was the Cabal's number one rule.

On the surface, it sounded almost benevolent. Protect the poor, unsuspecting mortals from becoming prey and causing a war that would devastate everyone.

But Mara knew better.

It had never been about protecting anyone except themselves. The Cabal needed secrecy to maintain its grip on power. If humanity ever discovered a hidden organization pulling the world's strings from the shadows, its control would shatter.

So they put boots on the necks of every supernatural being they could find, and that was how it had been for thousands of years.

Since the time of the Blood Queen.

She had dared to rule openly, wielding both magic and vampiric power with impunity.

And she had paid the ultimate price.

Even the Blood Queen had been brought down in the end, or so Davin said. He was the last of her bloodline, and he carried on the war against the Cabal in secret.

Despite the evening's coolness, Mara felt a spike of ice stab through her gut.

Her father was still out there, fighting—and now he was fighting alone.

He probably hadn't even realized she was gone yet.

He wasn't due for another visit to Houston for a couple of months. With luck, her employees would raise the alarm. Magic was rare on Earth, but if anyone could find her and bring her home, it would be Davin.

She just had to survive long enough for him to do it.

Her thoughts flickered to her restaurant, her one legitimate business. She hoped her people would keep it running smoothly in her absence. It had been her anchor to the normal world, even while most of her wealth had been built through more... *creative* means— strategically relocating valuables from owners who wouldn't miss them, or deserved to lose them.

On Earth, she wasn't a billionaire, but she had enough tucked away that she'd never need to worry about money again.

This world, though?

This was a different story entirely.

Which brought her thoughts full circle. She needed money, and while she *could* use compulsion, she hated doing it unless it was an emergency—or her target turned out to be a complete scumbag. Not that she was particularly religious, or even moral for that matter, but she'd always tried to steer clear of turning innocent people into victims.

Back on Earth, a hunt like the one she needed tonight would mean prowling around unpleasant places, looking for criminals whose absence would make the world a better place. Unfortunately, she was still mostly blind in this world. She'd have to ask around, play it smart, and find her opening.

A few careful questions as she moved south along the Mile started to point her the right way. There was no 'the' shady tavern—this wasn't some cheesy slice-of-life romance novel she'd occasionally indulged in. Daggerport had dozens of questionable watering holes. She just needed one close enough not to waste the whole night getting there, but far enough from the Dragon Inn that trouble wouldn't follow her home before dawn.

An hour and a half later, Mara found exactly what she was looking for.

She stood outside The Broken Fang and took a slow, steady breath. If there was a worse place in Daggerport to spend her evening, she hadn't seen it yet.

Not that two pubs are much of a sample size, she thought.

The squat, two-story tavern leaned visibly to one side, its timbers warped with age and neglect. A battered wooden sign swung overhead, the faded image of a wolf's skull bisected by a jagged crack barely visible in the flickering streetlight. The usual stench of stale ale, unwashed bodies, and cheap tobacco might have been scrubbed away by cleaning magic, but there was no mistaking a dive when you saw one.

Inside, the air was thick with heat and tension. Eyes lingered too long. Voices carried the weight of veiled threats.

The low ceiling pressed down, beams so darkened with age they looked half ready to collapse. The floor was sticky underfoot. Tables bore the scars of countless brawls: knife gouges, scorch marks, the occasional bloodstain no one had bothered to wipe away. Apparently, the cleaning spells stopped outside the walls.

The patrons weren't much better. Cutthroats, smugglers, mercenaries, and worse drank side by side. Even a few sailors hunched at the bar, their clothes a little too fine for common deckhands, their grins sharp and watchful.

A man in the back laughed too loudly. When his companion didn't join in, the laughter cut off, sharp and ugly. A ripple passed through the room—subtle, but real. The kind of ripple that meant someone had just made a mistake they wouldn't live long enough to regret.

Mara didn't flinch. She'd survived places like this for decades. The only difference was that back home, she could flash her fangs and make men tremble. Here? Flash the wrong thing and she might get a shockrod to the ribs—or a fireball to the face.

Still, if she wanted a good target—and answers—this was the place to find both.

Stepping inside, she moved through the crowd with the practiced ease of someone who knew exactly how much space to take up—not too inviting, not too threatening. Just another dangerous shadow among many.

She passed a group of men rolling dice over a pile of silver, their conversation low and heated. Past a woman with a scarred face who watched her with a little too much interest. Mara ignored them all, gliding toward the bar like she owned the place.

The bartender was a broad-shouldered man with a lazy eye and hands that looked better suited for strangling than pouring drinks. He wiped a mug with a cloth that might have once been white but had long since surrendered to the grime. He barely glanced at her, then did a double take, standing up straighter as if he'd just seen something that rattled him.

For a split second, Mara tensed.

If this bastard starts spewing cryptic bullshit like that dwarf did, I swear to whatever gods rule this world, I will kill him before he finishes his first sentence.

But instead, the bartender barked, "What do you want? I just paid day before yesterday—your boss shouldn't have any business with my pub right now."

She narrowed her eyes, thinking fast.

Okay. Not crazy talk, just mistaken identity. Who the hell does he think I work for?

Still, she knew better than to waste a good opening.

"I'm looking for someone," she said smoothly, letting just a thread of steel into her voice. "No concern of yours. But if you want to help, you could point me toward someone who knows things and answers questions. If they're useful, maybe I'll even consider it a small favor. A very small one."

The bartender's lazy eye twitched as he studied her, weighing something behind that battered exterior. Finally, with a grunt, he set the mug down and wiped his hands on the rag before tossing it onto the bar.

"Name's Luthan," he rasped, voice rough from years of cheap booze and shouting over worse.

"And if you're looking for someone who knows things, you might wanna wait a few minutes. Zariah usually sits right there." He jerked his chin toward a vacant stool at the end of the bar, the worn wood bearing the faint imprint of countless occupants. "She'll be back soon. Works outta here most nights. Knows plenty—so long as you got coin."

Mara filed the name away, already weighing how much information the woman might be worth. She was about to press for more when something else occurred to her.

"If I were looking for someone... let's say, someone no one would miss. Anyone like that around tonight?"

Luthan hesitated. His hand twitched toward the rag, then curled into a fist on the bar instead. He glanced around the room, his expression shifting from guarded to outright uncomfortable. "I don't like that question," he muttered. But after another glance toward one of the booths along the wall, he exhaled sharply and leaned in slightly. "See that guy in the far booth? The one with the greasy hair and the twitchy hands?"

Mara followed his gaze and found the man immediately. He looked exactly like someone up to no good, shifting nervously in his seat and glancing at the door every few minutes as if expecting trouble. His clothes were too fine for a desperate drunk, but his posture screamed desperation of another kind.

Luthan kept his voice low. "He ain't a regular. Came in an hour ago asking too many questions. Wants to hire someone to do a job, but from the way he's talking, it ain't a simple rough-up. He's looking for a killer." Luthan's expression darkened. "Shady business doesn't bother me, but he looks like an idiot, the kind that would make dumb decisions. I don't need the Watch sniffing around here. If he brings trouble, I don't want it landing on my head."

Mara smirked. "Good thing for you, I'm very good at handling trouble."

Luthan exhaled sharply, shaking his head. "Just keep it quiet." He blanched for a second, then added, "Sorry, sorry, I forgot who I was talking to. Of course, you will keep it quiet, unless you intend to make an example."

Mara didn't answer. She was already making her way toward the booth, barely sparing the bartender a second glance. After dealing with this soon-to-be wealth donor, she'd need to have a chat with Zariah, figure out more about the city, and—more importantly— who the bartender thought she worked for. She didn't need to get tangled up with the wrong people, not with everything else she had going on.

Sliding into the booth, she had to bite back a laugh as the shifty man nearly jumped out of his skin, his beady eyes darting around like a cornered rat.

"I hear you're looking to hire someone," she said smoothly, letting the corner of her mouth quirk up just enough to show a hint of fang. "I might be able to help. Tell me what you need and why, and if I like what I hear, maybe we'll make a deal."

The man's face drained of color so fast it was almost funny. He stammered, "Uh... ugh, that is—I... well, I need my father killed. You can—uh—do whatever you want with him, I don't care. I just need to inherit the family money before he changes his will."

Mara's fingers twitched. It took serious restraint not to reach across the table and wrap her hand around his throat and squeeze.

She exhaled slowly, keeping her voice even. "Why do you want your father dead?"

He hesitated, eyes shifting toward the bar like he was hoping someone might come save him. His body language screamed deception.

Mara didn't have the patience for this. She cast a quick glance around to confirm no one was watching, then leaned forward and let her power surge to the surface. She wasn't gentle about it.

"Tell me the truth," she ordered, her voice laced with compulsion. "Why is your father going to disinherit you?"

His eyes glazed over, his expression going slack. When he spoke, it was in the dull monotone of someone completely in her thrall. "He's about to cut me out of the will and leave everything to my sister. It's because of a scandal."

Mara raised an eyebrow. "What scandal?"

A long pause. Then, flatly: "Dog fighting. I own a dozen excellent fighters."

That was it.

Mara felt a cold fury coil in her gut, tight and sharp. She'd been prepared for the usual sordid reasons—gambling debts, cheating scandals, some pathetic noble dispute over an inheritance. But this? This was a whole other level of vile.

Her power surged again, heavier this time, suffocating.

"You will do anything to please me," she commanded, her voice silk over steel. "Now, pay your bill and meet me behind the pub. We're going to have some fun."

She released his mind and stood, striding out to the stables behind the building. The night air was crisp, but she barely noticed. The only thing on her mind was ensuring that this bastard never got what he wanted.

There were only a few horses in the stalls, and a single stable hand on duty. She caught the boy's eye and whispered, "Go take a nap in one of the empty stalls."

He slumped forward without hesitation, curling up in the hay.

A moment later, the would-be patricide rounded the corner, his steps eager and unquestioning as he stepped into an empty stall. Mara wasted no time.

"Would you please transfer all your wealth to my bank token?" she asked sweetly.

He was no longer under full compulsion, but he had been hit with the vampire equivalent of a post-hypnotic suggestion on steroids; he still wanted to please her. Without hesitation, he pulled out his bank token, held it up to hers, and muttered, "Transfer 53 gold marks, 10 silver marks, and 25 silver pieces."

The exchange worked.

Just like that, Mara had 58 more gold marks to her name—enough to live comfortably for years if she was careful. Not that she had any intention of being careful. She needed magic protections, and she doubted she could get them through legitimate means. Luckily, she was already in a place where she could find someone to make them for her.

She looked at the man in front of her, her fangs aching with the need to end him. A part of her whispered that it would be so easy. Just drain him, dump the body in the river, and move on.

But this world knew about vampires. If they found him, if they investigated, there was a good chance some kind of magic could trace his death back to her.

She exhaled sharply. "You're a very lucky man," she muttered, then slammed her will into his mind one last time.

"You will free your dogs and find them good homes where they will be treated kindly and loved. You will regret your part in harming animals for the rest of your life and dedicate yourself to helping them. You will forget you ever thought about killing your father. You will forget you ever saw me. And from now on, you will live a decent life—one where you do not harm people or animals."

The weight of her command settled over him like an iron shackle.

Mara stepped back and watched as the new reality took hold in his vacant, fogged-over eyes. She really hated crossing this line, it was one thing to rob someone or make them do something you needed done. That was temporary and didn't fundamentally contradict their nature. This was permanent, and it made her sick to her stomach. She wasn't sure what was worse—letting him live or forcing him to be a better person.

Maybe it balanced out?

Turning on her heel, she left him standing there in the empty stall, his fate no longer in her hands. She had more important things to do.

CHAPTER
TWELVE

STEPPING BACK INSIDE THE PUB, she made a beeline for the woman now sitting at the end of the bar, looking for clients.

"You Zariah?" Mara asked.

Looking her up and down, the woman raised an eyebrow. "You aren't exactly like my regulars, but I'm game. What are you looking for?"

Chuckling, Mara waved the question off. "Not what you think. I need information, and Luthan said you know things."

Zariah seemed to take that in stride. "If you're paying, I don't care how I earn the coin. Let's go." Waiting only long enough to see that Mara was following, the woman led the way toward an inconspicuous door in the back. Behind the door was an unexpectedly comfortable room, as neat and clean as the bar was dirty and seedy.

Taking a seat on the bed, Zariah gestured to a place next to her and to a chair that looked comfortable enough to curl up with a good book and relax.

SUNDERED SOUL

Overall, it was far from the impression that Mara expected from a lady of the evening, but then again, this was a very different world. With the Cleaning magic, perhaps they didn't view her profession so negatively here?

Taking a seat on the chair, Mara got comfortable. "First of all, Luthan mistook me as someone working for a 'boss'. Do you know who he meant and why he thought I was one of his people?"

Zariah blinked in surprise, and then took a closer look at Mara, and her eyes got big. "By the dragon's balls, I didn't realize when you walked up. The lighting at the end of the bar is pretty bad, but that pale skin. Are you a vampire?"

Not seeing a reason to deny it, she nodded confirmation.

"That explains it. There are gangs and criminals in the city, but one way or another, they all pay tribute to Noloris. He's an ancient vampire, been here since before the war that freed the city from Rydan. Luthan pays for protection to Noloris' people, but everyone knows his top enforcers are all vampires who live in the undercity. He must have noticed your lack of a tan and made a wrong assumption."

The woman thought for a second and then added, almost afraid, "You don't work for him, do you?"

Mara shook her head. "No, I just arrived in the city yesterday. This is the first I've heard anything about a vampire lord of the underworld. In fact, information like that is the thing I need most right now so I don't make any mistakes, offend the wrong people, or do the wrong things."

A wave of relief passed over Zariah. "Oh, thank the old ones! Sorry, I know better than to spout off like that, and I should have called him Lord Noloris, even in passing like that, so please forgive me. If his people thought I spoke disrespectfully– well, let me make up for it by helping you, however I can!"

Chuckling, Mara waved the woman's concerns away, "Don't worry about it, I have nothing to do with them, at least not yet. If all the city's vampires are part of his organization, I'm sure I'll run into them eventually, but hopefully it won't be soon. Tell me everything you think I should know about the city."

Still a little pale, Zariah hurried to comply, "That's probably the most important thing right there! All the organized crime in the city is controlled by Lord Noloris. I don't know what else to tell you about them, but I can give you general information."

Mara interrupted, "Before we move on, what kind of crime does he control, and how deeply does his reach go? Does every random criminal in the city have to have his permission to commit a burglary, or does he focus on groups of criminals?"

Knowing this would help her understand what she could get away with without drawing the underworld boss's attention.

Zariah shrugged, "Lord Noloris doesn't control every pickpocket and thug in Daggerport, but if a crime is organized, it either pays him tribute or is run directly by his people. Smuggling, gambling, illegal magic, blackmail, slavery, and assassination all fall under his domain...."

Mara interrupted, "Hang on, slavery? Is that legal here?" Her opinion about this place could hinge on the answer to that question.

The woman shook her head, "No, that's outlawed in all the southern kingdoms and the Free Cities. Still, the Valentros, Bane Elves, and others allow it, and Noloris is known to 'acquire merchandise' for such buyers, even if it is illegal here."

Disgusted, Mara wanted to spit. "Thank you. Go on."

"He's got enforcers running protection rackets, brokers selling secrets, and mages crafting enchantments that shouldn't exist. The brothels, the pit fights, the underground casinos—if it makes gold in the shadows, Lord Noloris has his fingers in it. Even the City Watch has its fair share of officers on his payroll. He keeps things running smoothly and makes sure the city doesn't turn into chaos, but make no mistake—cross him, and you won't just disappear. You'll cease to exist, like you were never born."

Zariah swallowed hard and leaned closer, "There was a group of street kids a couple of years back—called themselves the Black Rats. Thought they were clever. Thought they could run their own little gang without paying tribute to Lord Noloris. They started small— pickpocketing in the market, running cons on drunken merchants, even taking the occasional smuggling job from dock workers who didn't want to cut the boss in. For a while, it seemed like they were getting away with it."

She took a slow sip of her drink before continuing. "Then one night, the city woke up to a message. Every one of those kids—seven in total—was found nailed to the walls around that market square. Alive. Their hands were shattered, their tongues cut out, and Lord Noloris' sigil was carved into their chests. No one dared take them down until his enforcers came at dawn and put them out of their misery. That was the only mercy they got."

Zariah leaned back, eyes shadowed with remembered horror. "Since then, no one's been stupid enough to try forming their own gang without paying their dues. He doesn't just kill those who cross him —he makes examples of them."

Hmm... so he's your typical mob boss, but a vampire with centuries of experience at it. I've dealt with his type before on Earth. Shouldn't be anything I can't deal with as long as he leaves me be.

Back in Houston, there were more than half a dozen vampire elders, each hundreds of years old, and every one of them ran their own sections of the city. Thanks to her father, they left her alone; they all respected and feared him, or owed him favors. Here, she wouldn't have the shield of a powerful backer. Worse, with no competition, this 'lord' Noloris was sure to be drunk on his own power.

What she said aloud was, "I'm surprised the City Watch didn't intervene if they spent the entire night hanging from a wall like that. Seems like a challenge to their law and order."

Shaking her head emphatically, Zariah answered, "No, there were a surprising number of incidents that night that kept the Watch busy and away from the area. It seems like a lot of fights were breaking out. Also, like I said, there are plenty of people in the Watch who are either friendly with Lord Noloris or at least tolerate what he does because he keeps the criminals mostly under control. His people know not to cross the lines. The people of the city sleep well at night, knowing that, and so he's all but an unacknowledged Lord of the City. Some folks even refer to him as the Shadow Councillor."

Zariah leaned back in her chair, stretching her legs out as she considered Mara's question more and added. "Don't get me wrong, Daggerport's not like some of the real cesspits out there. This is the biggest trading city in the world, so the Watch does its job well enough, and they keep things safer here than even the other Free Cities north along the Maru River. You don't have to worry about getting knifed just walking down the street—not unless you've pissed off the wrong people. And even then, if you make a scene, the Watch will intervene. That's the difference between this place and somewhere like Valentros. Here, the law still matters. Mostly."

She tapped her fingers against her cup, her tone shifting slightly. "That said, the real Councilors only tolerate the Shadow Guild because Noloris keeps his people in check. Well, to be fair, I suppose

Lord Noloris doesn't like messes in his city any more than the Watch does. Bad for business."

"As far as other information that might help..." Zariah took a sip of her drink before continuing, her voice turning a little more thoughtful.

"Daggerport's split into four quarters, plus the docks on the seaside and caravan yards outside the north walls. The First Quarter is closest to the docks, so there's a lot of shipping-related business there, as well as the Citadel, the headquarters of the Spellswords Guild. The Second Quarter is where you get your laborers, working folk, and some of the less savory establishments, though nothing too lawless. Third Quarter's more middle-class—craftsmen, tradespeople, smaller guildhouses, and mostly respectable businesses. The Healers Guild also has its main branch there, so it's worth a visit sometime just to see their Heartwood tree." Zariah got a wistful expression on her face, "Just being near that thing can make you feel like everything is right with the world."

Shaking off the thought, she continued, "And then there's the Fourth Quarter... well, that's where the money is. You don't want to mess around there, as it is mostly filled with estates for the rich and the nobles who can't afford to live on the Mountain."

She smirked. "They call the dock area to the south, Seaside. Riverside is to the west. Both are always busy, always moving goods in and out. The northern caravan yards are just as packed with wagons and traders looking to offload wares or resupply before heading inland. They call that area Northside."

She leaned forward slightly. "What makes this place what it is, though, is the Dwarves. They own the mountains to the east, and everything beyond, but they let the city and undercity thrive here because it keeps their trade flowing. That's why this place is more stable than most—there's too much money at stake for anyone to let it fall apart." She tapped a finger against her head in a knowing way.

"Plus, all the major guilds have a presence here, but three of the biggest—Healers, Makers, and Spellswords—keep their main headquarters in Daggerport. If you ever need healing, gear, or protection, those are the people to know." She gave Mara a pointed look. "Just depends on how much you're willing to pay, and how many rules you're willing to follow."

Mara considered that and asked one of her most burning questions. "Speaking of that, I need a magic item maker. Someone who does custom work without asking too many questions."

Zariah snorted. "You don't want the Makers Guild, then. They'll charge you a fortune, demand paperwork, and probably rat you out to whoever asks the right questions, nor would they sell anything illicit. But if you want something made on the quiet, Toman's your best bet. He used to be Makers Guild, but faked his death to get out from under their rules. Now, he takes orders out of the First Quarter, near the old stone bridge. He doesn't come cheap, but he won't turn away business just because it's 'questionable.'"

She smirked, swirling what little was left in her cup. "He's a 'friend.' If you go see him, tell him I sent you. Won't get you a discount, but it'll at least keep him from trying to sell you junk."

Zariah went on for another half hour, going through more details of the city and highlighting things she thought Mara might want to know, but eventually, she looked toward the door reluctantly. "I'm sure I've got customers out there waiting impatiently. It has been nice talking with you, though. I wish I could give you more time, but I don't want to lose too much money tonight. I've got kids to feed."

Mara took the hint and stood. The conversation had gone a long way toward helping her understand the city and what made it tick. She quickly pulled out her bank token and presented it to the woman. "I don't know how much you usually charge for an hour, but take this, with my thanks."

When the other woman held out her own token, Mara transferred five silver marks. Probably more than necessary, but she appreciated the woman's honesty and helpfulness.

However, just as she was about to walk out the door, she turned back and asked, "One more thing, what's the deal with the Followers of the Dragon?"

An unpleasant look crossed the woman's face. "Bah, they go around preaching to the poor mostly about how the Dragon will lift up those who serve him when he returns. Bunch of shit, if you'll pardon me saying. Dragons don't care nothing about humans other than maybe as food or if we get near their lairs. Why one would help humans at all, I have no idea. The Followers seem mostly harmless though, if deluded."

That didn't jive with Mara's own experience, but perhaps the ones who had tried to assault her were just a group of bad apples. Regardless, they did sound like some kind of cult.

Grimacing at the thought of those pigs, she waved it off. "Some of their number tried to attack me right after I arrived in the city. They saw me as a defenseless woman that they thought they could get away with assaulting. They were wrong."

Zariah looked both horrified and amused at the thought of what must have happened to them.

On that note, Mara left the tavern, her bank vault substantially less empty, and with a decent basic understanding of the city, and she had two more contacts that could help her. Zariah would be a good source of rumors and news, and this enchanter, Toman, would hopefully be able to make items for her that she truly desired. Items that the City Watch might not be particularly happy for her to own, like a Scrying ward to prevent Seers from finding her.

But there's so much more than just that. If the ex-Maker is willing, I might be able to see the sun for the first time in over a hundred years!

CHAPTER
THIRTEEN

THE BROKEN FANG was located in the Second Quarter of the city, but Toman—the ex-Maker—operated out of the First, the same district as Greenstone, the pawnshop. Unlike Greenstone, which sat just off the main road near the southern wall, Toman's place was much farther north, closer to the mountain. Zariah had said it was near the Citadel—a massive stone fortress carved into the mountain's base— so finding the right area shouldn't be too difficult.

Still, before heading that way, it made sense to swing by Greenstone and unload the haul she'd picked up from the dog-fighting scumbag. The bastard had no idea how easy he'd gotten off. If she didn't need to keep a low profile, she would've gone full John Wick on him.

As it was, he would wake up tomorrow a changed man, having 'donated' all his worldly possessions to charity.

Mara laughed as she stepped out into the night and headed north toward the main road.

She hired a taxi—not that it resembled anything from Earth. It was closer to a rickshaw: three wheels, a small passenger bench that could seat two, and a driver up front. Except, this being a crazy magic world, the cart ran on magic provided by the driver rather than muscle. The skinny man didn't pull it, but rather steered it from a small seat while the thing hummed, rolling forward under its own power.

She had to admit, it was kind of impressive.

The man—Dunc, as he introduced himself—seemed constitutionally incapable of silence. He chattered nonstop as they rolled through the magic lamp-lit streets, oblivious to her lack of engagement. Still, Mara didn't mind. His gossip gave her a sense of the city's rhythm.

"The Healers Guild is still scrambling after that barge crashed into a ferry the other night," Dunc said, steering around a slow-moving merchant cart. "Big scandal! The Transportation Guild swears their pilot didn't fall asleep, but the Seers couldn't prove anything because there were anti-scrying wards on the barge. Can you believe that? Illegal as sin."

She made a noise of polite interest, which was all the encouragement he needed.

"Now the lords are all in a huff, dragging it to the Council. But Lord Tynin of House Tynos hasn't been seen in days—still grieving his wife and kids, poor man. Without him, the Council can't agree on anything."

On and on it went.

By the time they reached Greenstone, Mara felt like she had read half a newspaper. She climbed out of the cart and turned back to him. "Wait for me, will you? I've got a lot to do tonight, and if you stick around, I'll make it worth your while with a big tip."

Dunc blanched. "Oh no, no, can't do that! I'm a journeyman Transporter Mage—strict guild rules. I do this for extra coin in the evenings, but if the Guild caught me accepting gratuities, they'd hang me from the mast of the tallest ship in the harbor."

Mara raised an eyebrow. "Harsh."

He gave a sheepish shrug. "Eh, it's in the charter."

She gave him a grin, "Well, nonetheless, I've got a lot of ground to cover tonight if you don't mind sticking with me."

"Not at all! As long as you've got coin, I don't mind." The young mage chuckled in return.

After a quick word with Gavian, her business was done. He was much more cooperative this time, thanks to a strong post-hypnotic suggestion not to cheat her again. She didn't even need to compel him. He still skimmed a bit off the top, but she let it go—fences had to eat, too, and this was stolen gear. Her bank vault was seventeen gold marks richer as she left the store, and she was ready to go find that Maker.

She had just stepped outside and started down the steps when her danger sense flared—hard. A flicker of steel caught a lamp's glow at the edge of her vision. Instinct triggered her body to move before her brain caught up.

A crossbow bolt punched into her left shoulder and lit up with the sick glow of enchanted sunlight.

Not good.

She screamed, ripping the bolt free. It tore muscle and cartilage with it and scorched her right hand as it came loose. She flung it down the street with all the strength she had.

Rage surged through her, white-hot. Then came the bad news— there wasn't just one attacker. While she yanked the bolt out, three more figures stepped out of the nearby alleys, weapons raised. Two others were coming from the side, holding a glowing net between them.

Oh, hell no.

She surged forward, tapping her vampiric blood for every drop of speed and power she had to dive down the steps into a roll. Two more bolts hissed over her and thudded into Greenstone's wooden door behind her.

Reflex, instinct, and experience took over. Hundreds of fights had trained her brain to triage threats in an instant.

The net was the worst of it. If that thing had the same solar magic as the bolt, one hit and she'd fry, there would be no escaping. The others had fired—or were reloading. Crossbows were slow.

Go for the net.

She charged the man on the left, her useless left arm tucked tight, and her burned right hand extended, claws flared. She barely slowed as she passed him, raking his throat with two inches of razor-sharp bone. Blood sprayed in an arc behind her.

But the last crossbowman had anticipated her move. He fired—not where she was, but where she would be.

Thunk.

Another sun-damned bolt slammed into her abdomen. This one hit deep, barbs lodging somewhere behind her navel. Her vision blurred. Her knees buckled.

Can't leave it in.

She braced, screamed, and slammed her palm into the shaft, forcing it out through her back. The searing pain nearly made her blackout. She grabbed the blood-slick point and yanked the rest free.

Still crouched, she spun and jammed the bolt into the eye socket of the other net wielding man, who was running toward her, still fumbling with the oversized trap.

Two down.

But that little maneuver had cost her time. The remaining three were reloading.

Then she heard a voice she hated more than the pain.

"Finish her! For the Dragon!"

Drevan.

That greasy little bastard who tried to sic his followers on her the first night she was in this world.

I should've finished you the first time.

No doubting herself. No seer or Watch officer would call this anything but self-defense.

He'd already turned and run—coward. Covering his own retreat at the expense of his men.

She clocked the other three as they raised their crossbows.

Usually, she wouldn't be worried. Her speed made her a blur to shooters like these. But one had hit her already, and she couldn't take that chance again. Another bolt to the chest or the head, and it was game over.

Even now, it was only her vampiric ability to suppress pain and emotion that was allowing her to continue functioning after being hit with sunlight that had burned her internally.

That was when she saw it. The nearest man's crossbow was glowing with mana—so dense she could see it from forty feet away.

Shit. The crossbows are magic.

The man she'd just dropped was still falling, so she yanked his body up like a ragdoll and shoved it in front of her.

Just in time.

A bolt slammed into the corpse's chest with a dull thud. No time to waste—she charged the shooter, using the dead man as a moving shield. The other two still hadn't fired; she needed to keep a body between her and their sights until they did.

Only one arm still working, she tossed the corpse aside at the last second and lunged. The man tried to use his crossbow like a club, but she batted it aside and slammed her hand into his chest hard enough to punch through bone. His heart burst like an overripe melon. He dropped without a sound.

She turned just in time to catch another bolt—this one tearing through her left bicep. It punched clean through, burning like acid the whole way. Her arm went dead. More pain. More rage.

Grabbing the last man's corpse, she bolted for the fourth attacker, whose face had gone ghost-white. He saw the blood, the bolt that didn't stop her, and he knew.

But she didn't charge him. She pivoted toward the only one still holding a loaded shot.

"For the Dragon!" he screamed, loosing his bolt in a panic.

His god failed him. The bolt hit the corpse she was carrying—dead center in the skull. The head exploded in a red mist lit with rays of sunlight.

Perfect.

Both crossbowmen now scrambled to reload. Too late. They were already dead; they just didn't know it yet.

She dropped the body and lunged for the first one. He barely had time to shriek.

"You did this," she hissed, jerking her chin toward her mangled arm. "Now you pay."

She tapped the side of his skull just hard enough to drop him unconscious. Then she turned to his partner.

No hesitation this time. She sank her fangs deep, feeding until his heart gave out. Relief washed through her—hot, sweet, burning away the pain like whiskey through a cracked lip. She dropped the body and grabbed the next one.

Drained him dry, too.

No mercy.

Not for people who hunted her with sun-bolts.

———

Still bleeding, she one-handed her way through looting the corpses. She'd need an hour or more to fully heal, but she didn't have that kind of time. Drevan had fled, again. She'd deal with him later.

In the meantime, she'd collect her due. If people wanted to throw themselves at her blades, the least they could do was die with something worth stealing.

Too bad Dunc had vanished. Either someone warned him off, or he ran when the fighting broke out. *Can't blame him. I probably would've bailed, too.*

Ten minutes later, she hauled the loot inside Greenstone, cursing every painful step. The weapons were solid—enchanted, no doubt. Expensive toys for a bunch of suicidal cultists.

Gavian looked like he'd seen a ghost. "You killed them. Right outside my door."

"Still warm," she said, dumping the gear. "Now make it worth my time."

He started cleaning the blood off the items, muttering under his breath, too greedy to turn her away. She noticed the Cleaner he was using and felt stupid—she had her own and had forgotten all about it.

Might as well fix that.

She went back out and scrubbed the street clean. Blood, bolts, bodies —all vanished into a storage ring looted from one of the corpses. Ten minutes later, it looked like nothing had happened at all except for the bolt holes in Gavian's door.

Back inside, she leaned on the counter. "Don't lowball me again. I know what this stuff's worth now. Three enchanted crossbows. One of those bastards hit me mid-blur. He couldn't have even seen me."

Gavian raised his hands. "Hey, I'm not saying they aren't quality. But you literally killed them on my front step. That's hot merchandise. It's gonna cost me extra to move it."

"Bullshit. We both know you'll have this stuff downstairs and scrubbed clean before I hit the next corner. You'll ship it out to some other city where no one knows who died. Try to screw me, and I'll make sure your balls regret it."

Gavian winced. "There are bodies in that ring! You think dumping corpses in a city full of Seers is easy? If one of those floats to the surface—"

"You're full of crap," she cut in. "You'll toss them into that incineration circle of yours and have less than ash left behind. But sure, fine. I'll drop a gold mark per body off the price."

He faked a scowl, but she could see the glee in his eyes. Five gold marks saved. The man would dance on his mother's grave for half that.

In the end, they settled on seventy-two gold marks. Back on Earth, that would be worth close to three-quarters of a million dollars.

Mara took a long moment to consider the idea of hunting cultists full-time. If every group of zealots carried enchanted gear like this, she could be rich in no time.

But no—this had been personal. They'd come equipped with vampire-killer crossbows. Not standard-issue gear for your average true believer. Whoever had armed them either raided the church armory or dipped deep into their sacred stash just for her.

That meant Drevan had pulled strings.

For all she knew, he'd gone crying back to his superiors, claiming his righteous missionary group was ambushed by an evil vampire lurking in the streets. If they believed his version of events, then these men might have died thinking they were heroes.

Still complete bullshit, of course. But it made things... murky.

She couldn't shake the thought that not all the Followers might be like Drevan. Maybe he was the outlier–a rat in an otherwise clean house.

Then again, maybe not.

Either way, she couldn't go full John Wick on their congregation until she knew for sure. If Drevan was a symptom of something deeper, she'd find out soon enough—and then they'd see just how evil a vampire could be when provoked.

For now, she needed to find that Maker and get him to enchant something that would block scrying. If not, she'd be ambushed every time she stepped foot outside the Dragon Inn.

Just as she reached the door, a familiar cart rolled up to the front steps.

Dunc gave her a sheepish smile. "I hope you're not angry I left earlier. Things looked like they might get a little... heated." He looked around, surprised not to see any signs of violence.

Mara laughed as she descended the stairs. "Of course not. You made the smart call. Now take me toward the Citadel—the place I'm looking for is near there."

FOURTEEN

As she got closer, Dunc winced at the sight of her wounds. "Ouch. I guess things *did* get ugly. You alright? I can take you to a healer I know on the way."

Mara glanced down and frowned. By now, those injuries should've closed up—at least on the surface. They hadn't. Probably because of the sunlight damage. That crap was kryptonite to vampires, and Mara had gone out of her way to avoid tanning for the past hundred years. She didn't have much firsthand experience with what that kind of injury would do. Slower regeneration wasn't too surprising.

What annoyed her more was the state of her clothes. The blouse and corset were ruined. No patch job could fix damage like that. The cleaners might have perfectly removed the blood and stains, but those tears were beyond repair.

That's one more I owe you, you rat bastard. Drevan was going to have a very bad night once she tracked him down.

"Not unless they can heal vampires," she said dryly. Then, chuckling, "I'll mend up on my own. What I really need is a tailor."

The driver blinked. "Oh. I didn't realize... that is—sorry. I don't know any tailors near the Citadel, but there are plenty on the Mile. Not that there *aren't* any here; I just don't know them."

"No worries. I'll deal with it later."

The cart rolled on through the First Quarter. The buildings were tighter here, stacked closer together—this was clearly one of the poorer parts of the city. But the closer they got to the mountain, the more the scenery improved. Mid-tier homes, market squares, tidy little parks—everything she'd expect from a major city. It wasn't like the Merchant Mile, though. Other than restaurants and inns, most businesses here were shuttered for the night. Still, the streets were far from dead. It was only around 10:30 p.m., and the city still buzzed with life.

What really caught her attention, though, were the glimpses she caught of the Citadel.

The keep was enormous, carved right into the mountainside—larger than any medieval castle she'd seen back on Earth and a hell of a lot more solid. She never got a full view of it, but even the little she saw left an impression. Dunc was happy to fill in the gaps.

"The Spellswords are one of the Big Ten—most powerful mage guilds on Greymantle—and *that's* their headquarters. They say no one's ever broken in and come out alive. Those guys? They're something else. I'm with the Transporter's Guild, and our long-haul caravans usually pay the Spellswords for protection. I'm still a trainee—never done any ocean runs—but I've worked with 'em once or twice. I've *never* felt safer."

Mara found herself wondering how they'd stack up against Cabal agents. Earth's hidden masters had mage, vampire, and werewolf strike teams with the best training money and magic could buy. She'd love to see what a Greymantle Spellsword could do against *those* bastards.

"If people are coming at you in the street," Dunc added, "you might consider hiring one. Nobody messes with someone who's got a Spellsword watching their back."

"You might be right," she said. "But so long as they don't catch me by surprise, idiots like the ones tonight won't stand a chance."

She spotted the building she was looking for and sat up. "Stop! We've arrived."

The building looked unremarkable—plain and easy to miss—but it matched Zariah's description. They were in a small square now, and directly across from her destination hung a sign: *The Rook's Roost.*

It looked nothing like the Broken Fang. No shady figures loitering near the entrance. It had the warm, welcoming charm of a cozy Irish pub—friendly, lived-in, clearly a place for locals.

The square itself added to that impression. A large tree dominated the center, its thick branches promising generous shade during the day. Beneath it, people gathered at benches and tables, still chatting and drinking at this hour. Laughter drifted in the air. The whole space felt safe. Comfortable.

If she didn't have urgent business with the Maker, she might have stopped to enjoy it. But tonight wasn't that kind of night. Not yet.

"Dunc, please hang around if you would. I doubt there'll be any more incidents, and even those idiots wouldn't be dumb enough to cause trouble in a place like this."

The transporter mage smiled amiably, nodding his agreement—but he eyed the tavern longingly. "Will you be long? Mind if I duck in for a quick drink?"

"Not at all," she said, chuckling. "Just don't drink so much you forget how to drive."

Dunc laughed. "Don't you worry, miss! I never over-indulge. Especially not when I'm working!"

Waving him off with a grin, Mara turned toward the building—and toward her best hope of staying in the city.

She was counting on this Maker. Without anti-scrying protections, she might have no choice but to leave. The Watch and that dragon-licking cult were both hunting her now. After tonight, things had escalated. She couldn't keep looking over her shoulder every time she stepped outside.

She spotted the narrow staircase tucked into an alcove where the three-story building butted up against its neighbor. No sign. No indication of a shop. That made sense, given the man was working off the books. A real Maker—but hiding from the Guild—trying to keep his head down.

Still, to operate like this in the heart of the city? He *had* to be good at anti-scrying magic. Probably the only reason he was still alive.

A faint light illuminated the stairwell, just enough to keep someone from breaking their neck but too dim to draw unwanted attention. It reminded her of a Prohibition-era speakeasy. All it needed was a secret password and a jazz band in the back.

Smirking, she descended and knocked on the door, appreciating the irony that this 'underground' Maker actually lived below the ground in some kind of basement home.

A moment later, a metal slider scraped open at eye level. A gruff voice growled, "What do you want?"

"Rude much?" Mara arched a brow. "Zariah sent me. Said you might be able to help."

The man blinked in surprise. "Zariah? I haven't seen her in... well, never mind that. One second."

She heard locks disengage—both mechanical and magical—before the door swung open into a well-lit interior. The man stepped aside and gestured her in.

The man who opened the door was tall and lean, with the kind of build that made him look like he could slip through the cracks of the world if he wanted to—and maybe he had. He couldn't have been older than his early thirties, but something about the way he carried himself screamed experience. His eyes were sharp, too sharp, and when they locked on her, it felt like he saw *through* her, not just at her. Not in a creepy way—just calculating, precise, like a jeweler inspecting a gem.

His hair was short and neat, a deep brown that was almost black. No robes, no tools of the trade. Just a dark vest over a cream-colored shirt, sleeves rolled to the elbows, trousers tucked into scuffed boots. He could've passed for an off-duty professor or a very relaxed noble. Nothing about him said "mage," let alone "rogue enchanter hiding from one of the most powerful guilds in the world."

"Come in," he said simply, his voice low but clear, no wasted words. Then he turned and walked back into the room without waiting for her reply.

She followed him inside, taking in the space with a sweep of her eyes. It looked more like the front room of a quiet townhouse than a secret workshop. There was a heavy wooden table in one corner, surrounded by a few mismatched chairs, and a sitting area featuring a well-worn couch and two comfortable-looking chairs arranged near a small iron stove. Everything was tidy, quiet, and lived-in. Nothing sparkled. Nothing hummed. No enchanted trinkets floated in the air, and there were no arcane symbols carved into the floor.

If she hadn't just walked through a magically locked door with at least three types of protective wards layered on it, she'd never have guessed what kind of man lived here. That and the fact that Zariah directed her to him.

There were no books out. No clutter. No signs of business at all.

Clever bastard. Even the room lied for him.

As soon as the door shut and she stepped into the light, the man's eyebrows lifted at the sight of her injuries.

"I'd ask if you needed a healer, but your kind doesn't usually bother. Still... I'm surprised to see you wounded. You aren't bringing trouble to my door, are you? Because if you are, you can leave. Now. No matter who sent you."

He glanced toward the door meaningfully.

Mara waved it off. "No one's likely to come looking for me here—especially not with the kind of wards you've got around this place. Besides, I already dealt with the ones who did this." She nodded toward her injuries.

"I'm Mara, by the way."

"Toman," he replied simply.

Gesturing at the shut and locked door, he added, "Sorry, can't be too careful."

"I couldn't agree more. That's part of why I'm here. I need something to block scrying."

Toman gave her a once-over, gesturing at her clothes and wounds. "Looks like you need more than just that. I don't usually do warded clothing, but I can handle an anti-scrying item."

He dropped into one of the comfy chairs and gestured toward the couch. "Most Makers are pretentious pricks—too wrapped up in their own hype and chasing money. I'm not like them. I make beautiful things. I collect knowledge. Now, tell me what you need. If it sounds interesting, I might just bother with it."

"Top priority is the anti-scrying. I need it yesterday." She motioned to her injuries. "But I also want something to protect against fire, a good storage ring, something to mask my nature so I don't trigger detection spells, and... a daylight item. Something that lets me walk in the sun."

Toman's eyebrows rose higher with every word. "You don't ask for much, do you?" But there was a glint in his eye now. She had his interest.

"Let's say I'm intrigued. But you do understand how illegal all of that is, right? Not just Guild taboo. Actual, hang-you-in-the-square illegal. Especially the daylight enchantment."

Mara shrugged. "You haven't said no."

He smirked. "No, I haven't. I can make those things. But I want you to understand why they'll cost you. My prices are non-negotiable. And just so you know, the illegal ones will have built-in self-destructs if they're magically examined. If you get stopped by the Watch, don't let them take your gear—or it'll be gone. Explosively"

She narrowed her eyes, but he held up a hand. "Not the storage ring, though. Nothing illegal about that. I'll bind it to you, so even if they take it, no one else can access it. And I'll add concealment enchantments—make it invisible to casual detection. High-end stuff, but I'm good at what I do."

It all sounded reasonable to Mara—pricey, dangerous, but necessary. "And the daylight item?"

He leaned back. "Trickier. And yes, *more* illegal. Anti-scrying? Nobles and merchants use that all the time. But letting a vampire walk in the daylight? That's an automatic death sentence. That's why it needs a failsafe. But I can do it. The enchantment itself isn't that hard if you know the trick—which I do. The cost is all about the risk."

She found herself liking him. Not because he was kind—he wasn't. But he was upfront. That was rare. Also, he hadn't stared at her once, which was refreshing. Although maybe that had something to do with the gaping wounds in her shoulder, arm, and side.

She glanced down and frowned. She didn't have much experience with sunlight damage, but these wounds should've started closing by now.

Not good.

Toman noticed her frown. "I can check the wounds, see if there's lingering magic keeping them from healing."

That hadn't even occurred to her. "Ugh. Yeah, thanks. I'd appreciate that. I mean, it's kinda hard to see inside your own guts, after all, much less see if there's mana in there."

He laughed, but then gave her a strange look. "See? You mean *sense* the magic? Can you sense mana if it's inside you?"

"Yeah, no. I meant *see*."

She looked down at her shoulder, then shrugged. "Not inside me, but on the surface? Sure. No lingering misty grey energy that I can spot."

Toman's expression darkened. "Wait—you mean *actually see* the mana?"

He flicked his fingers and cast a tiny spell in the air next to him. She glanced at it instinctively.

His face went pale.

"Your kind can't see magic," he said slowly. "And I don't see any enchanted items on you that would give you mana-vision. How are you doing that?"

"Relax, Maker-boy. I *can* see it. I don't know why. I arrived in this world last night, and ever since, it's like magic has been visible to me. Must be something to do with the magic that brought me here, like the enchantments that let me understand your language. For the record, I wasn't able to see mana back on my world. This is new for me."

Toman sank back in his chair, stunned. "You're not from Greymantle? You were brought here... from another world?"

"That's right. I was kidnapped. And you're the only one I've told. So maybe don't make me regret it."

Her gut told her he wouldn't. She needed him—and more importantly, he hadn't set off any of her internal alarms. For now, that would have to be enough.

For a long moment, Toman sat and processed what she had told him. He cast another spell, which caused mana to hover in the air before his eyes, then asked, "Tell me the truth, you really aren't just messing with me? You really are from a different world?"

"That's what I said. My world is called Earth. I'd never even heard of Greymantle until I came here. Although I must admit that there has to be some kind of connection between our worlds. My world has stories of dragons, elves, and dwarves, but we don't have any of those and never did. So how else could we have such tales?"

Toman's lips pursed, and his brows drew together for a moment as he considered. "You're telling the truth. Considering that vampires on this world cannot see mana at all, I'll believe you. Dragon's Balls! That's crazy!"

He was out of his seat now and pacing as his mind raced with the possibilities. After a second, he stopped and asked, "But you do have magic on your world, so you know you couldn't see it before coming to Greymantle?"

"Yes, my world has magic, and I know I couldn't see it before I arrived. However, my world has only a tiny fraction of the mana that you have here. Mages were rare, maybe 1-in-100,000 or less?"

The Maker looked aghast. "How could you even live like that?"

Mara started, "We had technology, machines, and... you know what, that's not important right now. Can you scan me for magic inside my wounds, please?"

Blinking in surprise, he looked like he wanted to deluge her with questions but reined himself in and nodded. "You're right. Come with me, please."

He escorted her to the door at the back of the room and opened it. Beyond was a comfortable, lived-in space that immediately gave Mara the sense that this was a man who spent more time working than relaxing—but still valued comfort.

The lighting was warm, soft amber glowstones tucked into sconces that framed the walls like lanterns. The room had the feel of a cottage's den crossed with a workshop. A pair of overstuffed chairs sat near a modest hearth, and a low table between them held an open book, a still warm mug of something herbal, and a scattering of parchment covered in precise arcane notations.

Shelves lined nearly every wall, crammed with books, scroll tubes, crystal jars filled with glowing dusts, tiny bones, odd tools, and more than one magical contraption whirring softly to itself. A few of the shelves were clearly meant to be organized, but others looked like they had given up trying. Copper wires, rune-etched rods, vials of colored fluid, and broken bits of enchanted jewelry lay in little clusters on almost every available surface.

Mara's sharp eyes spotted a spellwork bench tucked against the far wall, with a half-completed ring suspended mid-air in a soft mana field, slowly rotating as if waiting for its next etching. The entire place felt like the inside of a magical tinkerer's brain—fascinating, overflowing, but surprisingly homey.

Despite the clutter, there was a quiet energy to the space. Not chaotic, just... busy. Focused.

"You live here?" she asked, genuinely curious.

Toman shrugged. "Safer that way. Everything I need is at my fingertips, and no one comes back here beyond the reception room unless I invite them." He gave her a wry smile. "And I like the smell of my own work."

Mara chuckled. "Smells like burned silver and tea."

"Exactly."

He gestured toward a padded stool near a freestanding crystal ring in the corner. "Sit. I'll run the scan."

The crystal lit up as Toman gestured, activating the device without a word.

Mara felt the mana wash through her body like a wave passing through every cell. It wasn't unpleasant—tingly, maybe—but eerily reminiscent of getting a CT scan back on Earth.

Toman's brow furrowed as he peered at something only he could see. "Fascinating. I've never examined a vampire before. There's magic in your blood—resists analysis—but it's not blocking me from seeing your physical structure."

She arched a brow. "Seeing what, exactly?"

Startled, Toman flushed. "No, not like that." He made a quick gesture, and an illusion sprang into the air between them—a translucent figure suspended in light.

It was her. Bones, muscle, organs—laid bare in ghostly detail. Like a magical MRI.

Mara's stomach tightened.

She saw the injuries clearly, but something else caught her attention. Scattered across her form, not just in her wounds but all over her body, were tiny pockets of... something. They didn't glow like mana. They didn't feel magical. But they didn't match the rest of her body either.

"What the hell is that?" she asked, pointing toward a small cluster near her ribs.

Toman didn't answer immediately. His frown deepened as he zoomed the image, adjusting runes she didn't recognize.

"Seriously," she pressed, eyes narrowing. "What is that?!?"

She concentrated, trying to feel it. Nothing. No burning, no resistance, no sense of invasion. After more than a hundred years living in this body, she knew when something was wrong inside her. Poison, sickness, curses—she could always feel the intrusion.

But this? This felt like nothing. And that terrified her.

Still silent, Toman turned the device toward himself and cast a second scan. The same image appeared—his internal form, healthy, alive—and everywhere in his body was the same pale substance.

The same stuff that had taken up residence inside her.

She blinked. "Wait... is that some kind of magical bacteria or something? Is that why people on Greymantle are so full of mana? Is that how you can see magic? Midicloriants or some shit like that?"

Toman looked between their two scans, his expression unreadable. Finally, he shook his head.

"No. It's not a parasite. Not bacteria. What you're seeing..." He paused. "That's living tissue."

She stared at him, unblinking.

"Living... *what?*"

"Your body's supposed to be undead," he said, voice quiet now. "But those pockets... they're alive."

Her thoughts short-circuited. For a second, she fixated on how casually he'd said it like it wasn't a punch to her entire reality. A ridiculous part of her wanted to snap at him for his casual tone. But the shock had taken her voice and most of her rationality with it.

Living tissue.

Inside a vampire.

That wasn't possible.

That wasn't how it worked.

The vampire blood didn't heal you—its magic preserved you. Converted your dead flesh into something that didn't rot, didn't age, didn't live. It sustained. It didn't grow.

And yet...

She looked back at the image. At her wounds. The outer damage still lingered, but inside—faint, fragile—she could see new tissue forming.

Living tissue.

"What the fuck," she whispered.

Her vampiric tissue wasn't regenerating.

Instead, living cells—actual *living* cells—were growing where undead flesh should've been knitting back together. What she was witnessing wasn't just unexpected—it was *impossible*. At least, by everything she knew about magic and biology.

Impossible. That word looped in her brain, over and over, like a stuck record. She couldn't shake it.

Toman's voice cut through the spiral. "I can give you an anti-scrying brooch now, a spare I already have. But for the rest, you'll need to come back. The brooch will run you fifty gold marks. And like I said —I don't negotiate." He paused, eyeing her wounds and the scan with interest. "Still... if you let me scan you again and record the results, I'd be willing to cut you a deal on the rest. I know this is upsetting, but... it's fascinating."

Mara shot him a warning look. Not hostile, but the kind that said *you're skating on thin ice.*

"Fine. I'll take the brooch. How soon can I get the rest?"

Toman pursed his lips, thinking. "Three days for the storage ring. As for the other items—the daylight enchantment, fire resistance, and masking charm—I can weave those into a single piece. But it'll take a week, maybe two. Not sure yet. The ring will be forty-five gold marks. The rest? One hundred."

Her eyes narrowed. "That's the *discounted* price, friend?"

"Friend? We're friends now?" he teased, a half-smile twitching at his lips.

"Hey, when getting this intimate with a girl, most guys at least buy dinner first," she said, jerking her chin at the illusion that had displayed every inch of her body in a high-res magic hologram. It was the interior of her body, but still.

Toman blushed again but relented. "Alright, I did promise a discount. Make it one-twenty-five total. But if I can offer a suggestion... as a friend?"

She arched a brow. "Let's hear it."

His joking tone vanished. "Go to the Healer's Guild. If anyone on Greymantle can make sense of what's happening to you, it's them."

Mara didn't like the idea, but she couldn't argue. She couldn't walk around with a non-healing shoulder and a hole in her gut while her body decided to reinvent itself from the inside out.

Without further delay, Toman retrieved the brooch—a platinum clasp set with a carved onyx bearing the glyph for *Obscure*. The enchantment would mask her presence from tracking or scrying, and like his other work, it was keyed to avoid detection unless someone knew exactly what they were looking for.

She clipped it to the center of her corset and transferred the fifty gold marks with a touch of her bank token.

"I'll be back in three days for the ring."

"Try not to get yourself killed before then," Toman said, already resetting the crystal for another scan.

Mara stepped back into the cool night and scanned the square carefully. If there were any assassins waiting for her, they were damn good at hiding. Nothing felt off.

Dunc's cart was already pulled up in front of the building. He looked up from his mug with a cheerful grin.

As she slid into the seat behind him, she said, "To the Healer's Guild, please."

CHAPTER
FIFTEEN

EVEN WITH THE magic cart going from the mountainside of the First Quarter to near the north end of the Third Quarter took well over an hour. It was nearly two o'clock in the morning by the time she arrived.

They had made a quick stop by the clothing store where she had bought her outfit previously. They took her old corset and blouse, promising to have them repaired for a small fee and deliver them to her room at the Dragon Inn. In the meantime, the saleswoman found replacements that were similar enough not to alter the overall look of the outfit. She also requested a spare set to be made from armored fabric, which would cost her an additional fifteen gold marks. On the bright side, it would include a basic self-repair enchantment but wouldn't be ready for at least a couple weeks.

Just to be safe, she picked up a complete spare outfit as well in case she ruined these new ones in another fight. She placed them in her storage pouch so she wouldn't be caught halfway across the city, only half-dressed. The tattered state of her blouse and corset had earned her quite a few stares from other late-night travelers on the streets.

The rest of the trip to the healers guild was somewhat more relaxed. While she was still very worried about what was happening to her, she felt much less exposed traveling the streets now that she had the anti-scrying item. The City Watch or the cultists might have people out looking for her, but they wouldn't be able to find her with magic and chase her down. They'd have to go about it the old-fashioned way. With that concern off her mind, she was able to better enjoy the drive.

The moment they turned onto the street leading to the Healers Guild, Mara noticed the shift.

The air felt different—lighter, cleaner somehow. The harsh edges of the city softened, the usual scent of stone and humanity replaced with fresh soil, blossoms, and something unnameable but deeply soothing. Even her nerves, raw and on edge from repressing the pain of her wounds, seemed to quiet slightly.

Gardens lined the street, not the showy kind, but carefully curated ones—stone paths, delicate flowering trees, and low shrubs sculpted into pleasing forms. The whole area felt... cared for. It was like walking into a living painting.

As they rode through the increasingly beautiful neighborhood, Dunc slowed the cart slightly, reverent in his tone. "We're close now. You know the Guild's near when the flowers start appearing on every windowsill. That's the influence of the Heartwood tree."

Mara arched a brow. "Heartwood?"

He grinned and fished a wand from inside his cloak. It was a slender, twisted thing—barely thicker than a pencil, with a natural curve that looked more like driftwood than a finely carved tool. But even from where she sat, Mara could feel the hum of power running through it.

"Heartwood," he said proudly. "Every guild mage on Greymantle has a focus item made from it. They say Heartwoods grow over the grave of someone particularly noble of heart. This one is older than the city, maybe older than the Guilds themselves. Some say it's aware. Not sentient like us, but close. Its aura calms people. That's why the Healers created their Guild around it."

Sure enough, a moment later, they rounded a final bend, and Mara saw the entrance.

It wasn't grand in the typical sense. There were no towering statues or banners, no armored guards or imposing gates. Instead, there was a tall stone archway that bore a distant resemblance to the Torii gates she'd seen at Japanese temples back on Earth. Through it, she glimpsed soft lantern light, lush green grass, and the massive trunk of a tree that rose in the center of the courtyard like a silent guardian. Its branches stretched impossibly wide, casting a dome of dappled shadow over the courtyard.

They stopped outside the gate, parking the small rickshaw-like carriage. Mara felt the shift the moment they passed under the arch.

Calm washed over her—not forced, but natural, like the exhale of a breath she hadn't realized she'd been holding. The pain in her shoulder and abdomen didn't vanish, but it faded to the background. Even her mind quieted, feeling more focused and relaxed.

At the entrance stood a girl in Healer's apprentice robes—simple but clean and well-tailored in green and white with a Heartwood leaf symbol over the left breast. She looked to be no more than sixteen or so, but her posture was straight, and her eyes were alert. A long braid of pale brown hair hung over one shoulder, and she had a concerned look in her eyes as the cart stopped before the gate.

"Evening," the girl said, though her eyes flicked to Mara's. "Are you hurt? Badly?"

Mara nodded. "Yes. I need a diagnostic. The damage isn't healing like it should."

The girl—Bryna, according to the name badge sewn into her robe—stepped forward with confident hands and a no-nonsense expression. "I'm just an apprentice, I'm not qualified to treat you myself, but I'll bring you in and find one of the Healers on duty."

Then, more hesitantly, she added, "You're... a vampire, right?"

Mara didn't bother to deny it. "Yes."

Bryna nodded, unfazed. "All right. Follow me."

As Mara looked back to Dunc, she said, "Thank you. I'll be okay from here." She paid him and tried again to tip, but he denied her.

"Be well, lady," he said, bowing his head respectfully. Then, with one last look at the tree, headed back out to his cart and quietly wheeled away down the flower-lined street.

Bryna led the way into the courtyard, guiding Mara toward one of the buildings on the right. Walking beneath the great tree's boughs felt almost meditative, the serenity settling into her bones like warm tea on a cold night.

Inside, she was ushered into a small room with a single bed and a pair of chairs. "Please, have a seat—or lie down if that's more comfortable. One of the healers will be with you shortly. We're a bit shorthanded right now; sorry for the delay." Bryna hesitated, then added awkwardly, "If you were human, uh... mortal, I mean, I'd offer to ease your pain. But I'm not sure how that works with your kind. Sorry."

She was halfway through the door when it opened again, and an older man stepped inside. His cuffs bore four white stripes—clearly indicating someone of high rank. Distinguished and confident, with white streaks in his goatee and at his temples, he studied Mara with a frown of concern.

Bryna bowed deeply. "Master Onaris. I was just about to find someone on duty. My apologies—I couldn't ease the patient's pain."

He raised an eyebrow at the girl's flustered report but didn't scold her. "That will be all, Bryna. I'll tend to our guest."

Once she was gone, Onaris took the opposite chair. "I sensed your arrival," he said, his tone flat but watchful. "Your kind rarely steps onto Guild grounds. I see that you're injured... but we cannot treat your condition."

Several snappy comebacks came to mind, but Mara wisely kept them in check. "Normally, no. My kind doesn't need treatment for wounds. It's one of our perks."

Onaris's expression didn't change. "Normally? So this time is different? Tell me what you're seeking, and if it's within our means, we will help you—as we do with all who come to us."

"I'm not regenerating," she said plainly. "The wounds were caused by sunlight-enchanted weapons—but I don't think that's the problem. Something is... growing inside me. Living tissue. Not just in the wounds—everywhere. Small patches all throughout my body."

That got his attention. His brow lifted ever so slightly.

Before he could speak, she pressed on, "I know how that sounds. It shouldn't be possible. I get that. But it's happening. And I need to understand what's going on."

Onaris gestured to the bed. "Lie down. I'll place one hand on your forehead and one on your abdomen wound—may I?"

"Go ahead." She lay on her back and got comfortable. This was a leap of faith, but for the second time in one night, she granted trust that had not yet been earned. She justified it to herself: *If he wanted, I'm sure he could end my existence with little effort.*

He had an aura of power to him that was hard to miss. Not the social kind that came from having a high position in a powerful organization, which he did, but instead, she felt a magical might within him that was almost palpable.

His face became a mask of focused concentration. Magic flowed through her—similar to Toman's scan but deeper, more complete. She forced herself to lay unnaturally still as he worked, letting him read her like a book written in flesh and blood and magic.

When it ended, he stepped back, clearly winded, and dropped into the chair as if the spell had drained him.

"Apologies," he said, catching his breath. "We've been overwhelmed since the ship wreck between the ferry and a barge. Many are still under care."

Mara sat up, shifting cross-legged on the edge of the bed, waiting quietly as he composed himself.

When he finally spoke again, it was with quiet awe. "You're right. I'd like another Guild Master to confirm it—but you do have living tissue growing inside you. And somehow, it's not being rejected by the magic in your blood. It's surviving. Thriving, even."

He hesitated, then asked, "May I bring in a colleague to examine you? There's more I could say, but I'd prefer a second opinion first."

That alone told her how serious this was. He didn't seem like the kind of man who asked for help lightly.

"Please do," she said. "I'm *dying* to know what's going on." She smirked faintly. The pun was absolutely intended and not lost on the Healer, who chuckled tiredly.

Roughly half an hour later, two women entered the room, both bearing the four white stripes on their sleeves that marked a Master of the Guild. One was older, with wispy white hair cut to her shoulders and a weary look in her eyes. The other was downright ancient—possibly the oldest mortal Mara had ever seen. Yet despite her frailty, she moved with confidence and purpose, her steps steady and sure.

Onaris rose respectfully and offered introductions. "These are Guild Master Dena—she was my own mentor when I first came to the Guild. And this is First Healer Margra Athne, the senior-most Healer in our ranks."

Mara believed it. Judging by appearance alone, Margra might actually be older than she was—counting her years before turning, which was saying something. She hopped down off the bed and offered them both a polite bow. "I'm honored. Thank you for coming."

Margra Athne sniffed. "Good manners for one of your kind. Most of the vampires I've met had an attitude." She took the remaining chair while Dena remained standing just behind her.

Dena got straight to the point. "Now, what's this about a vampire with living cells?" Apparently, Onaris had sent word ahead with magic—no surprise, given his rank.

Margra gave a short nod. "You were never one for foolishness, Onaris, not even as a boy. So, I don't imagine you're starting now. Still..." She turned to Mara, eyes sharp as scalpels. "Come here, girl. Let me get a look at you."

There was no malice in the command, only the bluntness of someone who had long since outgrown social niceties. Mara stepped forward without hesitation and stood still while the older woman placed her hands on her.

The magic flooded through her—stronger than Onaris's, like a river in full flood, and yet somehow gentler. More precise. Where Onaris had felt powerful enough to end her in a heartbeat, Margra Athne felt like she could unmake her with a thought.

Mara was suddenly very, very glad she'd decided to be respectful.

After a long moment, Margra withdrew and eased herself back into the chair. She looked a little more drained than before—clearly, the scan had cost her something.

"Dena, you have a go as well," the older woman said. "No point in only two of us seeing this."

The relatively younger white-haired Master stepped forward, her expression now curious, and repeated the process. When she finished, she sat down heavily on the edge of the bed, leaving Mara the only one still standing.

Part of Mara's brain found that funny. The one covered in wounds was somehow the last one on her feet.

"Well?" she asked. "What's the big secret?"

It was Margra Athne who answered. "First, let's be clear—there is no record, none, in any Guild archive, going back thousands of years, of anything like this ever happening. So don't misunderstand me—I am not saying your condition can be cured."

She held up a hand when Mara's mouth opened, cutting off any interruption with a look that brooked no argument.

"What I am saying," the First Healer continued, "is that the living cells inside your body are more vital than they should be. Somehow, they're surviving entirely off ambient mana. That's not supposed to be possible, but it's what the scans show."

She paused, then added, "And more than just surviving—they're spreading. Replacing your undead tissue. Slowly, yes. But steadily. There's no doubt about it."

Mara didn't have time to fully process what that meant before Onaris added, "I don't know if you'll see this as good news or bad, but if we heal your wounds, the process will accelerate. Instead of your body regenerating as it normally would, the damaged tissue will very likely be replaced with living flesh. That could raise the percentage of living matter in your body to twelve—maybe fifteen percent. The problem is, we don't know what happens if too much of your undead flesh is replaced while vampire blood still flows in your veins. You could turn mortal again... or you could simply die."

That rocked her. Hard.

She sank down into the seat he offered without a word. Mara blinked. She felt like she was being battered by one revelation after another, and none of them were minor.

She hadn't chosen to become a vampire. She'd been murdered. When she fought back, some of the bastard's blood had gotten into her wounds and her mouth. That had turned her death into a rebirth— one she never asked for. But in the century since, it hadn't been a bad life. She never got sick. Never aged. And her powers? They were more than just useful. They had made her dangerous.

And now, she might lose all of that.

If she did, how would she survive in this world? She already had bad people trying to kill her—and that was with her powers. Without them, she'd be a target with no way to fight back.

Dena must have seen some of that internal struggle on her face because she gently laid a hand on Mara's good shoulder. "Whether or not you accept healing is your choice. But know this—the Healers

Guild will be here for you, whatever comes. It's our calling to help those in pain and... I can see this is not easy for you."

That meant something. In a strange new world where she had no allies and no backup... It was enough to make her throat tighten for a moment.

For a hundred years, she'd fought in the shadows. She'd been forged like a blade, leaned on no one but Davin. She didn't break easily. She didn't bend. And she sure as hell didn't cry in front of strangers.

But looking up at the three Guild Masters watching her with concern in their eyes, she made a decision.

She'd already spilled the truth to Toman. Why not these three?

If they could be trusted with what they already knew, then perhaps the whole story would help them make a more accurate diagnosis. A better plan.

So she told them. Not everything, but enough.

She explained that she was from Earth. That she had been taken from her world without her consent. That she had translation magic and could see mana despite being a vampire. She kept it brief and straightforward.

The Masters didn't react with open disbelief—this wasn't nearly as shocking to them as it had been to Toman. If anything, her confession clarified what they'd already suspected.

Margra Athne looked the most unsettled by the kidnapping. That, at least, clearly got under her skin. But it was Dena who lit up, practically vibrating with excitement.

Dena spoke next, her voice gentler. "There may be at least one silver lining. If you survive the process, I believe you'll have a high potential to become a mage. For living tissue to survive as it is, it must be absorbing mana directly. That suggests a strong magical affinity,"

Seeing Mara's look of confusion, she added, "This means you can learn magic!" Her voice was urgent. "There's nothing stopping you. You may be weak now, with so little of your body capable of channeling mana—but as the change progresses, that will shift. You'll grow stronger. And that might be the thing that helps you survive the transformation. If, or when, the magic in your blood fails, that might be the thing that makes the difference."

It took Mara a second to catch up to what she was saying. When she did, her eyes widened.

She'd wanted to learn magic for as long as she could remember. Ever since she found out that Davin—her adoptive father—was a blood mage, she'd dreamed of following in his footsteps, but she didn't share his unique bloodline. Maybe this wasn't the same path, but it was a step in that direction. A way to finally touch the power she'd always been denied.

And maybe, just maybe, it would help her stay alive.

She looked at Dena, suddenly serious. "Could you teach me?"

Dena's expression fell, and Margra Athne's features turned stony. It was the ancient woman who spoke.

"Our Guild is sworn to train only those called to the path of healing," she said, voice clear despite her age. "To learn from us, you would need to be chosen by the Heartwood. She did not stir when you entered the courtyard, so I'm afraid... it is not possible."

Onaris's face was no less serious, though compassion softened the edges of his expression. "Just because we cannot teach you does not mean you can't learn. There are schools—institutes that teach magical foundations—but I'm afraid they're only open during the day. Most of their students are children newly discovered to have talent."

Well, that's out. No way I'm sitting in a classroom surrounded by spell-slinging preteens. I was done dealing with children even when I was alive.

What she said was, "I'll find a way. Thank you for the advice. In the meantime... I think I need to ask for healing. I can't keep walking around with one arm paralyzed and a hole in my gut and shoulder."

Onaris nodded. "Of course. I'll handle it personally. And if you survive the transition, you should return. If you ever feel drawn to the Healer's path, perhaps *She* will feel differently then."

There was weight in the word *She* and Mara caught it—the capital 'S' was for the Heartwood tree. Somehow, the Guild believed it could choose people. That it *knew* who belonged.

She didn't say anything out loud, but skepticism curled at the edges of her thoughts. How a tree, sentient or not, could detect someone's calling was a mystery she wasn't quite ready to explore.

Instead, she offered a quiet, "I'll think about it. But... I doubt it's my path. There's too much blood in my past—and probably more in my future."

"Of course," Onaris replied gently. "We all walk the path laid before us."

Without another word, the Master Healer stepped forward and placed his hands above her wounds. She felt the magic wash through her—not a shock, not even a tingle, just a calm, humming current that swept through every cell. Her body responded immediately. But not the way it used to.

Where once undead flesh would have simply knitted itself back together, now living tissue spread beneath his hands. Muscle and cartilage were recreated, new and vital, warm with blood that had no right to be there.

Oh shit.

The realization hit her like a punch to the gut. Living muscle and bone weren't designed to handle the forces her vampiric powers could generate. If she used her left arm to deliver a blow at superhuman speed or strength, it wouldn't just ache—it would tear, rupture, maybe even snap.

She might have full mobility back—but not full capacity. Her arm worked, but it wouldn't survive the strain of what she was capable of. That meant her life was only going to get harder from here.

Her enemies weren't going to go easier on her just because she was falling apart. And eventually, she'd reach the point where her vampiric powers would stop working entirely.

When that day came, what would she do then?

CHAPTER
SIXTEEN

IT WAS WELL after three in the morning, and Mara had taken one hit to her worldview too many. On any other night, she might've gone back out hunting to earn some of the coin she'd need for Toman's absurdly expensive creations.

Not tonight.

Right now, all she wanted in the world was to crawl back into that insane dragon's mouth and pretend none of this had ever happened.

After offering her thanks and goodbyes to the Master Healers, Onaris walked her to the street and flagged down a carriage. This one wasn't magic-driven, just a simple horse-drawn affair—but it was quiet enough, comfortable, and had decent suspension. She barely noticed the ride. One blink and she was back in front of the massive dragon's head entrance to the inn.

The night guard on duty greeted her with a nod. No crazy dwarf behind the bar this time, so she bypassed the common room and headed straight for her room.

Quiet. Cozy. Safe—as safe as anywhere in this insane world could be.

She lay there, staring at the ceiling until dawn pulled her under with the irresistible weight of the undead. Her last thought as she slipped beneath the veil of sleep was a bitter one:

Am I even still one of 'my kind' anymore?

Just like every evening since she had been turned, consciousness snapped back the instant the sun dipped below the horizon.

She sat up abruptly, determined not to let her situation drag her down. A dull twinge pulled at her abdomen where the bolt had hit the night before, a sharp reminder that she wasn't healing the way she used to. Her quick awakening and clear mind said she was still the vampire she knew herself to be, but the weakness where her wounds had been said something else.

Growling, she climbed out of bed and dressed quickly.

Three days. That's how long she had to come up with thirty-five gold marks—the cost of the storage ring Toman was crafting. Then, there was the daylight enchantment, the one she wanted more than anything. That one would run her seventy-two more with what she already had in the bank.

A thought crept in, and her frown deepened. If she really was turning mortal... did the daylight charm even matter anymore?

She hated that thought.

Mara wasn't the brooding, angst-ridden type who romanticized mortality or pined for sunlight with a poetic sigh. But she'd be lying if she claimed she hadn't missed it—deeply, at times.

And now, just when the chance to reclaim the day was finally within reach...

Fate's a bitch, she thought.

The universe, with its twisted sense of humor, dangled the prize right in front of her—only to make it irrelevant. She threw her fist toward the ceiling, defiant and dramatic like some half-mad Shakespearean heroine. "Really? Now you give me sunlight?!"

Whatever.

There was no time for sulking.

It was time to move—and earn some damned coin.

When she passed through the common room a few minutes later, the grumpy dwarf was back behind the bar, right where she'd left him the day before. He waved her over.

His gaze traveled over her, one bushy brow rising as it paused on her shoulder and her abdomen.

Did he see the changes?

He didn't comment if he did. Just lowered his voice to keep the conversation private.

"Things have quieted since Joram and the boy left the city yesterday morning," he said. "The Blood Mages are chasing after them—at least the ones who were showing their faces. Don't let that fool you. They've still got agents in the city. Keep your head down. The city's restless."

Then, almost like an afterthought: "Package arrived for you. Talk to the lad at coat check."

One of these days, she was going to sit that dwarf down and *make* him explain who the hell he thought she was.

But not tonight.

Tonight, she had work to do and a bank vault to fill

Mara made a note to herself to drop a donation off at the Healers Guild for all they had done for her the night before. With everything she had learned and been through, she hadn't even thought to pay them anything before leaving. She'd be sure to take a few gold marks out of her earnings for the evening and make a generous donation.

It took only a moment to retrieve the small parcel of repaired clothing from the coat check and tuck it into her storage pouch. Then she slipped into the night. Cautious, eyes sharp, cloak hood drawn up to hide her features.

Thanks to Toman, she now knew how to spot the signs of warding magic. The Dragon Inn's protections were strong—she wasn't being scried from inside; she was sure of that. But if the Followers had tracked her here that first night... or if they had someone posted nearby?

They'd never dare cross the threshold, not with Zak watching. But the street outside? That was fair game.

She kept to the shadows and scanned the alleyways as she moved. No tails, no watchers.

By the time she reached the main road, she was certain; no one was following her.

That didn't mean she was safe. All it would take was one misstep. One unlucky turn. One pack of cultists in the wrong place at the wrong time.

But not this evening.

Once she reached the main road, Mara flagged down one of the Transporter Guild's rickshaws and caught a ride back to the Second Quarter. The Broken Fang wasn't the only shady bar in that part of town. Sure, there might be more cutthroats and ne'er-do-wells near the docks, but the ones inside the walls would be more lucrative targets.

She grumbled to herself as the cart trundled along, missing the easy pickings back on Earth. There were plenty of rich bastards who'd made their fortunes through shady dealings, and relieving them of their wealth had been almost laughably easy. Here in Greymantle? Those same types probably had magical defenses—and she was nowhere near ready to play cat burglar in a world where wards and traps could melt your bones.

So, it had to be street thugs and mid-tier criminals. People like the bastard who'd run a dog-fighting ring. The kind of scum her conscience had no trouble robbing blind.

Once they reached the right part of town, she had the rickshaw driver drop her off. No way was he going to wait around while she poked her head into every dive bar in the district.

What followed was a frustratingly dry evening. She did manage to turn up a handful of dirtbags who deserved some karmic justice, but nothing close to the haul from the Followers the previous night. She relieved them of their valuables—carefully, of course. She'd learned fast that she couldn't afford to mess with the Dwarven Sovereign Bank. They were obsessed with the inviolability of their vault tokens and had a reputation for going full scorched earth on anyone who jeopardized that perception.

And she had no doubt others had figured out the same compulsion trick she'd used on that scumbag the night before. The fact that people still parroted the idea that tokens couldn't be used under duress told her everything. The Dwarves didn't just punish those who exploited the loophole—they buried the evidence and probably anyone who spoke about it, too.

Mara had no interest in finding out what their definition of "extreme retribution" entailed.

So, she left most of their tokens untouched. She looted their coin purses and snagged any magical items that looked unusual enough to fetch a decent price from Gavian, leaving behind Cleaners and other mundane gear. She only risked the vault if the payout justified it—and if she could be absolutely sure the owner would never report the loss.

All in, she cleared twenty-three gold marks worth of goods that first night, including a ten gold mark donation to the Healer's. Not bad, but not great either. She still didn't know the city well enough to reliably find her targets. She could spot trouble when it was in front of her, but knowing where to look? That took time.

The second night went much better. Turned out it was something called Restday—one of the three weekly off-days in the city's ten-day cycle. More people on the streets meant more predators, and Mara took advantage of it. She pulled in twenty-seven gold marks, a haul worth more than a quarter million dollars by Earth standards.

The third night settled back down to a more typical pace. Sixteen gold marks—not bad, just not as exciting as the night before. She still wasn't sure how the ten-day week mapped to a regular calendar, but Restday seemed to be the mid-week break. People seemed to treat it like a second Sunday of the week, probably saving up their energy for the next outing.

Still, she had what she needed for the storage ring and then some. So when she stepped into Greenstone, she expected a smooth transaction. What she got was a sour look from Gavian.

"Listen here, young lady," he grumbled, "If you keep this pace up, I might have to stop buying from you. I won't be able to move this much merchandise."

She scowled at him. "That's bullshit. I'm only bringing you the interesting pieces. You think I can't flood your shelves with Cleaners and trash gear if I wanted? And don't try to pretend I'm your only supplier. You're not moving more product from me than all your other contacts combined unless your other contacts are trash."

It was clear her original compulsion was starting to wear off. Gavian's greed gave his brain every incentive to push past the suggestion. She was just grateful he hadn't invested in any anti-vampire wards. Probably too much of a cheapskate.

He huffed. "Look, it's not that your gear isn't valuable," Gavian said, clearly irritated but trying to sound reasonable. "But every major city has laws requiring people to own a Cleaner. You know what that means? There's always some poor sod out there who can't afford Maker's Guild prices but still needs the basics. That's the real market —Cleaners, speech stones, light crystals, the stuff folks can't live without. What you keep bringing me are high-end pieces only a handful of people can actually afford. It's harder to move, and if it sits too long, it draws attention I don't want."

That gave Mara pause. He might actually have a point—though she didn't buy for a second that it was the real reason he was pushing back. More likely, he was trying to lowball her again.

Still, it was something to consider. She'd mostly avoided lifting the standard gear because she figured that much petty theft over a short span might draw unwanted notice. A couple dozen people showing up in just a few days needing replacement Cleaners and basic magic gear? That would start raising eyebrows. And magic items weren't cheap—taking someone's Cleaner or speech-stone wasn't like swiping a phone. It was more like stealing their car.

In other words, not petty theft but grand larceny.

Her only saving grace was that the people she was hitting weren't upstanding citizens. They were criminals, bottom-feeders, and scumbags. The odds of them filing a complaint with the City Watch were low.

"Alright, fine," she sighed. "I'll bring more balanced offerings in the future. Now, what'll you give me for tonight's haul?"

Gavian grumbled but tallied it up and offered her a number that was —generously—less than half of what it was worth.

She narrowed her eyes. "Are you sure about that?"

Straightening up like he was suddenly a model of honesty, he said, "Of course I am. That's a fair price under the circumstances."

Without hesitation, Mara blurred forward, grabbed him by the collar, stared him down with eyes like twin obsidian blades, and slammed her will into his mind.

"You will always give me a fair price when I bring you merchandise," she said, her voice low and thrumming with power. "Not what you think is fair—what an actual honest merchant would give. For tonight, you'll pay me triple what you just offered. If you try to cheat me again, you'll suffer an unpleasant accident. Do you understand me?"

He nodded, dazed and trembling.

"Good. Know deep in your bones that I'm not someone you want to mess with. Know that keeping me happy is cheaper than pissing me off. Know that you'd rather lose a few coins than what it'll cost if you cross me again."

Mara felt the compulsion settle, sinking into the core of his greedy little soul. Then she added the finishing touches.

"You will forget that I am a vampire. You will forget that I used compulsion. You'll only remember that I'm powerful and not someone you ever want to betray."

She released him, straightened his collar, and stepped back like nothing had happened.

Gavian blinked, and his expression shifted to one of strained politeness like a man trying to remember why he was scared. "On second thought, I made a mistake. These items really are exceptional. To make it up to you, I'll give you full price... and a little extra for the offense."

Even as he handed over the payment, his face twisted with pain. The man's greed was fighting her compulsion every step of the way.

Damn, she thought. *He's a stubborn bastard. Greed makes his mind slippery.*

Still, sixteen gold marks clinked into her account, and she left with the faint satisfaction of watching him wilt behind the counter.

Outside, she scanned the street, almost hoping the cultists had camped out again—because those magic weapons had been worth a hell of a lot more than what she'd hauled in the last few nights.

No such luck.

Back at the main road, she flagged down a Transporter mage and asked the first one she saw about getting in touch with Dunc. He'd been a reliable driver—and way more pleasant to ride with than the others.

The female driver frowned at the request but didn't argue. She used her speech-stone to contact her Guild, who passed the word along. Dunc would be there in twenty minutes.

Not a huge deal, but worth the effort. He had come back for her after that ambush, which said something. Maybe not loyalty, but a nose for good business. Either way, it was worth encouraging.

While she waited, she wandered along the small park that split the boulevard—too public to feed but peaceful enough to pass the time.

Dunc arrived chatty as ever, pleased that someone had asked for him personally. He even offered to attune their speech stones so she could call him directly.

Mara agreed.

"Thanks, Dunc. Take me back to that little square near the Citadel—the one with the big tree and the nice tavern."

He gave a theatrical bow and fired up the cart's enchantments. They sped off toward Toman's shop to pick up her first custom magic item.

She hadn't paid much attention to his chatter and almost missed what he said next.

"Did you hear about the fight near the docks? Big scuffle last night—gangs, longshoremen, and some of those Dragon cultists all brawling in the streets."

That got her attention.

"Wait. What? The Followers were in the fight? What would they want with longshoremen or gangs?"

Dunc shrugged. "I guess because they're always preaching to the working folks about how the Dragon's return will uplift the faithful and make them rulers of the world. Bunch of nonsense if you ask me. As if any Dragon—or Dragonlord—gives a damn about humans."

"Is that normal?" Mara asked. "For people here to worship gods or higher beings?"

He gave a vigorous shake of the head. "Some folks revere the Raëndil or the Dragonlords, sure. But it's not *worship* like you're asking about. None of those beings ask for it, and they sure don't grant favors in return. They say a Raëndil might show up in Daggerport once every century or so. As for Dragonlords—well, if a human meets one and lives to tell the tale, they're the exception."

He paused, then added in a darker tone, "And the Nameless One? They say he creates monsters. Started the last dark age and a few before it, too, but that was thousands of years ago."

Then, as if brushing off a shadow, he brightened and changed the subject. "Dragons—real ones, not the Dragonlords—are just animals. Hungry and territorial. People say they're smart like us, but smart or not, you get close, and you're dinner!" He chuckled.

Mara smiled politely. "Thanks. Like I said, Daggerport's still new to me. I appreciate the insight."

She didn't mention she had *no* context—because she wasn't from this world at all. Dunc didn't need to know that.

"Hey, Dunc," she said, leaning forward as the cart slowed. "If you hear anything else about those Followers, I'd like to know. I've had a couple run-ins with them since I got here, and I want to learn more."

"You got it, boss!" he said, tapping his forehead with two fingers in a mock salute. "Anything I hear, I'll pass along."

He looked for a moment like he'd say more, but then shook his head as they pulled up along the street opposite the small square—the one with the big tree and cozy tavern. Toman's place was just across the way. She transferred the fare with a tap of her bank token, then pulled a silver piece from her pouch and handed it over.

Dunc frowned and held up his hands. "No tips, remember? Guild rules."

"It's not for the ride," she said, pressing the coin into his palm. "It's for the news."

He hesitated, then gave a slight, grateful nod and slipped the coin away. With a grin, he tipped his head toward the Rook's Roost. "Well then, I'll just go spend that right quick and wait for you here in the square."

Mara chuckled and waved him off, then turned toward Toman's hidden door. Time to see if the Maker had delivered.

CHAPTER

SEVENTEEN

TOMAN LOOKED eager when he opened the door. "Come in, come in!"

He didn't bother with the sitting room this time but led her straight back into his living quarters and over to a workbench. "I might've gone a little overboard with this," he said, practically bouncing. "Since I'm interested in your condition, I added a bonus on top of the usual storage ring enchantments. This one also conceals your mana signature. Not perfectly, but enough to blur the edges. It won't stand up to a full diagnostic spell, but casual observers won't know what you are."

He held it up proudly. "It's not illusion magic—those leave traces—but this masks the signature entirely. Same concept that makes the ring itself unnoticeable. But this one extends across your whole body, and it's tuned specifically to your mana and your undead parts."

He was clearly proud of his work, and honestly, he had good reason to be. Given what she'd learned from the Healers Guild, that enchantment was going to be invaluable. It wouldn't do to have some random caster catch a vampire throwing spells. Toman's reaction alone to her mana vision had told her just how dangerous that exposure could be.

"Thanks. That's actually exactly what I wanted to talk to you about next. But first..."

She picked up the ring and turned it in her fingers, admiring the craftsmanship. A platinum signet-style band, the sides etched with thorny vines, and a flat slab of onyx where a family crest would usually go. It matched her brooch, and it was gorgeous—something she could have worn to a black-tie gala on Earth or with her hunting leathers here in Greymantle.

"It's beautiful," she said. "I love it."

Toman beamed and gestured at the stone. "The enchantments are embedded in the band. I left the face clean so you can imprint it with your mana signature if you want to use it as an official seal someday. And if you ever decide on a crest—or even just a favorite symbol—I can carve it for you. Make it yours."

She transferred the thirty-five gold marks for the ring without hesitation, then motioned toward the kitchen table. "Mind if we sit for this next bit?"

Curiosity flickered in his eyes, but he nodded and led the way.

"What's going on?" he asked once they'd sat.

"You remember that scan?" she began. "It's worse than I thought. The living cells... they're spreading. The wounds from the other night? They didn't regenerate. I had to go to the Healers Guild, and when they healed me, that living tissue filled in the gaps."

She didn't usually let her emotions show—that could be dangerous in vampire society, especially not the vulnerable ones—but her gut said Toman could be trusted. He wasn't a friend, exactly, but he was one of the few people in this world who knew the truth about her, and she had no one else to talk to.

"It looks like whatever magic brought me here did something to me, and now this living tissue is replacing the vampire parts." She gave a shaky laugh, a little too sharp at the edges. "And the stupid ironic thing is, it might actually kill me."

Toman blinked, the grin from earlier fading. "Damn."

Her voice was tight, and he picked up on it.

With as much empathy as he could, he said, "I was going to ask for another scan after the Healers, but... you don't have to. It's fine."

"It's alright. This sucks, yeah—but who am I to stand in the way of science?" Mara shrugged, though the motion tugged uncomfortably at the lingering soreness in her shoulder. "Go ahead and do your scan. Hell, I'll even come back and let you run more as things change. Honestly, it'll help me out. This way, I can track how far the condition's progressed and get a clearer picture of how much time I've got left."

Toman frowned. "You sound like you're preparing to die."

Mara snorted. "As if. There's no world where I just roll over and give up. This is about making sure I don't get blindsided when my powers decide to crap out mid-fight. I need to know when to switch to plan B."

Toman's expression softened. "I'm sorry. For what it's worth... if there's anything I can do, just say the word."

She gave a slow nod, accepting the offer. Maybe he'd only meant it as sympathy, but she'd take it at face value. "Actually, there is something. I mentioned Plan B? Well—this is it: I need to learn magic."

That caught him off guard. Her voice turned more serious. "If my condition keeps progressing, I'll lose access to my vampiric powers. Some are already weaker. But I can't afford to be helpless. I've got Followers of the Dragon hunting me, and because of them, I'm wanted by the City Watch. I need something to replace what I'm losing. Can you teach me?"

Toman sat there, stunned. "Of all the things I thought you might ask..."

He gave a rueful chuckle and shook his head. "A vampire asking me to teach her spellcraft. Now I've seen everything."

But then his smile faded. "I can't, though. Not because I won't—because I *can't*. I'm oath-bound. Standard Makers Guild procedure. The apprenticeship bond prevents me from teaching anyone else spells, even the basic ones. I literally can't speak the words. Anything that came from their training—every foundational concept—is locked behind that oath."

Mara's face darkened, and she cursed.

She sat there for a second, chewing on the frustration. Then, a thought struck her, and she leaned forward. "Hang on. What if the knowledge didn't come from your Guild?"

Toman blinked. "What do you mean?"

"Could you walk me through spellcasting if the spells came from another guild?" she asked, a spark of mischief glinting in her eyes. "I bring the spell books—you just help me learn what other guilds teach. That wouldn't be technically *teaching* anything from the Makers Guild."

He tilted his head, intrigued. "So... you'd bring spell tomes from another guild, and I'd... guide you through the learning process?"

"Exactly. If they're not Makers Guild spells, then your oath shouldn't apply, right?"

A grin slowly spread across Toman's face. "I like the way you think. I don't know if it'll work, mind you, but I'm willing to give it a shot."

Mara's smile was faint but full of hope. "Even if it doesn't work perfectly, just helping me not blow myself up in the process would be a win."

She didn't say aloud what the Healers Guild had warned her about— if casting spells could help her survive the transformation, then this wasn't just academic. Her life might depend on it.

"Any idea which guild I should target?" she asked.

Toman leaned back, pursing his lips and rubbing his chin as he thought aloud. "Well, the Makers are obviously out. Even if the oaths didn't prevent me from teaching you, you *couldn't* get your hands on their apprentice tomes. They go to absurd lengths to protect their secrets. Same for the other trade guilds—Teleporters, Seers, Builders, Transporters... most of those wouldn't make much sense anyway, not for someone with your background."

He hesitated and glanced at her, suddenly worried she'd be offended.

But Mara just laughed. "You're not wrong. My life's been... physical. Ten years of intense combat and spycraft training after I turned, and most of the last century spent fighting a shadow war against supernatural enemies. I'm not exactly the sit-in-a-tower type. Or the rickshaw-driving kind, either."

Relieved, he nodded. "Alright then. If fighting's your thing—and it sounds like it is—three guilds come to mind: War Wizards, Spellswords, or Nightblades."

She perked up. "Tell me more."

"War Wizards are probably the least useful to you," he said. "They *do* train for battle, but their spells are built for large-scale warfare. Think blasting down fortress walls, vaporizing platoons, levelling battlefields. Not exactly practical inside city limits."

Mara smirked. "Fun in theory. Catastrophic in practice."

"Exactly." He chuckled. "So that brings us to the Spellswords. They're mercenaries—combat-focused casters who enhance their bodies with magic and use spells to manipulate the battlefield: ice to trip someone, wind to deflect an arrow, a barrier to block a sword. That kind of thing."

That sounded very promising. "And you're saying they enhance their *bodies*? Speed, strength?"

"Yes, but here's the catch," Toman warned. "The Wasting destroys anything magic is cast upon—especially living tissue. No one outside their Guild can pull it off safely. You try casting on your own body, and you risk an aneurysm, organ failure, or worse. But Spellswords somehow do it. Their method is a closely guarded secret."

"Still," she said, "if they can boost strength and speed... even if it's not vampire-level, it's something."

He nodded. "It wouldn't replace everything you'd lose, but it'd get you part of the way."

"Sounds like a solid fit." She leaned forward; the last option also sounded intriguing. "What about the Nightblades?"

That gave him pause. "They're... different. Assassins, if the rumors are true. Stealth, illusion, shadow magic. No one knows where their Guild is. No official chapterhouses exist that anyone knows about. Honestly, a lot of people think they're a myth."

"But *you* know they're real," she said. She could sense his certainty.

He nodded. "Yeah. I do. The Makers craft Heartwood foci for all the mage guilds. The Nightblades have theirs commissioned anonymously, but they come. I've seen the orders."

That sparked a dozen questions about Heartwood items, but she tabled them for now. "Any idea where to *find* one?"

Toman gave a helpless shrug. "Not really. Best shot would be putting out feelers in the undercity. Maybe try to hire one. If they're real, they'll find you."

Mara sighed. "Pity. Their skillset sounds equally perfect for me as the Spellswords."

"Well, Spellswords are a lot more accessible," he offered. "Their local hall is just a few blocks from here. But even then, I doubt they'd loan you a spellbook. Guild members guard that kind of knowledge with their lives."

Mara leaned back, thoughtful. "Then I'll just have to get creative." She had already figured out that the unbreakable bank tokens were susceptible to her compulsion. Guild mages would never break their oaths, but what if they didn't think what they were doing was a violation of the oath?

A devious smile crossed her face at that thought.

"Looks like I need to find a Spellsword."

Even with the decision made, Mara wasn't exactly bouncing with enthusiasm. Learning magic had been a dream for most of her long existence—but having to do it now, as a matter of life or death, sucked most of the joy out of it.

Toman cocked his head and asked, "What's your plan?"

Chuckling, Mara gestured vaguely toward the walls around them. "The Citadel's just a few blocks away, and there are pubs nearby. Spellswords drink, don't they?"

The ex-Maker blinked at her determination to start immediately, then burst out laughing. "Well, get to it, then—and let me know when you've got the crystals."

"Crystals?" she echoed, confused.

"Most 'books' aren't books anymore," he explained. "Not physically, anyway. Paper wears out too fast. These days, they record spellbooks into data crystals. The term stuck, but no one's lugging around tomes anymore." He hesitated, then added, "Well, books are still made since the knowledge has to be written down in the first place, but after that they are transferred into crystals."

He stepped over to one of his benches, picked up a palm-sized crystal, and held it up for her to see. "These last longer. They're still affected by the Wasting, but only the enchantment used to record and access the contents breaks down—not the data itself. That means you just re-enchant the access function on a fresh section of the crystal."

Mara nodded, absorbing the info. "So, how long do they last?"

"Depends on the skill of the enchanter and the crystal's quality. A few hundred years, give or take—sometimes more. No degradation of the information, unlike paper, which fades or crumbles. Even when there's no room left to re-enchant it, you can still just copy the information over into a new crystal."

"Huh. Good to know. That'll make this easier." She started to turn toward the door, then hesitated. "Before I go, let's do another scan. I want to know what percentage of the infection we're up to. It'll help me gauge how much time I've got left."

Toman's mood visibly darkened at the reminder. "Yeah. Sure. Let's do it."

A few minutes later, the scan was complete. The floating projection of her body glowed in sections, highlighting the living tissue. At the top right corner of the display was a number: **16%.**

Two points higher than the Healers had estimated three days earlier. Not a huge increase—but enough.

That gave her a rough timeline. If the rate stayed steady, she had about 126 days before her body was completely overtaken. But she wouldn't have that long—not really. Her powers would start failing long before she hit 100%, and when that happened, every fight became a risk.

That was the real problem.

She'd need to learn magic fast if she wanted to survive.

Toman walked her to the door, a grim set to his face. "By the way—if you're going hunting Spellswords, there's a trick to spotting them. They don't carry wands or staffs like the other guilds. Their focus is their weapon—crafted from Heartwood."

Mara raised a skeptical eyebrow, glancing down at the dwarven-steel blade at her side.

He caught the look and added, "Stronger than that. No joke. Heartwood weapons are rare and absurdly tough. It's not just the enchantments— they're naturally dense with mana. I've made a few myself, back when I still took orders through the Guild. I know what they're capable of."

That got her attention. If she did manage to learn their magic, she'd definitely need to get her hands on one of those.

"Thanks," she said, "Speaking of magic items, I think it should go without saying I no longer need the other item I had commissioned, and I'll be a bit busy stalking Spellswords to go hunting to earn more gold for the moment."

Toman dismissed that with a wave, "Don't worry about it. I hadn't started on the other enchantments yet. Do what you need to do, and I'll be here when you're ready."

Mara gave him an appreciative smile and stepped into the street. "I think I'm gonna need all the help I can get. I'll be back as soon as I've gotten the crystals."

CHAPTER
EIGHTEEN

BACK OUTSIDE ON THE STREET, Mara looked around for her driver, but his rickshaw was still parked across the square, and he was nowhere in sight.

She chuckled, glancing at the warm glow spilling from the tavern's front windows. *Well, might as well start with this one since I've got to collect my driver anyway.*

She crossed the square and stepped through the wide, polished oak door of the Rook's Roost. Inside, the tavern was the very picture of cozy charm—low-timbered ceilings, worn but gleaming hardwood floors, and a wide central hearth with a lazy fire crackling inside. The smell of baked bread, roast meat, and spiced cider lingered in the air, along with the softer scents of pipe smoke and old wood.

Soft light gleamed off dark wood beams and glinted on the bronze fixtures lining the bar. Unlike Earth, there was no pounding music or rowdy crowds here—just quiet laughter, the gentle clink of mugs, and murmured conversation between regulars hunched over their drinks. Locals, mostly. A few merchants and what appeared to be a retired merc or two filled the booths along the walls. She noted at least two enchanted Cleaners nestled discreetly behind the bar and tucked in corners, keeping the place spotless without fanfare.

The overall effect was... homey. It was a distinct contrast to the half-hostile dens in the Second Quarter in which she had been hunting so far. This place wasn't pretending to be anything. It simply was.

Her sharp eyes scanned the room, not for her driver just yet, but out of habit—assessing threats, exits, and anyone carrying Heartwood.

Dunc was sitting at the bar, chatting amiably with a pair of older men who looked relaxed but not drunk. With her hearing, Mara picked up the conversation easily—something about House Tynos being too distracted by the search for their missing heirs to get anything meaningful done in the Council.

Unfortunately, none of the patrons were carrying Heartwood weapons.

Suppressing a sigh, she approached her driver. Dunc noticed her immediately, stood, and offered a polite apology to his companions. He placed a coin on the bar and set his mug on top of it. Mara clocked the gesture and wondered if it was a local custom but didn't ask.

"Apologies, Lady. I wasn't expecting you to be done so soon. Are you ready to depart?"

She waved off his concern and led the way outside. Once they were settled back in the rickshaw, she spoke. "Dunc, I hope you don't mind a bit of a detour. I'd like to visit all the pubs near the Citadel tonight before heading back to the Dragon Inn. I'm looking for someone, but I don't know which place they frequent."

What followed was a long, unproductive night.

She *did* spot a few Spellswords—easy to identify by the Heartwood weapons they carried—but none were viable targets. Some were seated in pairs or small groups, others alone but far too alert, scanning the room the way only trained fighters did. Always watching. Always ready.

She hadn't expected that, but should have. These weren't scholars or shopkeeps. Spellswords were battle-hardened mercenaries who operated as guards and bodyguards. That kind of work didn't leave much room for the unobservant to survive.

By the time the night wore thin and she was heading back to the inn, Mara was seriously beginning to doubt whether she'd ever get close enough to one of them to use her compulsion. Toman had warned her—mages had strong minds. Years of training and mental focus gave them a natural resistance, and Spellswords likely had enchanted gear on top of that. She couldn't count on being able to break through easily.

Worse still, one of those items might detect the attempt. Or block it outright.

That would be a disaster. Attacking a guild mage—even just mentally—could trigger a guild-wide response. The last thing she needed was the entire Spellsword Guild on high alert, hunting her down.

No, she thought grimly. *Best case is someone distracted, alone, and preferably too drunk to know they're being compelled.*

She could find someone like that. She'd hunted Cabal agents on Earth for months at a time before making a move to achieve her objective. But back then, she'd had time.

She didn't have that luxury now.

On the ride back to the Dragon Inn, she gave herself a hard deadline: one week. Ten days by Greymantle's calendar. If she hadn't found someone by then, she'd move on to another guild. Even if it was a worse fit.

She had to be realistic about her situation. She was lucky the dwarf innkeeper still hadn't started charging her for the room, thanks to whatever strange case of mistaken identity he was labouring under. But even that luck wouldn't last forever.

The following two nights played out much the same. Pub after pub, tavern after tavern, all in a slow semicircle around the Citadel. She saw plenty of Spellswords—mostly younger journeymen and journeywomen—but no opportunities. And then she ran into a Master.

He was in his prime, tall and confident, carrying a beautiful Heartwood spear. And the instant his eyes landed on her, his whole demeanor changed. Relaxed to wary in a single heartbeat. Not a step. Not a flinch. Just... alert.

She didn't know *how* he'd recognized what she was, but he had. And he saw her as a threat.

Too fast for even a spell to be involved but not fast enough to be supernatural.

He didn't raise the spear, but she had no doubt he could have staked her through the heart with it before she got within five feet. She couldn't help but consider that the spear being made entirely from wood was the mother of all stakes. Not a comfortable thought for a vampire.

Slowly, hands raised, she backed toward the door. No words. No sudden moves.

That pub was now officially dead to her. *Not going back there– not ever.*

Still, not every place she visited was crawling with Spellswords. Over those two nights, she encountered dozens of locals—merchants, servants, laborers, and more than a few minor nobles. Most of them were just out to unwind after a long day, enjoying drinks and conversation. In a strange way, it reminded her of Earth before tech took over—before TV and the internet slowly erased the need for face-to-face socializing.

It made her realize something else about Greymantle: for all its magical advancements, it lacked most of the entertainment infrastructure she'd grown used to. But it had its own flavor.

Many pubs had musicians playing in the early evening. Some even featured performers from the Illusionists Guild who used sound, light, and even scent illusions to enhance their stories or songs. A few upscale establishments had full-on visual illusions, projecting images to accompany performances. Although not even that came close to television or movies. These were just basic illusions to enhance a singer or storyteller's act.

She even attended a theater performance of *The Fall of Allard*, a historical tragedy about a king of Rydan, betrayed and murdered by his nephew two centuries ago. Illusionists provided the sets and atmosphere, shifting backgrounds with seamless magic that almost rivaled a movie set.

It wasn't Earth. But it wasn't bad either, and she kinda liked the 'in-person' nature of the performances. There was just something more satisfying about sharing an experience with others.

She chuckled to herself, thinking of sentiments on Earth– Introverts would probably hate it.

She only stayed for a few minutes—just long enough to get a taste—before slipping out. Beautiful as the magic was, no Spellsword would be vulnerable in that setting. Too crowded. Too public.

No time for indulgence, she reminded herself. *I've got work to do.*

And so, the hunt continued.

Counting the first night after her talk with Toman, this was now her third evening spent stalking taverns and inns, and her hope was beginning to flag. Still, Mara didn't give up. It wasn't in her nature.

Now that she knew the area like the back of her hand and had every pub and inn near the Citadel committed to memory, she'd taken to leaving Dunc at the Rook's Roost to idle away the evening while she made her rounds. The transport mage didn't mind one bit, especially since she was paying him to wait.

It was late—almost time to head back to the Dragon Inn—when she stepped inside the tavern to collect her driver and stopped cold just inside the door.

There, in the last place she'd expected, was her perfect target.

A tall, dark-haired, and dark-eyed young woman—late teens, maybe twenty—was slouched in one of the booths near the corner, very drunk and clearly furious, muttering angrily into her drink. But what caught Mara's attention wasn't the girl's attitude or her age.

It was the Heartwood spear leaning against the wall beside her.

Mara blinked. *There's no way I'm this lucky.* A lone, intoxicated Spellsword right across from Toman's house?

Not about to waste the opportunity, she quickly waved Dunc back to his seat at the bar and gestured to the bartender to pour her two mugs of whatever Dunc had been drinking.

She nodded toward the booth. "What's her name?"

The bartender gave a sympathetic look. "Olia. Comes in now and then. Poor girl's had a rough time lately. Good kid, though."

Mara offered a word of thanks, paid for the drinks, and made her move.

She approached the booth and slid a mug in front of the girl before settling into the seat across from her. "Hi, Olia. Mind if I join you? Brought you another."

The young woman blinked up at her, eyes bleary and brows scrunched in confusion. "Do... do I know you?"

Seeing her chance, Mara struck—not with brute force, but subtly, wrapping her compulsion around the girl's thoughts like a warm blanket.

"What do you mean, do you know me?" she asked gently. "Did you forget a friend now that you're a bigshot Spellsword?"

Using compulsion on criminals was one thing. Using it on someone innocent—someone hurting—was another. Mara hated herself a little for it. But survival was survival. Her life was on the line. She justified it to herself by promising—*vowing*—to help the girl however she could once this was over. Even so, it left a sour taste in her mouth. This power made her feel dirty sometimes... but dirty was still alive.

With effort, she pushed the guilt aside and focused on the magic. A moment later, Olia's resistance crumbled.

"We were close," Mara said softly. "Before you went to the Guild. You remember, right?"

The girl frowned, trying to conjure the memory. "The streets... of the Second Quarter? I... I think I remember..."

"Mara," she prompted. "We used to dream about getting into a guild, escaping the streets. You made it. I didn't, but I survived."

Olia snorted. "Lucky? *Me?* Hah!" Then, her expression faltered. "No... that's not fair."

She hiccupped and looked down into her mug, shoulders slumping.

Mara leaned in slightly. "You wanna talk about it? You know me—I always listened when you needed to vent."

That was the crack in the dam. Confusion gave way to resignation. Then the words poured out.

"You have no idea," Olia muttered. "Growing up in the Guild was brutal. I was this close to being cut. Barely passed the classification threshold for a mage. They almost didn't let me take the Trials at all."

She took a long pull from the mug Mara had brought her, then slammed it down and kept going, voice gaining force.

"But I *showed* them. Fought like a wildcat. Twice as hard. Three times as fierce. I made it. I passed. And I got assigned to the *Makers Guild* rotation—the highest honor a Journeywoman can get!"

Her pride was raw and real, and despite everything, Mara found herself impressed.

"That sounds amazing," she said honestly. "You worked your ass off and got the best post there is. So why are you here tonight? What happened?"

Olia's jaw clenched, and she waved her arm angrily, sloshing ale across the table. "They're *reassigning* me. Shipping me off to some backwater post in Canoldir. A punishment! And I didn't do anything wrong. Nothing! I gave *everything* to the Guild!"

Her voice cracked, and Mara saw the tears welling in her eyes.

It hurt to watch. This girl wasn't some careless drunk. She was driven. Determined. Talented. A fighter. Everything Mara respected. And here she was, drowning in disappointment.

"Are you sure it's a punishment?" Mara asked gently. "Maybe it's an opportunity instead. I don't want you to get in trouble sharing Guild business, but it sounds like something more's going on."

Olia blinked, clearly trying to process that through the haze of drink and emotion. "What d'you mean? They're *sending* us away. How's that not a punishment?"

Mara caught the keyword. "*Us?* So you're not going alone? Who else is being reassigned?"

The response was instantaneous. Olia's spine straightened as she fiercely growled, "*Jaran* would never do anything wrong! He's the best journeyman Spellsword in the Guild! Don't you *dare* say anything bad about him!"

Mara raised her hands in a calming gesture, more to hide her wince than out of fear of being struck. *Well, now I know what button not to push again.*

But still... this was working.

Olia was opening up, and she had her trust. All Mara had to do was keep the conversation going.

Holding up her hands in a placating gesture, Mara said, "Now, see, doesn't that prove this isn't a punishment? If you and Jaran are both being sent on this new assignment—even if it *feels* like a punishment —how could that be true? They wouldn't punish him just because of you, would they?"

Olia blinked, the fight momentarily draining from her shoulders. Mara could almost hear the gears turning as the girl muttered to herself, "They wouldn't punish Jaran... everyone loves him... but does that mean I'm hurting him?"

Mara cut in before that thought could spiral. "Hey, don't even go there. The Guild isn't vindictive like that. They wouldn't throw one of their best under the carriage just to mess with you."

She had no clue if that was true, but it was a calculated bluff—and one that landed. The doubt in Olia's eyes flickered, then faded as a spark of clarity took its place.

"You... you're right. They'd never do that to Jaran. There has to be something else going on. Something I'm not seeing."

"That's more like it," Mara said. "Don't treat this like a punishment. Treat it like a challenge. Another chance to prove yourself to the Guild. That's what you've been doing all along, right?"

Olia sat up straighter, a familiar fire lighting behind her bleary eyes. "Yeah! I *have* been proving myself. They didn't think I'd even pass the apprentice trials, and I blew past their expectations. I might have the weakest magic in my class, but I'm the best fighter. Even Jaran can only beat me when he leans on his spells!"

Those words, spoken under compulsion, would hit her deep. She'd wake up tomorrow with renewed purpose, driven to rise to the challenge. Whatever this assignment was, she would tackle it with everything she had.

That made what came next a little easier for Mara to stomach.

"Since you're here—and since fate dropped us together like this—I was hoping you might help me out, too. I just joined the Guild, took the oath and everything, but my training doesn't start until next month. I want to get a head start, you know? It was hard for me to get a handle on the magic, just like you. So... do you think you could lend me a copy of the spellbooks they give to apprentices and journeymen? Since we're both in the Guild now, that's not breaking any rules, right?"

Olia frowned for half a second, but then her expression warmed again as the suggestion settled in. "Sure! I can do that since you've already sworn the oath. It'll be so good having you in the Guild. It's a shame I'll be off on assignment when your training starts. I'd *love* to see you get put through the wringer like the rest of us." She let out a drunken giggle.

Mara forced a chuckle in return. "Yeah, I bet that would make the training way more bearable."

Gods, this sucked.

The more they talked, the more Mara liked this sad, scrappy firebrand of a Spellsword. Still, she had no choice. She'd made her move, and now she had to follow through. But she promised herself she'd find a way to repay this girl. Somehow.

"Can you bring the books here tomorrow evening? I won't be able to get back until an hour after sunset."

Olia tilted her head in thought, then nodded. "Yeah, I think I can manage that. I'm stationed at the Maker's Guild tomorrow, but I should be free by evening. Jaran and I have tickets to the theater, though. I'll have to stop by here before we head out."

"That's perfect," Mara said, her tone casual but her compulsion pressing down. "Just do me a favor and don't mention me to Jaran or anyone else, alright? I don't want people treating me differently just because I already know someone in the Guild. Let me prove myself without the extra attention."

Thin reasoning, maybe, but it didn't need to be airtight. Under compulsion, it stuck. Olia's mind offered no resistance; she believed they were old friends.

I need a damned shower!

This wasn't the first time she'd used compulsion on someone innocent, but it was one of the rare times it left her feeling genuinely filthy. This girl deserved better. And Mara owed her now.

"Drinks are on me tonight," she said, rising. "It was really good to see you again. I hope you feel a little better now."

Olia gave her a lopsided smile, her eyes glassy but warm. "Don't mention it, I never mind helping out a friend. And you helped me too. Before you showed up, I was in a bad place. Who knows what I might've done in the morning. I could've really screwed things up for both me *and* Jaran."

Mara smiled genuinely this time. Olia wasn't just a happy drunk now —she was hopeful. And that did help ease the guilt, at least a little. "Alright, I'll see you tomorrow night."

With that, she walked back to the bar, paid the girl's tab, and retrieved her driver.

Tomorrow, finally, she would begin learning magic.

CHAPTER
NINETEEN

It was with mixed emotions that Mara met with Olia at the Rook's Roost the next night. On the one hand, she was hopeful to be able to get the spellbooks necessary to learn magic, but she still felt like a terrible person for having used compulsion on her to make her think they were friends.

It didn't help that she absolutely hated people who pretended they were your friends only to stab you in the back. She had been betrayed by one such, and it had resulted in her death. She'd never gotten over that. And here she was doing it to someone else.

Damnit. Somehow, she would have to make this right.

Seeing Olia's face light up the moment she walked through the door turned the metaphorical dagger in Mara's gut—and twisted it.

She tried to put on a friendly face as she approached. The younger woman stood and greeted her with a bright smile, clasping her forearm in a warm, familiar grip.

It was the first time Mara had seen the journeywoman on her feet, and she was a little surprised to realize she had to look up to the girl. Mara wasn't short—5'6", or about 1.7 meters in Earth terms—but Olia had her by several inches. She had to be around 5'11", and with the outfit she was wearing, the girl looked every bit as strong as she was tall. Instead of the black-and-brown combat gear of a Spellsword, she was dressed to impress: a short sapphire-blue corset that matched her eyes and left her midriff bare, highlighting just how toned she really was.

Ah, Mara thought. *So she's not just partners with Jaran—she's into him.*

Thankfully, he hadn't come with her. That would've made this conversation a lot more awkward.

"Hope I'm not late," Mara offered.

"No, no. I'm just eager to meet Jaran at the theater. This might be our last chance for a proper date before we leave."

There was something in her expression that made Mara pause. Rather than just take the crystals and be on her way, she gestured toward the booth. "Why don't we sit for a minute?"

Olia blinked but nodded, and they slid into the booth.

"So," Mara asked casually, "what's wrong?"

The Spellsword's expression tightened. "What do you mean, what's wrong? Why would anything be wrong?"

The denial was instant—and unconvincing.

Mara dropped her chin and raised one eyebrow in challenge. "You really think I wouldn't notice something's bothering you?"

She meant it. She *liked* this girl, and if she could help, she would.

Olia looked down, then back up with uncertainty. "Is it that obvious?"

"Probably only to me—or someone who knows you well. Did something happen?"

"Besides the reassignment?" Olia hesitated. "Okay, fine. I'm not even mad about that anymore. It's just... there's this woman. She came to the Maker's Guild while Jaran and I were on duty. And she *flirted* with him. Right in front of me!"

Mara blinked. *Teen drama?* That wasn't where she thought this was going.

"What'd he do? Flirt back?"

"No," Olia admitted quickly, then frowned. "But I lost it. I was rude. On duty. She was a guest of the Guild, and I snapped at her in front of everyone. That's why I thought the reassignment might be punishment."

There was more to it. Mara could feel it.

"You worried Jaran might be interested in her?"

The tightening of Olia's jaw was all the answer she needed.

"No. I mean... not really. I don't *think* he is," Olia muttered. "It's just —she was so beautiful, a real noble type, and things have been rough between us lately. We've been under a lot of pressure. First trying to get the Maker's assignment, now getting pulled off of it. What if he blames me, or..." She didn't finish the sentence, but Mara knew where that thought was headed.

She gave the girl a sympathetic smile. Then she delivered the advice Olia wouldn't want to hear.

"Listen, Olia. You can't control someone else's heart. All you can do is control yourself. If his heart is wandering, then the relationship's already over—it's just a matter of when you both admit it."

Olia's eyes flashed, and Mara hurried to add, "I know you don't want to hear that. But think about it. You'll know it's true. Trust is the foundation of everything. Without it, what are you even fighting to keep?"

It stung to say it—she wasn't exactly one to talk about trust under the circumstances—but Olia needed to hear it more than Mara needed to preserve her own feelings. Mara's own troubles were of a more existential nature. She would worry about how hypocritical she was being when her life wasn't on the line. *Right?*

The silence stretched. Olia stared at the table for a long time. Then, finally, she looked back up, eyes misty but a little steadier.

"What if it's not too late? I don't want to lose him. I *think* he loves me. We've just... been fighting a lot lately. More than usual."

Maybe it was her century of hard-earned wisdom, or maybe it was just instinct, but Mara had a gut feeling that she was right about this next part.

She shrugged. "Then it's on you to break the cycle. You've been letting your insecurities fuel your anger, and that's poison in a relationship. Own your strength instead. You came from nothing and clawed your way to the top. You might not have the biggest mana pool, but I'd bet good coin no one in your class has your heart or your skill."

That got a flicker of a smile out of Olia.

Mara pressed the point. "You're not just some girl tagging along on a boy's coattails. You're the one they underestimated—and you proved them wrong. Don't forget that. Whatever comes next, walk into it like you deserve to be there. Because you do."

If Mara was right—and she usually was—then she'd just handed over a few hard truths. Now came the part where she waited to see how they landed.

The silence that followed stretched longer than the last. But Olia didn't explode or storm off in anger or denial. She just... sat there, quiet, contemplative, weighing herself against the mirror Mara had just held up. Mara thought for a moment she might cry, but then the girl's jaw clenched, and her spine straightened. She reined herself in, forcing control over the turbulent mess of emotions inside.

"I barely even remember our times on the streets together," Olia said at last, her voice quiet, "but I'm sorry we lost touch. You get me better than anyone else. I don't think even Jaran understands that part of me. I always felt like my weak magic made me not good enough for him. So I lashed out—pushed him away before he could leave me." She let out a bitter breath. "Damn."

She looked at Mara, her eyes wide with a mix of amazement and gratitude. "Thank you for helping me see the problem."

Mara could see it—the shift. Strength was returning to the girl, flowing back into her frame like sunlight breaking through a cloud. She'd be alright.

Bracing herself, Mara decided it was time to walk as close to the truth as she dared without cutting her own throat. "Listen... I wasn't really your friend back then. But I want to be now. I like you, Olia. A lot. And I'm here if you ever need me, okay?"

Olia blinked at her, momentarily confused. Then she waved the concern away as if it were a bad smell. "Bah, we all did what we had to on the streets. I don't hold that against you. What matters is now —and now we're friends."

That wasn't precisely what Mara meant; that had been a confession, and the girl's trust and acceptance stung in the face of her own choice to use her new friend. She shouldn't say more, but she couldn't live with herself if she didn't try.

"Even if I don't end up in your Guild? Or if you find out I'm not who you think I am?"

That gave Olia pause. A longer hesitation this time. But then she met Mara's eyes and nodded. "Whoever you are, you helped me tonight. You gave me perspective—twice now—when I really needed it. That's worth something. Hell, that's worth *a lot*. We're friends. And that doesn't change just because we might not wear the same colors."

Without ceremony, Olia reached into her storage ring and pulled out four crystals, laying them on the table between them. "Take them. Study. Use what you need. Return them to the Guild after you pass the trials. If you don't make it, well... the Guild'll erase the knowledge anyway. No harm done."

Mara felt like she'd been staked through the heart—not with anger or fear, but with guilt. The girl's trust hit harder than any blade.

Maybe, she thought, *maybe I really could get into the Guild someday. After I finish changing. After I stop being... this.*

Mercenary life wouldn't be such a massive shift from the war she'd fought against the Cabal for the last hundred years. Maybe this wasn't all just survival. Perhaps it was a chance for something different, something more.

Swallowing the lump in her throat, she reached out and took the crystals, sending them into her storage ring.

She made sure her voice wouldn't crack before speaking. "Thank you. Let's attune our speech stones. That way, you can reach me anytime. If you need advice or just someone to vent to, I'll be there."

She definitely did *not* need to wipe at the corner of her eye. Nope. Not at all. It was the wood smoke in the air. That's what it was.

Once their stones were synced, Mara waved toward the door, smiling faintly. "Now go. You've got a date with a handsome young man who's probably counting the minutes. Make tonight a memory he'll never forget."

Olia laughed, and to Mara's surprise, she leaned in and hugged her tightly. "He won't know what hit him."

Then she was gone, slipping out the door with a bounce in her step.

Mara sat for a long moment, staring after her.

In her hand, she held what she hoped would be the key to surviving. But maybe—just maybe—she'd also gained something more. A real friend. One who might actually stick, no matter how this had started.

Across the square, Toman welcomed Mara back with a wide-eyed expression and ushered her inside. "You got it already? Dragon's balls, that was fast!"

"Felt like forever to me." She summoned the four crystals from her storage ring, and they appeared in her hands in a shimmer of reflected light.

Toman took them with a kind of reverence, holding them like they were ancient relics. "Even though what I do is highly illegal, and my guild would kill me if they knew I was alive, I've never actually laid hands on another guild's spell tomes before. Individual spells, sure —but never a whole tome."

He placed each crystal carefully on his workbench, lining them up with precision. But instead of channeling mana into them to reveal their contents, he hesitated. His hand hovered above the first crystal, and Mara, watching closely, could just barely make out the ghost of a mana tendril poised in the air, shimmering faintly but never touching the surface.

"What's wrong?" she asked.

Toman inhaled deeply and slowly withdrew the strand of mana. He sat back, expression darkening with a rare seriousness that didn't fit his usual demeanor. "In my excitement, I almost did the dumbest thing of my life. Probably the last thing I'd *ever* do."

Mara's eyes widened, and she turned her gaze to the crystals with a hard squint. "Booby-trapped?"

"Yeah." He nodded grimly. "There's no way the Spellsword Guild would let anyone outside their ranks access these without a failsafe. At the very least, the crystal would self-destruct and crumble to dust. Worst case? Boom." Toman glared at the innocuous-looking stones like they'd insulted his mother.

Mara frowned, too, but for a different reason. "Tell me I didn't go through all that for nothing. I don't like what I had to do to get those."

He quickly shook his head and waved his hands in a frantic no. "No, no! Nothing's wasted. I'm a Maker—my Guild *creates* these data crystals for the other guilds. They add the content afterward. I can break the security—safely—it'll just take a little time. A day or so, tops. I have to work carefully so I don't fry the enchantment or destroy the data."

She gave him a skeptical look, waiting for the catch.

"If I had to guess," he continued, "I'd say the security's keyed to a Spellsword's Heartwood weapon. I remember something odd about them—unlike the other guilds, Spellswords don't start learning spells until after they finish weapon training and get their Heartwood focus. Stuck with me because it's so different. All the other guilds wait to give their foci until someone hits Journeyman."

"So I need to get my hands on a Spellsword's Heartwood weapon?" she asked, not hiding her irritation. That was not something she wanted to do. The deception it had already taken to get the crystals was eating at her. Stealing someone's weapon—especially someone like Olia—wasn't a line she could cross. Not unless she was attacked first. Even then, she didn't want it to come to that.

There was already too much change pressing in on her from all sides. Back on Earth, things had been cleaner. Simpler. There were monsters wearing human skin, and she never lost sleep when she took them down. If she needed gear or money, there was always someone who deserved to lose it. The lines were sharp and easy to follow. But here, in this new world, nothing was simple. Everything had weight. The choices she was making now had sharp edges, and she was already bleeding.

She shook the thought away and leveled a challenging stare at Toman.

He gave her a lopsided grin like he could see the storm behind her eyes. "Relax. I said I could break the security. No need to go hunting Spellswords. And it wouldn't work anyway. Their weapons are enchanted to return to the Guild if the bearer dies."

He caught her expression and added quickly, "Not that I thought *you'd* kill anyone. Just—don't worry. Come back tomorrow night, and I should have the protections disabled and the tomes safe to view."

Grateful, she let it go and pointed toward the scanning pedestal. "Fine. Let's do a scan. It's been three days since the last one."

A few minutes later, she stood with arms crossed, staring at the hovering projection. The glowing red number at the top right corner read **18%**.

Two more points. Again.

It didn't sound like much. Just a number. But it haunted her like the ticking countdown timer on a bomb. It felt like a creeping doom—like one of those horror flicks where you could run as fast and as far as you like, but the killer just kept walking after you. Slow, steady, and unstoppable.

And eventually, it would catch up.

CHAPTER
TWENTY

THE TRIP back to the Dragon Inn was made in silence.

As much as she usually loved to hear Dunc natter on about the latest gossip—how Baron Thildon of House Montanor had insulted some visiting queen and been rejected in the middle of the street or how unrest was brewing among the dockyard laborers—she just couldn't take it tonight. Her mind was too heavy, her thoughts too full.

She could have asked him to take her to the Second Quarter to go hunting, maybe build up more coin for an emergency. Or simply take a ride around the city to become more familiar with its streets and secrets. But that wasn't what she needed right now.

What she needed was time.

Time to come to terms with her impending mortality.

So instead of being productive, instead of doing what she *should* be doing, she rode in silence, letting the quiet stretch between them, grateful that Dunc had the good sense not to fill it. All she wanted was to get back to her temporary refuge at the inn, sit in the safety of the common room, and let her thoughts spiral in peace.

Just a few hours. That wasn't too much to ask, was it? A quiet corner, some soothing music, maybe a glass of whatever passed for Scotch in this world, and solitude amid a crowd.

Yeah. That sounded nice.

Unfortunately, that wasn't to be.

She arrived, found a seat, and tried to begin her evening of quiet contemplation—but the world had other plans.

Even Zak, the inn's eccentric dwarf owner, seemed to pick up on her mood. For once, he didn't pester her with cryptic nonsense. He just poured her a drink—something amber in a squat glass—and left her alone. It wasn't Scotch, not really, but it was close enough. The alcohol did nothing for her undead system, of course, but that wasn't the point. The ritual mattered. The faint burn on her tongue, the swirl of complex flavors—those helped center her. Ground her. Let her feel, if only a little.

She was halfway through her first sip when it happened.

Someone approached her table. Not just *someone.*

Everything in her went from idle to DEFCON 5 in the space of a heartbeat. The drink was forgotten.

The one approaching was a vampire.

Not just that—he was powerful. Maybe not by Greymantle's standards; she couldn't be sure yet, but by Earth's scale, he would be someone you shouldn't mess with. Possibly even older than her. She couldn't see auras the way her father Davin could—he could read a vampire's age and power at a glance—but she didn't need magic for this. Davin had taught her to see with sharper eyes.

There were signs.

The young and the weak moved with hesitation, not yet sure of themselves. But the old? The old were different. There was an economy to their movements. Precision. Confidence honed through decades—centuries—of repetition. It was in the way they stood, the way they scanned a room, the way they walked like the world itself would move aside.

And then there were the eyes.

Old vampires had dead eyes. Eyes that had seen too much, felt too little, and stopped caring long ago. Most of them wore that age like a shroud. The older they got, the deader those eyes became.

There were exceptions, of course. But not many.

This one? He ticked nearly every box.

In less than the time it took to draw a breath, Mara knew something was about to happen.

And someone was going to die.

This one's eyes were hard and mean.

He wasn't the kind of vampire who'd simply been worn down by centuries of existence. No, this was someone who *liked* being cruel. The type who went out of his way to make people's lives worse—not for survival, not for necessity, but because he enjoyed it. And it wasn't even a vampire thing. Mara had met plenty of mortals with that same look. The kind who would kick puppies for fun.

With a sigh, she rose from her seat. No way was she going to be caught sitting if this bastard decided to break the rules of the Dragon Inn and make a move.

Amusement flickered across his face the moment she stood, twisting into a sneer of contempt. "Relax. I'm just here to deliver a message... and escort you to a meeting."

Sure you are, Mara thought. And she had a lovely bridge to sell to anyone dumb enough to believe it. There was no version of this story where she let him "escort" her anywhere and lived to tell about it.

"Sit, then. Let me finish my drink, and you can deliver your message at least."

She didn't dare glance toward Zak. Couldn't afford to take her eyes off her visitor. But she hoped the dwarf was watching. He usually was.

The other vampire sat without hesitation. Lounged, really. Smug, relaxed, like she was no threat at all. The sheer *contempt* rolled off him in waves.

And it pissed her off.

But not enough to get her to do something stupid. Not here. Not in the Dragon Inn. And maybe that was what he was counting on—that the rules would keep her in check. Or perhaps he was truly that arrogant.

She took another sip of her drink, slow and deliberate, just to irritate him.

His sneer deepened. "I've never understood how any of our kind could stomach anything but blood. Disgusting."

She gave him nothing. No twitch. No frown. Just silence. Let him stew in it.

Eventually, her refusal to play along got under his skin.

"Fine. The message is this: You are summoned to the undercity to meet with Lord Noloris." His voice carried that self-important weight that came from knowing too many people had obeyed him too quickly for too long. "As a vampire in this city, you will either pledge him your allegiance and join his lieutenants to enforce his will..."

He paused. The sneer shifted into something hungrier. Meaner.

"Or you will die."

Ah, there it was.

Time to return the favor.

Mara leaned back, voice casual, laced with venom. "I'm already dead, you moron. I *hope* you're not what passes for one of Noloris' elite. If so, he's surrounded by trash."

His jaw ticked. He didn't move. Didn't so much as blink. To anyone else, it would've looked like he hadn't even heard her. But Mara caught it. The flash of fury. The tension behind the stillness. He wanted to leap across the table and tear her throat out.

Then, that subtle flick of his eyes toward the bar, just for a split second.

He was checking on Zak.

He was *afraid* of Zak.

Interesting.

That explained why he hadn't struck. The rules really did mean something here. Or at least Zak made sure they did.

Good to know.

The vampire's smile turned vicious, his eyes narrowing as some new decision solidified behind them. His posture shifted just slightly. Relaxed but eager now. Like a predator imagining the taste of blood.

Mara didn't flinch. Instead, she used the moment to study him more closely.

Shockrod at the hip. Boot knives in both boots—she could see the pommels. Sleeves loose enough to conceal forearm sheaths. She recognized the drape, the subtle bulge that betrayed hidden blades. Two more strapped to the chest of his tunic. Probably more behind his back. None of them were shiny—matte finishes, non-reflective. This wasn't some brute thug.

This was an assassin.

"I came here to deliver a message and escort you as a *courtesy*," he said, voice smooth but coiled tight. "Now, though, I think I'd like to test you. Personally."

His gaze flicked again toward the bar. "Join me in the ring. The inn has one outside in the old manor courtyard. We can settle things quickly, and we'll both know whether you're worthy of joining Lord Noloris' ranks."

Mara laughed. Loudly. Honestly. It rang through the room and made him flinch in the tiniest, most satisfying way.

"Wonderful," she said, eyes gleaming. "I've been dying to see what passes for vampire prowess in Daggerport."

His jaw tightened even further.

Perfect.

Just to rub it in, Mara took another slow sip of her whisky, savoring the flavor like it was the best drink she'd ever had. From now on, she'd remember this moment every time she tasted it. She'd have to ask Zak the name before she left tonight.

She could see it—the flickers of restrained rage rising with every sip. That made it all the more satisfying. She wanted to laugh. Hell, if she didn't have to fight in a few minutes, she might've ordered another just to watch him stew.

But eventually, the glass was empty. She placed it down with deliberate care and dropped a small silver coin on the table as she stood.

She only had one dagger and a shockrod. Against a vampire like this, the rod would be worse than useless—it would likely break before it ever slowed him down. No, this fight would come down to her dagger and her claws.

She hadn't paid much attention to the exterior of the Dragon Inn before, beyond its front doors. But as she followed him out into the courtyard, she realized it was actually worth a look. The marketing spin was that a dragon had crashed through and destroyed half the old manor, toppling stones and shattering trees. But now that she was seeing it up close, she could tell—none of the damage looked *old*. The broken walls hadn't collapsed further with time. The shattered trees hadn't rotted or worn. Someone was keeping it like this. Maintaining the illusion of ruin for ambiance.

Her gaze stayed sharp as they walked the cobbled path. "What's your name?" she asked casually. "I'd like to tell Lord Noloris who failed to represent him properly when I meet with him."

The assassin didn't even glance back. "Ewart," he said. "But you won't need to remember it for long."

She saw the subtle stiffening of his shoulders as they rounded a corner, approaching what had once been a horseyard. Now, it was a combat arena flanked by low stone walls. Where the stables had stood, there were now bleachers and seating for spectators. The fighting ring itself wasn't a true ring—not a boxing ring—but a wide oval of stone lined with packed sand and faintly glowing boundary runes.

Honestly, it was an excellent spot for an underground arena... except it wasn't underground. Anyone could walk in off the street if it weren't enclosed within the crumbling estate.

As they reached the stone archway at the entrance, a dwarf in formal Dragon Inn livery stepped forward. He had a large data crystal, a bright smile, and the eyes of a man who'd seen blood spill in every shade.

"One silver mark each for a match," the dwarf said cheerfully. "Three if a body needs disposing. One silver piece for those just spectating. If you're here to fight, you'll need to wait until the current bout finishes."

He gestured toward the ring, where two combatants circled each other under magical light.

The dwarf grinned wider. "All wagers must be placed through the bookie. Magically binding, of course." He gestured toward another dwarf seated near the front, flanked by two armed Spellswords—one wielding a Heartwood greatsword, the other a spear.

Smirking she pulled four silver marks from her storage pouch and made a show of passing them to the dwarf, "There you go, that will cover the removal of his body once I'm done."

If steam could come from the assassin's ears, it would have been.

Mara raised an amused eyebrow. That gave her an idea.

If this was going to be a life-or-death fight anyway, why not make it *really* worth something?

She turned to Ewart with a smirk. "Since you were planning to kill me anyway, how about we make it interesting? Everything I own against everything you've got."

The assassin gave a derisive snort, barely glancing at the bookie before sneering back at her. "Why not? I doubt you have anything worth taking. But I might as well get paid three ways instead of two." He was clearly trying to regain some ground after her stunt with paying for the body removal.

Mara tilted her head, asking mildly curious. "Three ways?"

Ewart chuckled darkly, clearly enjoying himself now. "Drevan—the Follower you tangled with—offered me twenty-five gold marks to put you down. Lord Noloris pays me well already and asked me to bring you to him. And now *you're* about to pay me too. This is shaping up to be a good night."

Drevan.

Of course. That greasy little bastard from her first night in the city. The one who'd tried to assault her in an alley. The one she *let* live because reinforcements were coming. She'd been too merciful. And now he was putting contracts on her?

Yeah. She'd be fixing *that* mistake real soon.

She laughed aloud, letting it carry. "Great! Then, when I take you down, I'll get paid *with Drevan's own money*. That's poetic, don't you think?"

Ewart's expression flickered, that smug veneer cracking ever so slightly.

Good.

He was mad.

And if he was mad, he'd make mistakes.

Her grin widened. *Let the games begin.* Mara laughed harder.

God, she *loved* needling guys like this. Arrogant pricks so used to being fawned over had no idea how to handle someone like her— someone who wasn't impressed, who didn't feed their egos, and who openly mocked them. They unraveled beautifully when they couldn't intimidate or impress.

Before she could deliver another jab, they reached the bookie's table.

The dwarf raised a brow and asked them to state the terms of their wager.

Ewart puffed out his chest, putting on a performance for the crowd. "When I win, I get all of her possessions, and there will be no recriminations from the Inn when she dies."

So sure of himself. Typical.

Mara gave a thoughtful nod, then followed with her own terms. "Winner takes all. But I want it on record that the loser gives full access to their bank token and any data crystals they own—no arguments later about who has the rights."

The bookie grinned like she'd just made his night. He turned to Ewart. "Do you agree to these terms?"

The vampire waved a hand, clearly bored. "Fine. I agree. Full access to accounts and data."

He took a cord from around his neck and placed his bank token and linked crystals into a secure lockbox next to the dwarf, then gestured at Mara to do the same.

She complied without hesitation. If she was betting her life, she might as well go all in.

With the formalities complete, the pair strode into the arena.

The previous match had ended, and the sand was freshly raked. The crowd buzzed with anticipation. It looked like at least twenty spectators were on hand. More than she'd expected for something this time of night—but then, maybe this sort of thing wasn't uncommon.

As she gave the bleachers a quick scan, she spotted a familiar face among the crowd and allowed herself a small, amused smile. No matter the outcome, she didn't think Ewart, the assassin, would be having a good night.

And honestly, the whole situation still made her shake her head. On Earth, the Cabal had enforced secrecy with lethal efficiency. No supernatural being would dare battle another openly in front of mortals. Not without wiping every witness' mind clean—or killing them outright.

Here in Greymantle? They were placing bets, eating snacks, and cheering as if it were a gladiator match.

The moment she reached her end of the oval, a mage she hadn't even noticed raised a translucent dome over the arena. A second, fainter shimmer followed it, encasing the bleachers.

The crowd erupted into cheers, but even to her sharp ears, the sound was muted.

Ah. Sound barrier. Keeps the neighbors from hearing the murder party.

And no doubt, the double-shield setup would also protect the audience from stray spells or flying debris. It was a clever, practical setup. Honestly, it made for a perfect small-scale arena. She could almost appreciate the ambiance—if she wasn't about to risk her life.

She pushed the thought aside. Time to focus.

The countdown had begun.

30 seconds.

CHAPTER
TWENTY-ONE

MARA DREW HER DAGGER, holding it low in her right hand, blade angled for close work. Her left hand curled as she extended her claws, and she was relieved to feel them grow out cleanly. Despite the living tissue now creeping through her shoulder and upper arm, her vampiric gifts still worked.

For now.

A reminder, if she needed one, not to lean too heavily on her left arm during this fight. The living tissue couldn't take the same punishment her undead flesh could.

She glanced at Ewart across the arena. He looked relaxed. Overconfident. Maybe even eager.

Big mistake.

She would have an advantage with this being an open arena, but she couldn't underestimate her opponent. Ewart might be an assassin, used to taking his victims by surprise, but he hadn't survived this long in Noloris' service by being sloppy. He must have had dozens of fights under his belt—real ones. Fights to the death.

Mara grinned as she loosened up.

Now, *this* was interesting.

Sometimes, the girl she used to be—the small-town kid who spent her mortal life mostly raising her siblings, who'd flinched at the sound of a belt being unbuckled—would rise up in the back of her mind in terror over the threat of violence. But that girl had died over a hundred years ago. The woman who stood here now had fought in both World Wars and probably seen more real combat than this vampire mafioso ever had.

World War II had been especially rough—there'd been a *lot* of werewolves in the SS that needed putting down. And after that? She'd hunted them across South America for three more years. Then came the Cold War, where she'd been both assassin and target more times than she could count.

That's why she knew what would come next.

15 seconds.

Ewart—God, she still couldn't believe someone had actually named their kid that—was going to open with thrown knives. Distract her. Blitz her with vampiric speed while her attention was split. He'd go for a flank, then a backstab.

It's what *she* would do in his shoes.

With a dozen weapons strapped to his body and probably twice as many in storage, he'd try to keep her off balance and reacting instead of attacking. Death by attrition.

10 seconds.

She reviewed her own options. Against a human, she'd have just tanked the hits and closed the distance. But against another vampire, that was a good way to lose a limb—or worse.

Her eyes flicked to the Spellswords beside the bookie. *What I wouldn't give for that wooden spear right now.*

Still, she had a plan. Get in close. Stay there. Keep him off balance.

Do the unexpected.

5 seconds.

More tactics ran through her mind, mentally simulating the first ten seconds of the fight half a dozen ways.

1 second.

Zero.

A sharp bell rang out.

As expected, Ewart's first move was a pair of knives launched from his sleeves at nearly bullet speed.

But Mara wasn't standing still. The moment the bell rang, she was already in motion—diagonal sprint, like a chess bishop. Moving off the line of fire, closing the distance, and shredding his range advantage.

She was halfway across the arena before he could adjust. Two more knives appeared in his hands and flew at her current path, trying to hit where she was about to be.

The crowd barely had time to react. To them, it was just two dark blurs and the *crack* of impact as the first pair of blades slammed into the magical barrier.

BANG! BANG!

With both combatants in dark clothing, it would be hard to tell which blur was which.

She expected his counter and zigged instead of zagging—cutting back toward the path of the original throws. It forced his new knives wide and brought her even closer.

BOOM! BOOM!

His rhythm changed. He produced another pair, but this time, staggered the throws, making the timing harder to dodge.

Smart. But she didn't zig or zag—she rushed directly toward the spot he'd just vacated.

BANG!

BOOM!

Close now.

Too close for ranged tactics.

Ewart finally seemed to realize the truth: he'd lost his opening tempo. He couldn't rely on distance anymore.

He adjusted again—backpedaling to get separation.

But Mara didn't give him the chance.

He threw two more daggers, but she was already inside the effective range. One passed close enough to ruffle her sleeve; the other flew wide.

BAM!

BAM!

The crowd flinched behind the barrier. The mage maintaining the wards was sweating now. Each impact lit up the shield with a flash of power as it absorbed the kinetic force. The last two had hit right near the bleachers—Mara could almost hear the startled gasps and cries of dismay.

She counted eight knives so far. Only the first two had come from his body; the rest had been conjured from twin storage rings—one on each hand.

He could keep this up all night.

It's a good thing I've only got living muscle tissue, she thought grimly.

Even with her enhanced undead durability, her shoulder and abdomen muscles were screaming from the strain. Moving at this speed was punishing, even for her. The G-forces were stacking up, and she could already feel the warning signs of overexertion in the living parts of her body. If she had any living organs, they would have been ruptured.

But she was closing the gap.

And once she was in clawing distance, *he'd* be the one on the defensive.

He surprised her.

Not with some fancy technique, but with how cleanly he moved— like a professional. Even as she came in fast and furious—claws slashing, dagger stabbing, a brutal kick aimed to neuter him—he dodged and countered without hesitation, pulling two longer blades from storage. Each was the length of his forearm, giving him reach.

She didn't care. She was going to *get inside that reach* and stay there until he was dead.

Finally, they stopped blurring across the ring, and the crowd could actually see them. But for the humans watching, the details were probably still a blur—just steel and black fabric flashing in arcs too fast to follow.

A dozen exchanges followed in seconds. His blades clashed against her Dwarven steel dagger, each hit gouging more from his inferior weapons. Claws deflected metal. Kicks and counters danced between them.

It didn't take long to realize the truth—he had the strength advantage. She had the speed. Not by much, but enough. Enough to control the tempo, to make him react instead of dictate.

Still, it was a stalemate.

That wouldn't do.

She waited for her opening—and when he swung in from his left with the same badly gouged dagger she'd already damaged, she stepped in. This time, instead of deflecting, she met it with all her strength, hammering into it.

The dagger snapped in half with a *clang*. The broken blade whistled past her cheek as she twisted and reversed the arc, slashing toward his neck.

She scored.

Blood arced from his torn neck—but only once. The wound sealed before the second beat of a heart.

Still, it startled him. He stumbled back.

She surged forward and raked her claws across his gut—but caught fabric instead of flesh. Her strike bounced off harmlessly.

Magically armored cloth. Damnit!

If not for that, the blow might've disemboweled him. It wouldn't have killed him, but it would've rattled him. Shaken his focus. And in a fight like this, one slip was all it took.

And Mara didn't let go of an advantage.

But Ewart had tricks, too.

He produced a glowing vial from his storage ring and smashed it against the stone floor.

Nope!

She was already moving before it hit.

A pulse of searing light erupted behind her, and even without turning, she *felt* the heat on her back.

Liquid sunlight! Seriously!?

She dove forward, charging toward him—only to realize he'd turned his back to the blast. Letting his enchanted clothing take the brunt while she got the worst of it.

It worked.

She reached him, but not fast enough. He had another dagger out, and now the fight was brutal again.

Harder this time.

The blast had burned the side of her face and her left hand. Not bad enough to blind her—but enough to *hurt*. Enough to slow her.

And that was all it took.

A blade slashed across her abdomen. Shallow—but it cut through living tissue. That part didn't heal like her undead flesh. It bled. And it hurt.

Claw. Slash. Kick. Claw. Dodge. Counter.

The sound of steel on steel. Of claws on bone. The arena echoed with it. The crowd was going *wild*.

She didn't care who they were rooting for.

She just wanted him dead.

If this were Earth, she'd have pulled out salt for the eyes. Or a flashbang. But here? She had only what she carried—and what she could improvise.

Which gave her an idea.

At the end of their next clash, she let go of her dagger—just *let it fall*. And in that same motion, she summoned a handful of copper coins from her storage and *threw* them point-blank into Ewart's face.

A shotgun blast of pocket change.

His eyes widened—reflexes betrayed him—he flinched just as they slammed into him with sharp metallic pings.

And that's when she struck.

Her hand dipped, caught the still-falling dagger, and without pause, she hurled it straight for his heart.

The dwarven-steel slammed into his chest with such force that even the crossguard punched into his ribs. Only the end of the pommel remained visible.

He staggered two steps back, eyes wide with pain.

But... not dead.

The blade had missed his heart.

Damn it.

She surged forward, ready to finish it—only for him to toss another sunlight vial at his feet.

Not this time, asshole.

She dove sideways and turned her back, shielding her face just as the second explosion of light seared the air.

No damage. But no follow-up either.

By the time the light faded, they were back at range. Resetting. Watching.

Ewart grinned, blood running down his chest. "Guess you missed. I'll keep it as a trophy."

Mara's lip curled. "That's a pretty morbid trophy."

But her eyes were locked on the pommel. Her dagger. Still embedded.

Still in reach.

And still sharp.

"But that," Mara said aloud, gesturing to the blade deeply embedded in Ewart's chest, "looks a lot more painful than this." She pointed to the burn seared across the side of her face.

It wasn't just trash talk—she needed to keep his attention away from her abdomen, where blood was still steadily leaking. If he realized she wasn't healing, he might start asking questions no vampire should inspire.

Still, she wasn't lying about the dagger piercing through his body looking bad.

And it did. Even missing the heart, any mortal would've dropped dead. There were six full inches of dwarven-steel protruding from his back.

The vampire assassin reached for another of his sunlight ampules, but Mara had been waiting for that. The moment his fingers twitched, she moved. Side-step. Forward-burst. She avoided the throw before it even left his hand.

As the flash exploded behind him, he instinctively turned to shield himself.

She was already moving. This was her chance. The light would burn —severely—but it wouldn't kill her outright, not if she angled it right.

Pain she could handle. Death she couldn't.

She kept her right side turned, using her position to shield the worst of it as she closed the distance.

Her left hand slammed claws-deep into his back, piercing straight through his armored clothing and sinking deep into flesh and muscle, and with her right, she drove her palm down onto the blade of her own dagger where it jutted from his back.

She put everything she had into that strike. It cut the palm of her hand in two lines, but it was worth it.

She felt the spine crunch. Felt the heart rupture.

Ewart dropped instantly, face twisted in agony and disbelief.

Just to be sure, she crushed his skull and then removed his head. This wasn't a movie or a video game. No EXP popups. No sparkly disintegration to confirm the kill. Dead was dead. Or it wasn't.

Mara *made sure.*

Afterward, she stood over the corpse, breath ragged, flesh still smoking from the sunlight burn that now blistered her neck, face, and left hand. The pain was excruciating, but she stayed upright. She had to. Show weakness now, and someone in the crowd would see it and remember – might even tell the wrong people about it.

The magical barrier dropped, and the roar of the crowd hit like a wave. She swayed slightly, willing herself not to stumble.

A minute passed. Then another.

A second dwarf stepped up beside the bookie.

Zak turned and faced the crowd, raising his stony voice. "This match was sanctioned by the Dragon Inn."

He looked at a nondescript young man in the crowd and spoke with calm finality. "Tell Noloris his man crossed a line. He threatened a guest *on the Inn grounds.* Everything he owned is forfeit. There will be *no reprisals* for his death."

The youth stood and gave a deep bow. "As you say, sir. He took a contract and attempted to fulfill it inside Dragon Inn walls outside of my lord's orders. I'll report what I've witnessed."

Zak gave a nod, then addressed the crowd. "One free drink on the house! To celebrate a proper match."

Mara finally forced herself into motion. She crouched beside the body, grimacing through the pain as she retrieved her dagger, wiped it on the corpse, and began looting with mechanical efficiency. Storage rings, speech stones, cleaner, everything. Even the clothes— enchanted and worth a good bit of gold.

She noticed with some amusement that the material was self-repairing even as she held it. *Well,* she thought, *that'll boost the resale value.*

She stood tall, every step toward the bookie a battle. She refused to let it show. These people knew she was a vampire. Let them believe these burns meant nothing. If anyone thought to wonder why she was still bleeding, perhaps they would pass it off as due to the magic sunlight damage.

The bookie opened the lockbox and passed her the contents.

She pocketed the assassin's bank token and data crystals without a word into her storage. She couldn't imagine the pain of wearing those on her melted flesh. She hated to even think about what her earrings looked like; they must be fused to her body.

Let the healers deal with it!

Zak said nothing either—but gestured toward the Inn's side door.

"Let's get you that drink while you heal. And if you ever want to fight in the ring again," he said, louder for the remaining guests to hear, "I'll waive the fee. That was damn good entertainment."

Her smile was stiff, half-melted. "Fine. But don't skimp on the drink. I want the *good* stuff this time. Not that whisky you gave me earlier."

The dwarf snorted, pretending to take offense at the insult, and led the way.

Inside, with the door closed behind them, he glanced over and muttered, "You look like dragon dung. Why aren't you healing? Tired of pretending to be a vampire already?"

She wasn't in the mood.

"I'm not pretending," she snapped. "I've *been* a vampire for more than a hundred years. Something about coming to this world is... changing that."

The words were out before she could stop them.

Damn it, Mara. Pull it together.

Zak gave her a long look. "You and the boy, both. Still. Go get yerself fixed up. You're bleeding on my floor."

The boy?

She'd follow up later.

Right now, she couldn't even think. She tapped her earring. "Dunc. I need a lift. How fast can you be at the Dragon Inn?"

The answer was instant. "Fifteen minutes. I was just over on the Mile looking for work."

"If you can make it faster, I'll give you a silver mark. I need to get to the Healer's Guild. *Fast.*"

"Right away!"

CHAPTER
TWENTY-TWO

THE HEALERS GUILD was soothing to her wounds just by walking through the gate into the courtyard under the Heartwood tree. Dunc had dropped her off at the curb and asked if she needed help getting inside, but she waved him off. He had seemed pretty squeamish looking at her face and winced every time.

She would not be seen leaning on someone. It was already risky enough just visiting the Healers Guild.

The same young apprentice, Bryna, was on duty at the gate again, and she blanched upon seeing Mara's wounds. "I know you are a vampire and all, but how can you be up and walking around with such horrible injuries?"

Mara didn't have the patience for small talk. "Please ask one of the Masters to attend me. I'm afraid they are the only ones I trust with my condition. It is a secret, after all." She said that last a bit reproachfully, and the girl stammered an apology.

"Of course. Right this way." Then, even as she escorted Mara, she asked, "Are you sure you don't want me to levitate you and carry you to the treatment room?"

"No, just take me there and then ask a Master to come as soon as they are able."

She had suffered worse injuries than these in her time as a vampire, but she'd never had the misfortune of her wounds not immediately healing. In those cases, she had only needed to suffer the pain for a short time at most.

Gritting her teeth, she maintained a steady pace and did not rush, but she felt some relief when the girl stopped fussing over her and hurried away to find the Master on duty.

Onaris, with his recognizable black and white beard and white streaks at his temples, made his way into the room after only a few very long-seeming minutes' wait. He looked imperturbable as usual, but she saw his eyes tighten when he looked at her burned face.

He immediately stepped forward and gestured toward her wounds, seeking permission to touch her. Seeing her nod, he wasted no time casting his spell to diagnose her condition, only to hiss a moment later and look at her with wonder in his eyes.

"How you aren't writhing on the floor in agony, I have no idea. Even if you are still mostly vampire, this is a lot."

Mara shrugged but regretted it instantly. After clenching her teeth for a long moment to get herself back under control, she said, "I do what I must."

The Master hadn't waited but touched the unburned side of her forehead, and relief washed over her body as the pain receptors were blessedly silenced. The injuries were still there, but the pain had vanished.

She chuckled and said, "Now that's a nice trick!"

Onaris frowned, "The pain is repressed, but don't move if you don't have to; you could make the injuries worse. Give me a moment while I address the most important ones first. Let's stop that bleeding."

What followed was a long hour of healing energies being focused on the various parts of her body that were damaged. The sliced palm and the slash across her abdomen were quick and relatively easy to repair. The burns took far longer and more effort from the Healer. More than three-quarters of the hour was spent just regenerating the flesh under the burns. Not vampiric regeneration, though, but actual healing. More of her body was now replaced with living tissue.

If she could resurrect Ewart, the assassin, she would do it just to kick his ass again. That fight cost her a lot. The amount of living tissue in her system was now at 23%. Almost a quarter of her body had been replaced by fragile mortal cells.

Mara didn't think she could get into another fight like the one with the assassin again and survive. Her left eye was now half-living, as were a lot of the blood vessels and arteries on the left side of her neck.

I don't know if I can move like a vampire in a fight and not rip my own throat out or pop my eyeball from the g-forces, she thought. Not to mention the muscles in her abdomen; they would rip apart if she tried half the maneuvers her vampiric body was capable of.

It was time to learn magic, and fast.

She had been summoned to meet the crime lord Noloris. She would have to meet him soon, or he would send people after her. Worse, he was expecting a vampire. If she waited much longer, she might not be able to pass herself off as a vampire; then what would he do? He had now lost one of his lieutenants and expected to get another in return.

She imagined he would not be too happy if he found out she couldn't fill that role.

Onaris interrupted her thoughts as he finally pulled his hands away and sat heavily back into his chair.

"That was a lot of work." Please don't do that again!"

Mara laughed. He had turned her nerves back on, and she could feel that she was whole, or at least as whole as she could be under the circumstances. "Thank you. I will try to avoid it."

Even as she said it, she wondered if that was a lie. She needed to hunt down that greasy bastard, Drevan, who had put a hit out on her. She did hope that there wouldn't be any *tests* from Noloris since she had already beaten one of his hitters. Other than that, she would certainly try to avoid getting damaged more. She couldn't afford it. She had already lost a lot of days in her timeline for learning magic.

"How much do I owe you, doc?" She asked as she got up and stretched.

"Healers don't charge for their services. We do welcome donations, however. Give what you see fit to the apprentice as you leave. No offense, but I hope I don't have to see you like this again. Even so, come back if you need us. One of the Masters will be happy to help."

Mara nodded her thanks and transferred three gold marks to Bryna on her way out. That had been a lot of work for the Master Healer. Thirty thousand dollars, or the equivalent, seemed pretty fair. She had given ten the last time, but there had been three Master Healers for that diagnosis and healing.

Dunc was waiting when she exited the courtyard. He brightened upon seeing that she was healed. The trip to the Healers had been made in near silence as the young Transporter mage sped through the streets in worry and sympathy for her pain. The way back to the

Dragon Inn was the opposite; the floodgates were open, and he chattered all the way, barely shutting up even for a minute.

She just smiled. He was a good kid, and truth be told, she appreciated the news and happenings of the city, as they helped her get a feel for the spirit of the place.

Some rumors were saying the Blood Mages were involved in the disappearance of Lord Tynin's wife and children. "Still, I doubt it. Everyone always blames them when something big happens. I figure it is more likely to be a rival House. House Tynos is in disarray with their lord so distracted right now. I'll bet that has cost them hundreds of gold marks, maybe thousands! The crazy thing is there are other rumors about the lord that say he has become infatuated with some young woman and plans to give his estate away to her and run off for a life of adventure."

Dunc snorted in derision at that rumor. "Ridiculous!"

And more.

And more, until she was finally dropped off at the Dragon's mouth. She thanked Dunc and gave him an extra gold piece for the speed with which he got her to the Healer's guild and for dropping everything to come get her. Most people still used horses to get around the city, and she couldn't even imagine how much worse the agony would have been if she was bounced around that whole way.

She shuddered at the thought and finally headed inside. She wanted to ask Zak who that boy was that he kept talking about but headed straight for her room instead. She needed some privacy and quiet to deal with what had happened earlier.

Plus, she needed to examine her loot.

Chuckling at the thought, she pulled out the vampire's storage rings first.

They did not react to her wishes. She put them on one at a time but had no luck.

Locked.

That was okay. She'd go to see her favorite Maker tomorrow night, and if anyone could break the security of the enchantment, it would be Toman. A little disappointed, she placed the rings back inside her own and moved on to the bank token.

She pulled out the token and put it around her neck, then commanded it to display the total.

1,372 gold marks.

That was well over a million dollars in Earth money. Without hesitating, she transferred the wealth to her own bank token. She didn't know if it was possible to have more than one token access the same account, but she didn't want to give anyone else a chance to plunder Ewart's vault. Her token then displayed the combined total:

1456 gold marks.

Damn! I've hardly been on this planet long, and I've got right at a million and a half dollars in the local currency. Not bad!

She sat, contemplating her next move. It had been one hell of a week.

Kidnapped to a new world where magic was everywhere. Nearly assaulted by cultists. Killed a few of said cultists and ended up wanted by the City Watch. Summoned by the city's crime boss. Killed one of his lieutenants. Oh, and let's not forget that scumbag Drevan put a hit out on her.

Then, a terrible thought occurred. What if Ewart had been a member of the Nightblades Guild?

Would they come after her? Would they honor the contract or consider it fulfilled, or would they see it as a challenge—a loose end to tie up?

She second-guessed herself and thought aloud, "If the Nightblades are a mage guild, would they even let a vampire like Ewart in?" she muttered.

The more she thought about it, the more she exhaled in relief. It seemed unlikely. No self-respecting mage guild would let one of their members moonlight as a crime syndicate enforcer. Too many overlapping loyalties. Too many ways it could go wrong. And someone like Noloris? He wouldn't want one of his people answering to anyone but him.

"Okay," she said aloud, "if worse comes to worst, I've got enough gold to move to another city and live like one of the rich."

Well, maybe not *that* rich. But definitely *comfortable*.

Then reality sank its claws back in: *First, I have to survive.*

That thought led to some decisions. Her nighttime hunting had clearly caught Noloris's attention—time to cut that out. Too late to avoid notice, but maybe if she didn't step on any more toes, he'd be willing to let bygones be bygones.

Drevan, on the other hand, had declared open war. Hired an assassin. Tried to have her killed.

That made her next target clear.

The Followers of the Dragon were his little cult buddies. She'd hunt them now instead of common criminals. Take them apart and, along the way, learn everything she could about their "faith."

If it turned out only Drevan and his goons were rotten, fine. She'd kill him and leave the rest alone.

Either way, someone was going to bleed.

But that could wait.

Tomorrow, she had a magic lesson to get to.

TWENTY-THREE

HER HEART WAS TORN the next morning. On the one hand, she was thrilled to learn real magic—not blood magic like her father Davin's, but true mana-driven spellwork.

Yet that thrill came laced with dread.

Every step forward in her training was also a reminder that her life— *unlife*—was on a clock. If she didn't '*git gud*'

fast, there might not *be* another birthday... or deathday.

She pulled on her nicest outfit—the one meant for looking social, not hunting scumbags through Daggerport's alleys in the dark. Her old clothes were still tucked away in her ring, just in case. But tonight was about magic... and maybe a little pretending to be normal.

Crossing the common room, she glanced around for Zak, hoping to finally ask him about that mysterious *boy* he'd mentioned. But the place was packed. The dinner crowd was flooding in now that the sun had set.

Meh. I'll ask him tonight when I get back. If he's not busy.

Dunc was waiting half a block away, parked just outside the worst of the crowd funnelling into the Dragon's Mouth. He looked up and practically *gawked* at her outfit.

He stammered, "S—uh, sorry. I'm just used to you looking like a... well, that is—"

She took mercy on him, holding up a hand. "Let's just go. You know the square."

No need to broadcast her destination. If Drevan had any brains, he'd have cultists watching the inn. Maybe even a Seer keeping tabs on her movements from afar. According to Toman, they couldn't scry on her directly, but if they knew exactly where she was, they could use remote viewing spells on that place and simply trail their clairvoyance spell after her. It would be a lot harder than simple scrying, but they could arrange it if they were smart. It would be like using traffic cameras to track a fleeing motorist back home.

Then again, the dipshit had already failed to kill her *twice. Hell, three times if you count the assault.* He might *not* be that smart.

As they approached Toman's square, she paid extra attention. She'd been in this part of the city too many times lately for it not to be suspicious. But no ambush sprang, no tail made themselves apparent. Dunc dropped her off at the Rook's Roost, and she crossed the square alone to the hidden alcove that concealed the stairs to her friend's home.

Toman greeted her as usual. Before anything else, he ran another scan.

"Twenty-four percent," he said, his eyes narrowing. "That's one percent higher than yesterday."

Her smile was grim. "Could be just the regular pace, or maybe it speeds up the further along it gets."

Dragon's balls, she thought. *I hope that's not the case.* She chuckled darkly at the new local curse, trying it out in her mind.

Toman gave her a sharp look. "Why the jump? What happened?"

"An assassin tried to collect on a contract when I got back to the Inn," she said matter-of-factly. "Incidentally, can you crack open storage rings?"

He looked torn—somewhere between exasperated and amused by her tone. "You casually mention someone tried to *kill* you, and now you want me to *loot* the corpse?"

Mara gave him a deadpan look.

Chuckling, he held out his hands. "Yes, I can unlock them. For me, it's relatively simple. I specialize in enchantment security as much as illicit crafting. Other Makers... not so much."

He gestured to her. "Hand them over. We'll do your lesson, then while you practice and study, I'll pop the rings."

She arched a brow. "That means you cracked those spell tome crystals, too?"

A broad grin spread across his face. "I said I would, and I did."

Then he hesitated and added, "Well, not exactly—but yes."

She narrowed her eyes.

Toman straightened with a modest puff of pride. "You see, what I had to do was..." And off he went, launching into a detailed explanation of how he had created fresh crystal matrices and carefully copied the contents over, one symbol at a time, preserving the enchantments without triggering their built-in defenses.

In other words, it is a piece of cake for a Maker specialized in the shadowy side of enchanting. For anyone else? Impossible.

She smiled, but her patience was starting to fray. Friend or not, she'd had enough exposition. "Okay, great. So, how do we actually *start*? I've been cramming every spare moment with those intro texts you gave me—you know, the baby mage stuff they drill into kids here. Now that we've got the Spellsword spells, what's next?"

Toman frowned slightly. "Well, you might not like it, but we start with the basics, one spell at a time. Even the Spellswords train their initiates with the same Tier 1 spells as every other guild: *Light, Fire, Cold, Wind, Water, Earth, Kinetic Force*. Each one uses a simple glyph pattern, and once you've got those down, we move on to modifiers—*Increase, Decrease, Explode, Push, Pull*, and so on."

Seeing that she was actually paying attention, Toman brightened and leaned into his explanation. "The only real difference between Tier 1, Tier 2, and beyond comes down to modifiers. You create fire—simple enough. Then you scale it up, tweak the behavior, maybe make it stick to surfaces or explode on impact. Eventually, you'll be juggling little dancing fireballs and changing their colors just to keep bored kids entertained at birthday parties."

He caught her unimpressed look and gave a sheepish chuckle. "Right, right. You probably already know all that. Fine, tonight we start at the very beginning—with Light. That's the most harmless of all the spells and the one that everyone starts with."

He lifted a hand and let mana pool at his fingertips. "I'll demonstrate a few times and talk through the process as I go. Nothing fancy. Just watch, ask questions if you need to, and when you feel ready, I'll walk you through your first attempt."

His tone shifted slightly, more focused. "Once you've cast it once, and you *feel* the shape of the spell, the rest is just repetition. Then practice until it becomes instinct."

Mara chuckled. She was eager to cast her first spell and knew she had to start at the bottom and work her way up, but what about the ones that could save her life?

"Yeah, okay, but what about the *real* stuff? The good stuff. Enhanced speed, strength, toughness? That's what I *actually* need right now."

Toman's enthusiasm dimmed. "That's more advanced. And... I've got bad news about that part. Looking through the Spellsword tomes, I found their secret."

Uh-oh. "How bad are we talking? I don't need to be baptized under a full moon and then bathed in dragon fire or something ridiculous like that, do I?"

Toman sputtered, choking on his own spit. "What!? *No!* Nothing stupid like that!"

She gave him a look.

He cleared his throat and continued. "It's just... they use their Heartwood weapons to channel their self-targeted spells. So when they cast something like *Iron Body*, they're not actually casting it *on themselves*. They cast it into their bonded Heartwood weapon, and the effect is channeled through it back onto them. That way, they don't suffer the Wasting."

Mara's eyes narrowed. "But they *do* still get the Wasting, right?"

He nodded. "Yes. But the weapon buffers them against the worst of it. They still take some minor damage to muscles and skin, but not their organs. And they undergo frequent magical healing to stay ahead of the damage."

She leaned back with a sigh. "And let me guess—getting a Heartwood weapon is... difficult?"

Toman winced. "Yes and no. I can do the enchantments. That part's easy. The hard part is getting the Heartwood itself. It's *insanely* expensive. Worth more than its weight in gold. Every mage has some kind of focus—rods, wands, orbs—but most guilds use tiny amounts. If you want a full-blown sword? That's *a lot of* Heartwood. Plus, you can understand why it's so hard to come by; you've seen the one at the Healer's guild; no one's just going to go harvest that thing to get focus items. We have to wait until they shed limbs naturally."

"There are others, of course—not just that one—but they are few and far between. Rarer than you'd think. That's why most mages end up using recycled pieces passed down from their predecessors. The wood's naturally dense and durable, but people like me? We make sure every inch of it is enchanted to be nearly indestructible."

Mara blinked. "But I thought the Wasting destroyed items that got enchanted. Isn't the mana toxic over time?"

Toman nodded, looking entirely too pleased with her question—like a teacher whose favorite student had just nailed a tricky concept. "Yes, exactly. But Heartwood's special. One of its best properties—aside from its ability to help mages focus—is how resistant it is to the Wasting. You can layer on enchantment after enchantment, and it'll barely degrade across a mage's entire lifetime."

He leaned forward slightly, warming to the topic. "Pieces last for generations. There are records of Maker rods being passed down for over three thousand years. That's the only reason there's even a supply at all. If it weren't so resilient, only the wealthiest or most powerful mages would ever get their hands on a shard, let alone enough to make a full focus."

That begged the question, "How much?"

"For a small focus, maybe a hundred gold marks. For a one-handed sword like some Spellswords use? Five hundred. A wizard's staff? Over a thousand."

Mara whistled softly. That was a lot to take in.

She actually *had* that kind of money now, thanks to Ewart and his unfortunate attempt to kill her. But still, she'd been thinking of that stash as her emergency *get-the-hell-out-of-town* fund. Not something to blow on a single piece of equipment.

"Well... easy come, easy go, I guess," she muttered darkly. Then, with a heavy sigh, "Okay. After last night, the money's not the issue. The question is—what kind of focus should I get? If I walk around with a Heartwood *weapon*, won't the Spellswords lose their minds?"

"Right. The other thing is, you could try to hide the spells—learn to cast without gestures and flourishes like most mages use. They aren't strictly necessary, just a crutch to help anchor the right mental focus. But if you can drop the theatrics, it'll help you fly under the radar."

Toman hesitated before adding, "And if you don't make your Heartwood into a weapon, that'll help, too. Something more discreet. Still... the really bad news is, if you're both casting and fighting in melee, someone's going to notice. Doesn't matter what spell you use or what shape your focus takes. The Spellswords don't let anyone outside their guild mix magic and close-quarters combat. That's their domain."

As if that wasn't bad enough, he dropped the other shoe. "And it's not just the guild. Most nations have formal contracts with them to keep a certain number of Spellswords on retainer for 'special duties.' The Spellswords make it part of the price of doing business— outlawing competition."

Mara groaned. "Son of a bitch! I go through all this trouble, and I won't even be able to use their magic in a fight?"

Toman shook his head quickly. "No, no—it's not that bad. Well... it is. But it isn't. You can still use their enhancement spells—boost your reflexes and reposition faster. Just don't fight like a Spellsword. Don't close the gap with a blade. Instead, fight like a Wizard—stand back, use force spells, barriers, clever tactics. Use the Spellsword enhancements to move when no one expects it. Be tougher than expected. Looking through their spell tomes, they've got some excellent stuff in there, and it's not all flashy and obvious."

He saw the skepticism on her face and rushed to clarify. "Look, there's always a risk. But if you're casting body-boosting magic without fighting in melee, most will assume you're just a Wizard who likes to dodge. Nobody's going to bring the hammer down on that."

She thought about it.

That would mean a change in fighting style.

But then again... wasn't she going to have to change anyway?

If she lost her vampiric body, going toe-to-toe with someone like Ewart again would be suicide. He'd paint the arena with her blood using speed alone. Her mortal form wouldn't be able to handle the kind of velocity vampires could generate—not even with Spellsword magic. She might get close. Might even surpass mortal limits. But she'd never match what she could do now.

Her mind kept circling the same brutal truth—this wasn't just about losing power.

Who will I even be anymore?

The thought hit like a blow to the solar plexus, stealing her breath and leaving behind a hollow ache.

For over a hundred years, her identity had been inextricably linked to being a vampire. Davin's daughter. The rebel fighting the Cabal—the bastards who ruled the supernatural world back on Earth with an iron fist. She hunted Nazi werewolves because only a vampire could. She was a thief, a saboteur, a predator in the night. All of it had been built on her vampiric edge.

What was left without that?

Sure, she was a restaurant owner. An art lover. But even in those things, her senses gave her an edge—heightened taste, scent, vision.

Without her powers... what was she? Just another woman with a complicated past and a bullseye on her back?

Across from her, Toman didn't say a word. He just waited—quiet, patient. Giving her space.

And even that, she noticed. She could still feel the subtle shift in his breath, the change in posture, the warmth of his body in the room... even while her thoughts were spinning out. Even that was beyond mortal senses.

She wanted to cry. Bloody tears welled in the corners of her eyes, but she blinked them back. She hated the mess. Hated the loss of control.

Come on, Mara. Get it together. You've been through worse. You went from death to unlife... how hard can it be to go the other direction?

For the first time, Toman spoke her name.

"I'm here for you, Mara. I like you, and I consider you a friend. But I think you're missing something."

She glanced up, wary but listening.

"You keep focusing on what you're going to lose—and yeah, you'll definitely be losing some cool abilities. But you'll *gain* something too. You'll be a mage. That means power, protection, *status*. If you join a guild, no one's going to mess with you. Hell, you don't even have to join one. Walk around in Wizard's colors, carrying a Heartwood staff, and most people won't question it. Wizards are loners. Most of them only know a handful of others because they train through direct one-on-one apprenticeships rather than through guild schools or academies. That is unless they're heavily involved in guild politics. Even then, I could help you fake it if you wanted to try."

He shifted slightly like he wanted to move closer—maybe offer a hug —but a single look from Mara made him wisely think better of it. So he just gave her a crooked shrug and added, "I'm just saying... you don't have to be a fighter. You could leave the assassins and enemies behind. Become someone new. Take your time figuring out who that person is."

Mara gave him a crooked smile. "You know, you're not entirely bad at advice. Or... comforting someone. Or whatever that just was."

Toman put a hand to his chest in mock hurt. "High praise from the scariest person I know."

She chuckled despite herself.

And just like that, the heavy weight pressing on her chest began to ease. Toman had done it. He'd pulled her back from the edge.

And more importantly... he was right.

She didn't have to have all the answers right now. She didn't need a perfect plan for who or what she would become. All she needed was to learn. To focus.

The decisions could come later.

CHAPTER
TWENTY-FOUR

An hour later, Toman had cast the basic Tier 1 Light spell at least two dozen times, walking her through every step with explanations even more detailed than what the spell tomes offered.

She had to give him credit—he was expertly skirting the edge of his former guild's restrictions on teaching outsiders.

Now, it all came down to her.

Was she ready?

The answer was an impatient *yes*. Honestly, she probably could've tried it a dozen demonstrations ago if Toman hadn't been so insistent that she watch, listen, and visualize with him each time.

When he finally gave her the go-ahead, she resisted the urge to jump for joy—very un-Mara-like behavior. She knew herself well enough to recognize how far outside her comfort zone this whole thing was. It reminded her too much of training with Davin after she'd first been turned, back when everything had been new and overwhelming. Since then, everything she'd learned or mastered had built on that solid foundation.

But this? This was something else entirely. Magic wasn't remotely like the physical training that had been stamped into her muscle memory.

But focus? That was something she had a century of developing!

With a sigh, she leaned forward in her chair, settling onto the balls of her feet like a predator preparing to pounce. She focused exactly as instructed and shaped her mana through the mental image of the pattern—the glyph for *Light*.

Controlling it was rough. She'd never tried to touch mana this way before. Still, thanks to Toman's exhaustive explanations, it wasn't as hard as it could've been.

The result, however, was pitiful. The tiniest glimmer of light flickered to life, barely bright enough for her to see even with vampiric senses. But it was *there*.

Toman leaped to his feet, clapping like a madman. "You did it! You *did it* on your first try! That's insane! No one does that!"

Startled, Mara blinked—and promptly lost control of the magic. The faint light vanished like it had never existed.

She rounded on him. "What the hell, man? I *had* it until you yelled."

She wasn't really mad, though. If his reaction was any indication, she had every right to be pleased.

"Seriously, kids spend *days*—sometimes *weeks*—just learning to touch mana for the first time. You did it on your *first try*. That's basically unheard of. Not even the best prodigies manage that."

That was flattering and all, but he was comparing her to literal children. "Ugh. You do realize I'm over a hundred years old, right? No snot-nosed kid is going to have the kind of focus I've developed in *my* line of work. If I were ten, I'd be thrilled. As it stands, yeah, I'm glad I pulled it off, but let's keep things in perspective. And thanks for hammering the visualization stuff. That helped more than I expected."

Toman blinked. "Huh. I guess when you put it that way, maybe it's not quite as legendary. But still—I *can't believe* you pulled it off so fast. Wait... why did you use so little mana? If I hadn't been watching it flow, I wouldn't even have noticed the light. Now that I *think* about it, maybe *that's* the impressive part. You used such a tiny amount."

Mara felt her stomach drop like a faulty elevator. That wasn't what had happened. "Uh, no. I didn't *try* to go small. That was about ten percent of my total capacity. I wasn't holding back."

Toman's face fell. "Oh. Crap. I'm an idiot."

He pinched the bridge of his nose. "Only twenty-four percent of your body is converted. Of *course*, you wouldn't be able to channel much yet. Think of it like water through a pipe. Right now, you've got a pipe the size of my Heartwood rod." He held up the slender focus item as an illustration. "Eventually, your full capacity will look more like..." He formed a wide circle with both hands, maybe twice the size of a basketball. "That."

Mara nodded slowly, still working through it. "Okay, but if I'm only channeling through *this*," she said, gesturing toward the rod-sized symbol of his guild, "why would it ever jump that far? Wouldn't the next stage be, like, grapefruit-sized at best?"

Toman grinned. "It's not linear. It's adaptive. As your body continues converting, and as you keep working with mana, you'll build tolerance and strength. Think of it like a muscle. You're weak when you don't use them, but the more you do, the stronger you get and the bigger the muscles grow. Not a perfect analogy, but close enough."

"Okay, I think I understand now. So I won't be pathetic when it's all said and done."

Toman nodded emphatically. "No, of course not. We haven't even begun to see your potential. That'll become a lot more obvious once you start tackling higher-tier, more complex spells. By then, your body and mind will be adjusting to the strain. It's hard to say for sure, but I'd bet you'll end up at least as strong as me—and I'm no slouch."

That was good to hear. There was hope. She'd managed this spell on her first try, and if Toman was right, she might eventually pass for a full guild mage—even as her vampiric powers failed. Maybe not exponentially stronger, but strong enough.

Encouraging.

Toman laughed, catching the flicker of hope on her face. "That's the spirit! Now, practice that spell as many times as you can until you run dry. Meanwhile, I'll start cracking open those storage rings you *acquired* and see what kind of goodies are inside."

What followed was two solid hours of concentration and trial and error. She failed here and there—one hundred years of learning to focus only carried so far when the task was new—but as the minutes ticked by, she started experimenting. More power. Less power. A few of the lights were bright enough to rival a light bulb, though those left her drained and aching.

It didn't take long to figure out that the limiting factor for mages wasn't some magic stat like in a game. The "Magical Aptitude" Toman kept referring to was really about how much mana your body could channel before you collapsed. Still, the irony was that this world did treat it almost like a stat—scaling aptitude from 1 to 100 to compare casters. Toman estimated his own somewhere in the mid-80s. Apparently, the Maker's Guild only recruited from the highest percentile. When you were the richest guild around, you had your pick of the best.

By the time her mana was spent and her head was spinning, Mara felt like she had a solid grasp of her first real spell.

Toman had long since finished bypassing the rings' security and now lounged in his chair, watching her. "Well done for your first session! You can cast it freely now. You haven't mastered it, but you're solid enough not to blow yourself up. Just... don't try any of the others yet. This room is heavily shielded. Out there, that's not the case. Never put innocent lives at risk."

He went on to lecture her—sternly—about the danger of altering a spell mid-cast. Apparently, that was how mages leveled city blocks.

"If you ever botch a spell, just stop feeding it mana. Let go, and it'll fizzle out. Try to finish a broken cast, and 'Boom' isn't even the worst-case scenario."

"Noted," she said dryly. "Now, what did Ewart, the dipshit, have in his rings?"

She held out her hands, and Toman passed the rings over with a grimace. "Not all of it's pleasant. Looks like some of this junk was taken as... *trophies*. From completed contracts. It's pretty sick."

Mara checked the contents for herself, mentally sorting through the stored inventory. He wasn't exaggerating. Some of it gave off real serial killer vibes. But there were also a lot of useful items. Maybe three to four hundred more gold marks in assorted coinage, a healthy stash of magic gear—likely looted off victims—and what looked like a small clothing emporium's worth of outfits in every size and style.

Apparently, he kept everything. Gross.

A thought struck her. "Wait, can stuff in storage devices be tracked?"

Toman raised a brow but answered. "Mostly? No. Some very high-level Seers might be able to, but it's rare. Why? Worried that loot's going to bring the heat?"

"Yeah, a little. I'm not part of the local crime syndicate, and I don't exactly have anyone backing me if they come knocking. Plus, you know... wanted criminal and all."

He waved it off. "The anti-scrying enchantment brooch I provided will block anything aimed at you. Even top-tier Seers won't break through. Besides, peeking inside someone else's storage ring is hard. It takes years of training and specialization, same as my work with bypassing security enchantments. Unless someone has reason to target you specifically, there's almost zero chance they'd even try. And even if they did, you're protected."

New fear unlocked—and immediately resolved. That was a relief.

"Alright then," she said, stretching. "I'm going to get some rest. But I'll be back tomorrow night to learn more."

Toman yawned and waved her off. "I'll be here."

She left and found Dunc waiting where she'd left him. Time to pay her greedy fence a visit and unload two rings full of junk!

TWENTY-FIVE

THE DRIVE to Greenstone Pawnshop was uneventful, but Mara had Dunc drive slowly and carefully as they approached the building. The last thing she wanted was another ambush upon arrival.

Thankfully, no one was lying in wait, and she was able to leave Dunc on the curb without too much concern. "If you see anyone approaching, just drive away. I can get out of here on my own if those Followers show up again. If that happens, just meet me on the main road. It won't take me long."

Nodding in agreement, Dunc tapped his earring speech stone, indicating that he would give her warning.

"Good man."

Mara entered the pawnshop, and Gavian looked visibly nervous upon seeing her.

"What, you don't like my business? Just tell me the name of another good fence, and I'll take my business elsewhere."

The pawnshop owner looked aggrieved. "No, no! That's not necessary, I appreciate your business—it's just that my profit margin is much lower with you for some reason."

Chuckling, she approached the counter. "Well, I have a lot for you today and need the services of that handy circle you have downstairs."

"Circle? What circle? I don't know what you're talking about." He spoke nervously.

She gave a sigh. Her compulsion had blocked his memories of the previous meeting's details. With an explosive burst of speed, she reached across the counter, grabbed his collar, and refreshed the compulsion. Just like that, Gavian was back under her sway.

Normally, this kind of use of her ability would leave her feeling uncomfortable—subverting someone's will like this wasn't something she liked to do lightly. But this guy was a cheat, and he had tried to exploit her lack of local knowledge to lowball his first purchase from her to a ridiculous degree. Her conscience wasn't even close to bothering her when it came to this greasy jerk.

"Okay, let's go downstairs, and I'll unload two storage rings. You make me an honest offer for everything, and I'll pay you a fair price for the use of your magic circle to destroy the less savory items I found inside."

He nodded reflexively and led the way to the back stairs.

Once below, she started with all the gross trophies the killer had collected. There were ears, fingers, eyes, and even whole skulls among the assassin's disgusting keepsakes.

If he hadn't been under compulsion, she was sure the fence would have painted the floor in the colors of Tex-Mex. Or whatever passed for the local cuisine.

Even a younger Mara might have done the same, but the years and sights she'd seen had jaded her to even something like this.

When it was all out and formed a sickeningly large pile, Gavian activated the incineration feature of the magic formation, turning his head to avoid looking any longer.

Only a minute later, nothing remained. Not even ash.

Unfortunately, she had to renew her compulsion again, as the unsettling sights had shaken the pawnshop owner's mind enough to void her power over him. She commanded him to forget what had just happened, other than the fact that she had asked him to dispose of some belongings of an assassin who had lost to her in a duel.

Even so, she had them move over to a large table to unload the sellable items in the rings. No sense in reminding him of the ugliness.

They did their usual dance, but since he was under compulsion, she only let him negotiate a fair price. The wardrobe alone came to 125 gold marks due to the sheer number of clothes and the fact that some of the higher-end pieces had enchantments like wear-resistance and self-repair. A few even had temperature control enchantments to keep the wearer comfortable regardless of weather conditions. Knowing they were the clothes of dead victims, they didn't even tempt her. However, they did give her some ideas for future clothes purchases.

That total was dwarfed by the value of the magic items. He surely had many more victims over the years, but at the moment, he'd been carrying around the equipment of at least three dozen people. Apparently, being an assassin with no moral compass was very lucrative. Gavian reluctantly agreed to a price of 220 gold marks.

The man acted like he was being bled dry and tortured as they concluded their deal. She subtracted a fair price of 10 gold marks for the use of his circle to get rid of the gruesome evidence of Ewart's obsession. That brought the total to 335 gold marks for the items she sold. Along with the loose coins of various denominations, which totaled 290 gold marks, the grand total for all she had obtained from Ewart, plus what she already had, was now 2166 gold marks between her bank account and coins.

Even under compulsion, the greedy fence bemoaned the cost. "This is nearly emptying my account! And now I have a huge shipment of merchandise to transport—and I've got to do it immediately instead of waiting the normal time. That's not going to make my buyers happy! I'm telling you, I can't buy anything more from you for a while, so please don't come back!"

"Fine. But I really do need the names and locations of other people in your line of work. I'm happy to take my business elsewhere."

And that wasn't a lie. Gavian had been useful, but he was about as trustworthy as a CEO who tells employees their jobs are safe—right before laying off half the staff and moving their positions overseas to "right-shore" them. In other words, she'd be more than happy to find someone else to work with.

She recorded the names and locations of the other fences into her data crystal and was just about to head upstairs when Dunc pinged her.

His voice came through the stone as if he were whispering under his breath. "Excuse me, lady, but there are some City Watch members loitering around the outside of the store. Just thought you should know."

Well, crap.

Turning to Gavian, she said, "I need a disguise. Something that will let me look slightly different than I really do. Not a big change—just small things. Hair color, eye color, different cheekbones. That sort of thing."

She already had the enchantment on her storage ring that would prevent anyone from detecting she was a vampire. If she could make herself look just a little different, she should be able to bluff her way out. She had a plan.

The fence chuckled darkly. "Of course. Illusion or actual change? The real thing will hurt, and you'll need to see a healer after—it'll almost definitely cause Wasting damage. Hair's not bad since it isn't living matter. Eyes and facial structure, though... that'll hurt like hell when the Wasting hits. You'll probably survive superficial damage like that since it won't affect any internal organs. You *could* go blind, but it's very unlikely before the spells wear off and you revert to your original appearance."

He coughed and looked vaguely embarrassed. "I'm an honest businessman, but sometimes my customers need items like this to avoid any... entanglements with the City Watch or people who are upset about losing certain items. If you know what I mean."

Mara almost laughed. The compulsion made him believe their business was all above board—and that *she* believed he really was an honest merchant.

"What about items that can fool a truth detector?"

Gavian puffed up in mock indignation. "What? I would never—"

She cut him off with a single raised eyebrow.

"Well, that is, I *might* have something like that. I just happened to acquire one in a bulk purchase. I'd never go looking for something like that on purpose, you understand." He actually looked like he believed it, just for a moment.

Not that she bought it for a second, but it was amusing watching him try

"I don't have long. Take me to the items and show me how to use them. Quickly."

He pulled several items from his own storage ring and coughed again, sheepish.

"Here you are. The ear cuff there will fool a Seer's truth sense. You'll still want to avoid telling outright lies if you can. Half-truths are better. If the mage isn't particularly skilled, you might get away with it. It's a one-time-use item, though—it'll only last for an hour. The other items are disguised as copper coins. They'll alter your hair, eyes, and facial structure enough to avoid recognition."

She used each in turn, and they *hurt*. The eyes were the worst—stinging like she'd been hit with pepper spray. But the pain faded after a few seconds. Her face burned like she'd rubbed it with stinging nettles, but thankfully, that too passed quickly. She pulled a small mirror from among Ewart's things she had kept and checked her reflection.

Mara still looked vaguely like herself, but now she had sky-blue eyes, blonde hair, and a heavier face like she'd gained thirty pounds. "This will do."

She held out her token and transferred thirty gold marks to him. "How long will the physical changes last?"

Gavian waved his hand from side to side. "Anywhere between a week or two. Everyone's different. They'll wear off if you get healed, though."

"Good. Then I hope I won't be seeing you again anytime soon. Remember, Lady Sorellin Vale came in and tried to sell you some jewelry. She's a minor noble who's fallen on hard times. You chose not to buy the items because she wanted too much coin for them. You will not remember *me* once I step outside."

He led her back up to the door, a conflicted expression on his face until she stepped through the front.

She saw the change come over him the instant she crossed the threshold, her suggestion taking hold. The greedy fence would no longer remember Mara from this moment on. There was nothing in his psyche that would resist the false memory. If anything, his greedy little subconscious would welcome it—happy to forget the woman who made him pay fair prices.

Waiting outside was a veritable SWAT team of City Watch guardsmen. Several were hidden in concealed positions nearby, wands raised and ready. Probably sunlight or fire, if they knew what she was.

At the base of the steps stood five officers, at least three of them mages. Dunc waited in his magic rickshaw just a few feet away, but the Watch stood in her way.

One of the mages stepped back just enough to allow her to descend into their midst.

"Please join us for a moment, if you please. We have a few questions."

If there was one thing Mara had learned over the years—whether infiltrating enemy compounds or robbing the corrupt—it was that confidence mattered most when you were most vulnerable.

It wasn't Mara, the vampire, who stepped down the stairs and into their circle.

It was *Lady Sorellin Vale*. A noble fallen on hard times, perhaps—but a noble nonetheless.

"Yes? What's this about? I have business to attend to."

The officer of the Watch, who seemed to be the highest-ranking—judging by the number of symbols on his gorget—spoke with a wary tone. "It's quite late to be out in a neighborhood like this. Moreover, we were given reason to believe a wanted fugitive was in this shop."

One of the other officers, a non-mage, was staring at an image projected above his data crystal. It was Mara's likeness from when she'd checked in at the city gate, next to a blurrier shot taken in the alley after she'd killed the cultist attackers.

The man's eyebrows drew together as he looked up at the woman standing before him, then back down at the images.

He held the hologram out toward one of the mages. "She's got a similar build, but the hair and eyes are all wrong. Is she wearing an illusion?"

The officer being questioned stepped closer to Mara and cast a small spell, a shimmer distorting the air between them. He frowned, then turned to address his superior. "Sir, I don't detect any illusion."

Mara frowned as if scandalized. "What's the meaning of this? You dare accuse a noblewoman of illusion magic? I never!"

The fourth officer, a middle-aged mage with a Heartwood orb focus in her hand, glanced at the ranking officer. "After we were informed, I performed a scrying, but I didn't detect the target in this location. The shop is warded against deeper readings, though, so it's possible the vampire slipped out the back when she saw us coming. Unfortunately, the tip came too late for me to get a remote view of the suspect arriving."

Frowning, the lead officer turned to Mara. "Pardon, my lady, but would you mind giving us your name? You certainly don't look like the target, but your presence here is... a bit too coincidental."

Mara sniffed with practiced disdain. "You may address me as Lady

Sorellin Vale. I'm visiting the city on business. It has been a long evening, and I was hoping to wrap things up after this stop."

She noticed the female Seer give her superior a subtle nod. Almost imperceptible—but there.

The officer's frown deepened. "If you'll indulge me, Lady Vale— where are your lands? From where do you hail?"

Her expression turned frosty. "That's a rather rude question. As it happens, my family no longer holds our ancestral lands. They were lost in the war—our castle destroyed in battle. We were from the West. You likely wouldn't have heard of it. It's been many years since the loss, but my father still holds title and hopes to rebuild one day."

Every word was true. Her adopted father had owned a castle in France near the German border. It was destroyed during a war, and he really did dream of rebuilding someday. Just not while the Cabal still breathed. As far as they were concerned, Davin was long dead.

The Seer nodded again—this time more firmly.

The dour officer gave her a tired, frustrated look. "I see. Thank you for your time, Lady Vale. Apologies for the inconvenience. We're searching for a vampire reported to be in this shop, and you do have... strikingly pale skin if you'll forgive me. It was only natural to assume—"

Mara feigned fresh offense. "Really now. Do I look like a vampire? Could a vampire do this?"

She cast a light spell, bright enough to bathe the Watchmen in its glow. She held it just long enough for the mages to clearly see her channeling mana through the pattern.

The lead officer muttered under his breath, but she caught it easily with her heightened hearing. "Dragon's balls. She's not a vampire— she's a human mage."

Speaking aloud, he called over his shoulder to one of the men loitering half a block away. "Arrest the one who gave you the tip about the vampire criminal."

Under his breath again, with less restraint: "Idiots."

Turning back to Mara, he offered a stiff bow. "Again, I beg your forgiveness for the inconvenience. Please enjoy your stay in our beautiful city. You're free to go."

She gave him a curt nod, then sniffed indignantly at the other officers before striding to the waiting rickshaw with her chin lifted high.

Hell hath no disdain like a noblewoman inconvenienced.

When they were well away from the scene and back on the main road heading north, Mara leaned forward and patted Dunc on the back. "Good man. Thank you for your loyal service despite the annoyances."

He glanced over his shoulder, confusion in his eyes. "I saw you cast a spell. But I thought you were a... well, you know."

Mara gave him her best mysterious grin. "A woman has her secrets. And the face she shows the world may not be the one you think it is."

Then she laughed. "Speaking of which, let's stop by the Healers Guild on the way back. I really need to remove this disguise."

An hour later, she was leaving the Healers Guild—relieved but frustrated. She hadn't suffered any Wasting from the short-term disguise spell, but the healing had accelerated the transformation of her body. More facial tissue had shifted, and her right eye was now fully living as well.

Her vampiric vision was failing. She could still see in the dark, but her long-distance clarity was gone. Her cornea had changed—too much to maintain supernatural focus.

She was now up to twenty-five, nearly twenty-six percent human. Onaris believed it would tick higher by morning.

Once again, fate had found a way to speed up her change.

It was nearing 3:00 a.m. when she returned to the inn, quietly slipping inside. To her disappointment, Zak wasn't working the bar. She'd wanted to know who he thought she really was—and who that boy was he kept mentioning.

Oh well, probably for the best. I'm not exactly in the mood for a cryptic conversation with him right now. Maybe I'll catch him tomorrow night.

TWENTY-SIX

RATHER THAN SIT in the common room and drink after the night she was having, Mara headed to her room to relax.

As she settled in, she frowned. *It's just a shame that Inn rooms on Greymantle don't really have bathrooms.*

They reminded her more of the places she'd stayed in during her first lifetime—places that hadn't even heard of indoor plumbing. Not that it mattered here. Who needed a shower or tub when magical Cleaners existed and could do a better job than any Earth-based hygiene ritual?

The inn *did* have a communal bath area, and it was undeniably impressive—designed more for soaking and socializing, like a Japanese onsen or a Roman bath, only with flair.

Dragon-themed flair.

She'd peeked inside a few nights ago and found a dark, grotto-style chamber with elegant carvings, magical lighting, and a fake dragon hoard glittering in one corner of the cavern-like room. Even the pools looked like natural springs—except for the suspiciously ergonomic seating and conveniently sculpted steps.

She'd almost gone tonight. At this hour, it was likely deserted. But she didn't have a swimsuit and wasn't feeling quite brave enough to test whether "clothing optional" was a thing on this world. Back in her original life, growing up in the Bible Belt, bathing suits hadn't even been a given—people swam fully clothed, if at all.

Instead, she changed into pajamas and stretched out on the bed, her thoughts wandering between her past and future.

She'd lived long enough to watch the entire 20th century unfold. First, ankles were scandalous, then calves. Bathing suits crept upward and downward in equal measure until bikinis were commonplace, and eventually, even they seemed too modest. Modesty itself became negotiable. Clothing-optional beaches and pools weren't just fringe anymore—they were practically expected in certain circles.

She chuckled. *I don't miss the bad old days when people expected you to marry someone if they saw your ankle.*

Now people threw around terms like Gen Z and Gen Alpha—"digital natives," as if being born with a tablet in your hand made you wise. Gen X, for all their smugness, liked to brag about bridging the before-and-after of the internet like they'd done something heroic.

Children. All of them.

Mara had been born when steam engines were cutting-edge. When ships were just making the jump from wood to steel. Her father had owned horses and a rickety wagon. No way would that cheapskate have bought one of those newfangled "automobiles."

She'd lived through the churn of invention: cars, airplanes, wars that turned those inventions into tanks and bombers. Then, not even twenty-five years later, nuclear weapons and men walking on the

Moon. The information age followed close behind. And now? People had access to all the world's knowledge in their pockets—and couldn't string together a coherent thought because schools no longer taught *how to think*.

Honestly, the last two decades have been the hardest. Not the technology—after everything she'd seen, switching to a world powered by magic barely registered. It was the *people*. The shifts in attitude. So much of it had been beautiful—people finding freedom to live authentically—but just as much had curdled into rage. Everyone seemed poisoned by hate. No one could stop drinking it.

Maybe coming to this world wasn't such a bad thing after all.

She laughed aloud at that thought, then shook her head. Cultists and vampire crime lords. *Yeah—every place has its monsters.*

But her smile faded as her mind circled back to the present. Her condition. Her transformation. Her uncertain future. She could deal with cults, crime syndicates—hell, she'd gone toe-to-toe with the Cabal. That wasn't the scary part.

The scary part was *who* she was becoming.

The only certainty was that her old life was gone.

The changes to her body were taking more than just her powers—they were taking her *identity*. No more compulsion. No more supernatural night vision. No more brute dominance. She was losing the edge that had made her *the* apex predator among prey.

And the hard truth was... she had *liked* being that predator.

As a mortal, she'd been powerless—forced to raise her younger siblings like free labor while her family chewed her spirit to pieces until she finally ran away from home to the big city. Only to then run right into the arms of that serial killer vampire.

Everything before had been fear, poverty, and a desperate desire for a better life — one filled with freedom. Freedom from fear, from expectations, and from the boundaries society had placed on her. It was only in her last moments that she had fought desperately, with tooth and nail, for all the things she'd never had in life.

She'd died. Been reborn, and it had all changed.

Sure, it had exchanged fear of men and society's expectations with a shadow war against mages, werewolves, and fellow vampires. The brutal training Davin had put her through, the battles, the bloodshed, the secrecy—it had all been worth it for one thing: *agency*.

From the moment of her death, she had never again let anyone else control her life.

Undeath had allowed her to have a life that was satisfying. She had freedom— she had a purpose.

And now? All that was draining away, entirely out of her control, just as her blood had done on the night of her death.

But the fire still burned in her heart. Just like that first night, she would not go down without a fight.

She wasn't going to lie down and let it end.

She wasn't that frightened girl anymore.

This Mara had survived wars, assassins, betrayals, and monsters. She'd carved a life out of shadows, torn down enemies, and stood her ground when the world told her to kneel. And if she had to do it all over again—reinvent herself from the ground up—she'd do it.

However long it took.

When she finally closed her eyes, she hadn't solved a single problem.

But her heart felt lighter.

Because no matter what happened—no matter what she became, or even if she lost all her powers—she was still a fighter.

And she would not be ruled by fate.

She would forge her own.

Nothing felt particularly hopeful when she woke that evening, but there was a new sense of resolve humming just under her skin. The night might not be brighter, but she was ready to meet it head-on.

Unfortunately, Zak was again swamped with customers, so she decided to skip the long overdue conversation in favor of getting her night started efficiently. It was a shame she wasn't allowed to hunt in the Dragon Inn; she was hungry again, not that she would have done that anyway, but her stomach was feeling insistent. Besides being against Zak's rules, she also made a habit of never feeding near where she slept.

At her direction, Dunc took her to her 'favorite' lowlife haunt in the Second Quarter: the Broken Fang. It was as much a wretched hive of scum and villainy as she'd ever seen, and finding a deserving donor was barely even a challenge. It only cost her an hour.

While she was there, she slipped Zariah a gold mark and asked her to start gathering intel on the Followers of the Dragon—and Drevan specifically. She'd danced around it long enough. It was time to learn more about the bastards making her new existence so complicated.

On the way to Toman's, she had Dunc take a meandering route— different streets, back alleys, and errant turns. The last thing she needed was to fall into a predictable pattern and let some high-priced Seer's Guild mage tag her through a routine. Drevan had already shelled out enough coin to hire an elite assassin in Noloris' syndicate. Who knew what else he was willing to pay for?

She had just stepped up to Toman's door when Dunc's voice whispered through her speech stone.

"Lady, sorry to interrupt, but you asked me to keep watch for your Spellsword friend. She's here tonight, in the tavern. Alone at a table."

Mara tensed. "Thanks, Dunc. I'll be right there. If she starts to leave, tell her I'll join her shortly."

She checked her ring to confirm the Spellsword crystals were still stored safely, then turned on her heel and hurried toward the Rook's Roost.

Inside, the familiar scent of ale and hearth smoke greeted her as she slipped through the crowd. The place was packed, locals crammed into every booth and table. But it didn't take long to spot Olia—alone at a table, sober, and dressed for a date that clearly hadn't happened yet.

Sharp girl. Her eyes swept the room the moment Mara entered, alert despite her expression. Olia stood and waved enthusiastically when she spotted her, none of the wary anger from before—just the open excitement of a young woman who thought she'd found a real friend.

Mara smiled back a little sadly.

Olia pulled her into a hug without hesitation, and Mara let her—for a moment. The warmth of it left an ache in her chest, and not the kind that healed. Because this was it. Time to rip the bandage off.

When Olia pulled back, still beaming, Mara took a breath and willed the four Spellsword spell crystals into her hand.

"I wanted to return these," she said softly.

Olia blinked in surprise, confusion knitting her brow. Her mind took a moment to catch up—processing not just the gesture but the reason behind it. She reached out and made the crystals vanish into her own ring, slow and reluctant.

"I gave them to you to help you get into the guild," she said, trying to keep her voice steady. "I'm no petty goblin trying to take back a gift."

But her expression betrayed the struggle beneath. Mara could see it —the subtle flicker of resistance, the tiny fractures of doubt. The kind that happened when a compulsion rubbed against a person's instincts when they tried to make peace with a memory that didn't quite line up.

That was why Mara had planted the reasoning so carefully when she'd used the spell. A believable justification was everything. Without it, the mind would splinter against the lie.

Even so... seeing that struggle on Olia's face was like a fresh stake through Mara's chest.

And it didn't make her feel one bit better.

"I don't want our friendship to be about what one of us can do for the other," Mara said quietly. "Last time we spoke, I told you the truth—I wasn't really your friend back then. And I feel like hell for it now, using you for what you could offer me. I wish we could just wipe the slate clean. No crystals. No false pretenses. Just two people who trust each other. I'm sorry for using you like that. I can't unlearn what I've already seen, but I'm here if you ever need me—big or small. Just call, and I'll do what I can."

Olia shrugged, brushing it off like it was nothing. "I already told you. The past doesn't matter."

But then her brows drew together. "Are you not going to try and enter the guild?"

Mara wasn't sure if that question came from a place of worry over broken rules or something more personal. She suspected the latter— Olia never struck her as someone who cared much for the letter of the law, only the result.

Smiling ruefully, Mara gave a slight shrug. "I don't know. I'd like to, sure. But I'm not sure they'd even consider someone like me. I was probably being too hopeful before. Would they really take a woman my age as a trainee? Or would they test me and shove me into some non-mage support role and be done with it? That's assuming they didn't just erase my memories and kick me out for daring to try."

Even as she spoke the words, she realized just how much she did want to join. The Spellswords were the only guild that actually made sense for someone like her. The Nightblades might have been a possibility, but she didn't even know how to find them, much less apply. And unlike most of the Spellsword initiates—wide-eyed kids raised from adolescence in guild doctrine—she was old, experienced, and very much not a blank slate.

Why would they waste time training her?

Olia, unsurprisingly, dismissed her worries with a wave. "I can't promise anything, but once Jaran and I get back from our assignment, I'll introduce you to Master Micah. He's one of the senior Masters and carries a lot of influence. If you impress him, he might be able to get you a proper trial—not just a screening to become Steelbound."

Seeing Mara's puzzled expression, she added, "Steelbound are what we call people who serve the guild without being full Spellswords. Staff, handlers, craftsmen, that sort of thing."

Olia gave her a determined look, full of the same fire Mara had once felt in herself. "With your age, that'd probably be your fate—even if you're good with a blade. But I'm not going to let that happen. I'll make sure you get your shot with Master Micah."

Damn. The girl just kept piling on the guilt.

Mara swallowed around the lump in her throat. "That sounds great. When will that be?"

Would it happen before the transformation took everything from her? Or after, when she wasn't even herself anymore?

Olia shrugged, all bright energy and optimism. "No idea. It's a field assignment, so we'll be gone for at least a few weeks. Could be longer. I wish I could say more, but... mission security, you know how it is."

Mara nodded, but before she could reply, Olia surprised her with a hopeful grin.

"Jaran should be here soon. We were going to eat dinner, then ride out to one of the parks and sit under the stars. Can you stay? I want you to meet him."

Mara's instincts flared like a flashing red light.

No. Absolutely not. Not because she feared being recognized—though that was certainly part of it—but because if Olia and her boyfriend were going through anything remotely rough, Mara wanted no part of it. She'd seen that triangle before, and she wasn't about to become its third point.

"Uh... sorry. I didn't expect you to be here tonight," she said, half-laughing, half-apologizing. "My driver just spotted you and let me know. I actually have a meeting, but I wanted to return your crystals while I had the chance. You two enjoy your dinner. I'm sure I'll have plenty of chances to meet your boyfriend when you get back."

Olia looked disappointed but nodded. "Alright. We've got our stones attuned, so if I don't see you again before the mission, just message me, okay?"

Mara gave her one last hug, warm but fleeting, and turned to go. Her timing was perfect—just as she stepped outside the tavern, a young man approached from across the square.

That had to be Jaran.

Even at a glance, Mara pegged him as dangerous. The way he moved was all balance and intent, the kind of grace that came from years of real combat experience. She'd seen it. She'd lived it.

Their eyes met. She offered a friendly smile and a polite nod in passing.

His expression didn't shift much, but she caught the faint narrowing of his gaze. He returned the nod without hesitation—but there was weight behind it. The unspoken kind. His hand stayed near the hilt of his Heartwood blade the whole time.

Smart boy.

Once he passed, Mara allowed herself a quiet laugh.

She couldn't wait to hear what he thought when Olia told him who he'd just missed.

The rest of the night was spent practicing each of the other basic Tier 1 spells Toman had selected for her. Just three: *Fire, Water, and Darkness.* Spells he deemed among the most useful to know immediately, especially for someone in her precarious position.

To both of their surprise, none were any more difficult to learn than *Light* had been. Even memorizing the spellforms and casting them with full concentration came easily enough. That wasn't the problem. The problem was mastery. That was where the grind began —slow, tedious, and utterly draining. Not just mentally, either. There was a deeper kind of fatigue that clung to her bones and settled into her flesh, the kind that left her aching long before the night was over.

It was subtle at first—just a heaviness in her limbs—but as the hours passed, it grew sharper. More insistent. A slow-burning strain in the parts of her body that were still alive: her shoulder, her abdomen, her eyes. Each throbbed like overused muscles forced to keep working without pause. Channeling mana was taxing for any mage, but for her, it was worse. Much worse. She barely had enough living tissue to handle the load.

Still, she pressed on.

She'd expected to collapse from the effort, but the real relief came when she checked her body scan—26%, just as she'd hoped.

A small victory but an important one.

It meant the transformation wasn't accelerating. Not really. If her theory held, the spikes in percentage were linked more to trauma and injury than to time itself. There wasn't enough data yet to be certain, but she planned to track it daily. Obsessively, if needed. She had to know what she was dealing with.

Before she left for the night, Toman officially certified her to cast all four spells—Light, Fire, Water, and Darkness—outside the heavily shielded training chambers of his home and workshop. A necessary step if she wanted to use them out in the world. Technically minor, but symbolically, it felt like something more.

Toman kept telling her she was moving at an incredible pace—well beyond what any guild apprentice could hope for. That she was learning in hours what others spent weeks or even months to master.

But it still didn't feel fast enough.

Not to her.

Not when every hour brought her closer to a future she couldn't predict. Not when her body was mutating under her own skin, and the magic she was just beginning to learn might be the only thing keeping her sane—or alive.

There wasn't time to celebrate small milestones. No room for moderation. Not when her life was on a timer with an unknown endpoint. Every spell had to be perfect. Every ounce of progress had to be earned. There could be no slacking, no letting up. Not until she could defend herself properly. Not until she knew what she was becoming.

It was maddening, in a way. She wasn't sure what terrified her more —how fast she was learning or how much further she still had to go.

But quitting wasn't an option.

She'd spent a hundred years adapting to the impossible. One more challenge wouldn't break her.

CHAPTER

TWENTY-SEVEN

A TEN-DAY GREYMANTLE week passed in that fashion.

Every night was spent in grueling repetition—learning more and more Tier 1 spells to build a broad foundation of single-glyph effects she could cast with little effort. Toman introduced three new spells each evening, but she didn't stop there. She practiced every previously learned spell as well, not just to keep them fresh but to burn the 'feel' of them into her mind, like throwing the same punch a thousand times until it became muscle memory. Only this was mental. Arcane. Deeper.

By the end of the week, Toman declared her first four spells mastered. She'd cast each of them over a hundred times, probably more. Not only did she know the glyphs by heart, she could now cast them purely by instinct.

Ironically, it was during that exhausting week that she realized the real reason she was progressing so fast. It wasn't her age. It wasn't even her century of training and focus from unlife. The secret was something far more specific—and obvious in hindsight.

It was the vampire in her.

Toman's reaction was immediate and loud. "Are you kidding me!?"

Mara threw up her hands, half amused, half annoyed. "Yeah. I know. I can't believe I didn't think of it earlier, either. But one of the lesser-known perks of being a vampire is having a near-eidetic memory. It's not glamorous, but it's the only way our long lives don't collapse under the weight of too much-forgotten detail."

She gave a dry, bitter laugh. "Think about it. You live a thousand years, and some guy you don't remember—but who sure remembers *you*—walks up and stakes you through the heart. Oops."

Shaking her head, she added, "The ability to remember even the smallest interactions is a survival trait for my kind. The real irony? I'm slowly losing all my vampiric gifts one by one—but this one, at least, is helping me prepare for what comes next."

Toman's brow furrowed. "But what about that ability? Will you lose all this work once it fades?"

She shrugged. "Maybe. But I doubt it. Repetition's doing more than short-term memorization. I'm etching these spells into my mind like muscle memory—more like the way people remember how to speak or walk, even if they forget their name."

She paused, expression serious. "It's like those amnesia stories— people can't remember who they are, but they still know math, how to cook or tie a shoe. If I lose anything, it'll be in forming *new* long-term memories, not in erasing the ones I've already made."

With a sigh, she added, "But yeah... I'll probably end up like any other mortal. Faulty memory, spotty recall, misplacing things. Just another piece of who I was... gone."

It hadn't really hit her until that moment. Among all the flashy powers she'd lost or would lose—super speed, compulsion, dark vision—this was one she was really going to miss. Quiet. Subtle. But invaluable.

So, from that night forward, she doubled her efforts.

During her rest periods, she stopped wasting time with idle thoughts and started devouring spell crystals instead—reading each pattern, absorbing each explanation, and committing as much as she could to memory while she still had the chance. Before the lights dimmed. Before her brain went back to baseline and this narrow window of perfect clarity slammed shut.

She wasn't going to waste this final gift. Not when it might be the only advantage she had left.

Late that night, Mara nudged Toman awake.

"Hey. I know the guilds are fanatical about protecting their secrets and all, but there has to be a black market where spells and guild knowledge can be bought, right?"

Toman blinked at her blearily, trying to parse the question through the haze of interrupted sleep. "Ugh... yeah, there is. But anything like that would be *incredibly* expensive. Hundreds, maybe even thousands of gold marks, depending on what you're after and how much detail you want."

He pushed himself up groggily and rubbed his eyes. "I've traded for bits and pieces before. Mostly so I can enchant items that do things I technically shouldn't be able to—like basic teleportation. That kind of spell? Off-limits unless you're a member of the Teleporters Guild. But a one-time-use emergency teleport enchantment?" He gave a tired chuckle. "That'll sell for a small fortune. And there are always people willing to pay to not die."

Now more alert, he added, "That said, I have to be *extremely* careful about selling anything like that. The Makers and the Teleporters would both want my head. Literally. They'd turn me into a cautionary tale to scare apprentices for the next five generations."

He gave her a pointed look. "Why are you asking, anyway?"

Mara gestured to the copied spell tome crystals. "Because I've got the full journeyman-level curriculum from the Spellswords, but nothing beyond that. And nothing from the other guilds. I don't need to learn 'Fire' again out of a different crystal, but if I could memorize *Teleport*, or learn higher-tier magic from the Seers Guild or someone else while my memory's still intact..." She trailed off meaningfully. "This is a once-in-a-lifetime opportunity—I just lack access."

Toman leaned forward, fingers drumming against the table as he mulled it over. "Well... I don't have much from the other guilds, aside from that one teleport spell, but I can compile what I've got into a crystal for you." He hesitated, visibly uncomfortable. "As for the rest... that black market you mentioned? It's real. But it's dangerous. Even for me."

He tapped his fingers again, this time with nervous energy. "Most people leave me alone because they figure they'll need me eventually, but what you're talking about—this kind of material— that's the rarest of the rare. Honestly? It scares me a little. The few times I've acquired that level of magic, it was only because I had a buyer lined up *and* protection. Or because the knowledge was handed to me by someone with enough pull to guarantee my safety."

Mara frowned. That wasn't what she wanted to hear. Now that the idea had taken root, she wasn't ready to let it go.

"What if I go with you?" she offered. "As protection. I act as your bodyguard."

He weighed that for a long moment, uncertainty warring with temptation. Finally, he nodded slowly.

"Yeah... actually, that might work. But there's one problem. The place we'd go is under Lord Noloris' control." His voice dropped. "Didn't you say that the assassin mentioned the boss wanted to meet with you? If you show up there and *don't* go see him..." He let the implication hang.

She'd already considered that. "What about disguises? Could you illusion me into someone else for the night? I've already done a real appearance change, and I'm not eager to speed up my transformation again with all the healing that would require."

Toman nodded, the motion growing more confident as the idea took shape. "Yeah—yes. I think we can manage that. I know a guy in the Illusionist Guild who owes me a couple favors. He's *good*, too. Better than most. His illusions don't leave the usual tells—no shimmer-blur to mana sight. He's discreet."

He leaned back, more energized now. "We'll need that kind of subtlety if we're going to visit *Deepcoin Hall*. That's the name of the auction house. It's down near the base of the mountain in the undercity, not far from Lord Noloris' palace."

He grinned, proud in that self-satisfied mage sort of way. "It's invite-only, but I've got a permanent invitation—occupational privilege. There are more than a few people in Daggerport's underbelly who wouldn't still be alive if not for the things I've made for them."

"Nice." Mara grinned as her plan began to take shape.

Toman sealed the deal with a casual aside. "You know... while we're there, it'd be the perfect opportunity to get you a Heartwood focus."

Her grin widened. "Funny you should mention that. I've spent the last few days thinking about it, and I think I've finally decided what kind of item I want."

"Oh?" The former Maker raised a curious brow. "Don't keep me in suspense—out with it."

Mara chuckled. "I want a staff. Or maybe a spear. I trained in martial arts for many years on Earth—became quite proficient with all the classic Eastern weapons. A bo staff would be a natural fit, and in my hands, it'd be pretty deadly. A spear would be even better... but that might draw too much attention."

Toman gave her a thoughtful once-over. "You know... it's rare, but possible, to make a shifting weapon. Something that could switch between a staff and a spear? That's definitely doable. Not easy, mind you—especially since weapons aren't really my specialty—but I could probably manage it."

He gave her a look. "Now, if you wanted something that could switch between a staff and a *sword*? That's pushing it. Might be beyond what I can do without weeks of prep."

Mara's eyes lit up, and for a moment, she let herself imagine it—wielding an enchanted Heartwood katana, elegant and deadly.

Knowing full well, she was poking the bear, she tilted her head innocently. "So... would a shifting weapon be limited to two forms? Or could you enchant it to shift between, say... four?"

Toman stared at her like she'd sprouted a second head. He sputtered. Actually *sputtered*. "What—? Are you *serious*? I just told you staff-to-spear would *stretch* my skills, and now you want *four* forms? What are you even thinking? You're insane!"

Mara burst out laughing, grinning wider as she saw him pale. "I notice you didn't say it was impossible. Just... difficult."

He groaned and muttered something under his breath. She caught the words, *"Ancients save me from this crazy vampire,"* which only made her laugh harder.

As much as she wanted access to more specialized magic to study and memorize, she had patience forced upon her.

Toman might have a long-standing invitation to the auction, but that didn't help until one was actually being held. Heartwood, as rare and valuable as it was, almost always made the list. But unusual spells—or better yet, guild spell tomes—were far less common. Toman warned her it could take anywhere from a week to several before something she actually wanted came up for sale.

Worse, even with a decent bit of coin—just over 2,000 gold marks—she suspected that might still be woefully inadequate. Especially if she hoped to acquire something as rare as a guild-level spell tome above journeyman rank. According to Toman, half of her money would go toward the Heartwood alone since she'd need a full staff-length piece. In other words, she'd be bidding on a relic taken from some dead wizard's cold hands. Not necessarily murdered for it, but the guild that staff once belonged to certainly wouldn't want it ending up on a black market auction block.

That left her with just over a thousand gold marks—enough for a couple uncommon spells, or maybe one rare one that fit her needs. But full guild spell tomes? Those were off the table.

So, she adapted.

Instead of spending every night locked away in Toman's shielded workshop, she began stopping by for just an hour or so—enough for a lesson—then spent the rest of her evenings riding around the city from one shady establishment to the next: dive bars, sketchy gambling dens, underground fight clubs.

In other words, she was hunting.

Not for blood, but for coins.

She wouldn't compromise her principles by preying on the innocent, so she focused on the lowlifes of the city—or the rich who liked to dabble in the darker corners of Daggerport's nightlife. If this were Earth, the job would've been easy. But here, the powerful protected their homes with wards, alarms, and magical defenses. Maybe someday, when she was a fully-trained mage, she'd be able to pull off a few juicy cat burglaries. But until then, she wasn't willing to take the risk.

For now, she hunted scumbags the old-fashioned way.

Another ten-day week passed in that pattern. Each night, she added to her growing hoard while also picking up bits and pieces of information about the Followers of the Dragon as she moved across the city. She wasn't ready to confront them yet, not without knowing more about their inner workings, but the picture was beginning to come into focus.

That meant the city's other criminals remained her primary prey. When she felt safe using compulsion—and had a solid justification —she hit her targets where it hurt: bank accounts, hidden stashes, loose purses. Now and then, she landed a decent windfall, but most nights netted her maybe twenty or thirty gold marks. By the end of the week, she'd added another 254 to her total—and uncovered even more about the cult's movements.

Unfortunately, her string of easy wins came to an end at the start of her fourth full week in the city.

That night, she crossed paths with the worst kind of filth she'd encountered so far.

Even worse than the cultists.

A slaver.

And while Mara wasn't some crusader hellbent on righting the world's wrongs... the moron made a fatal mistake.

He tried to make *her* his next victim.

CHAPTER
TWENTY-EIGHT

THE EVENING HAD STARTED like every other night that week. Mara swung by Toman's for a short training session—just enough to drill a new trio of spells into her ever-expanding arsenal—then hit the streets with Dunc, who drove her from one shady establishment to the next while she hunted for deserving targets with overstuffed coin purses and a poor grasp of morality.

It was in the second bar of the night that she spotted him.

One man in particular made her hackles rise the moment she walked through the door. Something about him tripped every internal alarm she had. He scanned each newcomer with a predator's focus—not just opportunistic like the other criminals scattered around the room, but methodical. Cold. He was hunting.

Mara had spent over a century being looked at by men—and women —but this wasn't that. He wasn't admiring her. He was evaluating her like a butcher checking the weight of a slab of meat. His eyes darted to the door after she entered as if expecting someone else to follow her. Then, to the other men in the bar, checking to see if anyone might intervene.

It was the same look she'd seen just before someone tried slipping something into her drink back on Earth. Unmistakable once you've lived through it enough times.

Normally, she might've just broken his nose and moved on with her night, but she was hunting. The creep practically had a sign around his neck that read, "Mug me, I deserve it!"

She smirked to herself and tried to look oblivious. *Might as well see what this asshole's story is.*

Sure enough, after she rebuffed a few other men and didn't seem to be meeting anyone, he stood and made his move.

The conversation was textbook—too smooth, too polished. He bought her a drink and engaged her in a fake sincere exchange, acting like he was just a lonely traveler who'd stumbled on someone interesting. He kept her laughing, asked a lot of questions that felt casual but weren't. Where was she from? Was she new to Daggerport? Did she have family in the city? Was anyone expecting her tonight?

In other words, *Would anyone come looking if she disappeared?*

She'd seen the playbook before. Bars were a great place to find blood donors when she was alive, and now they were equally suitable for finding scumbags.

When he judged her suitably isolated, he made his move—dropped something into her drink and watched her with calculated interest.

If she weren't a vampire, the whole thing might've been terrifying. Hell, it was this exact kind of situation that had gotten her killed the first time, although she had been led into that by someone she trusted. Which meant she had a special sort of loathing for guys like this.

Yeah, she thought as she feigned sipping the drugged drink, *this guy's about to have a terrible night.*

Only... her mind did start to go fuzzy.

Not enough to knock her out, but enough to worry her. Her thoughts wavered. Her eyelids fluttered. She blinked furiously, trying to will the fog away.

Son of a bitch used magic!

That was doubly despicable since the Wasting could kill or severely injure a person if you got unlucky, and this was specifically affecting the brain.

BASTARD!

It wasn't designed for someone like her—only partly alive—but it was still working. She just hoped that if she did get hit by the toxic wasting effect of magic being used directly on her brain, she would still regenerate from it, thanks to her vampire abilities. But maybe not! She now had living tissue in her brain, as well as the undead cells. Would she end up permanently brain-damaged? If so, she just hoped she could rip this piece of trash in half like a wishbone before she lost any capacity.

The blend of enchantment and drug slowed her thoughts, dulled her focus. She could fight it, but it was like wading through syrup.

Then, in her ear, Dunc's voice: "Are you okay? Do you need me to summon help?" Concern sharpened his usually sarcastic tone.

It took effort, but she realized he was communicating with her through her speech stone. She forced herself to respond carefully so as not to alert her captor. "Yesss... and nnno." She slurred the words deliberately. It was only then that she realized they were outside and moving down the street.

She almost changed her mind, but her only real ally was Toman, and he wasn't a combat mage.

Stumbling, she realized just how muddled her brain was. Toman wasn't her only option. Olia was her friend, and if anyone could bring vengeance, it would be her. She hesitated. She had already used the girl in more ways than one. She didn't want to burden the young Spellsword.

Mara fuzzily thought to herself, *I'll call her if it looks like they'll do anything to take away my magic items or make me unconscious.*

Besides, she wanted to deal with this herself.

The creep smiled like a spider welcoming prey. He was buying her act completely.

She shook her head violently, trying to clear it more. *Well, not entirely an act....*

He half-carried her across a few city blocks, down increasingly narrow side streets. She let her body go limp, carefully resisting enough to pass as drugged but not helpless. Finally, he led her into an alley so narrow it might as well have been a crack in the stone.

At the end of the passage was a plain section of wall—at least, it looked plain until he waved a hand, and the illusion dropped.

Behind it was a heavy wooden door reinforced with iron bands. Solid. Secure. Secret.

Sex dungeon? Her woozy thoughts offered.

But the answer came when a massive guard opened the door from the inside. He carried a shockrod and eyed her with professional disinterest.

"Strong will on this one," the man said with a chuckle. "Usually, they're half-comatose by now. This one still looks like she's got some fight left."

Mara didn't need her full faculties to know the truth.

This wasn't just some predator. This was organized. Efficient. Routine.

Slavers. Real ones.

And they had no idea what kind of monster they were trying to cage.

Her captor snorted, "Don't matter, none. She can't fight back. Barely conscious. Let's get her downstairs and processed. We only need a few more, and we'll be ready to ship 'em out."

Mara wanted to growl and tear out his throat—his and the guard's both. But the magic clouding her mind wasn't just numbing her thoughts—it was blocking her connection to her vampiric abilities. Apparently, having some parts of her brain as living tissue was bad enough to hinder her vampire parts. And that was one hell of an inconvenient discovery.

They shoved her through the door and down a long flight of stone steps. Around a few corners, deeper underground, then through a narrow corridor. She made sure to memorize the path, step by step, with the portion of her mind still functioning.

Eventually, they reached a four-way intersection in what was clearly part of the 'undercity.' Beyond it, two side halls branched left and right, where she could hear people talking and laughing. Beyond was a section of tunnel lined with four heavy doors per side. Each door had a barred viewing slit—iron prison doors by any other name. She had come to the cells where they kept their prisoners.

She couldn't see inside, but she could hear them. Quiet voices. Soft weeping. Adult men and women. Even a few children.

At the end of the corridor stood a reinforced door made entirely of iron. A peephole snapped open as they approached, and a guard on the other side scrutinized Mara as if checking the quality of livestock.

The door swung inward, revealing a mage with a broad, satisfied grin. "You brought us a good one, Derwin. We'll get her settled and have your pay in a moment. Just wait out there—shouldn't take long. All we need is to apply the bracelet and make a quick check for magic items."

Derwin's smooth tone vanished the moment he opened his mouth. "Morvek, you'd better pay me in full for everything this time! You only counted five items last time, and I *know* that woman had at least three rings and some other stuff!"

The mage, apparently named Morvek, looked irritated. "One of her rings was decorative. That doesn't count. Neither does a bank token or data crystals, and you know it." Then, a wicked smile curled across his face. "If you're that desperate for accessories, maybe start stripping them yourself before you bring 'em in. What you do in your own time is none of my business."

He let out a low, cruel laugh as Derwin's face flushed with humiliation. "You know I can't do that; some folks have trapped items."

Taking a deep breath to try and regain his calm, he added, "Listen, Morvek, if you're not gonna deal straight with me, I'll stop bringing you quality. Look at this one—she's *still* half-conscious, even after a full dose. That kind of fire brings top dollar."

Morvek didn't seem to care whether Derwin was angry or not, but he gave a begrudging nod. "Yeah, this is a good one. You did well tonight. I'll ensure you receive full payment for everything, so don't worry. Keep this up, and I might even introduce you to some folks who could help you out."

Derwin paled. "No, no! It's fine. I trust you. I'm good at doing what I do. I don't begrudge the tax."

That reaction was... odd. Then she heard him mutter under his breath, "Getting pulled deeper into the Shadow Guild is not my idea of fun."

Mara filed that away, even as she struggled to focus her thoughts and wrest back control over her body. One thing was certain—after this, she was getting Toman to make her something that shielded her mind from magical influence.

Morvek grabbed her roughly and dragged her through the iron door, slamming it shut behind them. It locked with a solid *thunk* that echoed through the stone.

Inside, the room looked like a cross between a dungeon torture chamber and a mad scientist's lab—only, in this case, a mad *mage*. A reinforced metal table sat against one wall, complete with thick iron restraints at the wrists, ankles, and neck. Above it, suspended by an arcane scaffold, was a device that radiated menace. Enchanted crystal nodes gleamed faintly in the gloom, and the threads of mana connecting them pulsed with a faint red light.

Morvek chuckled to himself as he half-carried, half-dragged her toward it.

From the moment she'd first felt the drugged magic dulling her thoughts, Mara had remained oddly calm. Now, it struck her as unnatural. Anyone else in her situation would be thrashing in terror or sobbing in fear. But not her. She *felt* afraid—knew it intellectually—but that emotion wasn't surfacing. Wasn't reaching her core.

Some of it could be chalked up to her experience—she'd faced death before, many times—but this level of internal chill felt artificial. It had to be another layer of the magic. Designed not just to sedate but to pacify. To make captives docile and compliant rather than eliciting a fight-or-flight response.

Most of their victims were probably unconscious by this point in the process, so whatever calm bled through to her must have been what leaked past the spell's influence—limited to what the vampire part of her still resisted.

Still, she knew one thing with absolute certainty: if they got her onto that table and used that device on her, it was over. Game over. No reset. No second chances.

They *had* to have a way of forcing obedience—and whatever hung above that table was the method.

Morvek's smug confidence and the cruel twist of his grin told her everything she needed to know—she *could not* let this happen.

In the precious seconds before she was dragged to her doom, she tried *everything*. Her thoughts were too foggy to summon fire and turn this stain of a man into ash. The same spell that dulled her mind clearly blocked access to her vampiric powers. She couldn't exert her will to bring him under compulsion. Couldn't even muster enough control over her body to tap into strength or speed.

That alone was terrifying—but what truly made her panic was the realization that, for the first time in over a hundred years, she had *no agency*. No means of resistance. Even her speech stones refused to activate when she tried, in desperation, to reach Olia, Toman, or Dunc.

She had relied too long on her vampiric nature. She hadn't been able to conceive of a way some mortal like Derwin could stand against her if she chose to exert her power. She could have asked for help then but had been arrogant in her sense of her own invincibility.

Morvek chuckled at her effort, clearly enjoying her helplessness. "I'm afraid you'll find that quite impossible. This room generates a localized null-magic field targeted specifically at 'guests' like yourself. Ingenious, really. Took me weeks to perfect, but worth it— for rare cases when someone like you isn't fully suppressed by the potion. You must've faked the drink, or you have a remarkable constitution. Either way, I'm impressed."

The gleam in his eyes betrayed the twisted soul behind the mask as he added, "Of course, it won't help you now. Let's get you on the table, shall we? Get the bracelet on, and then... we can have a nice, long *chat*."

Even through the drug-induced haze, she knew that "chat" would be anything but pleasant.

With what little clarity remained, she raged inwardly, promising herself that she *would* get free. She *would* end this piece of filth—and not quickly.

She was shoved onto the table, one iron restraint at a time, locking her limbs in place. Each sharp *click* rang in her ears like a funeral bell. Not even her vampiric strength, if she had access to it, would tear these free.

"There we go," Morvek said, rubbing his hands together. "Take your last breaths of freedom. After this, you'll belong to me... and then to whoever buys you next." He chuckled at his own joke. "Oh, but I suppose you're *already* not so free, are you?"

Above her, the magical rig creaked to life. The ray projecting the null-magic field shifted aside but still aimed at her head, and a second articulated arm lowered toward her right wrist.

Morvek beamed, practically vibrating with sadistic pleasure. "You know, most are unconscious by now. But when they're *awake* like you... oh, it's *so* much more satisfying. Watching the realization settle in. Feeling your dread... exquisite."

His eyes half-closed in rapture.

"I think I'm really going to savor our little *conversation* once you're nice and obedient."

She managed to turn her head, blinking away the haze just enough to see the gleam of a copper bracelet dangling from the descending mechanism. It was ugly, thick, and studded with three cheap gemstones.

Yet even dulled, she *felt* the dread what it would mean.

If she could move, she would gut Morvek and tear this place apart before that thing touched her. But she couldn't.

The bracelet opened with a quiet hiss and clamped around her wrist. It fused completely, leaving no seam. It was tight enough that not even dislocating her hand would allow escape. Even if she had her full strength, she'd rip her own arm off before it would come loose.

Then, the magic suppressor disengaged—just as the bracelet flared to life.

Agony tore through her nerves, like lightning racing through both her vampiric tissue and the living parts she so hated to acknowledge. Her body arched. She gasped as her mind cleared *violently*, forcing her consciousness back into full, painful awareness.

She thrashed—but the restraints held.

"Oh, *yes*," Morvek said, practically purring. "I *love* this part."

He leaned in close, his voice almost tender.

"Now, my dear, before you go trying anything stupid... know this: the band won't let you hurt yourself or others. It detects magic use and hostile intent. If you try anything you know to be against the rules your master gives you... well, when it does? It triggers your pain receptors. In waves. Stronger. And stronger. Until you're nothing but a twitching mess."

His smile was as vicious as the spell carved into her nerves.

And Mara, despite everything in her, felt fear. Fear that for once, she might be in real trouble.

If *that* was all it did, Mara could work around it. She could take pain. Hell, she'd endured worse for less. If stabbing a knife into Morvek's smug face meant enduring a full-body firestorm, she was willing. Her vampiric speed might let her move before the punishment kicked in. Her supernatural toughness might let her push through the backlash. She just had to get off this cursed table and try.

As if reading her thoughts, Morvek dashed her hopes. "We'll wipe your memories shortly. Make you far more obedient, pliant. But before that..." He grinned. "I want a few minutes with the *real* you. There's something delicious about watching that moment when someone realizes their old life is over."

He was savoring it. Dragging it out like a man enjoying fine wine.

"Now, I'm going to release your arms and legs. Know that you *will* be punished if you move too quickly or aggressively."

A few seconds later, her limbs clicked free.

Mara rose slowly, shaking out her arms as if stiff. What she was really doing was testing her limits—pushing the speed of her movements bit by bit to see where the bracelet kicked in.

She didn't have to wonder long.

At a brisk stretch, the pain hit level seven. A hair faster, and it ramped *instantly* to a searing spike that nearly dropped her. She staggered, barely managing to get her feet under her before collapsing again.

"Clever girl," Morvek laughed. "But as you can see, you'll never be fast enough to hurt anyone. Not before your muscles lock."

Now that her mind was clear, her rage surged to the forefront. She was furious—violently so—that some self-important *mortal* had managed to cage her like this. Her thoughts raced, clawing through options.

She tried her speech stone again.

Blinding agony exploded behind her eyes. She dropped to her knees, clutching her skull.

Okay. Nope. That's worse than I thought. Even my vampiric toughness can't brute-force that.

"Now stand," Morvek commanded. "Move to the other table. Let's get those memories scrubbed, but we'll have a little fun before that... once you are locked down again."

She rose on unsteady legs. Her eyes flicked around the room, scanning for *anything* she could use. A blade, a pipe, even a rock. If she could knock his head off—even if she blacked out doing it— maybe she'd recover fast enough to escape before reinforcements arrived.

The only object in sight was a large cleaver resting on a nearby desk. Some kind of torture implement? Didn't matter. It was too far.

Morvek saw where her gaze went and chuckled. "Stop."

She froze. Not because he said so—but because she couldn't afford another dose of the bracelet's pain yet. But she didn't speak. She would *not* give him the satisfaction.

To her surprise, he walked over, grabbed the cleaver, and approached. Then—grinning—he held it out hilt-first.

"Here. Take it," he said. "They always want to try."

Mara stared at him, not moving. But she reached out and accepted the blade. It was heavy. Solid. If she had her full strength, she could take his head off in one swing.

She *tried.*

She really did.

But pain lanced through her arm before she could even raise it to shoulder height. Her knees buckled. Her mind went white again. Somehow, she didn't drop the blade—her hand seized up from the feedback. She couldn't move her fingers, couldn't even *throw* the damn thing.

Morvek laughed, delighted. "Predictable. You *all* try, eventually."

She lay there panting, fury boiling beneath the surface. She'd never be fast enough. Never strong enough—not while that bracelet was active. And if he wiped her memories...

Horror and dread raced down her spine at that thought.

No! I will not let him win! I don't care if I am a vampire or nothing more than mortal; I'll never give in!

She ran through a hundred plans in half a second. None of them would work except maybe one.

And it would cost her. Dearly.

CHAPTER
TWENTY-NINE

GRINDING HER TEETH, she looked up at him and said, voice cold, "I'd rather kill myself than have my memories erased."

She lifted the cleaver—slowly—toward her throat. Not fast. Not aggressive. Calm. Controlled.

Maybe, just maybe, if she could fool the bracelet into thinking this was no different than brushing her hair...

It let her arm rise.

Right up until Morvek hissed, "Stop! You may not raise your arm any further! If you even *think* about killing yourself again, the bracelet will hit you so hard you'll wake up lying in your own piss and vomit! Do you understand?"

She kept the triumph off her face.

It worked.

As long as she didn't *think* about disobedience—as long as she believed she was following orders—she could act.

"Please don't command me to put the blade down!" she begged, layering her voice with trembling fear she didn't have to take.

Morvek sneered, smug and oblivious, sealing his own fate with his spiteful order. "Put the cleaver down. *Now.*"

She grinned, and in the half-second it took for his expression to shift —just long enough for him to register the mistake—she moved.

He gave me permission.

She dumped every ounce of focus she'd cultivated over a hundred years into *not thinking*. She wasn't rebelling. Wasn't fighting back.

She was *obeying*.

She was simply putting the cleaver down—*straight down*—as fast as she could.

Through her own forearm.

A mortal woman wouldn't have had the strength or speed. But Mara wasn't mortal. And Morvek had given her *permission*.

The bracelet and her severed hand had barely begun to fall, even as her left arm whipped around in a backhand meant to obliterate the slaver's face.

An automatic magic shield sprang up between them. It deflected her blow and sent the cleaver clattering off into a far wall with a ringing clang.

She snarled.

Morvek staggered back, eyes wide, just opening his mouth to scream or cast or both.

She never gave him the chance.

Her eyes narrowed. *Fine. You want a spell duel? Let's see who's faster.*

She forced mana threads, shoving them through the casting pattern for Fire at a pace only a vampire could manage. His casting was still halfway formed, threads of magic trickling like honey across a frozen surface.

Too slow, bastard.

Her spell burst to life.

The shield was still active, so she aimed for just behind him.

Flame detonated.

Scorching heat slammed into the chamber, hot enough to throw her backward. Ironically, Morvek's own shield blocked most of the blast from reaching *her*.

He wasn't so lucky.

He didn't die. But the entire back of his body blistered, blackened, and melted into a mass of charred flesh. There would be no casting now. No commands. No coherent thoughts.

Gritting her teeth, Mara hissed as she clutched her right arm. Blood poured freely from her stump. She pulled a belt from her storage and cinched it tight just above the elbow, twisting the end into a crude tourniquet.

Then she stalked toward the twitching mage.

She grabbed Morvek by the collar with her left hand and hauled him up off the floor. He screamed, or maybe gurgled. She didn't care.

The living tissue in her shoulder and bicep ached from the exertion —but pain was an old companion. A minor one compared to what the bracelet had done, or to her right arm.

Seconds later, she slammed him down onto the table he'd used on her.

Iron restraints locked into place with satisfying clicks.

He was barely conscious. Couldn't even cry out properly. Part of her wished he *was* lucid—awake enough to experience the same fear and despair he'd inflicted on so many others.

You deserve worse, she thought, but she'd settle for this.

She turned her attention to the device.

Fortunately for her, magic was *so much easier* than tech. No complicated programming, no multi-step activation. Just a guiding rune and a mana thread.

She fed a whisper of power into it.

The null-magic arm repositioned, angling downward over Morvek's chest.

Suddenly, the slaver was cut off from magic—completely.

Smiling grimly—or maybe it was a grimace—she called her driver. "Dunc, did you follow me?"

"Lady! You're alright! I got as close as I could, but I couldn't bring my vehicle any closer on those streets. I know where you went underground, though. I've got an item that lets me home in on your speech stone since we're attuned. Do you need help?"

Sneaky boy, she thought. "Yes, I'm going to need a healer. Soon. But you can't get to me, and I'm going to call in my Spellsword friend if she's available."

"I'll fetch a healer, whichever's closest."

The pain in her arm was distracting, but not so much that she couldn't anticipate the complications that would bring. So she replied quickly, "No! Don't do that, Dunc. I'll need to take me to see the masters at the Guild. They're the only ones who can treat my condition. I'll be fine for now. I can survive plenty long enough for the Spellswords to get here and wrap this up."

"If you're sure, lady?"

"I am."

She cut the connection and dashed over to scoop up her severed hand and send it into her storage. Items placed inside her ring weren't affected by time. She knew the healers in this world could regrow a hand, but if she could preserve her *undead* one, maybe—just maybe —she could avoid having the whole thing turn into living tissue.

The urge to spit on her unconscious captor was strong. Saving herself had definitely come at a cost. *How much would this accelerate her transformation?*

Shrugging off the thought, she activated her Speech Stone again. "Olia, I'm not disturbing you, am I?"

It was a surprised young Spellsword who answered. "No, Jaran and I were just finishing dinner. What's up?"

That complicated things, but probably for the best. She didn't want to put her friend in danger—and having her boyfriend as backup was a smart play.

"I'm sorry to ask, but I could use a little help if you don't mind. I hate to impose, but this is kinda big."

Concern echoed in Olia's voice now. "Is everything alright? You sound funny."

"Actually, no. I don't think I am. I got captured by slavers operating out of the undercity. I'm locked into a room with their mage who... well, that's not important. The point is, I don't know how many of them are down here, and there are a *lot* of captives. I'd estimate almost three dozen."

"Dragon's scaly balls, Mara! Seriously?"

Mara might've laughed if the situation weren't so grim. She could just picture the hot-headed Spellsword leaping to her feet and cursing loudly in the middle of a restaurant. She could even hear the girl relaying everything to her boyfriend, although that was done much more quietly.

"Yes, and I'm afraid I'm not kidding. No idea how many slavers or other Shadow Guild types are in the tunnels here. I'm safe for the moment, though. This room's designed to repel intruders, and the mage who chained me is about to suffer the same fate he tried to put me under."

She added under her breath, "*If he lives that long.*"

Olia's tone grew firm. "Good. That's great. Listen, we need to know exactly where you are. Slavers fall under the Spellsword mandate through our contract with the city. It won't take long to reach you, but we need coordinates."

"I was at the Golden Finch when I was drugged. My driver will meet you there and escort you to the entrance. It's in an alley, hidden by an illusion. His name is Dunc."

She went on to describe the precise path she'd taken underground. Despite the haze from the potion, the vampiric parts of her brain had recorded every turn and twist of the route.

"Fifteen minutes. Can you hold out until then?" Olia asked anxiously.

"Hah, are you kidding? There might not be *any* slavers left by then! I might not leave any for you to have fun with!"

Olia's voice turned stern. "*Wait* until you get reinforcements! I'm all for a glorious death, but a *stupid* one is unworthy!"

Mara chuckled, warmth blooming in her chest. It was good to have someone who cared. "Alright, I'll try. This slaver might not survive his injuries that long, but I'm sure there will be others left to question."

It sounded like Olia was running now. "We're on our way. Hold out."

She cut the connection, then quickly relayed the plan to Dunc, who confirmed that he'd meet them at the pub.

With that out of the way and Morvek no longer a threat, she used her mana-sight to locate his magic items and remove them one by one.

They could be dangerous, but Toman had taught her a thing or two about how security enchantments worked, so she was careful and didn't try to access them, only dropped them into her storage.

She finally had a moment to relax—at least as much as someone missing a hand and dealing with blinding pain could. No one was pounding on the door, so it was likely the cleaver blasting into the wall at half the speed of a bullet hadn't raised an alarm.

Spotting the bracelet on the floor, she grinned.

It was surprisingly easy to operate Morvek's disgusting invention. She just put the bracelet in place and added a single thread of mana, and the device moved on its own, inexorably descending toward the slaver's wrist.

With a deep sense of schadenfreude, she watched the enchanted bracelet seal itself to its creator.

Perhaps due to the artifact's magic, his eyes snapped open with sudden lucidity.

Mara smirked. "I'm surprised to see you conscious, considering your wounds. I hope you enjoy your fate. Now, for orders..."

She wove compulsion into his mind in conjunction with the magic of the bracelet, reinforcing the effect until there was no room for cleverness or escape.

"You will be a perfectly obedient servant who would never dream of disappointing your master—me. You will do nothing to escape or warn others. You will obey me without hesitation and follow not just the letter of my commands but their spirit. In every way, you will act to please me to the best of your ability."

With both the enchantment and her vampiric will pressing into him, she could feel the commands sink deep into his psyche.

"If you are capable, move to the other device and strap yourself in—but do not activate it."

He immediately began straining against the iron bands of the table he was already lying on.

"Wait until I remove the restraints," she added quickly.

She shook her head. She'd given him the best commands she could think of and was confident he wouldn't try anything. But now he was *too* compliant—lacking even common sense.

Subjecting anyone to this level of control disgusted her, but under the circumstances, she couldn't afford to be gentle with the bastard's mind. Not until she was safe. After that, she could loosen the grip.

Mara watched as the slaver painfully moved to the other table and began strapping himself in, all but one hand. When she clamped the final iron band in place herself, she let out a sigh of relief.

With him contained, she searched the room for anything useful or interesting. Several minutes later, she facepalmed. *Silly, Mara. The most interesting things will probably be on his data crystal. Or in his rings.*

Shaking her head, she walked back over to Morvek and pulled out the magic items. "Unlock them and give me full access. Also, transfer all of your money to me."

When he had complied, she asked, "Is there anything else of value in this room besides your evil enchanted items? What about in this base?"

Eager to please and avoid pain, he responded immediately, "Yes. There's a lockbox in the guard room that contains all the items taken from captives. We give them to the Shadow Guild as their cut for this operation. There are also the slaves, we sell them in Valentros and the Bane Nation."

"Bane nation? Who are the Bane?" She already knew about Valentros.

"Evil elves... Bane Elves."

He looked like he wanted to say more, but she silenced him with a hand. Her only hand.

Just then, Dunc messaged her that the Spellswords had arrived and would be at her location in five minutes.

That was good news. But it also meant she had very little time left to accomplish one more thing.

She checked her tourniquet to ensure it was still holding, then moved to the door. A quick peek through the sliding window revealed Derwin still posted outside, with no other guards in sight.

A grin of vengeance spread across her face.

It wasn't easy doing everything one-handed, but she managed to unlock the door, and then, with a burst of vampiric speed, she yanked the slimy trafficker into the room before he could react. She gently—*for a vampire*—tapped her forehead to his, and his eyes rolled back as he collapsed to the floor.

Unfortunately, she had forgotten that her face had been replaced with human tissue due to earlier injuries so that ended up hurting far more than it should have.

Grumbling, but with a casual motion, she closed the door again and let the lock click quietly into place.

No longer in a rush, she carried the trash that had tried to sell her into slavery over to the table that stole people's freedom.

He was unconscious, so she didn't even bother to lock him down. She simply pulled another bracelet from Morvek's storage ring and attached it to the device.

As she did, she muttered the old joke that had once been all the rage in the early internet days: *What I would do if I were a supervillain—Rule number 1: Do not monologue!*

Taking that advice to heart, she quietly fed a thread of mana into the arm with the bracelet. It descended without fanfare.

And just like that, Derwin was sporting a new piece of jewelry.

She slapped him awake and gave her orders to make him eager to comply, then added, "Transfer all your wealth to me. Unlock any items that have security spells."

While she'd been dragging Derwin in and fitting him with his new slave restraint, a thought had occurred to her.

"Now, tell me. Do you own any other property or valuables?"

He proceeded to spill everything—and then repeated the question with Morvek.

All in all, it was a profitable evening... even if it had quite literally cost her a hand.

Just as she was finishing her questioning, she heard screams outside the door.

The cavalry had arrived.

CHAPTER
THIRTY

WHEN SHE OPENED THE DOOR, Mara was surprised to see not just Olia and Jaran but an entire strike team of Spellswords.

She had planned to come out before the party was over and maybe participate a little, but less than a minute after the screaming started, it was already done. Bodies and prisoners lined the ten-foot-wide main tunnel all the way to the central four-way branch.

That warmed Mara's heart. But what made her feel even better was seeing the Spellswords throwing open the doors to the cells where the captives were stored.

However, that raised a concern.

Calling out urgently, she tried to stop them before they made a critical mistake. "Wait! Olia, make them stop!"

An older man stepped forward—still in his prime, though clearly nearing his middle years. His sharp eyes took in her missing hand, and concern softened his stern expression into something gentler.

"You must be Mara, Journeywoman Olia's friend. I'm Master Micah. We'll get our Healer to you right away."

Mara waved her good hand dismissively, pressing forward with what she'd figured out while waiting for them to arrive. "I'll live, for now. But you need to stop your people before you hurt the prisoners. The captives are all wearing obedience bracelets. They punish any thought of disobedience to the slavers. If you try to remove the bracelets, it'll cause terrible pain. If someone is too weak... it could kill them."

Micah's eyes narrowed in anger at that, and he reacted instantly. He tapped a device at his ear and barked in a voice that brooked no hesitation, "Halt!"

When he saw his team freeze, he relayed Mara's warning. The Spellswords immediately ceased all attempts to move the prisoners.

"There's a device in the room behind me that can safely remove the bracelets," Mara added. "It's easy to use. I'll show you. Just bring one of the prisoners."

In the moment—driven by urgency and concern for the victims—it didn't even register that she was issuing directions to one of the most powerful figures in one of the planet's top guilds. But to Mara, this was a combat op now, and her old instincts took over. She had led too many strike teams of her own not to speak to Micah like an equal.

He looked briefly surprised but then nodded, decisive and professional. Turning to one of his subordinates, he said, "You heard her. Bring one of the prisoners. Start cycling them through as we determine how long each removal takes."

Just then, Olia jogged out of one of the cells and made her way over. She clearly wanted to rush to Mara, but instead, she stood at attention beside her commander.

"Sir, I count thirty-three victims. Not including Mara."

Micah nodded gravely. "Thank you, Journeywoman. Assist your friend for now—she's injured but wishes to stay on duty until the captives are seen to."

That was when Olia saw her missing hand. Her breath caught. "Mara...!"

But she calmed herself almost immediately and stepped into place beside her.

"I'll help," Olia said. "Just show us how to use the device, and you can let others do the rest."

Mara patted her on the shoulder. "Thank you. It hurts, yeah, but I've had worse. Let's get this started. I'll go to the Healers after."

That raised a few eyebrows among the nearby Spellswords. Olia muttered under her breath, "She's had worse, she says..."

A few seconds later, Mara removed Derwin from the machine and—because it was petty and satisfying—ordered him to stand in the corner with his nose to the wall.

She introduced both Morvek and Derwin to Master Micah and briefly explained their roles in her capture and condition. She finished with: "When this is over, I don't care if they live or die. But they can *never* be allowed to go free again. They've destroyed too many lives."

Micah raised his chin in acknowledgment. "My guild will ensure there is justice."

"Thank you. Now, let's get those prisoners freed."

The first one in was a girl—maybe sixteen at most. She had the blank expression of someone who no longer cared whether she lived or died. She didn't even register that she was being rescued.

It hit Mara hard, but she kept her voice gentle as she and Olia helped the girl onto the table. They didn't strap her in. Just kept reassuring hands on her shoulders to make sure the device didn't harm her.

In less than thirty seconds, the cursed artifact was gone from her arm.

But the girl gave no reaction. Not even a flicker of recognition. She rose when prompted, moving as if by rote.

One of the female Spellswords gently guided her back down the tunnel to a waiting area where the slavers had been housed.

Micah's expression was grim as he said, "We'll get all of them to the Healers Guild. They have specialists who focus on the mind."

That sparked a dark thought in Mara, and she cleared the lump in her throat. She pointed with her nub of an arm toward the other device on the far side of the room. "That one removes memories. I don't know how effective the mind Healers are, but maybe they should take that device—just in case." She gazed at the back of the girl being led away and added, "If it were me, and I was that girl, I might want to forget it all and have a new start."

Beside her, Olia shuddered and then nodded, "Let me call the Healer now. I don't care how tough you are—that ought to be treated right away."

Mara sighed. She didn't want to reveal anything about herself in front of these people, so she absolutely couldn't let just *any* Healer near her—especially not one assigned to the Spellswords. That would be a disaster.

"No, wait. I can only be treated by Master Healers Onaris, Dena, or Margra Athne. I have a condition they're aware of. Any other healer could do me more harm than good."

Micah raised an eyebrow, not just at her refusal but at the fact she'd casually name dropped three of the Healers Guild's most powerful leaders. Still, he didn't question her. Instead, he turned and ordered Olia:

"Collect Journeyman Jaran, and the two of you escort the hero who saved all these people and exposed a den of slavers in our city."

He turned his attention back to Mara and smiled kindly. "Your friend and I have an assignment that'll keep us away for a few weeks, but when we return, I would very much like you to be my guest at the Citadel. We'll honor you properly for what you did here tonight. You may consider yourself owed a Minor Boon from the Guild. I'll have it recorded before the sun sets tomorrow. But for now... know that I am very impressed."

He gave her a sharp, formal salute with his beautiful Heartwood spear. It was a precise, military gesture, and she got the distinct impression it wasn't something the Guild offered lightly—especially not to outsiders.

A moment later, all of the Spellswords in the room echoed the motion, saluting with their own weapons.

She was touched. But still wary. So long as she remained in this hybrid state of limbo—neither fully vampire nor truly human—she couldn't afford to form ties with people like these. It was sad, though. She really did like the camaraderie she saw among the Spellswords. Not to mention the fact that they had crossed half the city in a matter of minutes to eradicate this stain on the city. That spoke well of their moral compass.

Maybe... she thought, but let the idea drift away as she allowed herself to be led toward the surface.

At the alley door, Jaran and another Spellsword stood guard. They both saluted the moment she appeared.

She wasn't embarrassed exactly, but it definitely didn't make her comfortable to be getting this kind of attention. Not for someone who'd spent a century living in shadows.

Stepping into the darkness outside, she was relieved to see that it was still three or four hours until sunrise—maybe more. The whole ordeal had *felt* like it took forever, but in reality, only two or three hours had passed since she had been drugged.

As they left the alley and made it back onto a street where they could actually walk, Jaran fell into step on her opposite side from Olia.

She didn't comment, but Olia spoke up. "Mara, meet Jaran. Jaran, meet Mara—an old friend from my days before the Guild."

He spoke to his girlfriend first. "Your friend is very impressive for someone with no formal training." Then to Mara: "It's an honor to meet you, friend of my Olia. I heard you chopped your own hand off to escape a magical binding?"

Jaran shook his head in stunned admiration. "That must have been incredibly difficult."

Damn, they had figured it out fast, and the word had even spread to Spellswords not in the room. Mara didn't want to talk at all— especially not about *that*. "Believe me, it was. Took everything I had not to think about what I was doing, just to keep the device from reacting and stopping me. That was the hardest part." Her voice turned stoney for a beat. "I'd willingly cut off both hands and feet before I'd let them erase who I am and turn me into some slaver's toy."

Jaran nodded in understanding. Up the block, he waved to Dunc, who was standing with another Spellsword guard. There was a Transporter mage behind him with her own vehicle as well.

Dunc jumped up the moment he spotted her and was already offering to help Mara into the passenger seat before she'd taken three steps. "I was so worried! I'm very relieved that you are alright, Lady!"

Seeing how things were playing out, Jaran stepped back and motioned for Olia to ride with her. "I'll follow in the other cart and watch your rear."

In as much pain as she was, she almost snickered at his phrasing. *Watch their rears.* A small, very ungrimace-like smile broke out across her face.

"Dunc, take us to the Healers Guild, please. As quickly as allowed."

His eyes went wide as he took in her missing hand. The blood drained from his face.

"Right... right away!" he stammered, then gave the other driver a challenging look as if daring her to keep up.

The drive was a blur, and Olia—bless her—was mercifully quiet. She didn't pepper Mara with questions or nervous chatter; just sat beside her, a steadying presence.

In short order, they were through the gates of the Healers Guild compound. Onaris stood waiting at the entrance to the usual building, arms crossed and shaking his head.

"Again? You're starting to make a habit of this."

Mara shot him a pointed look, then subtly gestured back toward her Spellsword escort.

The Master Healer cleared his throat, shifted to a more professional tone, and addressed them. "I'm sorry, but you'll have to wait outside. Once treatment is complete, perhaps you can see the patient."

Half an hour later—after a good deal of focus and effort on Onaris' part—her hand was back. Unfortunately, the reconstruction wasn't without complications. About an inch and a half on either side of the severed wrist had converted from vampiric tissue into living flesh.

Onaris frowned, studying the result. "I swear, even with your... unique condition, this is madness. The living tissue is behaving like an infection—spreading at every opportunity."

He sobered further, meeting her gaze. "I'm afraid you're up to thirty-three percent."

Grim news. It would enhance her magic, yes, but she was approaching the tipping point. Her vampiric abilities had already started glitching, though not often enough yet to be a significant concern. Still, at this rate, it wouldn't be long before they became unreliable altogether.

She grunted in frustration. "Thanks, Master Onaris. By the way... would it be possible to attune my speech stone to yours? If I ever need emergency treatment, it'll almost certainly be at night—and you might not always be on call."

He chuckled. "Certainly. Your case is... well, let's say I find it fascinating." He caught himself and added, with a touch of embarrassment, "Sorry, I get a little carried away when I'm learning something new. But don't worry—I live here at the compound. I'm not technically on night shift, but I am a night owl, so they often wake me for the difficult cases."

"Well, thank you. It's not lost on me what an honor it is to be treated by one of the best Healers in the world every time something bad happens."

He waved off the compliment. "Nonsense. This is what Healers do."

Still, Mara suspected even the wealthiest nobles wouldn't get this level of personal care—or had earned a major favor.

Once she was discharged and had tipped the apprentice at the gate, they rode back to the Dragon Inn. As they dismounted in front of the dragon's maw, Jaran raised a brow and gave her a sidelong look.

"You must be wealthy if you're staying here. This place isn't cheap."

Mara chuckled, shaking her head. "Not really. I've just been lucky lately—like tonight. Those two scumbags were very generous in their shame over what they'd done. That, and the owner is letting me stay here for free—for now."

From Jaran's reaction, she realized she may have said too much.

"Zakkarius IronEater is letting you stay here for free?" He started ticking off fingers. "And you get private treatment from three of the most powerful Healers in the world. And you just happen to foil a slaver ring—just like that. And you grew up on the streets with Olia?"

His expression was amazed. "Who are you?"

Damn. This guy was too sharp. No wonder Olia was infatuated with him.

She gave a rueful smile and offered an honest—if unhelpful—answer. "Well... not really *with* Olia. But yeah, all of *this* started a few weeks ago. One night, I got jumped by some cult members—Followers of the Dragon." She stopped and yawned. "And, I think that's a tale for another night."

Both Olia and Jaran looked impatient to hear every last detail. But they weren't going to get lucky tonight.

"I'll tell you all about it—at least the parts I'm comfortable sharing. But that'll have to wait until you get back from your mission. Right now, I need to lie low and catch up on about a week's worth of sleep."

It wasn't a lie. The living parts of her body ached with deep fatigue, even after Onaris' healing.

Olia looked like she might protest, but Jaran stepped in. "We should head back, too. The City Watch will have taken over by now, and they'll probably want our statements."

Mara fought to keep her worry off her face. If the guards made the connection between Mara the vampire and Mara the heroine, things could get complicated fast. She doubted they'd arrest her outright— Zak wouldn't allow it—but the scrutiny could blow her cover, and those secrets could put her carefully guarded life in jeopardy.

Olia finally let her guild professionalism drop and pulled Mara into a fierce hug, which Mara returned. After that, they said their goodbyes, and Mara stepped inside the inn. Zak was at the bar, but she didn't approach him. She was beyond spent, and talking to him now would open a whole new can of worms.

She chuckled to herself, bone-tired. *Besides... may be best not to clear up his misconceptions right before the City Watch might come sniffing around.*

Sanctuary mattered more than curiosity tonight.

Tomorrow, I'll see what I managed to get out of those two slavers for my troubles.

CHAPTER
THIRTY-ONE

TOMAN WAS incredulous as Mara tossed Morvek and Derwin's storage items onto the workbench and launched into a rundown of the previous night's events.

He gave her a sympathetic look when she mentioned that her transformation had now overtaken a full third of her body. "I'm so sorry. It's insane what you've been through in just the short time you've been here."

She chuckled darkly and shrugged. "I'm not the kind of person who sits idle while the world burns. Going out night after night hunting scumbags for coins was bound to land me in trouble eventually. I'd already caught the crime syndicate's attention. Honestly, I'm surprised they haven't sent another representative yet."

The ex-Maker looked even more sorrowful on her behalf than she felt. But after hearing her full explanation, he surprised her.

"You're on a race against the clock now. I thought your learning speed was already ridiculous, but we need to push it even harder."

He stood abruptly and began pacing. "I was planning to get you through all the Tier 1 spells before introducing modifiers, but now..."

He dug into his storage pouch and pulled out a glowing crystal, slamming it gently onto the workbench. "Okay. Here's what you need to know."

A holographic diagram flared to life above the crystal, displaying the spell pattern for *Light*. Branching from the base glyph was a series of marked variations—one had a sharp line extending upward, and another had a looping curve that gave an impression of motion or change. Each branch represented a different modification to the base pattern.

"Spells are basically a language," he explained. "The foundational sigil is like the action word in a sentence. But just like in any sentence, you can modify the verb with—well—modifiers." He winced at his own phrasing but pressed on.

"Anyway, this core glyph just makes a ball of light. That's all it does —it floats right where you cast it. But what if you wanted it to shoot upward and illuminate an area?"

He pointed to the branch with the vertical line extending from the glyph.

"Or if you wanted it to follow you around, hovering just overhead?" He gestured to a more complex variation with two added marks.

"Each new addition increases the tier of the spell. That following light? It's Tier 3. One modifier to make it move up, another to make it track your position." He grinned as he settled into his teaching groove, and she leaned forward, fully engaged. She had read about all this, of course, but seeing it visualized like this clicked it into place in a new way.

He continued, "Spells can be as complex as your imagination allows, but there's a limit. Add too much and your mind can't hold the pattern clearly enough to cast it. A Tier 15 spell, for example..." He shook his head grimly.

"Just imagine the mana you'd have to pump into something that convoluted. Now imagine you screw it up and don't release that mana properly. Every couple of years, some idiot tries it and takes out themselves *and* their neighbors." He gave her a knowing look. "I don't think you'd be that stupid—but you're moving faster than anyone I've ever heard of. Keep that in mind."

Mara nodded thoughtfully, then gestured at the diagram. "So if it's a language... how flexible is it? Like, can you mix base glyphs? Could I combine fire and water to make steam?"

Toman smiled. "Good question—and yes, absolutely. You treat the second base glyph like you would a modifier, except it takes more mana to complete."

That was exactly the kind of answer she'd hoped for. She'd been itching to move on to modifiers for over a ten-day.

"I've already memorized all the modifiers from the Spellswords' training tomes. Can I try one?"

Toman blinked, then gave a theatrical sigh and rolled his eyes. "Of *course* you have. Because you're Mara. Why *wouldn't* you already have done something that takes most students over a year?"

There was sarcasm in his tone but also amusement.

She grinned and prepared to cast—but he raised a hand to stop her.

"Hang on. Start with just one modifier. In fact, don't learn any new spells tonight. I want you to go through every spell you already know, one by one, and cast them using whichever modifier makes the most sense."

He crossed his arms and looked serious. "Tomorrow, we'll push into Tier 2 more thoroughly. But tonight? Muscle memory. That's what this is about. You talk about it all the time—well, this is where it matters. Just because you *can* rush doesn't mean you should. In combat, those modifiers have to be instinctive. Otherwise, you'll end up killing yourself or your allies instead of your enemies."

It was solid advice. But Toman was forgetting something.

"I still have my vampiric recall," she reminded him. "It's not just memory—it's experiential. I can internalize this stuff way faster than a normal student."

He gave her a flat look. "Sometimes, I *almost* hate you."

But it was spoiled by the grin and an incredulous shake of his head.

A couple of hours into practice, Mara finally had to call it. Her body needed a break—channeling mana in her current state was a special kind of exhausting. She motioned Toman over to the workbench.

"Hey, come look through these with me."

She dropped two storage rings onto the table with a metallic clink. "Got these off the slavers last night."

She started pulling out everything they'd been carrying—standard-issue Cleaners, speech stones, and a handful of other day-to-day enchanted tools. The usual junk. But one item she immediately flicked over to Toman.

"Check this out. I tried to kill the bastard, and this thing created a force-field around him. It reacted instantly—there's no way he activated it himself. It had to be automatic."

Toman caught it, turned it over in his hands, and narrowed his eyes with interest. After a long moment, he gave an appreciative nod.

"This is solid work. Actively monitoring for threats will wear it out factor, but it should still have several years of life left before the Wasting degrades it. And the fact that it stopped a hit from *you*? That's a high-tier defensive item. You should definitely keep this."

Mara was pleased—it was rare she found something she didn't already have a better version of. But she hesitated, tapping a finger against the workbench.

"Actually... maybe you should take it. We're heading to the Deepcoin auction soon, and that place isn't exactly safe. You'll probably need it more than I do."

Toman looked genuinely touched. "Thanks. I'll wear it for the trip, yeah. But you should still keep it for yourself after. Or sell it—it could easily go for fifteen or twenty gold marks."

She examined the item again: a belt-worn metal badge etched with delicate floral patterns she didn't recognize. Honestly, it wasn't something that screamed *slaver*. More likely, Morvek had taken it off one of his victims. With a sigh, she clipped it onto her own belt and studied the way it sat.

Toman smiled. "Looks good on you." Then, shifting gears, he added, "Speaking of the auction, the next one's happening Restday evening. I know for sure they've got Heartwood. And I've heard rumors about illicit spells, too—but they won't say what. Not until the bidding starts."

"Of course they won't," Mara muttered.

"Right? They're worried about guild interference. It's happened before—Spellswords, Makers, or one of the other Big Ten raiding the event to reclaim restricted items. Got messy. So now, the auctioneers never leak what they're selling in advance. Keeps the heat down. When the Guilds find out about something, they feel compelled to act or risk losing face. Not that they want their secrets getting out, but sometimes they feel it's better to ignore a problem if it doesn't cost them reputation."

He turned his attention back to the pile of gear from Derwin's ring and let out a snort.

"This guy was ridiculous."

She raised an eyebrow. "How so?"

Toman held up a ring with an ornate design, clearly unimpressed. "Every single one of these is flashy. Too flashy. He blew a lot of coin to make his stuff look high-end. Function-wise? You could've bought everything here for thirty to fifty percent less if you didn't care about showing off."

He gave her a sheepish glance. "Sorry, as a Maker, this just bugs me. These are the kinds of accessories you'd expect from low nobility, not some gutter thug luring people into slavery."

Mara snorted. As if she needed more reasons to hate the bastard. She made a dismissive shooing gesture at the pile.

"Meh. As long as I can get decent coin out of it, I don't care. He's out of my life. Let the Spellswords mete out justice. Besides, I already did what really mattered. I used compulsion to ensure he would never be a threat again. Even if they wiped his memories, those commands would still be lingering, buried deep in his brain."

She gave Toman a grim look, "Not something I would normally do, but for scum like him, I made an exception."

But despite her words, a chill threaded down her spine. The memory of how close she'd come to losing everything—her identity, her mind —was still too fresh. And not in the same way her slow transformation was already stealing pieces of her. This had been worse.

Much worse.

She understood trauma. Understood how to face it, process it, work through it in a healthy way.

She really did.

Tonight, though? Tonight, she didn't care. She didn't want healing. She didn't want introspection. She wanted action—something tangible. So she did the one thing she could stomach.

After finishing up an exhausting round of spell modification practice at Toman's, she took a detour. She would make two stops, going to the slaver's homes. They were both in custody never to be released, making their residences ripe for pillaging. She was going there partly for loot but mostly for closure. And maybe, if one of them had a decent place, she could commandeer it for a while. There'd be a certain poetry to that—her taking over the home of the monster that tried to take her life away.

Derwin's apartment was first. She found it tucked away in the Second Quarter, surprisingly upscale and worlds away from the grime of places like the Broken Fang. The more she explored Daggerport, the more it felt familiar. Like any city back home—gritty districts, solid middle-class neighborhoods, and enclaves of the rich who bought silence and safety with coin. Derwin clearly wanted to be one of the latter, but like his magic items, the place screamed knock-off. Flashy, shallow, trying way too hard. He was close to one of the well-off merchant enclaves, but it was apparent he didn't belong. Faux-gilded trim, imitation silk, cheap illusions to make the place look bigger than it was. It had the desperate stink of someone playing at wealth instead of living it.

She searched the place anyway. Every drawer, every false panel, every floorboard. Hopes weren't high, and they weren't wrong. No hidden stash, no dark secrets—just ego and bad taste. In the end, she left most of it untouched. Almost nothing worth stealing, much less selling.

Morvek's place came next. Third Quarter this time, not far from the Healers Guild compound—but too close to the river for her taste, and tucked into a side street near a cluster of taverns and inns that catered to visiting merchants. Perfect place to meet with them while looking to avoid notice. His home was... normal. Painfully normal. The sort of place someone chose when they didn't want to be remembered. Which, considering his line of work, tracked perfectly. The location was strategic too—close to the docks, yet just random enough to seem innocent.

Between Dunc driving her around and a worn, leather-bound journal tucked into a drawer, she got a decent picture of Morvek's routines. No names. No shipment logs. Just scraps of notes: "Roasted Pheasant – 1 a.m.," "Docks, Workday sunset," "S. arrives w/ coin." Oblique and coded, but not meaningless. It painted a picture of a man constantly in motion, doing far more business than she'd even guessed. She documented everything, even the mundane stuff. It might help the Spellswords or Watch understand the bigger picture —assuming they couldn't beat it out of him before he died.

The strangest part? Walking through Morvek's place almost made him seem... ordinary. Except she knew better. She knew what he was. That knowledge killed whatever guilt might've crept in. She took some of his clothes, a small piece of art or two, then left the rest. She wasn't here for souvenirs.

And despite the fantasy, she dismissed the idea of claiming either place for herself. They were rentals. Temporary shells with nothing to anchor her. If they'd been owned outright, she might've turned one into a bolt hole, a safe house for a rainy decade. But paying rent to squat in the homes of soon-to-be-dead slavers? No thanks.

With nothing else to gain there, she paid a visit to one of the fences Gavian had told her about—a name Toman had also vouched for, along with one other. This one was Metner.

She liked Metner almost instantly.

Old—seventies, maybe even older—but not feeble. Still sharp, still moving, still kicking up the dust of younger men. He had that air about him—the kind that said he'd spent his life swimming with sharks and had long since stopped caring if they bit. Not jaded. Just done pretending. He wasn't cruel or grumpy, just very clear: he didn't give a shit. All that mattered was his comfort and a reasonable profit. Not an obscene one, not a scam—just fair enough to make him smile and keep his bones from aching.

He also loved to haggle. That was fine. So did she.

And she was good at it.

"Eighteen?" she said flatly, holding up the bracer etched with light runes on iron. "Don't insult me."

Metner gave a raspy snort. "You brought me a piece that's been melted and reforged three times, girl. Nineteen."

"It's got an automatic response function," she said, tapping the underside. "Plus, it's got auto-adjusting fit. It's worth double that on a bad day. Twenty-one."

He grunted. "Nineteen gold marks and Five gold pieces. My final offer."

She smiled. "Done." Then, she added under her breath, "Old bastard."

The visit went smoothly. She offloaded both their gear, enchanted storage rings, and everything of value she'd pulled from Morvek's house. The total take from him alone—thanks to records in his data crystal, which confirmed he ran the Slavers' operations—came out to **1,322 gold marks**. A huge sum.

Derwin, for all his flash, had only **179 marks** between his gear and coin.

That brought her total to **3,667 gold marks**.

By Earth's standards, she was holding roughly **thirty-six million dollars**. She knew the $10,000 to 1 gold mark wouldn't really translate that conveniently, but it helped her keep the value of the coins straight in her head.

It should have felt like a victory. But mostly, it felt... strategic. Useful. Cold.

She tucked aside what she needed for the Heartwood staff and still had more than **2,500 marks** to invest in spellcraft.

She just hoped it would be enough.

CHAPTER
THIRTY-TWO

THE NIGHT BEFORE THE AUCTION, Toman took Mara to visit his Illusionist friend, and together, they pulled off something close to a miracle. It would complement her current setup nicely. Her storage ring already masked her from scrying and hid her vampiric nature. Now, she'd have something to shape what people saw when they looked at her.

The new pendant, enchanted by Toman and filled by his friend Blaize, let her access a library of custom illusions with the flick of a thought. More than just toggleable glamours, it came with multiple preset versions. She could turn them on or off at will.

Thanks to Blaize's finesse, she could pass for either a man or woman, shift skin tone through every shade from pale to deep umber, and alter her eye color, hair, apparent age—even her weight. The only thing the illusion couldn't adjust was height.

"Still working on that," Blaize muttered, annoyed. "It's the perspective. A short person's eyes look up, a tall person looks down. That part's subtle, no problem. The real issue is the arms—angles get all wrong. A short illusion reaching *up* to grab a drink when your real arm's coming down? It breaks the immersion. The illusion jitters, or your hand clips through it, and there goes the ruse. Too many contingencies, and I can't anchor that many into a single spell without losing focus."

Toman chuckled. "It's like casting a Tier Fifteen spell. You can't hold the complexity in your head long enough to finish the weave."

Mara nodded, fully understanding. What they *could* do was already remarkable.

Blaize gestured toward her outfit. "There are a dozen clothing sets bound to the pendant—noble wear for either sex, a merchant's outfit, a traveling cloak, even a ratty tunic and scuffed boots that look like they belong to a stable grunt. You'll have options. Could be the difference between vanishing into a crowd or getting arrested by the Watch."

He smirked, clearly proud of his work. "And I disguised the mana haze on purpose. Normally, someone walking by could spot the shimmer, but I layered the illusion's core into the pendant and built in an interference pattern. It distorts the visual aura just enough that it's practically invisible. Unless a mage is actively scanning you, no one will notice a thing."

Mara gave a low whistle. "I'm impressed. This'll be insanely useful. But... is it legal?" She looked at Toman with raised eyebrows.

"Not *technically* illegal," Toman replied. "But if you commit a crime while using it, it's treated as contributing to the commission of the illegal act—so, yeah, harsher sentencing."

Blaize snorted. "There's a social stigma against appearance illusions. They call it *Tweaking*. But unless you're courting nobles or trying to marry up, no one really cares. The upper class pretends to hate it," he added, leaning in with a conspiratorial grin, "but I've got contracts with two dozen noble ladies and more than a few lords."

Mara nearly choked on the whisky she'd just sipped. *Tweaking* meant something quite different back on Earth.

Once she'd stopped coughing, she managed, "I see. Well, I just need it to avoid attention from certain groups. Groups I'd rather not chat with unless it's on my terms. You understand."

"Oh, no judgment," Blaize said, grinning. "I make more off this kind of work than most people realize. I'll never be Maker-rich, but it keeps my workshop warm and my pantry full." He threw a mock-scornful glance at Toman at the word *Maker*, but Mara caught the friendly undertone.

She wasted no time trying it out. With just a few gestures and a whispered phrase, she could selectively pick between individual appearance traits with ease. Dozens of them. Each one crisp, convincing, seamless.

The feeling it gave her surprised her—warm, almost nostalgic. If she'd had this kind of tool back on Earth, she could've *wrecked* Cabal black sites. Infiltrated without effort. Exfiltrated without risk. No fingerprints, no camera footage, no heat. Her identity would've been a ghost. A legend.

And now, it finally could be.

Grinning, she clapped both Blaize and Toman on the shoulder. "This is a masterpiece. Thank you both for collaborating."

Blaize actually blushed at the praise, his chest puffing ever so slightly, while Toman just looked smug—he knew how damn useful the pendant was. Mara paid the illusionist seven gold marks and five gold pieces, then Toman fifteen for his share of the work.

Afterward, once they'd left Blaize behind and the door had shut behind them, she gave her mentor a sly grin. "I'm going to have Dunc drop you off, and then I'm paying a little visit to our local chapterhouse of the Followers of the Dragon. Might be a chance to earn a bit more coin before tomorrow night's auction."

Toman blinked. "Wait—*what?* I thought they didn't have buildings or any kind of headquarters. Wasn't the whole point that they were just regular folks who pledged loyalty to the Dragon in hopes of some vague reward if he ever returned? Isn't that what you found out?"

It was, in fact, what Mara had uncovered after two weeks of poking around in the alleys and smoke-filled corners of the city where she did her hunting. She'd questioned informants, leaned on contacts, even paid for a few tips. Everything pointed to the same conclusion: the Followers were relatively new—only a decade old—and had shown up in Daggerport and other cities across the realm at roughly the same time.

But unlike the firebrand religions back on Earth, these people weren't looking to convert the masses. No shouting in the market squares. No pamphlets. No sermons on street corners. They worked slowly and quietly, targeting the desperate. The hopeless. The people who had nothing left.

And they *helped* them. That was the part that made her stomach twist.

Addicts got clean. Gamblers paid off their debts and somehow never went back. People on the edge found jobs, housing, even friends. It was real, tangible aid. They *built* lives.

On the surface, it looked like salvation.

But Mara didn't buy it. Not for a second.

Maybe it was her experience on Earth, where cults had been studied, dissected, and documented like diseased organisms. Or maybe it was just instinct—the same itch on the back of her neck that had kept her alive during field ops when something didn't add up.

Whatever the cause, her gut told her this wasn't what it seemed.

First clue? They only recruited locals. In a city like Daggerport, where the population grew and shrank every week with trade caravans and sea traffic, that wasn't just odd—it was strategic. According to Zariah, the Followers had groups in every major city. *All* of them. All in the last ten years. But every chapter only pulled from locals.

If the goal was to spread the word and do good, make new converts, why not travelers? Wouldn't that help your message spread quickly?

It didn't make sense.

Mara wasn't sure what it meant, but it definitely didn't pass the smell test. The ironic thing was, if she hadn't had her encounter with the group of cultists that had wanted to assault her, she might never have looked into them or noticed anything off.

Like the money.

How did a disorganized, leaderless grassroots movement afford a Seer to track her movements? Or a high-level assassin?

Maybe Drevan had rich friends. Maybe he was slumming it as part of some redemption arc.

Except Zariah—bless her twisted little heart—had used her network in the sex trade to dig into Drevan's past. Her clients knew things. And the things they knew were fascinating.

Drevan owned a warehouse in the Second Quarter. Not a rented space. Not a flat. A whole damned *building* inside the walls. Nearly 10,000 square feet.

Strike one - property values in this city hadn't decreased in over 400 years, they were more insane than New York City or LA.

Zariah's contact confirmed he hadn't inherited it—he bought it outright five years ago. Before that? Just a loud-mouthed drunk who started fights at the docks and pissed off every barmaid from here to the river. Then, almost overnight, he turned into a zealot. Quiet. Disciplined. Clean. Two weeks later, he bought a warehouse with cash.

That didn't smell like salvation. It smelled like funding.

Mara could spin theories all day. Puppet for a hidden master. Front man for a larger organization. Maybe even possessed. It didn't matter. What did matter was that while the average cultist might just be some poor bastard who'd gotten clean and found meaning, people like Drevan were something else entirely.

Which made them fair game.

She had no intention of knocking over some reformed dockworker who gave up gambling. But she'd happily rob the ringleaders blind.

That was why she was now jogging through the quieter streets of the Second Quarter, dressed as a young male laborer in scuffed boots and a worn tunic.

Her goal: poke around Drevan's warehouse and, with any luck, find him home. If he was, she'd rob him and his creepy little cult blind. If he wasn't, well... she'd settle for whatever valuables were left behind. Either way, she planned to walk away richer than she started, both in information and coin.

Something was rotten in Denmark, and she was going to find out what!

THIRTY-THREE

THE BUILDING SAT CLOSE to the juncture where the southern and western walls met. An odd choice.

Mara would've expected something more central if it were meant to serve as a meeting place. Somewhere easier to reach, easier to blend in. But this? This was deliberately out of the way.

Standing in the shadows of a narrow alley entrance two blocks out, she studied it from a distance, one eyebrow raised. The structure was three stories tall and took up nearly a quarter of the block. But what stood out most wasn't its size.

It was the color.

The entire building had been whitewashed from top to bottom. A bright, sterile white that clashed hard with the rough, natural stone of its neighbors. The effect was... unsettling. It stood out like a bone among stones.

Of course, that might've been the previous owner's doing. She couldn't assume it was the Followers. Their colors were red and gold —none of which appeared anywhere on the exterior.

Hmm... now that I think of it, there's no dragon symbol either. Nothing like the emblem on their cloaks or any other identifying details.

Keeping a wide berth, she circled the surrounding blocks. She had no intention of getting close yet. Not until she had a clear picture from every angle. Unfortunately, the layout made that difficult. The structure was boxed in tight. Only the eastern and northern sides were accessible. The south and west were pressed up against neighboring properties—businesses and homes that cut off all direct lines of sight.

She couldn't spot any magical traps from a distance, so she moved in casually, strolling down the east-facing street. That side had three massive wooden doors, easily large enough for freight carts. The ground in front was worn with grooves from old wagon wheels— though the wood looked weathered, and it was clear they hadn't been opened in some time.

No windows on the first floor. But several dotted the second and third. Those, at least, were possibilities.

Once she turned the corner and was out of sight, she swapped appearances. This time, she chose an older man, blue-eyed, rough around the edges. Not rich—no one flashy in this district would last long—but clearly not a beggar either. Someone who belonged.

Casing the north side was just as easy. That façade held the main entrance. Again, no windows on the lower level. Several above, but all were shuttered or sealed tightly. Nothing looked ajar or forgotten. It might be possible to squeeze through one, but she'd need a better route.

Midnight had already settled in, and only a few faint lights still burned inside.

She didn't like what she saw. Not one bit. There was excessive security for a warehouse that was supposedly just a glorified clubhouse for a religious movement. Every door and window was warded. Even the high windows—hard to see from the street—were laced with magic.

But the shift in her body was proving useful. As her vampiric essence gave way to living tissue, her sensitivity to mana had grown sharper. It was getting easier to see magic, not harder.

Toman had even said so. He'd been impressed at how well she could trace the flows of energy at her stage. He still had her beat, of course, but he was genuinely pleased with her progress—and tonight backed it up.

The problem was that she now had a decision to make: go in loud and brute-force her way through the wards or sneak in through one of the neighboring properties and approach from the rear.

She snorted and gave a half-hearted spit onto the cobbles as she walked on toward the end of the block.

There *was* an alley on the west side, but it was narrow—claustrophobic—and definitely warded. The southern edge of the warehouse, meanwhile, was built flush against the building beside it. No access there.

Grumbling under her breath, she completed the circuit. Only a couple of the buildings flanking the warehouse had gone dark for the night.

Hmm... I could wait until everyone's asleep. Or slip through one of those vacant ones now.

It wasn't a hard choice. The more time she had inside, the more thorough her search would be. And if she didn't trip an alarm or wake a neighbor? Even better.

Circling back the way she came, she stuck to the shadows, keeping close to the walls and deeper in the gloom. When she reached a good vantage point, she stopped and cast a Tier 2 spell: *Levitate*.

Her body lifted smoothly into the air, rising above the roofline of the two-story home next door. She glided over it, soundless as mist.

The lights inside were off. Someone was likely asleep below. No point in risking footsteps on roof tiles when she could just float silently overhead.

Soon, she passed above a quiet courtyard behind the house, and beyond that, the back wall of the Followers' warehouse came into view. Just as she'd hoped, the rear security was sloppier—clearly not the side they expected anyone to approach from. The windows back here weren't warded at all. No glowing glyphs, no enchantments humming through the stone. Just simple, mechanical toggles.

Old-school locks.

The only hitch? She was still maintaining *Levitate*, and that meant no new spellcasting until she dropped it. If she wanted in, she'd have to muscle through.

She drifted to the wall and grabbed hold of the window frame, her fingers gripping the ledge with precise force. Her vampiric strength made it possible—barely. It wasn't hard, exactly. Just awkward. Hanging there with her toes dug into the frame below, her body held up by tension alone, was not the ideal casting posture.

She tried anyway.

The first attempt failed.

Balancing like a bat on a wall and trying to cast was harder than it sounded. Her concentration slipped at the final moment, and the spell fizzled out.

She clenched her jaw, breathed deeply, and let go of the frustration. Anger wouldn't help her balance. Fear wouldn't make the magic flow.

On the second attempt, she focused hard and sent a small kinetic force through her fingers—a tight, deliberate pulse aimed directly at the latch.

Click.

The lock popped free.

Next came *Silence*. She wrapped the area in magical hush just in case the window shrieked like a banshee as she moved it. She immediately recast *Levitate*—this time on the window itself.

It resisted at first, the frame stiff from age or disuse. But after a few seconds of steady upward pressure, it shifted with a reluctant groan —muted entirely by the silence field.

With a quiet breath of relief, Mara slipped through the opening and landed on the floor inside, solid and silent.

One thing was certain—she loved her vampiric powers and wouldn't trade them willingly. But she had to admit, having magic was starting to grow on her, even if she was still fumbling through the basics.

Speaking of which... you're here for a reason, Mara. Stop gawking and find their stash. We need spells, and spells cost coin.

She swept her gaze around the room she'd landed in—and dismissed it almost instantly. The thick layer of dust on the floor made it clear no one had been through here in a long time. That gave her the confidence to move forward without worry. She dropped the *Silence* spell—it wouldn't follow her anyway. She wasn't advanced enough yet. That would require at least Tier 3 magic with two modifiers: one to tether the spell to her and another to allow it to move.

Yet another reason she needed to move on to Tier 3 spells. Once the auction was over tomorrow night, she had work to do.

Still, her current mission didn't rely on spells. She might be in transition, slowly bleeding away her vampiric essence, but her skills and experience weren't affected. Silent as a shadow, she crept to the door and listened.

Silence. Not magical—just real, honest quiet.

She pulled a vial of oil from her belt and dabbed a few drops onto the hinges, waiting for it to soak in. When she finally eased the door open, it moved with a muted creak that still felt loud to her ears.

But instead of stepping into a hallway, she froze in the doorway.

There was no hallway.

Just empty air. A straight drop all the way down to the ground floor.

She stood there, stunned, trying to process what she was seeing. The entire interior of the warehouse had been gutted. The outer shell of the building remained intact—windows, doors, façade—but everything inside had been hollowed out. Floors, walls, rooms— gone.

What in the Nine Hells?

Her mind spun through wild theories. A staging area? Storage? Ritual space? The cult called themselves the *Followers of the Dragon.* Were they actually planning to summon one?

No. That didn't track. The dragon corpse mounted over the entrance to the Dragon Inn was massive—far larger than anything that could fit inside this building. Whatever they were planning, it wasn't a dragon. Or at least not a big one.

She edged closer to the threshold and peered down. Good thing she wasn't afraid of heights. One step forward without checking, and she would have plummeted three stories. That would've made a hell of an entrance.

Estimating the space in imperial terms, the cleared area below stretched roughly 80 by 80 feet on the ground floor—maybe more. The first floor didn't have perimeter offices all the way around, just along the front wall near the main entrance. The rest was stripped bare. And the height? At least forty feet to the ceiling.

A hell of a drop. Good thing she had *Levitate.*

Still, one thing was clear: she wasn't going to find any treasure in these upper-floor rooms. Whatever the cult was planning, the upper levels were just for show—a mask to keep up appearances in case someone peered through the windows.

If there was anything useful left behind, it would be in the first-floor offices... or possibly in a basement, assuming one existed.

Grinning, Mara cast *Levitate* on herself and stepped out into the void. She hadn't seen or heard any movement below, so she felt confident enough to descend calmly, gliding through open air like she owned the place.

She was really starting to enjoy this spell, like having her own private elevator—albeit a slow one. And with no walls, the view was incredible.

As she drifted lower, she was relieved to find that her night vision hadn't failed her yet. To her eyes, the warehouse interior was dim but clear—no lurking threats, no hidden surprises.

In fact, what surprised her most was just how empty the space was. The ground floor was utterly clean. No crates. No ritual markings. Nothing. Just that row of offices along the front wall near the main entrance. Everything else had been scrubbed spotless.

Once she touched down, she made a slow circuit of the open area, checking for traps or residual spells. She wasn't expecting to find much, but she still hoped for some kind of clue—anything to explain why this massive building had been gutted.

No luck.

But she did spot something else: heavy-duty wards on every loading dock door. And complex anti-scrying spells etched into the inner walls.

Serious ones.

Thanks to the last thirty days of training with Toman, who specialized in dismantling wards, she could now recognize not just their function but also their complexity. And these weren't your average merchant-grade barriers. These were intricate, high-tier defenses.

More evidence.

You didn't hollow out a building and line the inside with industrial-strength privacy spells unless you were doing something deeply sketchy.

Sure, maybe they're changing lives and helping the hopeless—but they're sure as hell doing it as a front.

Still... she hesitated.

Maybe it wasn't the Followers themselves. Maybe someone else was using the cult. Manipulating them. Just like the way the outer walls of this warehouse disguised the vast hollow core within, maybe the Followers were nothing more than a convenient mask.

Could be corruption at the top. Or something worse pulling the strings.

Withholding judgment—for now—she turned her attention toward the offices along the front wall. Quiet as breath, she moved toward them and pressed her ear to the door.

There were four doors along that front wall, so she decided to start with the one closest to the main entrance.

CHAPTER
THIRTY-FOUR

Voices inside. Two men, one woman—arguing. With her enhanced hearing, Mara could pick out who was speaking, but the words themselves were garbled. Sound-warping magic. Must've been implanted into the walls, or one of them had some kind of personal privacy item.

She could likely have barged in and taken them all down before they raised the alarm—but that felt premature. Starting this off with a brawl might blow whatever advantage she had. And she wasn't entirely sure she *wanted* them to know she'd found their secret.

Whatever that secret was.

This vast, hollowed-out structure had to serve some critical purpose. She just didn't know what yet. The longer she studied it, the more she began to lean toward leaving the cultists in the dark. Let them keep thinking they were unnoticed.

Still... that didn't mean she couldn't rob them blind.

Suppressing a grin, she slipped to the next door.

Nothing.

No sound, no movement. Same with the one after that. She considered breaking in but held off until she'd checked the last.

This one was different—soft, steady breathing. A low snore, rhythmic and slightly wheezy.

Apparently, sleep apnea wasn't exclusive to Earth.

It had to be a bedroom. And with the occupant asleep, it was the perfect place to start.

Smiling faintly, she pulled a thin, flexible strip of metal from her belt pouch and eased it into the space between the door and the frame. No lock visible on the outside, no magic she could detect—just a basic latch. She worked it upward with slow, practiced pressure. It caught slightly, then gave with a gentle click.

Child's play. After decades of infiltration and cat burglary, simple mechanical locks like this were second nature.

A sliding bar would've been trickier—but only a little.

She dabbed oil on the hinges, waited a beat, then nudged the door open just wide enough to scan the room.

No wards. No traps. No glow of magic, not on the door, not on the floor. Just a quiet, mundane bedroom.

Apparently, the cult felt confident no one would ever find their little hideaway.

Within three heartbeats, she took in the space—cheap furnishings, a mismatched desk and chair, a narrow bed. The room felt like an afterthought. As if someone had been told, *"You'll stay on-site,"* and they'd just dragged in whatever furniture was lying around.

More evidence something wasn't adding up.

Her eyes settled on the man sleeping on his side, one arm under the pillow, the other tucked against his cheek. It looked uncomfortable to her, but whatever. He hadn't stirred, and that was the important part.

She closed the door behind her, latched it, and tucked the tool away.

He had the standard items—Cleaner, speech stones, data crystals, and more—but two items stood out. A belt-mounted shield charm, not unlike the one she wore now, and a cloak draped over the chair with a brooch pinned at the collar. She couldn't tell what the brooch did, but if he wasn't wearing it, it wouldn't help him.

She crossed the room in silence, then moved fast—grabbing a fistful of his hair with one hand while pinning his arms down with the other.

He jerked awake, eyes wide with panic—and that was all she needed.

She drove her will into his groggy, half-aware mind, locking eyes as the dim glow of a light crystal bathed her face in pale fire.

There was no resistance. No mental defenses, no counter-spell, nothing. He didn't even have time to try.

Child's play.

With a crooked smile, she asked softly, "How much money do you have on you—and in your bank account?"

His subconscious made no effort to resist. Her will wrapped around his like chains.

"One hundred and seventeen gold marks," he murmured. "But most of that belongs to the Followers."

"Is there any money or valuables stored in this building?"

"Yes." His voice remained flat.

"Do you have access to them?" If there was a vault here, she wanted every coin of it.

"No."

Her eyes narrowed. "Then explain it to me—like I'm a trusted member of your organization who's just arrived and needs to be brought up to speed. Someone you want to impress."

His dull eyes and slack features grew more animated, lighting up as the compulsion reframed the situation into something positive. That was one of the most important tricks to deep control: if you could make someone *want* what you wanted, even subconsciously, they'd give it up without a fight. No resistance. No mental gymnastics to dodge your command. Just eager cooperation.

"Of course! I'm so sorry—I didn't recognize you," he said, sitting up straighter and giving a clumsy bow from the bed. "Here in this base, we've gathered all the magic items over the last four years, preparing for the Day of Return. They're secured in the rooms next door. We also keep a healthy reserve of gold, silver, and copper, to assist with the transition of the Faithful Remnants...."

That last phrase triggered something.

He shuddered mid-sentence as if his mind slammed into a wall. Mara felt the compulsion stutter. She clamped down on his will, hard—too hard. His body reacted violently, his limbs jerking as convulsions overtook him.

"Damn it," she muttered.

She hadn't hit a resistance like this in decades. The last time had been during World War II—back when certain Nazi officers had undergone magical indoctrination so deep they couldn't divulge classified intel even to allies. Some kind of arcane failsafe—magical keys tied to bloodline, allegiance, or presence. Without the right identifier, their minds shut down—or burned out.

It wasn't just conditioning. It was kill-switch loyalty, embedded like a tripwire.

"Let's talk about something else," she said calmly. "Best not to speak of such things aloud—even among ourselves."

His body gradually stilled. A few more seconds passed before his breathing returned to normal. He hadn't even realized he'd been dying. The fail-safe was that deep.

So, she mused, *the term "Faithful Remnants" was the trigger.*

That meant someone—some group—was coming. From somewhere else. And these people were prepping the field for their arrival.

Interesting.

He'd also mentioned the *Day of Return*, but that wasn't exactly a secret. The Followers shouted that bit in the streets. Their god, *the Dragon*, would come back one day and uplift the faithful. That was the cult's entire sales pitch.

This was different, though. This wasn't just religious optimism. This was *logistical preparation*. Stockpiling magic items. Banking gold. Coordinating an actual arrival.

Preppers, she thought wryly. *Every world has them.*

She stifled a chuckle. *Or maybe it's like a reverse Rapture since this is religious. Stockpile gold and enchanted relics for the chosen ones.*

Funny how the end of the world never quite arrived. Back on Earth, every dire prediction turned out to be overblown. Sure, preppers weren't *entirely* wrong—natural disasters happened—but so far, they'd been regional inconveniences at worst. No complete societal collapse. No dragons.

But these people?

They were building for something real. Or believed they were. The Dragon wouldn't be coming alone—he'd be bringing the **Faithful Remnants** with him. And they'd need resources when they arrived.

Unless this is one hell of a long con, she thought. *These people are all in. Deluded, maybe. But committed. And that mental conditioning? That's industrial-strength!*

It was a thread she could pull later. But not tonight. There was no sign of urgency or imminent movement. No timeline. Just preparation.

She leaned in. "Can you access the gold and items?"

The man gave a cheerful nod. "Of course! All those assigned to the Arriv—"

His voice caught again. Choking. She held up a hand quickly.

"Stop. Don't say anything that would be inappropriate."

He nodded, breath hitching in his throat as the fit passed.

"Do others check the contents? Or do you just deposit everything and let it sit, locked away?"

This time, no reaction. Good.

"I keep inventory," he said. "I track coin and items and maintain records."

Now we're getting somewhere.

"Does anyone verify your tally? And if so, how often?"

"Once a year," he said, then paused, clearly reluctant to name who. "Last check was three months ago.

Mara's eyes gleamed in the near dark. *Nine months* before anyone would notice the theft. That was excellent news. By then, her current half-vampire life would be over—she'd either be living under a new identity... or she'd be dead. And even if they brought in a Seer to look into the past, she was wearing anti-scrying enchantments. According to Toman, the best they'd see was a blurred, unidentifiable figure.

Now for the real question. "Are there any magical wards on the storage? Anything that would trigger an alarm or prevent you from removing items or coins?"

Morren blinked, confused. "Why would there be? Only the Faithful are allowed in the base. Anyone who enters through the doors or windows without the badge of the faith is killed."

Mara felt the cold tickle of blood sweat threaten to form at her brow. She forced herself to stay calm. Coming in through the third-floor window might've been the only thing that saved her life.

She took a breath. "Who's in the office? Will they be leaving, or staying the night? And what's your name?"

She activated her data crystal for a quick visual scan—just long enough to record his face and name.

"I'm Morren, quartermaster of this base." He straightened with pride. "The others are Drevan, Edris, and the woman is Seren. Edris is on watch tonight. The others will likely go home soon."

Her blood simmered at the name *Drevan*, and she fought back the heat rising in her throat. She wanted him dead—but that could wait. Now that she knew where he operated, she could track him. Or hire a Seer to follow his movements and ambush him somewhere *safe*.

Now was the time to hurt them.

"Morren, can you access the storage rooms without alerting the others that you're awake?"

"Of course."

"Then take me there. Show me the storage." She was ready to drain this place dry.

Morren hesitated. "You must have left your cloak in the office. Without your badge, the wards will kill you."

Of course. There had to be traps. And she didn't have a badge.

"Alright," she said coolly. "Listen carefully. Take this ring and fill it with all the gold and coins and in your treasury. And since we're such good friends, you want to transfer all of your banked gold to me as well."

She held out her bank token.

Morren looked momentarily dazed, then nodded. "Transfer 117 gold marks," he said aloud.

Next, he unfastened a pouch from beneath his cloak and poured the contents into her waiting hand. Thirty-two gold marks in mixed coin. She slid them into her storage ring without hesitation.

Smiling, she added, "And Morren... you want to please me because I'm very important among the Faithful. You won't set off any alarms or do anything that draws attention to your actions. This is so inconsequential, you won't even remember my visit. The coins were transferred temporarily to meet an urgent need—they'll be replaced before anyone notices."

She nearly referenced *the arrival* but caught herself. After how he reacted to *Faithful Remnant,* she didn't want to trigger another episode.

"Of course! We all live to serve. None of this is ours. We're stewards for the Return."

Crazy bastards.

She waited, counting the seconds as Morren donned his cloak and reattached his belt. Then he approached the far wall. As he neared, an illusion fell away, revealing a heavy, iron-banded door crackling with enchantments.

He placed one hand on the badge over his chest, and the other on the doorknob. A pulse of light surged through the metal as he touched it. The door creaked open.

Suddenly, Mara was very happy she had chosen to hit the room with the sleeper first. She bet every gold coin Morren had just given her that those doors to the storage room visible from the warehouse floor were trapped decoys. It made sense from a security perspective. This way, anyone wanting access would have to go through this room or would be killed via some nasty magical trap.

Putting those thoughts aside as she watched the quartermaster open their storage vaults. Beyond was a chamber built of thick stone blocks—fused, not stacked. Solid. Secure.

They're not playing around.

If she'd tried to break in herself, she'd be a smear on the floor by now. Everything here was tied to those badges. And if she was right, they weren't interchangeable. Each was keyed to a specific bearer. It's what Toman would've done. Just like her storage ring—only *she* could access it.

Speaking of rings—she'd given Morren one from the matched pair she'd taken off Ewart, the assassin. It was empty, and more than capable of holding all the coin this little operation had on hand. She'd *considered* cleaning them out completely, but flooding the city's fences with even more enchanted gear was starting to draw attention. Besides, she couldn't offload any more tonight—not with the auction looming tomorrow.

There was time. If she still needed coin, she could always come back for the rest. In fact, if her investigations into the Followers turned up any evidence that they had nefarious motives, beyond just serving a god called 'the Dragon', she would want to come back and hit them strategically once she had a good plan and a reason to justify it to herself.

Morren returned quickly, sealing the door behind him and reactivating the illusion that hid it. He wore the same vacant smile as he handed her the ring.

"Here, mistress. It is an honor to support the Dragon. This gold is still in the treasury as far as I'm concerned. You'll return it once your need is resolved."

"And you won't remember any of this," Mara said smoothly. "You'll have no idea the treasury was ever touched, even during the next accounting. And you won't care—because the gold was placed in the hands of the Faithful, who used it to prepare for the Return."

His brow furrowed slightly, then his voice dropped into a trance-like murmur. "I won't remember, but I won't worry. It is for the Glory of the Dragon."

"For the Glory of the Dragon," Mara echoed.

His face relaxed completely.

Holy crap, she thought, stunned. *These idiots have been deeply mind-fucked.* Her own compulsion didn't even seem to *compete* with whatever mental conditioning had been baked into this guy's skull. She shook her head in disbelief.

If there had been any doubt about this cult's legitimacy before, it was gone now. Seeing the way Morren had changed when she repeated the catchphrase. It was like Nazi Germany all over again. You didn't program people's minds to accept anything that deeply and have it be a good thing.

Shaking her head and trying to hide the disgust she felt, she ordered the cultist, "Lie back down," she told him. "Go to sleep. Forget this ever happened."

No harm in reinforcing it.

She slipped out silently, levitated up to the third-floor window she'd come through, and made her way back through the empty night streets. A few blocks away, Dunc's rickshaw picked her up without fanfare, and she rode in silence back to the Dragon Inn.

On the way, she finally peeked into the storage ring.

Her eyebrows shot up. Then kept climbing.

Between Morren's personal coin purse, his bank transfer, and the cult's treasury haul, the total came to **3,781 gold marks**. Combined with what she already had stashed, that brought her reserves to **7,470 gold marks.**

Roughly **74 million dollars.**

She whistled under her breath.

No way in hell this was just some grassroots workers' cult scraping by on faith and handouts. *Somebody*—someone *very* rich—was pumping coin into this operation 'Faithful Remnant's return.'

Still, she couldn't deny it felt *good* to have real wealth again. Back on Earth, she'd never hit that kind of figure. Even with vampiric advantage, fortunes like that had always come with strings.

This, though... this was hers.

And she'd need it. Spells weren't cheap—especially adept-level spells for the Spellswords. She wanted teleportation, enchanting, lie detection, remote viewing... maybe even healing spells if she could get them without a Healer's license. She had no idea what they'd cost—but she was ready to find out.

When dawn came, she collapsed into bed with a rare smile on her lips.

For the first time in weeks, she felt like she could *breathe*.

THIRTY-FIVE

Mara was in a hurry the next evening, needing to meet up with Toman before the auction, so she didn't have time for the long-overdue conversation with the Dwarven innkeeper.

Ah well. I'll catch up with him eventually. Maybe even later tonight if the auction goes well. I'll want to get back to my room and start reading whatever spells I manage to buy. Might as well kill two birds with one stone.

With that settled, she stepped out onto the street just as Dunc pulled up in front of the Dragon's Mouth.

They made their way toward Castle Boulevard, giving Mara her first real look at the ritzy thoroughfare. Like the North Road, it was divided with greenery—parks, gardens, even small fountains—but this stretch was clearly a step above. It resembled the Merchant Mile, but the businesses catered exclusively to the rich and the noble-born. The closer they got to the base of the mountain, the more the neighborhoods transformed—modest shops gave way to mansions and walled estates.

The city might have been built on a perfect grid, but the true center of power was the castle carved into the mountainside. Castle Boulevard terminated at its base and took its name from the fortress that loomed above all else.

They didn't go all the way to the castle—only about half a mile short. Toman had instructed her to meet at a particular business, a very respectable-looking one, tucked in among the upper-tier storefronts.

He was already there, seated at a table outside and sipping tea when she arrived. Dunc peeled away quickly, clearly eager to avoid the judgmental stares of the elite Transport Guild drivers.

Mara had seen the way people looked at them as they rolled past. She caught Dunc's faint blush and patted his shoulder as she stepped down.

"Don't worry about them. You've got a fine ride, and someday you'll make it as fancy as you like. But I'd still rather ride with you than any of *them*."

Her words brought a grateful, if subdued, smile to his face.

"Thank you. Just call when you're done, and I'll be right there!"

A few moments later, she was seated across from her friend and mentor. The tea was a little bitter to her enhanced palate, but a splash of tart juice from a local citrus-like fruit mellowed it into something richer and more complex. Not perfect, but good by human standards.

She sighed, thinking about the senses she would lose—the subtle flavors, the enhanced smells—once her body became fully mortal again.

Toman noticed her expression and tilted his head. "Everything alright? You're not having second thoughts about tonight, are you?"

She shook her head firmly. "No, I'm more eager than ever. This could change everything for me. I just hope they have something that makes all the effort worthwhile." She leaned in slightly, voice low and pointed. "Speaking of which, we'll need to talk later. About *that group*."

His brows shot up. "I can't wait to hear it!" Then he looked around and his face fell. "Damn. I guess I'll have to wait a few hours...."

She smirked, having *intended* to bait him like that.

Toman scowled, realizing she had done it on purpose. "You bitch! Just wait—I know how impatient you are. I'll get you back for this!"

Her laugh drew a few glances, but she didn't care. A moment later, a liveried servant approached their table and gave a respectful bow.

"Your reservation is ready. If you'll follow me, please."

They stood and followed the young woman through the refined interior. Mara had been briefed, so she wasn't surprised when they were led to a luxurious room with no visible exit.

"The way will open in a moment," the woman said. "When it does, please proceed into the shaft and you'll be transported down to the Market."

There was a subtle emphasis on the word "Market." Mara didn't miss it.

The Market.

The Shadow Market.

The illegal heart of the Undercity's black-market trade.

She took the opportunity to shift her face and body once again. Now she was a man—broad, scarred, and mean-looking. A deep slash ran from hairline to jaw across his right cheek, just missing the eye. The illusion wasn't any taller than her usual 5'6", but the build was stocky and hard, someone you wouldn't want to cross. She changed quickly into a set of enchanted leather armor—damage-resistant, blow-deflecting, and looted from the late Ewart, may he rest in pieces.

She still chuckled thinking about how much she'd gained from that duel. The armor was one of the few items she'd decided to keep, and tonight, she was glad she had. It even had a sizing enchantment, which adjusted perfectly to her body.

Appraising herself in a tall mirror, she nodded. She looked exactly like what she meant to portray: a competent and dangerous bodyguard. Blade on one hip, shockrod on the other. The only thing missing was a sword to complete the ensemble, but with any luck, she'd fix that before the night was over with a large piece of Heartwood she could call her own.

Toman gave her a speculative once-over. "I wouldn't have recognized you if I hadn't seen the shift myself. More importantly, you look intimidating enough to keep people from trying anything. The auction's set up well—we'll be escorted to a private booth, and all bids are anonymous. Distribution of purchases is handled afterward in a way that even the staff won't know who picked up what. That way, no one can be pressured by Guild or Noble to give up our identities."

Mara nodded, impressed. That level of discretion didn't come cheap.

"Their whole reputation hinges on that," Toman continued. "Even the nobles and guilds prefer it this way—they might not admit it, but they use the auction just like everyone else. The only time they get aggressive is when something big goes up for sale, something that threatens someone's domain or position. Rare, but it does happen, which is why the auction house goes to such extremes."

He gave a confident grin, "Don't worry, I'll let you know if a listing crosses the line."

As he finished, a section of the wall slid aside like a pocket door, revealing a lavishly adorned elevator shaft. A platform floated in the center, unsupported, though Mara could see the magic woven through its structure.

Toman stepped on without hesitation, and the platform didn't so much as sway. It was more stable than any elevator she'd ever ridden back on Earth. Even with her enhanced senses, she couldn't detect a single vibration when she joined him.

Just like that, they began to descend.

At the bottom, another panel slid aside to reveal a vast cavern chamber as bright as a cloudy afternoon. Wisps of cloud drifted across an illusionary sky so convincing she had to blink to remember it wasn't real. This was the peak of the Illusionist's craft.

The chamber held dozens of buildings designed to mimic an open-air market square, though many were built into the cavern walls. It was busy—at least two hundred people moved between the stalls and shops. A proper black market, though the sign overhead declared it the *Shadow Market*. Same difference.

The elevator they'd just exited was cordoned off by security, clearly a VIP-only route.

"There are other exits," Toman said casually. "I know of at least six. I could walk all the way home through the tunnels without ever coming above ground until I reached my neighborhood. But this is more convenient—and it shows anyone watching that we've got the kind of backing it takes to use this path."

He nodded toward the west. "That's Lord Noloris' palace."

It loomed—grand, overdone, and carved directly from the rock by hands far more skilled than human. Dwarves, most likely. It wasn't Mara's style—too much flash, too much power on display—but it did its job. It made a statement. She'd give Noloris credit for that.

Despite the setting, it reminded her of Petra—Earth's long-dead city of stone palaces, abandoned in the desert heat. It had the same carved grandeur... only this one wasn't abandoned.

The other place of note stood out precisely because it didn't. A pair of plain stone doors sat flush against an otherwise unremarkable stretch of wall—no signs, no symbols, nothing to suggest it was the entrance to what might be the most exclusive and illegal auction house in the world. Nothing, that is, except the guards.

There were a lot of them.

They weren't clustered together, and they weren't in uniform, but they were far too alert, too tense, too ready. Mara casually counted twenty, all milling about with the kind of energy that only came from professional paranoia.

And Toman was heading straight for the doors.

As they drew close, the guards started to react—one at a time, subtle, but unmistakable. One of them tapped his ear and murmured, "The Maker has arrived with a bodyguard."

That was it. No names, no questions, no fanfare.

Half of them resumed scanning the area for external threats, but the other half locked their attention on Mara, reading her as the only real unknown.

There were no introductions. No challenges. And most curious of all —no welcome.

The guard standing closest to the door just raised an eyebrow and glanced at her.

"My guest," Toman said simply.

The guard nodded, then stepped aside and opened the left-hand door.

It was only once they were inside that the welcome finally arrived.

An elegant older woman, composed and dignified, stepped forward to greet them.

Toman withdrew a large gold coin from his storage ring and presented it without being asked.

Mara's eyes caught the shimmer of intricate mana threads woven tightly into the metal. As the woman approached, the coin flashed and a shadowy rune flared into view above it.

"Welcome, honored guest. It is always a pleasure to serve you, Maker," the woman said warmly, offering Toman a genuine smile before turning a curious gaze toward Mara.

Toman gestured toward Mara dismissively, as though she were of little importance. "I have a commission," he said smoothly, "and the buyer sent an impressive guard to ensure my safety and to hold his gold."

"Of course," she said with a gracious nod. "Are you selling anything today, or just bidding?"

"Bidding only."

While they spoke, Mara took the opportunity to study the surroundings and was quietly impressed. The auction house lobby was elegantly understated, with fine furnishings and carefully curated opulence. A bar occupied the left side of the room, its leather seating gleaming with polish and age. There were more doors than she expected—many of them discreet—but it was the double doors at the far end that clearly led to the main auction floor where the crowd of general bidders would be seated.

She scoffed inwardly. That was where the low-stakes players sat. Anyone bidding on illicit spells or rare magical contraband wouldn't risk being seen. For buyers like Toman and herself, there were private booths—magically shielded and entirely anonymous.

And that was where they were headed next.

"Right this way, then." The woman turned and led them to a black door on the right. Behind it, a compact lift large enough for five or six waited. It rose one floor before curving into a lateral tunnel, eventually stopping before a blank section of wall. The woman waved her badge, and a hidden door slid open, revealing a small but luxurious room.

It was about the size of a private theater box, complete with two plush chairs and a modest table. A well-stocked wet bar glittered with two dozen rare and no-doubt expensive spirits.

Mara raised an eyebrow. They weren't just getting white-glove treatment—they were being coddled.

For a moment, she wondered whether the woman would remain to serve, but that thought was quickly answered.

"I'll take my leave," the woman said. "If you need anything, speak my name into your badge and I'll return immediately." Turning to Mara, she added, "I'd normally explain the rules, but the Maker has dealt with us for years and knows them well."

Shrugging, Mara watched her go. Once the door shut, she muttered, "Bit rude, isn't she?"

Toman chuckled. "Not really. Maré simply understands how this works. Most guards—or mercenaries, as you currently appear—don't merit much attention. They can't bid, don't make decisions. She likely sees you as furniture."

"Fair enough," Mara admitted. "At least they gave me a chair instead of making me stand guard the whole time." She dropped into the seat and blinked. "Dragon's Balls! This might be the most comfortable chair I've ever sat in! I need one."

Toman laughed aloud. "I say the same thing every time. But they refuse to name the craftsman or the workshop." He rubbed his chin thoughtfully. "Hmm... I wonder if I could buy that information. They do deal in more than just goods here—though secrets don't come cheap."

That caught her attention. *Information might be useful—especially about the Followers.*

But she dismissed the thought just as quickly. She already had leads now that she'd breached one of their bases. Once she had time, she'd investigate on her own—and save the gold for spells.

They had half an hour to wait before the auction began. When it did, the lights in the main hall dimmed, and bright spotlights illuminated the stage below.

THIRTY-SIX

FROM THEIR VANTAGE POINT, Mara saw the main floor and its crowd of seated bidders, but no sign of any other private booths. Just stone walls and illusion—clever enough to suggest they were the only elite guests in attendance.

Of course, she knew better. Toman had already warned her—there were dozens of booths like theirs, cloaked in illusion, silenced by magic, and completely hidden from view.

She had to admit, it was a clever setup. No distractions, total anonymity, and all attention directed toward the stage, which was brightly and almost theatrically lit.

Toman poured himself a drink and offered her one as well. "They're complimentary. The house hopes a few stiff drinks will loosen wallets and fuel some bidding wars."

She gave a soft chuckle and accepted the glass. While more of her body was becoming alive by the day, most of her brain was still undead, meaning alcohol would barely touch her. But as she raised the drink, she paused mid-motion.

Was that still true?

Nearly forty percent of her tissue was living now—maybe it wasn't safe to assume anymore. With a reluctant sigh, she lowered the glass, setting it aside, and settled back to wait.

Fortunately, she didn't have to wait long.

A striking human woman in her early twenties stepped onto the stage, laying a piece of Heartwood on a table draped in rich black velvet. She had deep brown skin, a curtain of straight black hair down her back, and wore a sleeveless crimson gown embroidered with subtle arcane symbols that shimmered when she moved. Mara had seen few enough dresses on this world to take note of the elegant gown, still, it seemed to rather fit the atmosphere of the auction house.

The Heartwood was only the length of a wand, but from their second-floor booth, Mara could still make out the gorgeous grain of the wood.

Then a gentleman emerged from the curtains behind the stage and stepped behind a gilded stone podium that rose smoothly from the floor. He was tall and broad-shouldered, the kind of man who might have once worn armor as easily as a coat. Though age had touched the temples of his black hair with silver, it only added to his presence. He had the refined bearing of a statesman but with the grace of someone who'd survived real battles. He reminded her a little of Master Healer Onaris—if Onaris had chosen war over medicine.

"Welcome, all, to the Deepcoin Auction House." His voice carried easily through the chamber—smooth, assured, and professional. "We have a great many desirable items for you tonight, so I'm sure your fingers are already twitching. That said, let me remind you: any attempt to discover the identity of a fellow bidder, whether driven by curiosity or spite... will not end well. Such actions will result in a lifetime ban and a bounty placed upon your head should you ever set foot in the Undercity again."

He smiled, but it was the kind of smile that promised ruin, not forgiveness.

Mara didn't need her enhanced senses to tell—this was not a man to cross.

"I am Allar," he continued, that smile now warm and charismatic, "and I will be your host this evening. As always, we begin with our Heartwood selections—ever popular, ever in demand. Tonight's offerings are among the finest you will find anywhere."

He gestured to the wand, which floated into the air, expanding in size until it hovered in the center of the stage. Somehow, it was illuminated and shadowed all at once—glowing softly at the edges while shadows curled behind it. It was as if someone had applied both an inner glow and a drop shadow, a visual trick that reminded her of photo-editing software from Earth.

She had to admit, it was an impressive trick. Someone was paying their in-house Illusionist very well.

The wand was lovely—but useless to her. Still, it was a good opener. It set the tone.

Allar's voice deepened with apparent admiration. "This wand is a singular piece, well cared for, owned by only one mage. Upon his passing, it was surrendered in repayment of a private debt, rather than being reclaimed by his guild. A mage of taste and discretion will find pride in its legacy. The bidding will begin at 175."

A glowing number *175* appeared in the air to the right of the stage, clear as day and impossible to ignore.

Down on the floor, a figure lifted their hand, displaying a copper badge. It flashed, and the bid was recorded.

"Copper?" she asked Toman quietly.

"Entry-level," he replied. "Copper badges go to first-timers or clients who just barely meet the house's standards. Above that are bronze, silver, and gold. Most never get past silver. You need deep connections, or a long spending history to make it to gold."

He said it with just a hint of pride, and she chuckled.

"Well," she said, stretching out in her seat, "I'm glad you made the cut. I like the privacy... and these chairs are absurdly comfortable."

The price of the wand steadily rose five gold marks at a time, and then by ones once it reached 200 gold marks and bidding slowed down. It ended up selling for 206 gold marks. Not bad.

Thirty minutes passed as more pieces of Heartwood were brought out and auctioned off until finally, one appeared that made her sit forward on the edge of her seat. The announcer repeated a variant of the same spiel, playing up its beauty and functionality, but this time, he focused on its size. However, there was a surprise when he spoke of the provenance.

"This staff is old, as you can see from the wear. However, we were unable to find records of its previous owner or owners. That said, our appraiser believes this Heartwood was shaped at least 5,000 years ago. The enchantments had been removed before we received it, but given its age, it almost certainly had a very skilled invulnerability enchantment to have lasted so long with so little degradation. I have seen Heartwood less than a hundred years old that bore more effects of the wasting than seen here."

"Bidding starts at 950."

"Toman. Do you see anything wrong with this one?" She tried to keep the eagerness out of her words, but it was difficult. The staff was just over six feet, or two meters long, straight, and unadorned. It would be perfect for fighting as a quarter-staff and had enough mass to be reshaped into a spear without becoming too delicate. More than its usefulness, she had a feeling that this was the one. It was not something she could put into words, but she had felt a chill down her spine when it appeared.

The ex-Maker took a moment and nodded slowly. "It looks excellent. I see no flaws from here, but of course, an auction house like Deepcoin would not list something that didn't meet their standards. I think it should be great if you want me to bid."

"Yes, please!" She deliberately held herself still so she wouldn't fidget.

Raising his token slightly, it flashed golden. Then Toman gave her a reassuring smile. "There are likely to be one or two more if this one doesn't work out."

The price rose quickly until it hit 1000, then it began to slow.

Mara watched intently at the area just below the number. Each time someone placed a bid, it would flash a character to represent the bidder. That way, even though the bidding was private, the audience could tell when different bidders raised the price.

By the time they reached 1000, there were only three people left, but it kept slowly climbing. Toman frowned when the price topped 1015.

"If it goes higher than 1025, we should let it go. There should be more, and beyond 1025, we will be getting into the territory of paying too much. I know the age of this one is unusual and interesting, but if this weren't already so much like a fighting staff, rather than a more decorative Wizard style, I would have already suggested we drop out."

Mara jerked her head from side to side. "No! Keep going. I don't know why, but this one calls to me. I want this one, even if it goes a hundred marks higher."

Giving her a skeptical look, he shrugged and raised the token again, eliciting a new flash and the number on the stage incremented to 1016.

At 1020, there were only two bidders left: Toman and some unknown competitor.

Thankfully, whoever they were, they gave up at 1030, and Mara became the proud owner of an ancient Heartwood staff that had seen better days.

And she couldn't have been happier. She was eager enough to get her hands on that staff that, if she didn't need the spells so badly, she would have hurried to leave and collect her winning prize.

What followed was two hours of mostly boring items. There had indeed been more Heartwood staffs, and one of them was especially eye-catching—decorated with inlaid gold and gemstones, the kind of staff a Master Wizard might carry into a royal court. It even came with a dramatic story: its previous owner had been a famous mage who gave his life to save an entire village during the last Bane Elf incursion into human lands, more than a hundred years ago.

Allar, the ever-sly auctioneer, delivered the final flourish with a theatrical gleam in his eye. "It is even speculated that within the next one hundred years, a new Heartwood tree may grow over the grave of that brave wizard, nurtured by his sacrifice and noble spirit."

Toman gave her a look that practically screamed, *I told you so! Why didn't you listen to me?*

She didn't care. None of the other staffs—shiny, heroic, or otherwise —had given her chills or stirred the strange sense of certainty that hers had. No story, however noble, could change that.

After the last of the Heartwood lots, other items cycled through. Most were forgettable. A few, though, caught her eye.

There was a rapier called *Soulpiercer*—a sleek, wicked blade enchanted to bypass most armor, even magical kinds. The seller claimed it could wound the soul itself, though she wasn't sure she believed in souls. It went for 246 gold marks, a steep price, but not unheard of for a weapon with that kind of mystique.

Another curiosity was a single-use item labeled *Wand of Dragon's Breath*. Certified to unleash a superheated flame capable of melting stone and armor in a fifty-foot cone, the blast would last a full ten seconds. That was enough to incinerate half a street. No vampire could survive in that kind of fire unless they were so loaded down with protective artifacts they lit up like a Christmas Tree. She was mildly tempted by that one, especially considering the possibility of a future confrontation with a certain vampiric crime boss who ruled the Undercity. Still, *mildly* was the keyword.

The one that truly tempted her was the *Whispercloak*—a rogue's dream. Shadow-draped armor in the form of a cloak, enchanted to muffle sound, dim presence, and render the wearer nearly invisible in low light.

What she wouldn't have given for one of those back when she was fighting the Cabal.

Even so, she talked herself out of bidding. First, she really did need to save every last coin for spell purchases. And second, she had a Maker sitting right next to her who could build a cloak like that—if she brought him the right materials.

Of course, he'd make her pay for it.

It sold for 111 gold marks, and in her opinion, it was worth every coin. That was nearly ten years' wages for a common laborer.

She sighed and gave Toman a look, then tilted her head toward the Whispercloak and raised a questioning brow.

He harrumphed but eventually gave in. "Fine. But you'll owe me 100 gold marks. Earliest I can get it done is a month out—I've got too many commissions in the queue."

Mara gave him a sweet smile, the kind a spoiled daughter might give an indulgent father. Then she spoiled it with an impish grin, and the ex-Maker burst into laughter at her antics.

Despite the nerves that came with waiting and hoping for usable spells to appear on the docket, she was in good spirits. Buying that staff had given her a glimmer of hope—that she could rebuild a credible persona before her transformation reached the point where her powers would be more glitch than function.

That sobering thought deflated her a bit, but only for a moment.

Then the announcer said the words she'd been waiting for.

CHAPTER
THIRTY-SEVEN

"As ALWAYS, we save the best for last. The rarest. The most sought-after. Spells—unavailable to the public. Spells that cannot be obtained without guild affiliation! But tonight, they are available to a lucky few who have the coin."

Mara straightened, leaning forward, heart beating faster.

Toman cautioned her, "Remember—they'll dribble them out one at a time. Singles first, weakest to strongest. The final item will almost certainly be a spellbook or bundle from an important guild."

She sighed but nodded. "I know. Still, anything that looks like it could serve my future—single spell or not—I want it."

They didn't have to wait long. The crowd below erupted the moment the first spell was announced, a frenzy of flashing badges and overlapping bids.

The first spells were exactly as Toman had warned—useful, but not thrilling. Most came from guilds like the Transporters or Builders. One created sustained winds; another fused materials together and strengthened the resulting structure. Interesting additions to any magical toolkit, and she wouldn't have minded having them in her repertoire. But none of them were worth parting with her limited funds—not when there might be spells up for bid that could save her life or keep her hidden when it mattered most.

Speaking of that—one spell finally made her sit up straighter: *Veil of the Forgotten.*

Allar's voice took on a reverent tone as he sang its praises. "This magic renders the target completely unmemorable for twenty-four hours. It falls under the rare and tightly controlled class of mind-affecting spells. So effective, in fact, that its use is banned by the Seers Guild." He let that statement hang in the air, milking the silence as if it were part of the show.

Then, with a sharp smile, he added, "Let the bidding start at one hundred gold marks."

Gasps rippled through the audience on the main floor, and Mara understood the reaction. Up to now, most spells had gone for between twenty-five and fifty gold marks. This one started at double that. On Earth, it would've fetched close to a million dollars from any black-market buyer. They were officially into the high-stakes segment of the night.

And she *wanted* it.

This spell would be a game-changer for someone like her—investigating cults, infiltrating dangerous places, robbing the right kind of people. The spell didn't erase memories or knock people out —it simply made it impossible for their brains to *register* the target long-term. Like trying to remember the face of someone you passed on a crowded street. Utterly forgettable. Practically invisible.

She did wonder how it worked without damaging the minds of everyone it affected. Mana was mildly toxic, and tampering with the brain could be risky. Maybe that's why it was banned. Still, too useful to pass up.

She gave Toman a nod.

He sighed but raised his token, and their bid flashed—105.

Several competitors jumped in, then dropped off as the price climbed in steady intervals: 120... 130... 135... 140...

It kept rising. She leaned forward, heart thudding. Another flash. Another bid. And finally—

She exhaled sharply and shook her head. "No more."

Toman looked visibly relieved, which made her chuckle despite the sting of walking away.

It would have been an incredible asset, no question. But it wasn't worth putting a dent in her purse this early in the game—not when she was chasing spell tomes that could run into the thousands. She had to keep her eye on the prize.

The next spell to grab her attention was *Echo Step*—a short-range teleportation spell with combat applications. It lets the caster pre-cast. When triggered, it would instantly return them to where they had stood ten seconds earlier. Used correctly, it could change the flow of a fight in a heartbeat—sidestep, bait, reposition, then *bam*—reappear behind your enemy and end it with one well-placed strike.

Toman gave her an understanding look, but warned, "If I didn't already have a basic teleportation spell, I'd advise you to pass. Spatial magic is tricky. One wrong cast, and... well, you don't want to see what's left after that. But with a foundation already in place, this one will help you understand the field. The two complement each other."

They bid—and won—but it didn't come cheap. The final price: 163 gold marks.

Between the Heartwood staff and this spell, she was now down to 6,233 gold marks. Still a huge sum by most standards, but considering how fast the high-tier spells were climbing in price, she felt a gnawing unease in her gut. If there *was* a spell tome up for auction tonight, the competition for it would be brutal.

Her gaze drifted to the drink still waiting on the side table, untouched. She eyed it for a moment, tempted to take the edge off her nerves.

Just one shot. That's all.

But in the end, she left it sitting there.

She completely missed the next spell as she came to a sudden and startling realization—the sensation twisting in her gut wasn't the cool, calculated nervousness she'd grown used to over the last hundred years. No, this was something else entirely.

A stomach-churning, full-body reaction. One she hadn't felt in so long that it took her several seconds to even recognize it.

Damn it.

It was *anxiety*. Real, physical anxiety. The kind that came with a racing heart and fluttering stomach—symptoms she hadn't experienced since she was human. Her living tissue was catching up with her, and this was just the beginning. The more her body transformed, the more of these inconvenient sensations would return.

Worse, it brought other feelings along for the ride—emotions she hadn't needed to manage in her unlife. Fragile things. Unwanted distractions.

Toman nudged her. "Hey, do you want this one?"

She blinked, dragged back into the moment. Another spell was already being auctioned, and it was a doozy.

Chains of Binding. A War Wizard spell. It conjured ethereal chains to lash out in a fifty-foot radius, attempting to restrain every target in range. Even if the targets were strong enough to resist the bindings, the chains would still deliver a paralyzing shock—one designed specifically to disrupt spellcasting.

Bidding started at 150 gold marks.

Mara hesitated. It was tempting, no question. A powerful area control spell. But she knew better.

War Wizard spells were notoriously mana-hungry. She wasn't even sure she had the reserves to *cast* it, let alone wield it effectively in a real fight. And if she ever found herself surrounded by a few dozen enemy spellcasters? She'd already be dead.

No thanks. She had no interest in large-scale battles. That wasn't her style. Never had been.

Another tempting spell came and went: *Blood Price.* A brutal, high-risk enhancement that temporarily boosted the caster's speed and strength by fifty percent. But the cost? Possible internal injury, or worse. It essentially mimicked what Spellswords could do—minus their safeguards against the Wasting. Fifty percent was a huge gain, much more than the journeyman-level Spellsword spells she'd memorized.

Still, it was a last-ditch kind of spell. A gamble. Not her thing. She passed.

Then came the final individual spell—and this one *did* make her sit forward.

Writ of Unmaking.

It allowed the caster to safely unravel a single enchantment without triggering a catastrophic failure.

Not just *nullify* it—*unmake* it. Neat. Clean. Controlled.

The possibilities were endless. Disarm traps, remove curses, strip enchanted armor... and do it *quietly*. No backblast. No mana flare. Just... gone.

Toman seemed equally impressed. He was already perched on the edge of his seat, his posture alert.

He didn't even ask—just raised his token.

Then he turned to her, a touch of urgency in his voice. "I'll go half on this with you. Or if you're not interested, I'll buy it myself."

She grinned at his boyish eagerness. "Half, then."

Come on, mama needs a new spell! She chuckled at the thought and leaned back to watch.

Bidding opened at 175 and surged quickly to 230 before slowing down. At 250, she found herself gripping the armrest. It was a hot item, no doubt about it. Four bidders were still active at 275, and it didn't drop to single-increment increases until 290.

Toman looked slightly pale as he lifted his token again—final bid: 312 gold marks.

When no counter came, the tension broke like a snapped string. He slumped back with a heavy sigh.

Turning to her, he looked sheepish. "I'm *so* glad you agreed to go half. I couldn't have afforded that on my own."

Mara gave him a wink. "What are friends for?"

Still, that was another chunk out of her bank account. Minus 156 gold marks from her total, leaving her at 6,077.

The thought of not having enough coins for what she really needed was causing butterflies to do gymnastics in her stomach.

Damn, this nervousness.

Other than a few theatrics to stir the crowd, there were no further delays before Allar announced, "And now for the highlight of the evening. The rarest of the rare. We have on offering not one, not two, not even three, but *four* guild tomes tonight."

The auctioneer raised fingers dramatically, punctuating each number with flair, before launching into a hasty disclaimer no doubt meant to keep the auction house in the guilds' good graces.

"This is unprecedented, and the Deepcoin Auction House was incredibly fortunate to receive these from an anonymous seller. Where the seller received them is unknown. Nor did we ask questions. And so it is your good fortune that you have attended tonight on such a rare occasion!"

Unlike the usual mystery that shrouded individual listings, this time all four spell crystals were brought out at once and displayed center stage. The house Illusionist cast gleaming labels beneath each one.

- *Illusionist – Basic Apprentice Tome*
- *Maker – Journeyman Tome*
- *Spellsword – Adept Tome*
- *Seer – Master Tome*

And they were *glittering*. The interplay of light and shadow made each one shine like the finest diamond, glowing from within like the jewels in the crown of some forgotten dark lord.

The room was so quiet she could hear her own heartbeat—then came the wave of whispers, mutters, and sharp gestures as the crowd buzzed with growing anticipation.

Once the audience had calmed, Allar spread his arms. "We bring these all out before you so you may choose wisely which to invest your efforts into." He smiled magnanimously. "The Deepcoin Auction has no doubt that bidding will be fierce on each of these."

The radiant illusions dimmed, shrinking the crystals back to their normal size.

"And so we will begin. They shall be auctioned in order of rank."

He raised his hand again, and the Apprentice spell crystal floated upward.

"I am sure our bidders are aware, but these are not mere lists of spells with diagrams and visual aids. These are guild-standard tomes —designed to teach and shape the next generation. This one, for example, contains not only every basic Illusionist spell list up to Tier 3 but also the core philosophy and spell crafting theory taught to all new initiates."

He beamed with paternal pride. "Let us begin the bidding at 2,000 gold marks!"

Mara choked. That was *not* a good sign. Starting the bidding that high for an *apprentice* tome did not bode well. On the other hand, she counted herself incredibly lucky that one of the four was the very tome she needed most.

If there hadn't been four available, she might have started to believe some higher being was looking out for her.

Toman gave her a questioning look.

She shrugged. "I want it. I think it would be incredibly beneficial— but I *need* the Spellsword tome."

He nodded, regretful. "I wish I had the coin. I'd buy it for myself."

Surprisingly, the Apprentice tome sold for only 2,800 gold marks.

"That's a good price," Toman said. "The spells may be basic, but that tome gives someone the entire foundation of what it means to be an Illusionist." He stared wistfully as the crystal dimmed and floated back to its pedestal.

"What about the others?" Mara asked.

The ex-Maker considered carefully while the auctioneer extolled the virtues of the Illusionist tome and how fortunate the buyer was.

After a pause, Toman shook his head. "The Maker and Seer tomes are worthless to you. You'd need the Apprentice-level foundation to even touch that Journeyman Maker crystal. Without the—"

He stopped abruptly, face twisting, gagged by the oaths he'd sworn.

Mara caught the slip and quickly pivoted. "What about the Seer tome?"

He gave her a grateful glance, cleared his throat, and began to breathe again. "Also... also worthless. Master-level spells with no Seer background? You'd never cast them. The only ones who'll benefit are Adept Seers trying to push ahead without permission."

That just left the one that mattered. The Spellsword tome.

Mara was practically vibrating with tension as the Maker tome came up next. It sold for a staggering **5,320** gold marks.

While they were preparing for the next one, Toman leaned closer and explained, "Unlike you, any Wizard worth his staff knows enchantment theory. Many make a side hustle of selling magic items. They are the only ones the Makers Guild legally allows to do so. It goes back to a very ancient treaty. So, for them, this tome is invaluable. It helps bridge the gap between what they learned on their own and what's taught in the Maker's Guild. If that Wizard specializes in enchanting going forward, they'll make that investment back in a couple of years—and likely become renowned among their guild as an expert enchanter someday."

That made sense.

Mara wished Toman weren't under such strict oaths—she would

love to dabble in enchanting. She had a hunch that her Earth-based technological knowledge would come in handy in that field.

And then the announcer gestured at the thing she had dreamed of acquiring.

"We have another wonderful item here—the Adept-level tome of the Spellsword Guild..."

He went on to sing its virtues and how amazing it would be to learn their secrets and become the world's greatest fighter.

All bullshit, of course.

What Toman had said about the Seer Guild crystal held true here—*even more so.* Without the foundation provided by the Apprentice and Journeyman spell books, there was no way she'd be able to cast the advanced spells safely. The Spellsword Guild's real secret wasn't in the *spells* themselves—it was in the *process* of casting them. And that wouldn't be included in the Adept crystal.

Not all the audience members seemed to understand that. The bidding was *fierce.* It started at 3,500 and climbed fast—by ten and twenty gold mark increments, surging past 4,000 with no sign of slowing.

She was tempted to tell Toman to jump the bid by 500, just to weed out the amateurs, but she was afraid it might have the opposite effect—*spur them on harder.*

Toman was constantly raising his token, his arm starting to droop from the effort.

At 4,500, it finally began to slow. Bidders dropped away.

Mara was *bouncing* in her seat now, barely able to contain herself.

Toman gave her a pitying look but kept at it.

4,750... 4,800... 4,975...

One by one, the competition fell away—until only two bidders remained.

"5,090—do I hear 5,100?" Allar called.

Toman raised his hand.

So did their opponent.

Again.

Again.

Again.

At 5,150, the rival bidder finally hesitated.

And when Allar made the closing gesture, Mara felt her entire body sag with relief.

She didn't hear whatever praise the auctioneer poured over the sale.

She was hugging her knees, trembling from the adrenaline crash— an emotion she hadn't truly *felt* in a century. A warm tear slid down her cheek.

Toman placed a hand on her shoulder—gentle, steadying.

"I've called Maré. She'll meet us shortly and take us to the exit rooms, where we can pay them a *mountain* of gold."

Mara angrily wiped her face—and froze, staring at the clear smudge on her hand.

"...*real* tears?"

She sat still, stunned, as the full weight of that hit her. So much of her body was living now that she no longer cried blood.

And that realization?

It almost made her cry again.

She cleared her throat and stood abruptly, forcing the storm down.

No.

She didn't have the luxury to fall apart. *Not here. Not now. Not in enemy territory.*

They needed to grab their wins and get the hell out of dodge.

When the knock came and the panel slid open, revealing the auction greeter, Mara was composed again. A rigid wall of willpower held her emotions at bay.

She still wasn't fully mortal. That meant she could *still* control her own mind—if barely.

This is like being a damned teenager again. Raging hormones throwing my brain chemistry all out of whack.

As before, the servant barely glanced at Mara. Her attention was on Toman.

"I hope your evening was successful. If you'll follow me, I'll escort you to the exit rooms."

CHAPTER
THIRTY-EIGHT

THE EXIT ROOMS were magically scrambled—or so Toman said. As you stepped toward the entrance, a teleportation circle would activate, sending each individual or group to a randomly assigned exit chamber. Then, after the purchase was complete, a second teleport would deposit them at one of the building's many public exits— shared by all attendees. It was timed with such precision that no one, not even the staff, could say who had collected what, or where they had exited.

Mara was sure the auction house *could* cheat if it wanted to, but they had a reputation to protect. Besides, this gave them plausible deniability—so when one of the four major guilds inevitably came knocking, demanding to know who had walked away with their spell tome, they could honestly claim ignorance. It protected the buyers *and* the sellers.

The exit room they arrived in was plain but well-warded. Mara noted dense layers of protective and anti-scrying runes carved into the stone. There was only a single table in the center of the room.

The clever part was the circle etched into the table's surface, labeled simply: *Place bidding token here, and then transfer the owed amount. Once transfer completes, items will be deposited on the table.*

Toman, clearly an old pro at this, stepped forward and placed his gold badge in the circle. Followed by Mara, who transferred a painful 6,653 gold marks. That was more money than most minor nobles had, but she didn't regret it. She only had a slight fear of a double-cross, but it was immediately put to rest as their purchases materialized one at a time—three glimmering spell crystals and the ancient Heartwood staff. Mara verified each, lightning-quick, then slid them into storage.

Only the staff lingered in her hands a moment longer. The second her fingers closed around the smooth wood, she felt a surge of calm —*rightness*. A forgotten warmth filled her chest. It was like being handed a sword she'd forged herself. It felt like *hers*.

Reluctantly, she tucked it away.

Toman was beaming. "That staff is perfect. Like it was made for you. Let's get home—I've got work to do. I need at least a week for the enchantments, but most of the prep's done. I just need to set the circle and begin casting."

His excitement warmed her again. She'd heard the legends— Heartwood doubled a caster's mental clarity and focus. Now, after just a few seconds in her hands, she was a believer. With that staff, she'd be able to learn and cast spells faster and more reliably than ever before.

They stepped into the spell array at the far end of the room—and in a flash, they were back at the auction house's grand entrance.

But they weren't themselves anymore.

Mara appeared as an older woman—stooped slightly, thin white hair pinned back in a tight bun. Toman looked like a young, broad-shouldered man with a heavy illusory sword at his hip.

Other guests merged with them in a slow-moving crowd. Plenty of onlookers tried to catch a glimpse of who was coming out, but thanks to the booth system and post-exit disguises, it was nearly impossible to connect purchases to faces. Besides, this was only *one* of many exits—any attempt at an ambush here would spark a riot.

Still, they didn't take chances.

They exited through a different VIP lift, back up to the starlit night of the surface. Soon, Dunc arrived with the cart—this time at a separate location entirely—and the group meandered through the city in a roundabout route before stopping at the Dragon Inn.

Early evening foot traffic made their presence less suspicious. The inn, with its noisy tavern and transient guests, was perfect for shaking any Seers who might've been trying to remote view their departure.

Extreme paranoia?

Definitely.

But in Mara's world, that just meant *good sense.*

Once inside, Dunc was dismissed. Toman lingered for a while, sitting in her room as they examined the spell tomes. Finally, with a yawn that nearly cracked his jaw, he got up to leave.

Mara pressed the staff and the Writ of Unmaking into his hands.

Letting go of the staff again stung. It was absurd, but it felt like parting with an old friend after a single evening together.

Toman gave a sleepy grin. "Don't worry. I'll take good care of it. Next time you see it, it'll be so enchanted it'll glow like the sun."

She snorted. "Please don't *actually* make it glow. I'm trying to be *subtle*."

He laughed, tired but happy. What he was planning would push the limits of his skill as a Maker—but she trusted him completely.

"I'll be staying in tomorrow," she said as he packed up. "Memorizing the spells in the tome."

He raised a brow.

"And no," she added, "I won't cast anything yet. Even if they seem simple."

"Good," he mumbled, halfway through another yawn. "I'll probably fall asleep in the carriage anyway. I can barely keep my eyes open."

It was nearly dawn. After seeing him out, Mara slumped into her chair, pulled out the Echo Step spell crystal, and turned it over in her fingers.

Time to crack the mysteries of teleportation.

Learning the spells—or at least memorizing everything—took more time than she'd liked. For the next week, she spent almost every waking hour either sitting in her room at the inn, poring over the spell crystals, or at Toman's home practicing what she'd learned.

Fortunately, her vampiric memory was still going strong, even as the rest of her powers began to glitch without warning. She could no longer trust that her speed or strength would be there when she needed them. That uncertainty was maddening for someone who had spent more than a century relying on those very abilities to survive. Even feeding was happening less frequently as her blood had less need to sustain her unlife.

Still, she was incredibly thankful for her vampiric memory. Before the week was out, she had fully memorized every spell she had access to—including the full Teleportation spell and several random, likely illegal spells that Toman had collected over the years.

The sad part was that just because she had them all memorized didn't mean she could cast them.

Far from it.

In the week since the auction, she'd progressed from Tier 2 spells— basic single-glyph spells with one modifier—to Tier 3, adding a second function. From there, the difficulty spiked. Every additional layer required more focus, more concentration, more willpower to prevent the casting from spiraling out of control.

The vampire part of her brain still helped with that, at least a little. It let her lock down stray thoughts and push distractions aside—but it wasn't enough on its own. This was a skill she had to build from scratch.

As Toman put it one evening, "Don't beat yourself up for not being perfect. No one starts out as a master. We all have to crawl before we can learn to walk or run."

It was true, and she knew that. Intellectually. But it didn't help when she could *feel* the self she'd always been slipping away, piece by piece, replaced by something unfamiliar. It felt like she was in a race for her life. Could she gain enough skill before it was too late?

Toman tried to be empathetic, but he didn't understand. Not really. She told him as much.

"Well, then explain it to me," he said, frustrated but earnest. "I've never been a vampire, sure—but I *am* a mage, and I know how great it feels to be able to cast spells and make a living doing something I love. I get that you're losing what you're used to, but try to look on the bright side: what you're gaining is incredible. Whether it was the spell that brought you here or your innate genetics, you're one of the lucky ones. It's already clear you'll have top-tier mana potential when the change finishes. Dragons' balls, Mara—you're already stronger than a third of the mages I know, and you're only halfway through your transformation."

She sat still, focusing hard on staying calm. The hormones running wild through her system wanted her to lash out, to scream in frustration—but she wouldn't let them. She took two extra-deep breaths, then forced herself to speak.

"I told you about video games, right? Do you remember?"

He tilted his head. "Yeah... those illusion-based stories where you play an adventurer?"

She laughed softly at his warped version of the truth. "Close enough. Anyway, one of the concepts a lot of games had was passive abilities versus active ones. Active abilities are things like spells or attacks— you have to use them. But passive abilities? They're always on. Always working."

She pointed at the magic item on her belt. "Take this, for example. It raises a force shield automatically when it senses danger. If you were attacked by an assassin, would you rather rely on that, or have to manually cast a shield spell? Remember, you won't know you're under attack until it's too late."

Toman's eyes lit up as understanding clicked into place. "So your abilities were like passives. Always on. You didn't have to think, didn't have to plan. They just worked."

Then he frowned, and his voice lowered. "And now you're scared— because magic doesn't work that way. You're switching to a system where everything's *active*. You have to choose. You have to react fast. And if you hesitate..."

She nodded. "Yeah. If I hesitate, I die."

Mara knew it was true.

She had been avoiding thinking too deeply about it. Deep down, she'd been hoping someone would come along and fix her. Make it stop.

She *loved* casting spells—she found it fun, despite how tedious the work was to master them.

But still, Toman was right.

She was scared.

This wasn't just about becoming mortal. It was about changing *who* she would be.

Active spells couldn't replace passive abilities.

This was a fundamental shift in identity—like changing classes in a game. You couldn't just pick up new skills and keep playing the same old way.

Damn it! Screw that analogy. This is my life.

She didn't *want* to change. Being forced to hurt. And she had to admit it to herself—it scared the hell out of her.

Toman gave her a sad look. "I was going to wait until later, after your practice, but... I have something that might cheer you up."

Mara gave him a skeptical glance—then lit up in amazement as he brought out her Heartwood staff.

It looked different, but she *felt* it instantly. That same connection was there, immediate and deep—but richer now. Before, it had felt raw. Empty. Now it had a complex aura she didn't recognize but instinctively understood.

She barely restrained herself from snatching it out of his hands and hugging it to her chest.

Toman, maddeningly slow, held it back, wanting to explain first.

"This was the hardest thing I've ever enchanted," he boasted, proud. "It changes form—staff to spear and back. That's not something I've done before. Not as complicated as storage enchantments, maybe, but still... a serious challenge. I think I did a good job."

He demonstrated, and Mara was impressed.

As a staff, it resembled a slightly ornate quarterstaff: scrollwork along its length and two intricate finials on either end. It could pass as a wizard's tool, but those finials? They could *crush* a skull. Elegant and deadly.

It would be devastating in her hands—giving her reach over a sword or knife fighter. She was trained for this.

And then there was the spear form.

Sleek. Deadly. Beautiful.

The same delicate scrollwork adorned the shaft, but the blade was a work of art—two feet long, just two fingers wide, and razor-sharp. Though designed for thrusting, the twin edges meant it would slash just as well. Opposite the blade was a shorter spike—deadly in its own right. Both looked vicious. And being Heartwood, it could ruin a vampire's night. Their *last* night.

Even with its density, the weapon was lighter than steel and perfectly balanced. She might've been afraid of it if it didn't already feel like part of her.

Toman, of course, was still talking.

"Besides the shape-changing, I added the indestructibility enchantment and a moderate mana pool. It's not huge, but it'll save your hide if your own mana gets disrupted."

Resting his hand on the staff, pride creeping into his voice. "It does more than just that. I built in a shock enchantment—same effect as a shock rod. Touch someone with either end, and they'll be twitching on the ground, completely locked up."

He gave her a sideways glance. "There are two settings. The regular charge will drop most people cold. The high one... well, that's for something like a vampire. It hits a lot harder—could kill a human, but definitely should incapacitate even the undead for a bit."

She raised an eyebrow.

He continued, "You switch modes with a thought. Just don't overuse the big one—it drains mana pretty fast. I built in a limiter, but still. Save it for when you really need to make a point."

Toman grinned then—smug and satisfied at her approval, but he wasn't done.

"I also added the *Writ of Unmaking* as an enchantment. Three uses per day, directly from the staff. It eats mana, which is why I had to build the internal mana pool. It recharges slowly, but you *can* refill it manually—though that'll tire you out fast."

Mara's eyes widened.

That was huge. She'd worried about casting that spell herself. Right now, she didn't even have the capacity to cast it *once*, not without exhausting herself. With it embedded in the staff, that limitation vanished.

It changed everything.

Against wards. Against traps. Against people.

She knew the dirty little secret of the spell–undocumented in the spell crystal–but she'd figured it out. If targeted at a person, it could scramble the mana in their body—damaging them, short-circuiting their ability to cast until they rested or got healed. Using it offensively as a self-cast spell was a pipe dream—it required too much time and concentration to use in combat. But with the staff...

"Toman," she said, voice thick with emotion, "you've made me a very happy woman."

He blushed, but finally handed it over.

The moment it touched her hands, it was like a puzzle piece snapped into place. Her mind cleared. Her connection to mana expanded. It flowed through her with newfound grace and ease.

"It feels like mana *wants* to obey me," she whispered, awestruck.

Toman grinned. "Welcome to the wonderful world of having a Heartwood foci."

The rest of the night, Mara practiced spells with her new staff—and everything came easier.

Her focus sharpened. Her grip on complex patterns solidified. It even seemed to boost her ability to memorize. By dawn, she was casting Tier 5 spells with confidence. That was a two-Tier jump in a single night—an extraordinary leap. Considering that each new Tier meant juggling one more modifier and exponentially greater complexity, it was nothing short of remarkable.

For the first time in weeks, she felt like she was becoming a real mage. The road ahead was still long, but for once, she didn't dread it.

She had hope.

So, bolstered by that success, she decided to try something riskier—the Spellsword technique.

She picked the most basic strength-enhancement spell and aimed it at her Heartwood staff, willing the effect to bounce back onto her body.

Toman's eyes narrowed as he watched the mana threads twist through the staff, then rebound into her, threading power through every muscle and bone like a living circuit.

What followed was *agony*.

Pain flooded her body. It was as if her muscles were being torn from the inside out. She screamed until her throat went raw.

When it finally stopped and she slumped, drenched in cold sweat, Toman winced.

"Well... on the bright side, you didn't blow yourself up. So that's... something."

She flipped him off.

He didn't know the gesture, but he got the gist from her face.

"That can't possibly be the right way to do it," she growled. "That was *excruciating*."

Worse, she could *feel* the damage. The mana had ravaged her tissue, disrupting cells like a storm. And judging by the way her limbs still throbbed, she had a terrible suspicion it had accelerated her transformation.

"Let me scan you," Toman said, already heading for the diagnostic device.

Mara stood still and waited, silently daring the results to be good.

They weren't.

The projection showed micro-tears across her body—concentrated in the undead tissue. Her still-living cells were mostly untouched, but the rest...

"Dragon's balls," she muttered. "That was a *very* bad idea."

She was furious—not at the Spellsword spell, but at herself. She hadn't stopped to think what bouncing mana through a living conduit might do to a body made of half-dead flesh.

That might've just shaved another five, maybe ten percent off what little vampiric essence she had left.

She'd need a Healer. *Immediately.*

"I'm really sorry," Toman said, genuinely shaken. "I didn't think that could happen."

"You and me both." She let out a slow breath and rolled her aching shoulders. "Well, that's that. I'm done for tonight. I'll head to the Healers Guild, get checked out. I'll be back tomorrow, but from now on I'm sticking to regular spells—nothing that enhances my body using their secret technique until the change is done."

Toman nodded, still looking guilty. "There's plenty to work on. But... just so you know, if you ever *did* want to force the transformation forward, well—*that* would do it. You'd just need a healer on standby."

She didn't answer right away.

That idea *had* crossed her mind. But it wasn't one she wanted to entertain—not yet.

"I still want to master what I can *before* I lose the rest of my powers," she said finally. "If I'm going to turn mortal, I'm not doing it half-trained. I've got too many enemies. I can't afford to be vulnerable."

On that note, she left.

She found Dunc waiting where she'd left him and instructed him to take her straight to the Healers Guild. It was late—so late it was nearly morning—and Onaris had to be woken from sleep.

She waited nearly half an hour before he arrived, looking rumpled but concerned.

THIRTY-NINE

ONCE DONE, he gave her a rueful smile. "I'm afraid you've passed the halfway point already—53%. I thought you'd have around a hundred and forty days left. A normal person probably would. But you?" He shook his head. "I think it's more likely you've only got three or four months. You can't seem to stop getting injured."

Mara didn't like hearing it, but he wasn't wrong.

"Yeah, I get that. To be fair, what happened tonight wasn't due to violence. It was a freak circumstance. I tried casting a spell, and it interacted with my body in a very unexpected way. I definitely won't be doing that again until after the transformation."

Onaris gave her a sad smile and echoed something Toman had said, but added a new idea she hadn't considered. "When your transformation gets further along, you should come back to the compound and let me guide you through the final stages. The percentage doesn't matter—whether it's seventy percent or ninety-five. Just come when your vampiric powers are practically unusable."

He placed a comforting hand on hers. "Whatever spell you used tonight... if we cast it again, under controlled conditions, we can finish the process safely. That final moment could be dangerous. Doing it here could save your life."

That was... a good idea, actually. Not one she liked, though. She wanted to hold on until the last possible moment, to squeeze every drop of usefulness out of her vampiric memory while she still had it. Every extra day of magic practice might make the difference later.

A typical mage might spend twelve to fourteen years training to become a full guild member. Mara was trying to cram all of that into a matter of months—pushing herself through relentless hours of study, relying on the cheat code of her vampiric memory to make up the difference. The more time she could give herself, the better.

"I'll keep that in mind, Doc."

She was already rising to go when the Master Healer added one more thing—and it sent chills up her spine.

"I hesitate to bring this up, but now that you've passed the halfway mark, I'm becoming more certain. The mortal tissue growing inside you... it's not normal."

She turned to look at him fully. Her voice was calm but deliberate. Too calm. "Please clarify. Are you saying I won't be human?"

Mara had never seen the older man look so serious—or so uncertain.

"Not exactly," he said at last.

That was *not* the answer she wanted.

This world had orcs, goblins, and who knew what else.

"If I'm not becoming human again, like I was before... then what the hell am I turning into?"

"Hang on," he said, raising a hand. "I'm not saying you're turning into something non-human. I'm saying the living tissue has odd properties. It *looks* human. But it has..." He searched for the words. "It's too potent. Living flesh shouldn't be able to overwhelm undead tissue like this. It's like it's energized with mana somehow. But that shouldn't be possible. If it were, the Wasting would be ravaging you by now. And I'm not seeing any signs of that."

She took a long breath. Then another. Her heart was pounding from the spike of adrenaline, but the fear was slowly receding.

"Okay," she exhaled. "That was *not* the best way to start that conversation, *Master* Healer. You scared me half to death."

The older man had the grace to blush. "Ah... sorry. It's just baffling. This defies everything I know, and I thought you should be aware. It *is* good news, though. The more this progresses, the more convinced I am that you'll survive the final transition. It's still going to be an ordeal—but I don't think it'll kill you."

Mara nodded slowly. "Well, I guess that *is* good news... as long as I'm not turning into an orc or something."

Onaris scoffed. "I'd *tell* you if you were turning into an orc. I know orc genetics. You're not. And if you start transforming into a fish, I'll give you a proper warning."

There was a twinkle in his eye as he said it.

Snorting, Mara rolled her eyes. "Fine. But for the record? That could be a thing. So I had to ask."

She pulled her cloak back on and was turning to leave when another thought struck her.

"Master Onaris, I've heard the Healers will train anyone in medicine, even if the Tree doesn't choose them. Would it be possible for me to learn basic healing spells?"

She added with a dry smile, "So I can heal myself. As you mentioned earlier, I do have a nasty habit of getting injured."

He chuckled but shook his head. "I'm sorry, but that's not possible. We can teach you medicine—non-magical methods—but healing spells are restricted. The guild doesn't permit non-members to practice healing magic. It's partly about protecting our reputation; we can't risk people passing themselves off as Healers. More than that, healing knowledge can be twisted—used to injure just as easily as to heal—and we won't put that kind of power in the hands of anyone who hasn't committed to the Calling."

He gave her a rueful smile. "Not even for you, and I don't believe you would misuse our gifts."

"I see. Thank you, then. I'll see you next time—or when I've managed to hurt myself again. Whichever comes first." She offered him a wry smile, and he laughed in return.

The trip back to the Dragon was almost calm enough to lull her to sleep, but she was too paranoid for that. With so many enemies in the city, she never let her guard down.

It was a good thing she didn't.

A woman stood a block from the Dragon Inn, directly in their path. Pale skin. Still posture.

A vampire.

Mara reached forward and tapped Dunc on the shoulder, signaling him to pull over. There was no outrunning this one, even if she weren't blocking the way. No sense in getting Dunc killed. The only real question was whether this was another assassin—or just a messenger.

She hopped down from the carriage and walked the rest of the way. "Looking for me, I presume?"

The other woman nodded.

Mara took in her outfit at a glance—tight blood-red blouse with a plunging neckline, black leather corset cinched tight enough to double as armor, and pants so snug they looked painted on. Crimson trim traced each leg like warning stripes. Her knee-high boots gleamed with obsidian polish, the kind that could crack a rib with one good stomp, and the red ribbon laced up the back screamed, look at me. No cloak, no attempt at subtlety—just raven hair, pale eyes, and a body dressed to dazzle and kill.

Huh. Not my style, but she stands out like a rose full of thorns you don't expect until it's already bled you.

Then again, Mara *had* been expecting this. Ever since Ewart delivered his summons—then tried to cash her in.

"I'm Laris," the woman said. "And Lord Noloris wants to know why you haven't come to visit him."

No threats, no preamble—just blunt delivery. Mara appreciated that, but it didn't make her any less wary. This one looked competent. And old enough to be careful.

Mara glanced at the sky. "Shall we step inside and discuss it over a drink?"

The vampire frowned, eyes narrowing with insight. "Trying to reach safe ground, or trying to get me in trouble with Zakkarius for 'threatening' a customer on Inn property?"

Mara smirked. Wary, yes—but she kind of liked this woman. Not that she trusted her any more than she would a viper.

"Neither," she said. "It's just been a long night, and I'd like a drink. You're welcome to join me and explain what's on your mind. I'm not avoiding Lord Noloris—but that idiot Ewart tried to cash in a bounty on me, so you'll understand if I'm a little cautious."

Laris smiled for the first time. "I could drink—if you're buying."

She looked no less guarded, but maybe a bit more relaxed. Mara hadn't made any threatening moves, after all.

Not surprising. Ewart had been at least two centuries old, and she'd beaten him. They probably thought she was just as ancient. Noloris' people would approach her with care now.

Sure, they could have come in swinging, but this? This was the smarter play. Noloris hadn't built a criminal empire by being stupid.

Mara turned to Dunc. "You're dismissed. Be here tomorrow at sunset."

Normally, she'd have thanked him or cracked a joke, but this was for his safety. Let Laris assume he was just another enthralled servant. Inconsequential. Unworthy of being used as leverage.

Without further hesitation, Mara stepped toward the inn and fell in beside the other vampire. It was a risk—but a calculated one. Even outside the Dragon, Zak wouldn't want bodies dropping on his doorstep.

She was right. No ambush came. The two of them walked the red carpet into the Dragon's throat and descended into the common room.

Surprisingly, Zak was behind the bar despite the hour. Or maybe, from his perspective, it was early.

Didn't matter. She ordered two whiskeys—the good stuff—and joined Laris at the table she'd claimed.

As she turned to go, Zak spoke in a low voice. "Don't start trouble in my inn. You might be changing back into your old self, but you know I won't play a part in one of your games."

Mara paused mid-step and gave him a sharp frown, nearly a glare. "I've been meaning to ask you about all these cryptic remarks, and this just bumped it to the top of the list. Unfortunately, I've got a guest to deal with, so it'll have to wait—but we're going to talk." There was an edge to her voice, not quite a threat, but close.

The dwarven innkeeper just snorted and went back to cleaning glasses.

And why the hell did he even bother with that, when he had Cleaners?

Damned annoying Dwarf.

She shoved the irritation aside, returned to the table, and slid one of the drinks in front of Laris before taking her seat. She was mildly amused to see they'd both picked spots that gave them a clear view of the door. Professional instincts.

Once they'd each taken a sip of whiskey and settled in. Laris gave an appreciative look at the glass and saluted Mara for her choice of drinks, then got straight to it.

"So why haven't you shown Lord Noloris respect by presenting yourself?"

Mara shrugged. "No disrespect intended. First and only time I heard of a summons was when the assassin showed up—and then tried to kill me. What was I supposed to think? Does Lord Noloris really not care about one of his own disobeying orders, or should I show him the ultimate respect by getting out of his city?"

Laris let out a dry, humorless laugh. "If my lord wanted you dead, you'd be dead. And it would be messy. Public. Right now, he's deciding what to do about a vampire in his city disrespecting his authority by not meeting with him."

That tracked. On Earth, the elders didn't tolerate unannounced guests in their territory either. Back there, she'd had the backing of someone just as powerful as the elders. Here? She had a couple of friends. None of them strong enough to stand against the criminal lord of Daggerport. If she planned to stay, she'd need to give him face.

She understood the politics. The real question was whether he'd consider her an enemy now—or if a belated bow and a few words of respect would be enough.

And there was a perfect person to ask, sitting right across from her so she posed the question.

Laris smirked, amused but not mocking. "Good question. After what happened with Ewart, you've proven your value. If you present yourself soon and show him proper respect, I believe he'll forgive the delay and permit you to stay—provided you follow the rules."

That was the best outcome Mara could hope for.

But one problem loomed: if he found out she was turning mortal. That kind of curiosity could be deadly. She doubted a man like Noloris would let something like that walk away free. And with her powers waning, fooling another vampire might not be possible.

She'd passed the 50% mark. Her abilities were unreliable. Strength beyond a certain point would tear her muscles or snap bones. Speed could rupture organs. At most, she could safely tap into thirty percent of her old performance—and even that was a gamble. It might fool humans, but not vampires.

This was it. She had to choose.

Disappear from the city and change identities—or bluff her way through and hope she can finish the transformation before her secret gets out.

She nodded, decision made. "Tomorrow evening, then. But I've never been near his palace. I'll need directions."

One more thought struck her. "By the way, does he require tribute to remain in his domain—or just presence and respect?"

Laris gave an approving nod. "Presence is enough, but tribute shows good faith and willingness to play by the rules. If it were me, I'd bring something meaningful—coin, items, or valuable information."

She paused, then produced a card from storage and slid it across the table.

Mara picked it up and examined it—an engraved invitation, gilded and literal. It would get her past the Undercity lifts and grant safe passage to Lord Noloris' palace.

She made it vanish into her storage with a flick of her fingers. "Then I'll do that. Lord Noloris can expect me tomorrow evening."

CHAPTER
FORTY

Mara messaged Toman first thing the next evening to let him know what was happening.

"Are you going to be okay? I deal with folks in his organization from time to time who want illegal items made, but I've never dealt directly with him or his lieutenants. Everyone's scared shitless of dealing with them."

She chuckled. "That's very comforting, thanks. Super helpful."

She could practically hear him flush as he rushed to add, "Listen, I've got an item. It's one I'd never sell, but I could lend it to you for the evening if you want. It's a one-time teleportation enchantment— completely undetectable. I've tested it. Even the most invasive scans haven't picked it up. Use it, and it'll jump you to a small village two days ride outside the city. They've got a healer there, but no Teleporter's Guild station, so you won't be tracked."

She hesitated. She was tempted, badly.

It was smart. Practical. Safe. Exactly the kind of backup she should have. But it would take time—more than she had. If Laris was any indication, Noloris operated like a king, and you didn't tell a king "tomorrow" and then show up late. Not unless you were already planning to vanish forever.

Besides, Mara didn't think he would kill her tonight. Not unless he knew. Not unless she slipped and gave something away.

"Thank you, Toman. That means more to me than you know. But I don't have time. Everything should be fine."

She just had to keep her head down, show the proper respect, and let him think he was the one in charge. That's what men like him wanted. Authority. Deference. Acknowledgment of power.

Zak was behind the bar when she crossed the common room, so she veered toward him.

"Listen. I feel like a conversation is overdue. But I've got to meet with Noloris right now. If you're here when I get back, I want to talk." She muttered under her breath. "Assuming I survive."

The dwarf just gave a shrug and that same unreadable stare. "Go play your games. I'll be here. I'm always here."

Shaking her head, she continued outside where Dunc waited with the cart. She had him deliver her to the same VIP platform she and Toman had used the week prior to access the Undercity.

The staff barely glanced at her invitation before snapping to attention. No waiting. No questions. The young woman who escorted her to the platform even showed a flicker of fear, keeping her eyes politely downcast.

Mara didn't blame her.

She'd be lying if she said she wasn't scared, too.

The Shadow Market was quieter than auction night but still alive. At least a hundred and fifty people wandered through the outer stalls, and probably triple that number were inside the shops. That seemed pretty good for what was basically an illegal version of the Merchant Mile.

She moved carefully through the crowd, making mental notes. Exits. Obstructions. Who looked dangerous. Who didn't. Just in case.

Soon, Noloris' palace loomed ahead—dark stone and deep crimson glass, cut with angled metalwork and subtle runes that shimmered faintly in the torchlight.

She straightened her shoulders and walked forward.

No fear. No hesitation. The only way out of something like this was to never show weakness. Make them believe you were dangerous and they'd treat you with respect.

Problem was, push too far, and someone like Noloris might decide you were a threat—even if you did bend the knee.

The guards took her invitation and barely glanced at it before gesturing for a servant. He stepped forward immediately and offered to escort her.

Of course, the bastard would have a throne room. Pretentious prick.

She gave a single nod and followed, moving with calm, measured steps—neither meek nor arrogant.

Her nerves were jittering under the surface, but she clamped down. There was still enough vampire in her to lock her body chemistry into line.

Barely.

She was grateful this meeting hadn't come a week later. Any more degradation and she might not be able to suppress the tells. A pounding heart or a bead of sweat rolling down her forehead would spell her doom.

Right now, she could still fake it.

She found herself wishing she had her staff. Holding it would help her center, channel her focus, keep her expression steady no matter what. But even carrying it would raise eyebrows—and if she transformed it into a spear? No way Noloris wouldn't see that as a threat. Even an elder might get nervous facing a vampire holding a seven-foot-long magical stake.

The servant led her through several grand hallways, each more ornate than the last, until they stopped before a towering pair of gilded double doors—carved wood and iron inlay, silver runes laced through like veins. It was magnificent. And way too much.

He turned to the guards and murmured her name.

Mara took a slow breath and waited as they announced her.

She had been too focused on her thoughts to pay much attention to the palace's halls and corridors—other than counting the turns and committing the route to memory. Still, between that winding path and the gilded, overdone antechamber she waited in now, Mara was forming a pretty clear impression of Lord Noloris.

He was trying too hard.

This wasn't the austere, timeless elegance of old money. This was gaudy. Flashy. More *Florida nouveau riche* than *New England aristocracy*. And for a vampire who had to be at least a few centuries old, that struck her as... odd. Shouldn't someone like that be secure in their power by now? Not putting on airs for the sake of appearance?

Unless it was intentional. Some performance for effect.

Or maybe the man just has bad taste.

The doors swung open with slow ceremony, and a crier announced her like she was attending a royal gala.

"Mara, vampire. Visitor to the city, come to pay respect to the Lord."

She kept her face still, but it took effort. No eye roll, no grimace. The urge to smirk at the theatrics was strong. This guy was really committed to the whole *Lord of the Underworld* thing.

Sure enough, he was seated on a raised dais at the far end of the room, perched on a throne that looked like it belonged in a stage play. The rest of the hall was filled with people—two dozen at least —lounging, drinking, whispering, posturing. A parody of a noble court. It reminded her of vampire nightclubs back on Earth.

She recognized Laris near the foot of the dais. And another vampire too, sprawled across a lavish sofa with three human women draped over him, each trying to charm their way into becoming his next meal. Probably thinking it was an honor.

Mara resisted the urge to sneer. This wasn't her kind of scene. Too many sycophants circling too little power, all trying to catch the attention of their betters. She'd seen this kind of thing back on Earth —only the names and accents were different.

Her gaze flicked to Noloris.

He sat tall, lean, and broad-shouldered, the peak of human strength frozen at the moment of undeath. He had been lucky enough to be turned in the prime of life, rather than young like most vampires– like she had been.

His throne was intricately carved, and above it loomed a stone relief of a dragon's head-worn and unpolished, as if it had been salvaged from some ruin. Whether it was heraldry or art, the roughness of it stood in distinct contrast to the overdesigned trappings around it. Oddly enough, it worked. It gave the elder vampire an edge of gravitas, as though despite all the showmanship, something ancient still rested at the heart of him.

His face, though, told another story.

Sharp lines, hard eyes. A man who'd seen too much, and cared too little. He looked cold and ruthless. The kind of predator who fed on fear and obedience in equal measure. She'd met men like him before. They didn't care why you disobeyed—only that you did.

She doubted he'd make an exception for her.

All eyes followed her as she approached. Her escort offered a brief bow and backed away, leaving her alone at the foot of the dais.

Noloris watched her in silence, pale grey eyes tracking every movement, every breath. The weight of his gaze pressed down on her like a physical force, as if daring her to flinch or falter.

She held steady, but couldn't help noting the resemblance to Laris. That same pitch-black hair, those sharp, symmetrical features. It wasn't just a shared style or grooming—it was blood-deep. A familial echo.

Was Laris one of his descendants? A daughter, perhaps, or a favored progeny? That would explain her authority—and her confidence.

Forcing out those stay thoughts, she took a step forward and offered a low, formal bow. "Greetings, Lord Noloris. I've come to pay my respects."

His voice was slow and deliberate, each word carrying the weight of judgment. "Did you not think to do so sooner? I'm told you've already been doing business in my city. That's... bold. Some would say disrespectful. And now you arrive dressed for war?"

Mara had chosen her enchanted leather armor carefully. It offered solid protection and didn't scream *threat*, especially with her cloak thrown over her shoulders to soften the silhouette. But she knew how this game was played. Any choice could be used against her. Too formal, she would've been accused of mockery. Too casual, of insolence.

Here, even practicality could be twisted into offense.

She met his gaze calmly, choosing her words with care.

She went to one knee.

"Lord, please forgive my tardiness in appearing before you. After Ewart tried to kill me and I killed him instead, I wasn't sure what kind of welcome I would receive. It wasn't until I spoke with your lieutenant, Laris, last night that I understood he hadn't been acting on your orders. So I committed then to come immediately, to offer you my deepest respect—and present a tribute worthy of the circumstances surrounding my stay in your city."

She removed pouch after pouch of gold from her cloak and spilled them out across the marble floor. The coins gleamed in the torchlight, dozens of eyes following the cascade. "Three hundred and seventeen gold marks. Seventy percent of what I earned while operating in your territory. I meant no disrespect by the delay. When I arrived, I was destitute, having lost nearly everything in a tragic accident. I needed time to re-establish myself, else I would've come to your court looking like a pauper. This way, I demonstrate both respect—and that I can be an asset worth keeping."

Laris stood with arms folded near the throne, her smirk all amusement. Noloris, however, looked thoughtful.

"Pretty words from a pretty vampire," he said at last. "I enjoy beautiful things here in my court. For that reason alone, I will accept your tribute—and consider your delay a form of respect. You did not want to seem weak before me."

It took everything Mara had not to let her reaction show. Did he say that just to watch her squirm, or was he truly a thousand-year-old creep?

She bowed her head low, giving the elder face, all while picturing the smug bastard with her spear rammed through his heart.

When she looked back up, he was smiling. "That has earned your forgiveness. However, no vampire may reside in my city without serving me. If you wish to make Daggerport your home, you'll replace Ewart as one of my lieutenants."

There it was. The offer. The trap. Exactly what she'd expected—and dreaded. Depending on what he asked of her, she might have to run. There were lines she wouldn't cross. Slavers. Murder for sport. She'd torch his entire empire one minion at a time before becoming that.

But she didn't actually have to serve. She just had to survive. Pretend long enough for the transformation to finish. When the time came, Mara would die—publicly, loudly, in front of plenty of witnesses— and then she'd vanish and become someone else. And, hopefully, never have to deal with Noloris or his ilk again.

The question was, how long could she fake being a vampire with her powers already starting to fail?

Noloris's voice snapped her out of her thoughts. "Well, girl? Will you serve—or leave my city?"

She bowed her head again. "What would you have of me, Lord? While I can fight, my true strength is in hunting. I doubt I matched Ewart's skill in assassination, but I have some ability in that arena."

Noloris laughed, and the crowd laughed with him, sycophantic and eager. The sound cut off the instant he raised a hand.

"You must jest. You killed Ewart in open combat, in front of many witnesses. That speaks to more than mere ability."

Mara smiled modestly like she'd been trying to downplay it. "As I said, I do have some skill. Ewart was no slouch, but his strength was stealth, not the ring. His pride was his downfall—he lost his temper and got careless."

Another chuckle from Noloris, this one more genuine. "You amuse me, young Mara. I'll enjoy having you here. You will swear loyalty to me for one year. After that, you may leave if you wish."

There was steel beneath the smile. She had no doubt—refusal meant death.

"Of course, Lord," she said, voice even. Words meant nothing. She began, "I, Mara, swear—"

"Stop," he said, eyes gleaming with malice. "The oath will be binding."

He produced a crystal orb traced with gold filigree and held it toward her. "Place your hand upon it. The oath will be inscribed into your vampiric flesh. Should you betray me, or try to leave before your year is up, the magic will burn you alive."

Oh, this was bad.

Mara searched for an out but came up empty. Her vampiric flesh wouldn't last much longer, and that could be a death sentence. Enchantments like this didn't react well to disruption—especially not ones designed to enforce loyalty. She had no doubt it came with built-in safeguards. The kind that exploded. So what happened when too much of her undead tissue vanished? Would the spell collapse and take her with it? That seemed likely.

Worse, what if it didn't bind at all? What if there wasn't enough vampiric essence left in her to anchor the oath? Would the spell fail gently—or would it burn her alive for trying to deceive it? And if it did fail... would Noloris know why?

His voice cut through her spiraling thoughts, sharp and cruel. "Well? Were you planning to flee without paying your due for hunting in my city these past weeks without permission?"

She forced calm over her face and rose smoothly to her feet. Climbing the steps with measured confidence, she approached the crystal held out in his hand. There were moments in life when hesitation was death. This was one of them.

So she placed her hand on the gold-banded stone and spoke clearly. "I, Mara, pledge to serve from sunrise, for one year, giving my undying loyalty to Lord Noloris. To follow his commands to the best of my ability."

Nothing happened.

The magic waited, hungry but inert, like a beast on a leash.

Noloris narrowed his eyes. "From sunrise? Do you think to run before the dawn and weasel free of your oath?"

She shook her head firmly. "No, Lord. I only meant not to cheat you. This night is already half gone."

He chuckled, clearly pleased. "Good, good. A strong oath. I approve. I will enjoy your service."

There was something in the way he said it—something that set her every instinct on edge. If she didn't find a way to break this soon, the sunrise would kill her.

He spoke with finality, "So let it be."

The words rang like a bell through the chamber, and the magic struck.

Threads of invasive mana sank through her hand like burning needles, scouring her body for every shred of vampiric flesh. They found what they needed. Then they began to carve. Glyphs etched themselves into her bones, her nerves, in her brain.

True vampire flesh would quickly regenerate from this. Mara wouldn't. The spell sat inside her like a poison, slowly killing her from within. But Noloris couldn't know that. He couldn't see it.

She didn't scream. She didn't twitch. She let the agony wash through her, clenched her jaw, and stood still.

It felt like it lasted forever.

In truth, it was less than a minute.

When the initial pain passed, she willed herself to move, ignoring the scorched and damaged tissue that wasn't regenerating. She had to get out. Now.

Noloris waved her away, a cruel satisfaction in his expression. "Go. Settle your tab at the Dragon Inn and return tomorrow evening. You'll take Ewart's home—it's yours now, by right of conquest. Then you'll attend me. I have tasks for you."

Even through the haze of pain, that last comment told her everything she needed to know. He didn't care about her skills or loyalty. He wanted obedience. Domination. The kind that turned her stomach.

She would die before she let that happen.

No—she would kill him first.

But the oath was written into her bones, and she could feel it even now, coiled and waiting. Disobedience wouldn't just hurt—it would burn her from the inside out. Actively, not passively like it was now.

She had to find a way to undo it. Before dawn.

Gritting her teeth, she bowed low. "Until then, Lord."

It took every single ounce of her will not to flinch or show that the oath was still eating her alive from within because she couldn't regenerate.

Every step was agony, and the walk to the big double doors felt like a death march. She kept her pace slow and deliberate, holding herself rigid so nothing would give her away.

It wasn't the worst pain she'd ever endured, but it was the hardest—because she had to hide it. No clenched jaw, no stumble, no twitch.

Weakness in front of these people meant death.

And if she faltered under the elder vampire's gaze, if he sensed anything was wrong, she'd never be allowed to leave.

When the heavy double doors finally slammed shut behind her, she didn't hesitate. She flashed through the palace halls at vampiric speed. Not her full speed—she couldn't manage that—but fast enough that none of the human servants could react or even register what passed them.

She burst out the palace doors, and no alarm followed. No one tried to stop her. She was a vampire, and in Noloris's Undercity, all vampires served him. A blur of motion was seen with fear, not suspicion.

The lift to the surface was waiting, but the minutes she stood there might as well have been hours. Her vampiric tissue was burning away piece by piece under the binding of the oath. And she wasn't healing. If the Healers didn't help her in time, she wouldn't survive the night.

She called Dunc. He promised to be waiting on the curb.

She called Toman and told him to meet her at the Healers Guild.

She called Onaris last and didn't waste words. "It has to be now. Tonight. As soon as I arrive, or I'm dead."

Each of them shouted her name or demanded an explanation, but she hung up without answering. She didn't accept their return connections. She couldn't afford to. Not here. Not where eyes and ears might still report back to the crime lord.

If she let her guard slip, even for a moment, she was finished.

Dunc was already pacing when she emerged from the surface entrance. He looked between her and the storefront that hid the lift with wide eyes.

She gave a tiny shake of her head. No time. No questions.

"Healers Guild. Quickly." Her voice was low and hoarse.

He went pale and nodded fast, then leaped into the driver's seat and threw the magic rickshaw into motion.

Anyone watching would assume she was returning to the Dragon Inn—most of the trip followed that route. But just before they reached the main intersection where Castle Boulevard met the main road, Dunc veered off, avoiding the guard tower and the City Watch stationed there.

Too many guards. Too many questions.

They took a wide road north, weaving through side streets.

The entire ride was a blur—not just because of their speed, but because it took everything she had not to black out. Her tissue was tearing apart inside her, leaving scorched, rotting holes that would never regenerate.

At one point, the rickshaw hit a stray rock. The jolt sent a white-hot bolt of agony through her chest and she screamed before she could stop herself.

Dunc flinched hard and nearly crashed.

"I'm sorry, miss! I'm so sorry! I'll get you there—just hang on!"

He meant it, too. When the roads were clear, he pushed the rickshaw dangerously fast—maybe fifty miles an hour or more.

Finally, after what felt like a century wrapped in agony, they screeched to a stop, nearly parked in the Healers Guild gateway itself.

Onaris was already there, standing with tension in every line of his body. The moment he saw her, his eyes went wide and he didn't waste time.

With a flick of his fingers, he levitated her from the seat and ran with her into the building, straight to one of the shielded treatment rooms.

He didn't wait. Didn't ask questions. He dropped her gently to the padded table, cast a diagnostic, and swore.

Loudly. Creatively.

"Gods below, Mara—you're going to die. There's a spell burning through your vampire flesh. It's moving faster than I can heal. I may not even have enough mana to keep up."

She choked out, "Oath enchantment... into vampire flesh. It's burning me... from the inside out. Toman... on the way... can negate the enchantment."

Onaris shook his head grimly. "If he doesn't get here soon, it won't matter. I'm calling Dena to assist. I can't handle this alone."

Some distant part of her mind marveled at that—two of the most powerful Healers in the world were needed just to keep her alive. And there was a chance even they wouldn't be enough.

Relief didn't come when healing began. It got worse. Much worse. Mortal tissue began forming to replace the scorched vampire flesh, and with it came new nerve endings, pain receptors, all firing into raw pathways. She screamed until her voice broke.

Onaris looked stricken. "I'm so sorry. I shut off the pain, but the new pathways are forming as fast as I can suppress them. Every time I cut one off, more grow back. This is going to be bad, Mara, and I'll do everything I can—but you have to hold on."

He activated his speech stone. "Master Margra, I'm sorry to wake you, but I need you. This patient is more than I can handle."

A moment later, blessed silence. Her voice rasped through the haze. "Damn. It's so bad not one or two, but *three* of the most powerful Healers in the world are needed. That's got to be some kind of record."

She tried to laugh, but it dissolved into another ragged scream as more nerves lit up in her mind.

Then Dena swept into the room. She took one look at Mara and didn't hesitate, stepping opposite Onaris as he quickly brought her up to speed.

Seemingly long minutes later, the door opened again. Toman came in supporting Margra Athne, the ancient Master Healer. She walked to the head of the bed, sat on a chair that Toman moved into place for her, put a hand on Mara's brow, and without asking a single question, shut off the pain entirely.

Mara gasped in relief, drawing a deep breath like surfacing from underwater. "Thank you."

Margra simply nodded, calm and impassive, like this was nothing more than her duty.

Toman, on the other hand, looked like a wreck. "What's going on?"

Now able to speak clearly, if hoarsely, Mara said, "Noloris made me swear a magical oath. It carved the enchantment into my undead flesh. And that's going about as well as you'd expect." She grimaced. "Remember when I used that *secret* technique?"

Another spike of pain flashed through her—just as quickly cut off again. She gave Margra a crooked smile.

"To put it mildly? This is worse. And it's still happening. The oath is still burning through me. I need you to use Writ. Strip it out."

He nodded, though his hands shook. She could see the worry behind his eyes, the doubt, the panic.

So she summoned her staff from storage and pushed it toward him.

The sudden appearance of the large Heartwood weapon interrupted Dena mid-healing. She blinked in surprise but caught on quickly and resumed without comment.

Toman gripped the staff like a lifeline, then turned to the others. "I need to purge the enchantment. Please step back. If it reacts, I don't want any of you caught in it."

The Healers hesitated only a moment before withdrawing their hands and retreating. Instantly, the agony returned, fire clawing through her body from the inside out.

Toman placed the staff gently on her shoulder and activated the magic within.

Writ of Unmaking.

Threads of glowing mana spiderwebbed out, weaving around the oath enchantment embedded in her flesh. The matrix formed, encapsulating the invasive spellwork like a cage—and then collapsed inward, compressing the energy before dispersing it into harmless motes that vanished into the air. It took a long moment of agony for the spell to do its work.

Mara barely followed the process. She was too far gone. But the instant the burning stopped, she knew it had worked. The damage remained, but the fire was gone.

Toman withdrew the staff and nodded. "It's done."

The three Master Healers immediately resumed their work. This time, the results were almost miraculous. The pain didn't return. Margra's hand remained steady on Mara's forehead, shielding her from even the slightest sensation.

For the first time in what felt like an eternity, Mara could breathe without flinching.

She let herself relax, her body loose, her mind hazy. Onaris and Dena continued rebuilding her, one cell at a time.

Two hours passed. The work was slow, precise, exhausting.

At last, the three Healers sat back, spent and pale from the effort.

Mara could already feel the difference. She didn't need to hear the words.

The damage was done. And whether it was her doom or her salvation would depend on what came next.

But Onaris said them anyway—his voice soft, resigned.

"There's only about five percent of the vampiric tissue left," Onaris said with the calm, professional assurance of a lifelong Healer, but the words still landed like a blow.

Not that it changed anything. The oath was gone, but Noloris would still expect her return by sunset. There was no going back—not now.

The next words out of her mouth might have been the hardest she'd ever spoken.

"Finish it," she said. "I'll cast the spell I mentioned. Let it destroy the rest. I'll be fully mortal."

Onaris had walked every step of this journey with her, and he understood what this meant. So did Toman.

Her mentor leaned in and gently took her hand. "I'm sorry it has to be this way," he said, his voice thick with sympathy. "But it'll be okay. You'll still have me to teach you. And once the transition's done, your mana capacity might hit near max. You'll be a powerful mage, Mara."

The words helped, not for what they promised, but because of the true friendship they represented. The warmth of his hand was grounding.

Her hand. Warm.

That hit her harder than expected—warm skin. Human skin. She swallowed against the lump in her throat and nodded. Then, wordlessly, she gestured for him to pass her the staff.

The Healers stood nearby, watching, curious but respectful.

No hesitation. You can do this, Mara. It wasn't magic blood that made you who you are.

She tried to steel herself with the thought. It didn't help.

She cast anyway.

Channeling the Spellsword's body-enhancing magic, she focused it through her staff. It rebounded cleanly, flooding her system. Mana surged through her veins, empowering every living cell—and annihilating the last remnants of vampiric tissue.

The pain was immediate. Excruciating.

She screamed and dropped the staff as her spine arched, her entire body rebelling. She felt herself being torn apart from the inside.

The Healers didn't hesitate. Onaris and Dena moved instantly, magic flaring brightly as they fought to keep her alive. Onaris focused on rebuilding what was destroyed, layer by layer, while Dena stabilized her internal systems, protecting organs on the verge of failure from the shock.

Only Margra Athne remained seated, impassive as a judge, watching in silence from her chair by the head of the bed.

Mara barely noticed. The pain roared for a time, then slowly faded, replaced by the cool hush of healing. As her breathing steadied and the agony passed, she realized the truth: if Onaris had tried to do this alone, she'd be dead. No question.

It had taken both of them.

At last, she lay still. No more pain. No more burning. Just quiet.

She closed her eyes as hot tears slipped down her cheeks. It was done.

She had lost something fundamental. Irrevocably. A part of her that had shaped every moment of her life for more than a century.

Who she would become now... that was a question for another day.

She still had enemies. Powerful ones. Distant ones. Petty, irritating ones. But all of them were still out there.

And she still had no answers for why she'd been pulled into Greymantle. No explanation. No prophecy. Just a chain of choices leading her here.

But she wasn't alone anymore.

She had friends now—a welcome change from her solitary life on Earth—Olia, Toman, and even Dunc. The fact that they were each loyal to her and cared about her warmed her heart.

And that mattered more than she could say. Other than her adopted father on Earth, that was not something she'd had in a very long time, and it felt good.

It wasn't everything. But it was something.

A small light in the darkness.

———

———

Mara had almost gotten used to the idea that she was not so slowly changing into a mortal, but thought she still had many weeks to go. Then the fateful meeting with the city's ancient vampire crime lord shot that all to hell.

Now she's mortal again, but what will that mean for her future?

Join us in the second installment to find out how Mara juggles this new threat while also settling her debt of vengeance against the Followers of the Dragon.

———

Sign up for a free short story and receive the newsletter to stay current on what's happening with Greymantle and the other worlds of J David Baxter's imagination.

Support me on Ream to get early access to works in progress and exclusive content not available elsewhere. (It's like Patreon for authors).

AUTHOR'S NOTE

Please leave a review here! Help other fantasy readers and tell them why you enjoyed this book.

I would love it if you would tell your friends so they can join us on Mara's dark epic adventure to learn the truth of the Followers of the Dragon and survive her transformation from Vampire to Mage. If you do leave feedback for Sundered Soul where you purchased the book, Goodreads, or your blog—I'd love to read it. Don't hesitate to email me the link at info@jdavidbaxter.com.

ALSO BY J DAVID BAXTER

VISIT THE AUTHOR'S PAGE TO SEE ALL THE GREAT BOOKS BY J DAVID BAXTER.

About the Author

David's journey through his career has been anything but conventional. Transitioning from the exhilarating world of Renaissance Festival Jousting, where he braved falls from horses, to orchestrating teams and projects at Fortune 500 companies, he's held diverse roles. Armed with a degree in English and teaching certifications in English, History, and Professional Pedagogy, he's ventured into the realms of education and literature. David embodies versatility and a passion for storytelling, leaving an indelible mark on every path he treads.

www.ingramcontent.com/pod-product-compliance
Lightning Source LLC
Chambersburg PA
CBHW071640260626
47170CB00001B/180